My Wicked Aunt

COLLEEN NOONAN

First published by Busybird Publishing 2025

ISBN: 978-1-923501-25-6

This is a work of fiction. Any similarities between places and characters are a coincidence.

Cover image: Colleen Noonan

Cover design: Busybird Publishing

Layout and typesetting: Busybird Publishing

Busybird Publishing
2/118 Para Road
Montmorency, Victoria
Australia 3094
www.busybird.com.au

For my family
Lisa, Wade, Eugene, Julie,
William, Mackenzie, Henry,
Archer and my most valued
critic Bill.

Love Always
MMM.

+

Life could have turned out differently,
if only her aunt hadn't died.
But her aunt had died.
That was the painful truth of the matter.
And as Margaret
had been so much more than just an aunt,
Elizabeth felt angry and needed
someone to blame.
The difficulties that were to follow
also led Elizabeth to wonder
if her aunt was truly as wicked
as certain people would have her believe.
And if so,
had Margaret unwittingly
brought about her own untimely demise?

Content Warning

Readers are advised that the story contains depictions of sexual assault and mental illness.

1

A Troubled Departure

Barefoot, showered and wrapped in a towel, Elizabeth stepped from the doorway of the steamy ensuite. The scent of her fragrant, sweet-smelling bodywash accompanied her entrance into the bedroom, where, with less than an hour to pack and do all that was needed, she raced around in a state of panic.

Positioned between the open doors of the wardrobe, she riffled through the coat-hangers.

Unable to find her favourite shirt, she stepped back and stubbed her toe on a discarded, size eleven sneaker. 'Ouch!' The shrill pitch of her voice seemed quite an extreme reaction even to herself, when she'd been struggling to keep her emotions in check.

Gary, stretched out on the bed, wasn't helping. Especially as he didn't bother to offer one word of sympathy or ask after her toe.

She bent down to retrieve the offending shoe and aimed it directly at him.

He ducked as it whizzed by and bounced off the headboard. 'What was that all about?' he asked.

Elizabeth knew he was pissed off because she was leaving. 'You haven't seen my favourite white shirt have you, Gary?'

'Aw yeah!' he replied. 'It was on a stopover in Dubai. I can vividly recall getting a lot of compliments from the flight crew last time I wore it out to dinner.'

'Smart-arse!' Elizabeth scoffed.

'How the hell would I know where your frigging shirt is, Liz? What's with the favourite shirt thing anyway? You're not thinking of doing a runner on me, are you?'

'I can't believe you actually said that,' Elizabeth fumed, as she bundled rejected items of clothing in a heap and dumped the lot on top of an overflowing laundry basket.

Gary could be such a pain when things weren't going his way, Elizabeth thought. Yet, as he reached out and pulled her onto the bed, pinning her down beneath him, there was an expectation that all would be forgotten as the towel fell from around her to expose her naked body.

Well-practised hands went into immediate overdrive as he seemed hellbent on delaying her departure. His movements slowed in, what she believed, a deliberate ploy to prolong whatever it might take to keep her from packing.

'Relax, Liz. What's the hurry? You're getting yourself all worked up.'

Gary was right. Gary was always right. She'd had no time to take in the news. Stressed and broken, Elizabeth allowed herself to indulge in a temporary lapse of pleasure to enjoy a welcome surge of relief as he traced the soft contours of her breast, causing every nerve-ending to tingle. Closing her eyes she sighed when he gently slid his palms over the curve of her hips and reached behind to sink his fingertips into the firm rounded muscles of her buttocks.

Elizabeth knew it would be so easy to fall under his spell once he lingered to expertly knead, massage and seductively prepare her to fully comply with his wishes.

Compliance, yes it was all about compliance. Not just to appease Gary's wishes, but also her own. Elizabeth would be lying if she admitted otherwise. Especially when knowing how susceptible she was to his touch, and at any other time, finding their lovemaking hard to resist, she would have willingly succumbed to his attention. But not now … *this isn't right*, she thought.

'Stop! Stop it, Gary! I'm in no mood for play,' she said, as she wriggled out from under him, dragging the towel behind her.

'Could have fooled me!' he replied.

'I'm sorry!' she shouted. 'But in case you haven't noticed, I'm in a bit of a rush right now.'

A look of profound disappointment spread across Gary's face. Rejection, she knew, was not a word he included in his vocabulary.

'Wow! Once you would have been begging me not to stop. What've I done to deserve this?'

'It's more about what you haven't done that's the problem. My aunt has just died, for God's sake. Have a little respect, Gary.'

All Elizabeth could think about was the phone call from a Constable Madden at Mariners Cove Police Station to inform her of Margaret's sudden death. Still in shock, this news had really thrown her. It seemed impossible, and her immediate response was, 'No, you must be mistaken.' But there was no mistake, the police officer assured her. Yet, when she'd later spoken to Gary, he'd acted more concerned about his own selfish needs.

'I wasn't even aware you had an aunt, Liz.'

'Most people have an aunt, Gary. Even you, I suspect. But Margaret raised me from childhood. I thought you knew that.'

'Not sure I did. What more can I say apart from I'm sorry?'

The sentiment seemed a little empty and Elizabeth felt grateful Gary hadn't been at home to see her in tears. Her face a mess and nose running, she'd managed to put on a brave front before his return, that happened to coincide with a phone call to arrange six weeks extended leave from her workplace at the publishing house.

Forever demanding, life was all about Gary alright, and when Elizabeth had finally dressed and finished packing, she reminded him, 'It's a long drive and I want to get there before dark.'

'You worry too much, babe, that's your problem.'

'Easy to see it's not your problem, Gary,' she frowned. 'And don't call me babe by the way.'

'Really! Don't call me babe! When did that happen? And when were you planning to tell me you'll be away for six weeks?'

'Just covering my tracks. I'll be looking to get everything sorted quickly. The last thing I need is to lose my job.'

'What about me?'

'Couldn't get that lucky,' Elizabeth scoffed. 'We both know on the few occasions that you're based in Melbourne there'll be no shortage of willing admirers only too eager to rustle you up a slice of toast and marmalade to share in bed. But I'm warning you, Gary, don't go leaving any crumbs on my side.'

Still comfortably stretched out on the bed, hands behind his head, he looked a little hurt. 'Travel is my livelihood, Liz, and sometimes I wonder what you expect. I'm a pilot in case you've forgotten.'

'The fact that you're a pilot is pretty hard to forget, Gary, but by the time you get back from Singapore you won't even realise I've been gone.' Then, with a fleeting peck on the lips she again repeated, 'I really do need to get on the road.'

'What sort of way is that to say goodbye?'

Placing her overnight bag alongside the suitcase, Elizabeth said, 'Come on, Gary … you really are a selfish bastard at times. Do you think I'm looking forward to this? It's not exactly a walk in the park for me you know.' The words caught in her throat, and she reached for a tissue on the bedside table. 'Give me a break will you and stick my luggage in the boot.'

Gary leapt off the bed and threw his arms around her. Elizabeth leaned into his shoulder. He held her close. Brushing the hair back from her forehead he gently lifted her chin and wiped away a tear. 'Let's not leave each other on a sour note. I know that I might seem an insensitive bastard at times, Liz, but I really don't want to lose you.'

'Now's not the time, Gary. Maybe we can discuss this when I get back.'

'There's only one thing we'll be discussing when you get back, and I'm sure you know what that is.'

When Elizabeth was buckled up in the driver's seat and about to back the car out the driveway, Gary popped his head through the open window. 'Don't forget to call when you get there. My flight's not leaving till late tomorrow evening.' Kissing her tenderly, he stepped away and shouted at the top of his voice as if she was hard of hearing, 'Love you, babe!'

Oh no, Elizabeth cringed. Why did he always broadcast an intimate message like 'Love you, babe' so that the words would literally bounce off the walls and echo around the entire neighbourhood?

Not content with just one goodbye, he moved to the rear of the car and in between waving and blowing kisses, turned up the volume to repeat the same embarrassing line loud enough to disturb old Elsie Gordon in the house next door from her afternoon nap.

She pulled the curtain aside and with a cranky look on her face, threw open the window and told him to keep his voice down. 'Some of us are trying to sleep!'

Moving off down the street, Elizabeth glanced in the rear-view mirror and recalled how once she would have been overjoyed at Gary's antics and wild declarations of love that he shouted in the streets. But the novelty had worn off and this sort of grandstanding behaviour irritated her. His words of love sending a mixed message given his unreasonable resentment at being left. Would he have preferred she ignore her aunt's passing?

The early evening light began to fade when, hours later, she reached her destination. Exhausted, she entered the cold unwelcoming surrounds of a house left unattended. Elizabeth shivered when something far more sinister than the emptiness of the house without the presence of her aunt overwhelmed her. Only once before in her childhood had she ever experienced such complete abandonment. Something was amiss, and in that moment, she felt she would require a certain strength of courage to get through this.

Alone and bone tired, she didn't bother unpacking but reached inside the overnight bag to withdraw her warm pyjamas. The fleecy material offered a small degree of comfort against her skin and when her head hit the pillow, she closed her eyes in the hope of sleeping right through the night.

Forgetting to charge her mobile, not once did it enter her mind to call Gary.

2

Nightmare

A key turned in the lock.

A source of restless confusion, the sound penetrated the gloomy passageways of a dream interrupted.

Eight years old, a frightened child again, hide—she must hide. Terrified, she buried her head beneath the blankets and cried in a muffled plea, 'Aunt Margaret, where are you?'

But Margaret was gone. There was no Margaret.

Alone, Elizabeth found herself trapped, neither in one world nor the other. A battle between wakefulness and slumber, she became captive in an all too familiar nightmare.

The floodgate opened and a rising tide inched its way up the walls.

No, she didn't want this. She clung to the bedpost. A soggy sheet slapped against her face. The mattress, cast adrift, began to float – a lifeboat about to be caught in a storm. Up and over, it ploughed, up and over through the turbulent waters, her journey carrying her away to the centre of the raging sea.

A cry for help sounded amid the swirling depths of the ocean. Someone was drowning. She rolled on her tummy and stretched her arm as far as it would go to try and save them. 'Mummy, Daddy!' she screamed. 'You promised to come back. Please don't leave me.'

Skeletal claws dripping in slime desperate to grab on to her reached out from a murky tomb. 'Hang on!' she shouted. 'I can almost touch you.'

Round and round she circled, caught in a whirlpool, the wind then carrying her across the waves. Tears streamed down her face. Gone, they were gone – swallowed and sinking like stones beneath the surface of the angry tempest. Gone to rest forever in the silence of the distant seabed below.

Click, the release of a catch, the squeak of a door hinge. Startled, she sat up in bed alert, alarmed, eyes wide open. Her fear confirmed – absolute terror, no longer alone, no longer a child.

Her heart racing, she stared into the darkness and listened like a frightened deer in the forest, a hunted prey, her body tense, unmoving, frozen.

Floorboards creaked, footsteps wandered, a shuffle along the hallway – a pause, a silence, the scuttle of a mouse. Doors opened, doors closed, movement drawing closer – a stranger approaching. Breathing, heavy breathing.

Beneath the door, light filtered into the bedroom.

A soft tap, she cringed and huddled against the padded bedhead, her knees drawn up beneath her. Terror, absolute terror. She reached out to the side table in search of a weapon, her hand fumbling blindly along the surface. A turn of the brass knob – her only protection a bolted door refusing to budge. Eerie whispers along the walls of the hollow hallway echoed. 'Margaret, are you awake? Margaret, it's only me … it's only me.'

But Margaret was gone. There was no Margaret.

Silent, still, a chill in the air, sweat on her nightclothes, she shivered in fear. A tap at the door now more insistent – the intruder intent on entering. Louder he called, 'Margaret, it's only me.' He waited, he paced, he circled.

Drawing the covers up to her mouth, she prevented herself from crying out.

A movement, a shuffle, the light faded beneath the closed door. Footsteps receded down the passageway. The squeak of a door hinge, the click of a catch, the house fell into darkness.

She crept out of bed and peeked through the curtain. A crunch on the gravel, a shadowy figure in the moonlight, the hoot of an owl. A surge of warmth trickled down the inside of her legs.

A key turned in the lock.

3

An Update

When Elizabeth charged her mobile the following morning, the screen lit up with countless missed calls and worrying text messages. At this rate she expected to be met with some seriously bad vibes when she contacted Gary and he greeted her with a less than welcoming, 'About effing time, Liz.'

'Before you say another word, Gary, I want you to know I had every intention of calling. But more importantly you're not going to believe what happened last night.'

With no immediate response, Elizabeth asked, 'Are you still there, Gary?'

'Yeah, I'm listening! But this better be good, Liz, as I'm really in no mood for any of your bullshit excuses right now.'

'Well, it wasn't in the least bit good, if that's what you're asking. But you will be pleased to know I stopped off along the way and picked up a cheeseburger and fries as well as a chocolate sundae to give me a sugar hit.'

'Then what happened?' Gary asked in an impatient *I've got more important things to do* kind of voice.

'By the time I drove a few more k's up the road, I was struggling to keep my eyes open. Totally stuffed, when I finally arrived, I fell straight into bed and the minute my head hit the pillow, I was out like a light.'

'And that's it? That's what you're calling to tell me? About a cheeseburger and fries, with not a care in the world that I was almost ready to send out a search party when I didn't hear from you?'

In her defence, she said, 'So, I forgot to put the phone on the charger. Is that a crime, Gary? 'Cause last time I looked, I'm pretty sure you've messed up once or twice in your less than perfect existence.'

Hearing a lot of noise in the background, it seemed obvious that she was talking to herself. Gary's phone was on speaker and his mind elsewhere. *So much for his undying concern*, Elizabeth thought when trying to dismiss the fact that his preoccupation was annoying the hell out of her as she added, 'The story didn't end there.'

Met with no reply, 'Hello!' Elizabeth shouted. 'I am literally trying my best here.'

An ongoing clatter was doing nothing to relieve her tension when eager to tell him about her awful ordeal and wanting his full attention. This was the important part that she should have mentioned at the start. Why had she rambled on about a cheeseburger and fries, when what she had really wanted to say was, 'I thought I was going to get my throat slit last night.'

Already he had lost interest and sounded a million miles away with more important matters to attend to, as she had earlier detected. And then, as if out of breath, his voice came back on the phone. 'Now, you were saying, the story didn't end there.'

'I can't believe you, Gary. I've been chattering away here talking to myself while you're obviously doing something else. What in God's name is going on?'

'If you really want to know, I've been having a bit of a moment in the kitchen. The shelf in the dishwasher collapsed. But it's all under control now.'

'Okay … are you sure you've got that sorted? Because I was about to tell you a noise woke me in the middle of the night. I was so petrified my body broke out in a cold sweat after having that horrible nightmare about my parents.'

'Not again!' Gary cut in. 'You really should talk to someone about that.'

'After all these years, I'm sick of talking about it to be honest. But it wasn't the nightmare that was doing my head in, so much as the noise. Then I realised … '

'Look, babe, sorry about this, but I've really got to go,' he again interrupted. 'Been waiting on a call about a change in the flight schedule, and someone's trying to get through. Don't forget I fly out to Singapore this arvo and then on to London. We'll talk about these nightmares later. Stay safe and keep me posted.'

Stunned, Elizabeth didn't even get the chance to finish the sentence or say goodbye when the phone went silent.

'Worried my arse! I hope he fries in his Singapore noodles or gets mugged when out to dinner in my favourite white shirt, because I swear, he won't be hearing from me again in any great hurry.'

Later when Elizabeth sat back and thought about the ghastly nightmare and frightening incident that took place the previous evening, she realised she had lost count of the times that the *if only* scenario had played out in her mind. *If only* her parents had listened and not gone on that trip to Europe.

If only she had booked a room last night at the Cove.

If only her aunt hadn't died.

She recalled how as a young child in her grief-stricken state, she had blamed God. Why not? Who else could she blame? He alone wielded the power to intervene and prevent her parents from drowning. Yet God had chosen to look the other way.

Not long after, she forgot about the God theory and decided her father was to blame. She begged them not to leave, and her mother had shed a tear. Her father promised they would return in no time. Yet, not once did he look back when she'd chased the car and fell to her knees sobbing as she watched them drive away. Broken-hearted, she hated him in that moment and didn't care who knew it.

Her grandfather, when learning about this talk of hatred, gently tried to explain. 'You mustn't blame your father, Lizzie. I know it's hard, but sadly certain things are meant to be and there's nothing or no one who can change that. It's called fate, you see.'

Convinced that all her yesterdays and tomorrows were already mapped out, Elizabeth wasn't at all happy about fate. Because Grandpa had also said, 'Depending on a person's destiny, when least expected, fate has a habit of stepping in and taking charge to determine good fortune or bad.'

'That's enough, Dad! Please don't fill the child's head with things she's far too young to understand,' her aunt said, fondly placing a protective arm around her and comforting her in a time of need.

Elizabeth had since grown old enough to think for herself and now cursed the fact that fate could again take control and treat both her and her aunt so unkindly. This thought giving rise to her childhood tendency to reassert itself. And with all due respect to Grandpa, she preferred to believe that bad things happened because someone was to blame.

4

An Official Complaint

Elizabeth stepped up to the counter and made herself known to Constable Madden – a plain, freckle-faced young woman. She then stated the nature of her complaint and was handed a form to fill out. Completing the details she passed it back to the constable who then ushered her into a boxy, stale smelling room furnished with a metal filing cabinet, two spindly chairs and a pine table. Inviting her to be seated, Madden swiftly scooped up the browning remnants of an overripe banana and greasy paper bag from under her nose.

When offered tea or coffee, Elizabeth politely refused. She then met with Senior Sergeant Ian Henderson in charge of the Mariners Cove police station as he entered the room and took a seat opposite. A rotund and beady-eyed man whose prominent moustache defied the sparse strands of oily hair combed across his balding crown, he dispensed with any pleasantries while Madden hurried away. No sooner had she gone than she returned to place a steaming mug on the table in front of him. Only then, after she left the room, did he begin to interrogate Elizabeth.

In a gruff and officious manner, his questions were shaped in such a way as to treat her like the perpetrator of the disturbance as opposed to the guilty party she was there to report.

With an obvious look of dislike, he glared at her sternly and asked, 'Did the said intruder threaten to hurt you in any way?'

Elizabeth shook her head.

'I take it that's a no,' he scowled and told her to speak up. 'Can you recall his exact words?'

'Yes! *"It's only me!"* he said. *"It's only me!"*'

'Sounds like this intruder expected you to know him. So, you're quite certain these are the words he used to identify himself?' The senior sergeant paused and slurped his coffee in a loud and undignified manner.

Scalding the roof of his mouth, he coughed and spluttered, spilling the liquid down his shirtfront. 'Confound it, Madden!' he shouted. 'Why do you persist in making my coffee so damned hot? Even the devil himself would be hard-pressed to swallow it.'

Armed with a towel in one hand and a folder in the other, the constable rushed from her position at the front counter. Flustered, she passed both items across the desk. 'Sorry, Sir! Would you like me to top up your coffee with a drop of cold milk?'

Ignoring her request, the senior sergeant dabbed at his shirt and thrust the towel aside in yet a further unguarded display of anger. Clearing his throat, he opened the folder and scanned the details. 'A few too many typos here for my liking, Madden.'

With deliberate intent to belittle and embarrass the poor girl, Elizabeth thought, *what sort of a lowlife is this man?*

'Well, you see, Sir,' Madden replied, 'I had to dash it off in a bit of a hurry. Sorry about that!'

'Well don't just stand about gawking,' he snapped. 'That'll be all, Madden!'

'Yes, Sir … thank you, Sir.'

'Close the door behind you, Constable. Now, where were we? Oh yes, *"It's only me!"* So, I take it the said intruder was no stranger to your aunt?' The sergeant fumbled back through the folder to check the paperwork before emphasising the words, 'One, Margaret Amy Thornton, deceased. A person who he … I presume we are speaking of a male here … fully expected to recognise his voice. Would I be correct in saying this, Ms O'Connell?'

Senior Sergeant Henderson again lifted the mug to his mouth and cautiously blew into his coffee.

'Go ahead, Ms O'Connell, go ahead,' he demanded. 'Should you be unsure of the answer, I would like to hear whatever else this so-called intruder had to say.'

With such words as *so-called* being bandied around as if to undermine her credibility, Elizabeth pulled back her shoulders to make herself appear taller. 'Yes, it was a man's voice, and he asked, "*Margaret, are you awake?*"'

'Interesting! So yet again, we can quite positively ascertain from this simple statement that the said intruder not only knew your aunt but also had no knowledge of her recent death.'

'While it does seem that he knew my aunt, perhaps he was already aware of her circumstances but might have wanted to convince me of his ignorance to the fact.'

'This hardly seems likely, Ms O'Connell.'

Annoyed with the senior sergeant's negative attitude, gruff manner and air of superiority, Elizabeth took a further moment to compose herself.

'I'd like to make this quite clear, Sergeant Henderson ...'

Raising his hand, he rudely interjected. 'Correction, Ms O'Connell! I would ask that you please address me by my full title, Senior Sergeant Henderson, if you don't mind.'

What a pompous arse. 'My mistake, Senior Sergeant Henderson. But no matter who this person might be, I can't excuse or think it proper for him to enter my aunt's house unannounced in the middle of the night. And I'd like you to investigate the matter.'

'You have failed to mention the point of entry in your statement. Did he climb through an open window? Or did he prise a window open?'

'No, he unlocked the backdoor with a key.'

'With a key you say! Goodness me, could this be a spare key conveniently hidden under a mat or in a flowerpot for just this very purpose? With all due respect, Ms O'Connell, Mariners Cove is a small town, and your aunt was known to mix with various male acquaintances,' he sneered in a self-righteous manner. 'She was also an unmarried lady who may have been intimately involved with any one of these friends to whom she could have handed a key.'

Being made to feel like an empty-headed schoolgirl for coming here in the first place, Elizabeth was finding it difficult to control her anger. 'My aunt's personal affairs were her own business and I'm not sure I like the nature of your insinuation. Especially since Margaret is no longer able to defend herself. Also, I feel it important to question whether there were any suspicious circumstances surrounding her death.'

'None whatsoever!' Henderson scoffed.

Elizabeth jumped to her feet and scraped the chair back jarringly across the floorboards. 'Then might I request a written report supplying the details about who determined the cause of death, along with the exact location and name of the person who discovered my aunt's body?'

'I'll speak to Constable Madden. But let me tell you, I strongly recommend you think twice about living alone in that isolated house. A woman on her own will always be an easy target for drifters and the like who camp along the foreshore.'

'I appreciate your concern, *Senior* Sergeant Henderson, but I will not be so easily frightened away.'

'Well then, should you experience any further problems, I would suggest you contact the station immediately.'

Henderson came from behind his desk to place the folder and a biro in front of Elizabeth. 'A signature is required before you leave.' Stepping back to open the door, he asked, 'Have you neglected to inform me of anything at all unusual about this person? Was there anything distinctive about his speech for example?'

'Not really. His voice was muffled, and he mainly spoke in no more than a whisper saying only the few words I've already mentioned.'

'Well, there's little reason for concern. Whoever was outside your bedroom door, I believe presented no threat and was on familiar terms with your aunt. In which case there can be no charges laid. The man had a key, stole nothing, assaulted no one and left quietly without any sign of forced entry, leaving no evidence to suggest any intent to act out a crime.'

'You make this sound like an open and shut case, Senior Sergeant Henderson. Nothing more serious than an inconvenience brought about by a foolish woman.' Elizabeth remarked while scratching her signature across the dotted line and tossing the pen down on the desk. 'Oh, and be sure to call in at the bookshop. My aunt always stocked a vast selection of crime novels which should prove great reading to interest someone employed in the investigative side of the business. To uphold the law is a most admirable profession,' Elizabeth concluded with an air of sarcasm.

Barely able to stifle her anger, she hurried out through the doorway and walked in the direction of the hardware store to buy a batch of sturdy locks and bolts. A far better option than relying on any help from the likes of Ian Henderson.

5

A Bad Start

Returning to the normally peaceful surrounds of her aunt's house, the last thing Elizabeth expected was to be greeted by the deafening intrusion of a ride-on mower. The noise resounded across the hillside and ripped through the forest like the roar of an untamed beast.

A stranger seated behind the wheel of the mower could be mistaken for the owner by anyone who knew no different. And, given the death of her aunt, she felt incensed at his inappropriate behaviour. How dare he just wander in unannounced and carry-on with business as usual.

She unlatched the chain on the gate, and noticed the stranger look up to catch sight of her – probably curious to know who she was and why she had disregarded the private property sign. His ignorance about the matter provided her enormous satisfaction, as with an air of authority, she returned to the car and made her way up the driveway.

When she pulled in at the top and stepped out from behind the steering wheel, the man shut down the motor and hanging his goggles and earmuffs on the handlebar, he strolled across the garden to meet her.

Elizabeth watched him remove his cap and wipe his brow, while she struggled to hide her annoyance at his misplaced

19

sense of belonging. It was as if he'd taken ownership of the place before her aunt was cold in her grave.

'G'day there! Can I help at all?' he asked.

'I really don't think so.' Her dismissive manner being quite clear as she turned her back on him and busied herself unloading packages from the rear seat of the car.

She then took a moment to look out across the valley and ocean beyond. It wasn't difficult to see where he'd been, as rows of circular patterns, carved through swathes of overgrown grass, had left their mark on sections of neatly trimmed lawn. However, thinking it best to guard against showing any sign of approval, Elizabeth took pleasure breathing in the fragrance of freshly mown grass while secretly admiring the precision of the finely clipped hedges.

'Can't say I recall ever seeing you round these parts. Are you new to the area?' he persisted.

'Just the opposite, I grew up here and could ask the same question of you.'

Elizabeth didn't care if he thought her rude as she deliberately treated him in a haughty and offhanded manner. But seeming undeterred by her cool reception, he tried to break through her barrier of icy aloofness, perhaps in the hope of befriending her.

'Forrester's the name … Lenny Forrester, of no fixed address,' he said, reaching out his hand.

Of no fixed address. Elizabeth noted while ignoring his offer of polite introduction.

'A handshake is usually the norm around these parts when strangers meet for the first time. But I'm guessing that's completely out of the question,' he added, rubbing his palms self-consciously down the side of his jeans. 'Hands get a bit grubby in my line of work.'

With no response forthcoming, he continued. 'I stop off here to do odd jobs whenever passing through. Move around a bit as you can understand. Then again, it's obvious you're not here to discuss my movements. You must be looking for Margaret?'

'Looking for Margaret?' Elizabeth raised an eyebrow.

'Well yeah! Why else would y'be here?'

Thinking him the intruder who'd entered the house on the previous evening, Elizabeth snapped, 'I could say my being here is none of your business. And much and all as I'd love to see Margaret, the answer is no. I'll be staying for several weeks, but I'm not certain that your services will be required.'

'Hey, hang on there a minute, one of us must be confused. Because you drive in here from out a nowhere acting like Lady Muck and treating a bloke like some sort of second-class citizen, then have the nerve to tell me my services are no longer needed. Just who do you think you are?'

Elizabeth stopped fussing with parcels and looked Lenny straight in the eye. He had certainly captured her attention in the past few minutes, and as she took in his animated facial expressions, she guessed him to be aged somewhere around his mid-thirties. Self-assured and articulate for a knockabout odd-job man, it hadn't escaped her notice that an enraged Lenny Forrester was rather nice looking in an off-beat and assertive sort of a way.

Seemingly unfazed by her lack of response, he said, 'Look, lady, I'm not quite sure what your problem is, but I'd have to say you strike me as having a diploma from the university of bad manners. My advice would be to think carefully whoever you are because the last time I looked, Margaret Thornton was the owner of this house. Which leads me to believe that her decision is the only one that counts. And as there was never any discussion about her ending my employment, I would prefer to hear these words from her own mouth.'

'I'm afraid, Mr Forrester, that's no longer possible. I'm her niece, Elizabeth O'Connell, and a little surprised that no one has thought to inform you of my arrival.'

'Well, excuse me, Your Royal Highness! Had I known of the importance of this occasion, I would have rolled out the red carpet, declared it a public holiday and lined the driveway with a rent-a-crowd of flag waving admirers. But if you'll forgive my ignorance, I can't really say it's a pleasure to meet you. Especially given the news that I'm no longer welcome here.'

Lenny paced back and forth and finally came to a standstill right in front of Elizabeth's nose. 'I'm not sure what in the hell I've done to upset you, lady, but am I correct in saying that Margaret's away? Because it strikes me as a bit odd that your aunt, who struggles to manage on her own, might suddenly want to let me go.'

Stepping back a pace, Elizabeth sighed. 'Yes, she is away and there may be changes made in the future. So, in terms of settling whatever you are owed in wages, what time did you arrive may I ask?'

Lifting his eyes to the sky, Lenny shook his head. 'I don't believe I'm hearing this. But if you really want t'know, I reckon it was around nine or maybe ten.'

'Would that be am or pm, Mr Forrester?'

'Of all the snooty, stuck-up females I've had to deal with in my life, you'd have to be the worst. The truth is I don't usually make a habit of working in the dark if that's what you're asking. And I don't charge Margaret by the hour. I get free board and lodging in the shearers' cottage on my visits.'

'Look, Mr Forrester, I'm not interested in your sleeping arrangements, just give me a rough estimate of how long you've been working, and I'll settle the account. The reason for my visit is not a social one and I don't have the time to quibble over a few dollars.'

Lenny threw his hands in the air. 'Who's quibbling? Surely Margaret's not selling the place, is she? She's not ill or anything, I hope!'

'No, she's not ill. But selling could be the case in the future. The purpose of my visit is to sort out her affairs. You see I thought you knew, but it would seem you are unaware that my aunt has only recently passed away.'

The colour drained from Lenny's face, and he staggered back in shock. 'What! That's not possible … she can't have.'

Surprised by his reaction, Elizabeth watched him closely as he sat on a log and lowered his head into his hands. 'This is terrible! I can't believe it,' he mumbled. 'Are you sure about this? What was the cause of death?'

'I'm not exactly certain. But it seems her heart may have given out.'

'That amazes me,' Lenny replied, shaking his head. 'Margaret was always such a healthy and robust woman.'

For the first time, Elizabeth felt a little sorry for Lenny. 'Look, Mr Forrester, perhaps I've acted unfairly towards you. If you want to stay on for a bit and get the garden into shape it will probably benefit the both of us. I need the place to be in good nick if, and when, I come to sell and I'm happy for you to continue using the facilities in the cottage.'

Picking up a splintered stick, Lenny drew a circle in the dirt with a line down the middle. 'What's with the sudden change of heart?'

'Let's just say, I had a lot of faith in Margaret's judgement. If she was happy with your work and trusted you, then that's a good enough recommendation for me.'

Lenny looked pleased about this unexpected change in her attitude until she added, 'Although should I discover otherwise.'

Cutting Elizabeth off mid-sentence, he jumped to his feet. 'You really are a piece of work, do you know that? I think it best all round if I collect my bag and head off. I'll pack up the tools and put the mower in the shed.'

Elizabeth watched him walk away - his shoulders slumped. Upset with herself for acting in such a high and mighty manner, she shouted, 'Wait, Mr Forrester … wait. What do I owe you?'

'Forget it, lady! You owe me nothing. It's on the house. And I'm sorry about your aunt.'

Although Elizabeth felt certain that Lenny Forrester was without doubt the person on whom she had just filed a complaint, he did appear to be genuinely saddened when she had broken the news of Margaret's passing. Yet, when she'd left for Mariners Cove earlier that morning, there was no sign of life at the cottage. If he was there at the time, she hadn't noticed the tradie type ute in which he later sped away amid a cloud of dust.

6

A Challenging Day

Following Lenny Forrester's departure, Elizabeth slept without incident on the second night and woke to the familiar sights and sounds of the fresh dewy countryside.

The view beyond her window held the promise of a heavenly summer's morning and the cloudless sky appeared to shamelessly flaunt a land made solely for rejoicing. The glorious weather, being a timeless reminder that the chirping of birdsong continued regardless of another's mortality, and the misery of those who felt their world had ended due to the death of a loved one.

It had long been foretold that should the rain fall upon the hour of one's burial, it could be seen as a sign of respect. Was this then a cruel trick of fate or simply a glimpse into paradise and the future of her aunt's soul beyond the gloomy depths of the grave?

No matter the interpretation, this morning was one that clearly marked the beginning of a perfect day with little chance of a single drop of rain – a day for building castles in the sand. For others going about their normal business, it would be perfect also. But for Elizabeth O'Connell, it would be a day as grey as winter – a day to bury the dead.

By mid-morning Elizabeth had discarded her sombre black jacket and now looked at home in a colourful cap, jeans and flimsy white blouse that billowed in the breeze.

The salty sea air and pleasant aroma of the fishermen's catch reminded her of the past as she wandered along the stony-faced jetty and slowly made her way towards the end of the pier. Young boys and old men equipped with buckets and tackle cast their fishing lines over the side, and moored boats bobbed and rolled in rhythm with the ceaseless swell of the tide.

'Lovely morning for a stroll,' greeted a leathery faced gentleman, tipping his cap.

'Couldn't be better,' Elizabeth replied in a cheery voice that belied the gravity of her true feelings.

Across the universe entire villages ceased their normal activities to gather and weep for the dead. Yet the people of Mariners Cove continued in ignorance with business as usual.

Staring vacantly into the distance, the sunlight danced on the water. Her eyes filled with tears, blurring her vision of the white capped ocean. *Doesn't anybody realise a life has ended?* she thought. *Doesn't anybody care that the one person I have loved so dearly now lies buried in the darkness?* Lower the sails, lay down your rod, put aside your foolish playthings, she longed to shout … it's time to mourn.

With no one to comfort her, Elizabeth thought of how she had walked from the direction of the graveyard where the private burial had earlier taken place, with none of the usual formalities of a funeral service. She'd stopped when reaching the war memorial to pay homage to the list of young men who died in battle and gazed up at a carved figure of a lone soldier who stood in silent vigil – a rifle by his side. Sadly, their sacrifice was rarely acknowledged by those passers-by who seldom paused to spare a thought for the forgotten heroes and the price they'd paid for freedom. Her aunt, perhaps a hero to no one apart from Elizabeth herself, had lived a simple life and in time would lay forgotten also.

Mindful to allow ample time to arrive for her appointment with the solicitor, she turned to retrace her steps along the pier. But unlike the carefree visitors who invaded the popular camp sites and beaches, she had taken this journey with a heavy heart and would return to the emptiness of a silent house.

The kindly fisherman waved. 'See you again,' he shouted.

'Good luck with your catch,' Elizabeth replied.

Mirrored in her sunglasses, the rolling hills swept down to meet the small coastal township that skirted the pristine waters of Mariners Cove. The peaceful countryside being in sharp contrast to the bustle of the main street as a swelling influx of summer holidaymakers filled the shops and lined the colourful sidewalk cafes. The weeks ahead ensuring the normally sleepy community of a healthy income to tide them over in preparation for the more solitary seasons to follow.

Elizabeth wandered the grassy foreshore and admired the strange formation of the trees which so uniquely typified the identity of this pretty village. Flat cypress heads spread atop gnarled trunks and wayward branches. Yet like proud old seamen, although arthritic and bent, these ancient sentinels remained defiant and dug their roots deep in a bid to anchor themselves more firmly into the soil. Only the strong survived the ravages of the buffeting wind – their grey-green canopies a shady refuge and welcome relief for the benefit of all who passed beneath them.

Like so many to have come before her, Elizabeth had picnicked with her aunt beneath the trees of Mariners Cove. Together they had wandered the clifftops, explored the hidden valleys and fern glades where the cooling waters rushed down the gullies to enter the pebbled creeks and sandy riverbeds. *Why must everything end?* she thought.

With a painful sadness, she realised there was no alternative other than to accept her fate and face the grim reality of a life without her best friend and a world with far less purpose.

Elizabeth joined the throng on the leisurely stroll along the esplanade – some licking ice cream, some lounging outdoors at the various coffee shops, wine bars and up-market restaurants. Others walked their dogs, jostled to be served in the bakeries, browsed in the real estate windows or tucked into a counter lunch in the beer garden or balcony of their favourite pub. Her mouth watered as she noted the roast of the day and crayfish written up in chalk on a prominently displayed blackboard. Loud music spilled out onto the pathway, and she heard a distinctive wolf whistle come from a group of beer swilling youths who invited her to join them for a drink. Elizabeth quickened her step and passed shops selling swimwear and postcards prior to turning down a side street to reach her destination – Graeme Jenkins & Associates.

She tapped on the door and entered a quiet space with a small unattended reception area where a notice on the countertop informed visitors to please ring the bell and take a seat – which instruction Elizabeth followed.

After waiting for five minutes, she walked across to the hallway tapped on a closed door and shouted, 'Hello, is anyone there?'

A kindly looking man dressed in an open neck business shirt and slightly crumpled trousers appeared from a room at the farthest end of the corridor.

'I'm so sorry,' he warmly smiled. 'My receptionist is on leave, and I didn't hear you come in.' But then as he drew closer the smile turned to a look of surprise. 'Margaret!' he said. Then quickly realising his mistake, his face turned red. 'Oh dear, forgive me for staring. For a moment, I thought you were Margaret. But of course, that would be impossible. You must be her niece, Elizabeth. The likeness is incredible.'

'It's quite okay. My aunt and I have often been mistaken for sisters.'

'Well, I do feel rather silly.' The solicitor said prior to introducing himself and greeting her with an enthusiastic handshake. He then led Elizabeth to his office and invited her to take a seat.

'Without my glasses,' which he retrieved from his desk, 'my eyesight's not what it used to be.'

When he placed the rounded, almost Dickensian style bifocals midway down his nose, he took on the studious appearance of a college professor. And despite a distinguished mane of slightly tousled, snowy white hair, his cheeks glowed with a youthful almost boyish freshness. Elizabeth, guessing him to be aged in his late fifties, decided that she liked him immensely and felt relaxed in his company.

Jenkins, positioned behind his desk, said, 'Before we get started, allow me to offer my condolences. Your aunt was much admired in the community and her sudden passing is a sad loss for all.'

'That's very kind, Mr Jenkins.'

'Most clients just call me Jenkins. I know it sounds a bit like the butler, but we don't stand on ceremony in Mariners Cove.'

Elizabeth was to later learn that Jenkins was an independent character who'd never married. A former partner in a Melbourne law firm, some years earlier, he decided on a quieter lifestyle where he could spend his weekends golfing and fishing. And now in semi-retirement, he worked three days a week.

'I hope you don't mind me asking, but has there been any history of heart disease in your family?'

'Not that I know of.' Elizabeth hesitated before addressing him as Graeme. 'It's okay to use your Christian name I suppose.'

'Go right ahead,' Jenkins laughed and nodded in agreement.

'It's just that I'd feel a bit cheeky calling you the butler. But getting back to your question, I'm hoping for further information about the details of Margaret's death in the coming days.'

'That's good to hear.' Jenkins agreed. 'It's important to know of any pre-existing health condition in the family. Not just for your own benefit, but for those that follow. Who informed you of her death by the way?'

'A Constable Madden from the local police station.'

Jenkins sounded a little puzzled when hearing this. 'Why a police officer I wonder?'

'That's a good question. But I just assumed, as there is no family in town, they must be expected to pass on this sort of information.'

'Ah … yes … perhaps you're right!' Jenkins said scratching his head. 'But I would fully agree you should look further into the matter, and ask the pertinent questions needed to ascertain the exact details and satisfy yourself about what occurred.'

Feeling a little shaken since Jenkins raised this concern, she desperately wanted to tell someone her story. And as he seemed a genuinely caring person, she decided to confide in him. 'I'm not sure if you know my aunt became my legal guardian following the death of my parents. Only eight years old at the time, I grew to love her in a way that any daughter might love her natural mother. Now I have no other living relatives and can't imagine how I will manage without her.'

Jenkins shook his head in despair. 'How cruel life can be. The loss of all three of the most important members of your family is tragic. This is a sad day, and I'd like to offer my support if ever you're in need of help.'

'Gosh, I feel bad for burdening you with my woes.'

'We all need someone to talk to,' Jenkin's replied as he shuffled through the paperwork on his desk. 'The one thing I can tell you, is that Margaret's concern for your welfare was clear, and after your grandparents passed away, she did draw up her Will. I also assisted her with various business matters.' Adjusting his glasses, he added, 'More recently she arranged an appointment in relation to a separate issue and hinted she had something on her mind you should know about. She wanted my advice but refused to tell me about a secret she'd kept for years.'

Elizabeth leaned forward in her chair. 'A secret!' she repeated. 'So … what did you say to her?'

'I told her the truth has a way of making itself known, and it would be in her own interest to reveal whatever was worrying her. With that, she later entrusted me with an envelope which she instructed me to hand to you should something happen to her.'

Elizabeth raised her eyes to the ceiling. 'This all sounds most intriguing. Why would she suddenly think in these terms if she had no reason to believe her life was in danger?'

Tipping back in his chair, Jenkins clasped his hands together behind his head. 'This sort of thing is not unusual. She was probably just being cautious. Because, as we so often hear, there are no guarantees in this life.'

'Yes, you're so right. But what are the odds of losing my entire family before I've reached the age of thirty? It's as if we've all been cursed.'

'Unfortunately, we may never know the answer about why certain things happen,' Jenkins replied. 'But at least your aunt's wishes over which she did have control are quite straightforward. Her first request specifically pointed out that she had no desire for a funeral service and simply wanted a private burial in the grounds of the Mariners Cove Cemetery.'

Elizabeth said, 'I did receive the message and carried out Margaret's wishes this morning. I'm sure her friends would have wanted to pay their last respects and will be disappointed. But she must have had her reasons.'

Jenkins nodded. 'It was you she was mindful of and wanted to make this difficult task as quick and easy as possible.' Then lowering his head to read the Will, he continued. 'The rest of her assets as listed, include the sum of an unspecified amount currently in the region of eight thousand dollars held in a savings account. Together with a thirty-thousand-dollar fixed term deposit along with the title to the bookstore, plus the house and contents.'

Elizabeth's mouth dropped open when Jenkins went on to say, 'As there are no other known living relatives, the estate in its entirety is bequeathed to her niece, Elizabeth Jane O'Connell.' Peering over the rim of his glasses, 'Namely yourself, the sole beneficiary,' he concluded, as though she may have at that moment been suffering doubt as to her own identity.

Jenkins then corrected himself. 'Oh, my mistake, Elizabeth. There is a codicil that was only recently added. It specifies a payment of three thousand dollars be handed to a Mr Philip Anderson.'

Elizabeth looked puzzled. 'Philip Anderson? I have no idea who that is.'

'All I can tell you is that he and his brother, I believe, live at Misty Headland. Jenkins then passed a sealed envelope across the desk. 'Maybe the contents of the enclosed letter might be of further assistance.'

Checking the envelope, Elizabeth noted her name and recognised Margaret's handwriting. 'Do you know what this is about?'

'I suspect it could have something to do with the secret we spoke of earlier. But no matter what the letter contains, if you want my advice, don't be too hasty in making any decisions. Think things through carefully after you've had time to come to terms with your grief. If you then choose to stay at the Cove with the plan of re-opening the bookshop, it should prove a rewarding venture.'

'You seem fairly sure of that.'

Clearing his throat, Jenkins explained, 'There's no library in this region, so you can be assured that both the locals and visitors alike will be at a loss without a decent book to read. But if you decide to return to the city, I'll be happy to arrange the sale or lease of either property on your behalf.' He then handed Elizabeth the keys together with copies of relevant papers and documents while confirming the original deeds were to be filed in a vault with his former law firm in Melbourne.

'Thank you for your kindness, Graeme.' Elizabeth got up to leave. 'And just out of interest, how many employees do you have working in the firm?'

Jenkins laughed. 'Don't be fooled by the, & *Associates*, on the window, Elizabeth. I'm running a one-man show here apart from Rita my receptionist, who works part-time.'

Taking her hand in his, 'Please take care, my dear, and whatever you decide, my best wishes go with you. It's been a pleasure to meet you and I'm only sorry that this introduction was brought about by necessity and under such painful circumstances.'

7

Slightly Tipsy

Unable to face returning to an empty house, Elizabeth delayed this extra burden in favour of visiting a nearby café. Selecting an out-of-the-way table, she ordered a hot meal and noticing a wine list, decided on a glass of the house red to help settle her nerves.

'Could I interest you in a small carafe at no extra charge? It's a special promotion on offer to our customers for one day only,' the waiter smiled.

'Why not!' Elizabeth agreed. A little pick-me-up wouldn't hurt given everything she had undergone. Yet, by the time the waiter returned with her order, the emotional turmoil of her aunt's death was threatening to engulf her. Fighting back tears she discreetly placed a Valium tablet on her tongue and washed it down with a good measure of wine.

A light-headed sensation suddenly took hold, and Elizabeth realised that swallowing the medication on an empty stomach had not been very clever. She asked the waiter for a glass of water as he served her lunch. But the pungent aroma of garlic began to turn her stomach, and she struggled to finish.

Before Elizabeth knew it, she had emptied the carafe and pushing the plate aside, she held her head in her hands. Her shoulder collapsed as one elbow quite unexpectedly slipped off the edge of the table. Hoping no one had noticed, her mind in a muddle, she thought about how her life had been turned around in the space of a few days, all because of … all because of … Elizabeth couldn't think straight and was becoming increasingly uncoordinated. All she could fathom was that now she had a house and a bookshop, but no aunt. What was she going to do with a house and a bloody bookshop, but no aunt? She wanted Margaret back. 'Give her back,' she said out loud. 'I demand my Margaret back right this minute,' she repeated.

Losing all inhibition when people turned to look at her, she scowled at a family across the way. 'Easy for you lot. This is a trajedy … a trajedy, do you hear me?' *It was so unfair. Where was my family?*

Feeling drowsy, her elbows now slid across the table knocking the dishes aside and narrowly missing the wine glass. She slumped forward, fighting a longing to lay her head down.

'Pardon me, dear … would you mind if I join you?'

Elizabeth tried to focus on what she at first believed to be two elderly ladies bent over a walking stick and ghosting into one another.

Loosely waving her arms around with little control, 'Of coursch not.' She rallied in a bid to show a little dignity. 'Jus-cht about t'finish and be on me way.'

'Please don't rush off on my account, dear. I do hope you won't mind me interfering, but I couldn't help thinking you seem a little distressed. Are you okay?' The lady, seating herself at the table – and now graduating into one and the same person – asked with a look of concern.

Bleary eyed, Elizabeth shook her finger at the nearby family chatting over their coffee and milkshakes when they rudely stared her way and the children giggled.

'Wha's so funny?' Elizabeth said to them.
Slurring her words, her eyes rested on her companion. 'I'm a liddle upshet. Yeah, upshet … that's what I am right now. Y'see,

it's Margaret! She's gone! Kaput! Jus' like that without a word of goo'bye.' Elizabeth's eyelids drooped. She swayed in the chair and reached inside her purse to withdraw a hankie which she struggled to connect with the end of her nose. 'Can you believe that? Kaput!' Her lifeless hands flopped on the table.

She then pointed a shaky finger to make a further point. 'Scnuffed out … like a light.'

The old lady gently placed her bony fingers on Elizabeth's arm. 'Oh dear, I'm so very sorry. Would you prefer to be left alone?'

'Shirtenly not!' Elizabeth hiccupped and gripped the woman's sleeve in desperation. 'Don't leave me. I'm all alone.'

'I can tell you, dear, you're not alone.'

Elizabeth again hiccupped and smiled. 'You're susch a nice lady. I really, reeally, like you. No … crossch that out. I really, really love you.'

The lady reached out and brushed a tear from Elizabeth's cheek. 'There, there, now, let's wipe away those tears.'

'Whatch y'name?'

'I'm Beatrice Barry. But you can call me Beaty.'

'Susch a lovely name.' Elizabeth patted her hand adoringly to Beaty's face.

The family got up to leave. The little boy nudged his sister and pointed a finger to the side of his forehead then turned it round and round in a circular motion. They both looked at Elizabeth and again giggled behind their hands.

Elizabeth placed a finger at either corner of her mouth, spread her lips wide and poked out her tongue.

Their father shook his head and frowned before shunting the children away.

The waiter came to collect the dishes and wipe the surface of the vacated table. He turned to Elizabeth and asked, 'Can I get you a coffee?'

'Nope, but me frien' mi' like one.'

The waiter gave Elizabeth a strange look and moved on. It didn't occur to her to ask why Beaty never ordered anything. Although she did look abnormally pale. A cloud of soft white hair surrounded her wrinkled face, and her skin like powdered parchment reminded Elizabeth that apart from a tinge of rouge painted on each cheek, Beatrice Barry was quite surreal in a way.

'You're an anjel, Beead-dy!'

The two chatted for a short time and Beatrice urged Elizabeth to drink more water. 'Never fear now, Elizabeth, and always remember you are not alone. I've enjoyed our little chat, and should we not have the good fortune to meet again, I wish you well, my dear.'

Elizabeth felt calmer and more able to cope with the thought of returning to an empty house as the waiter tapped her on the shoulder and introduced the manager. 'Are you okay, young lady? You've only had a few drinks but seem really under the weather. I think you might've nodded off for a while.'

'Don' worry bou' me. I'm fine, jus' fine … really,' Elizabeth replied. 'But wha' happened to my frien' Bead-dy?' Elizabeth swayed.

'What friend?' the waiter shrugged.

'Have you ever been drunk on red wine before, darlin'?' The manager asked. 'Because I'm going to have to ask you to leave. You're disturbing the other diners,' he said, pulling her from the chair. 'And if you're ever planning on returning, next time I might need to see if you're old enough to drive.'

Elizabeth laughed. 'Tha's crazy! I'm twen'y cheven,' she tried to tell him as he unceremoniously escorted her to the door.

'Yeah, aren't they all. Nice try, darlin', you did manage to fool the waiter who also saw you popping pills. Come back when you turn eighteen and can hold your liquor. And think yourself lucky I don't report you to the police.'

Elizabeth still had enough presence of mind to assure the manager she wouldn't be returning even though she was having trouble standing, let alone capable of seeking out her driver's licence. And as she staggered into the open, a sudden rush of air caused her to wonder, had she been hit with a brick?

Almost losing her balance, she reeled back to steady herself against the wall of a neighbouring shopfront. Feeling wretched, she then caught sight of herself in a mirror. Her hair looked a mess, and mascara had blackened the hollows beneath her eyes, but she somehow managed to weave her way towards the cemetery.

Hesitating alongside the chapel, she noticed that since earlier in the day, a small bunch of wildflowers had been laid at the foot of Margaret's gravesite, and as the interment had been a private affair, her curiosity outweighed her desire to rest her head down in the back seat of the car. So, she decided to investigate.

Scanning the grounds, she caught sight of a man watching her in the distance. Impossible to define his facial features hidden in the shadow of a cap and sunglasses, he turned to leave once seeing Elizabeth had spotted him.

'Stop! Stop!' she shouted.

The stranger looked back over his shoulder. And Elizabeth couldn't blame him for fleeing when afraid of being accosted by some drug-induced mad woman. She'd felt too weak to follow and her legs buckled under her. Hot and feverish, a painful cramp caused her to double over as a bitter tasting bile came rushing up her throat. The sour content of her stomach burst forth from her mouth and she fell to the ground exhausted.

Completely lifeless she rested against the base of a headstone and asked herself whether she was about to join her aunt and die right here in the graveyard. Too young to die, this thought gave her the incentive to drag herself to her feet and stagger back to the car where she curled up in a ball on the back seat and fell asleep.

Having locked the doors, Elizabeth woke with a start to the sound of persistent tapping and jeering at the window. Distorted faces of three teenage boys with their noses squashed against the glass leered at her. But thankfully they ran away when someone called, 'Oi! What are you blokes up to? On y'way or I'll call the coppers.'

Still groggy, head pounding, Elizabeth, surprised to see the sun setting, checked her phone. She climbed into the front seat, turned the key in the ignition and headed away from town while praying not to run into the local booze bus around the bend. Senior Sergeant Ian Henderson would be beside himself with joy if she got charged for being over the limit and thrown in the local lock-up.

Just think, drunk and disorderly and driving over the limit wouldn't be a great place to start.

A sense of relief came over Elizabeth when she reached the turn off and entered a section of unsealed track that snaked its way beneath the towering gums where, tucked away at the edge of the forest, the house sat carved into a hillside. It seemed strange, even in summer, not to see smoke rising from the chimney or Margaret rushing out to greet her. This evening the place appeared especially gloomy and stood in silent mourning without the ring of her aunt's laughter.

Elizabeth wandered through the rooms in the hope that this had all been a mistake and Margaret might suddenly pop her head out from somewhere unexpected and shout surprise, you can wake up now. But no, that was not about to happen. The dim interior lacked any of its usual cheer and an unwelcome chill crept into Elizabeth's bones as the evening shadows stretched before her and nightfall descended. She boiled the kettle and searched the cupboard for a painkiller to relieve the throbbing in her head. Only then in the stillness of the kitchen did she think to reach for the envelope and with shaking hands removed the letter.

Dearest Elizabeth,

No doubt the unthinkable has happened, and as you read these words, my time to walk this earth has ended.

Perhaps I have deserved my fate, but I want you to know I loved you more than any other person in my life.

I am truly sorry to leave you, but don't be afraid to embrace the future. Also, never forget to enjoy the moment.

As a young girl, I didn't heed my own advice, and since you have been in Melbourne, a second chance for happiness came my way. Sadly, fate has decreed that this important period of my existence be snatched away and left unresolved. It will now be up to you to decide the truth.

Apart from yourself, there are three very dear people I have grown to have a deep affection and concern for. Then there is Phyllis of course. Our friendship did run into trouble, but don't be too hard on her. And due to my departure, the suffering of those I have mentioned may increase as they have each in their own way come to rely on me. Brothers, Philip and David Anderson, who now live at Misty Headland in the old Gentry place will benefit from a meeting with you. And you with them I should think. The other person will make herself known. Whatever follows will be left to your own discretion.

Part of a long-held secret which I intended to someday reveal to you will surely come to light. However, the missing pieces, still hidden, I intended to destroy as the truth has never sat well with me. Yet should some twist of fate lead you to stumble on that which holds the answers, all I ask is, please don't judge me too harshly.

Farewell, my darling. There's no need to be afraid – you are not alone. I am with you in spirit and beside you always.

Your loving aunt,

Margaret

How extraordinary, when even though Elizabeth may have been a little tipsy, her aunt had ended this letter with Beatrice Barry's exact words about not being alone. Yet, left intrigued and unsettled about the content of this mysterious and somewhat vague letter, she felt little the wiser. The question of the Anderson brothers left her really puzzled. Who were they? How had they won their way into her heart? And what of the third person? Obviously, a woman. Was she connected to the brothers? And perhaps the biggest question of all being, what possible secret could Margaret have chosen, even in death, not to reveal?

Elizabeth's priority in all of this was to rest as she had really beaten herself up today, and the ghost of her aunt must now be allowed to lay at rest also. Yet, given this latest development, this somehow seemed unlikely.

8

The Bookshop

With the unsettling happenings that had occurred over the past few days now behind her, Elizabeth put the embarrassing episode at the cafe aside and focused on the bookshop and financial situation.

Wearing sensible walking shoes, it was on this the third morning of her stay that she passed a string of airy retail premises, low rise holiday apartments, trendy boutiques and galleries. These newly developed establishments having injected a renewed confidence in her as they should surely provide an added enticement to lure the curious shoppers down the side streets.

The leafy setting on her approach to the historical stone church housing the bookshop, re-enforced Elizabeth's belief that the building held an age-old appeal to attract the passers-by and those who were prepared to explore the back streets of Mariners Cove.

A shingle bearing the words "Telltales Bookshop – Proprietor M. A. Thornton" hung prominently displayed alongside a board that once informed patrons of the times of Sunday services. The former notices now replaced with information about the latest bestsellers and upcoming literary events.

The original owner who sold the business to Margaret had chosen to keep the aptly named "St Thomas Bookshop" title.

Yet, her aunt decided to ditch St Thomas in favour of the far less secular name, Telltales. Perhaps having been attracted to a change or simply preferring to put her own stamp on the place.

A paved path led the eye from the gate to an impressive arched porchway and solid oak door. Inserting the key in an ornate lock, Elizabeth entered the cool interior. 'Beeswax and dust jackets,' she said, as she took in the well-stocked shelves and inhaled the pleasant aroma.

Between the leaded windows, books lined the walls and soared to the height of the vaulted ceiling. Ladders, equipped with roller-casters, ran along tracks to enable access to volumes that would otherwise be out of reach. While at the rear, a spiral staircase climbed to the choir loft from where a narrow cast iron walkway extended along either side of the building to provide a second level. The former altar area, complete with baptismal font and pulpit, had been left as a multi-purpose hub with well-placed church pews used for seating.

'I really had forgotten this place could be quite so charming,' Elizabeth said, smiling as she stumbled over a misplaced book lying at her feet. Placing her bag down on the counter, she rolled up her sleeves and searched for a vacant slot along one of the upper shelves.

Teetering uncertainly on the fourth rung of the ladder, Elizabeth – being somewhat new to this endeavour – was trying to replace the book into position when an unexpected tinkle of the brass doorbell caused her to almost lose her balance.

'Oh my God,' she whispered. 'Why didn't I remember to bolt the door behind me.'

The book slipped from her grasp and dropped to the floor below.

In obvious annoyance, she cursed beneath her breath and peered back over her shoulder to capture a glimpse of a tall red-headed woman framed in the doorway.

'Shop's closed, I'm sorry.'

A closed shop appeared to pose no deterrent to the stranger as she continued to enter, while obviously not in the least concerned about such a minor detail.

Beads, bangles and earrings jangled with her every movement. And when the stranger drew closer, Elizabeth was struck by the colourful combination of her clothing and quick to notice this woman's bold choice of accessories worked in her favour to complement a pretty face.

Hesitating for a moment, the stranger reached down to retrieve the book. Careful to inspect the cover, 'No damage!' she said while watching Elizabeth step down from the ladder and brush off her clothing.

'Here you go,' the woman placed the book in Elizabeth's hand.

'Thank you! But I'm not sure if you heard me … the shop is in fact closed for an extended period.'

'I do realise this to be the case, darling, and did read the "Closed until further notice" sign. Forgive me for my forwardness, but being a bit of a rebel, when I turned the doorknob to find it unlocked, I just couldn't help myself and had to take a quick peek inside. Who knows … you might even be glad of the company?'

'Well, maybe you're right,' Elizabeth agreed, extending her hand to introduce herself. 'I'm Liz … Liz O'Connell.'

The young woman clasped Elizabeth's hand in her own. 'Thorny's niece … yes, I know! To be honest this is the real reason for my visit. As for the rest, well let me just say, I have been keeping an eye out for you. Tilt Jacobson, at your service.'

'Tilt, did you say?'

'That's right, darling, you've got it in one. Few ever do first up you know. Oh, you don't mind me calling you darling, I hope. Of course, it's only a nickname … Tilt, I mean.'

'And a quite unusual one.' Elizabeth replied when realising the discussion had moved on and no longer needed to respond to the question of whether she objected to being referred to as darling.

'My real name is so pedestrian. I just loathe it with a passion.' An expression of disgust spread across her face. 'It's Eileen, you see. Now I ask you, darling, do I look lopsided to you?'

Tilt became so intent on the telling of her story that she didn't bother to wait for too many answers.

'Can you believe that anyone in their right mind could inflict an ugly name like that on their own daughter? But there's worse to come. My maiden-name was, "Overton" … I lean bloody Over-ton, darling! If you'll pardon my French? At school the kids all called me "Tilt" and it has stuck ever since.'

Elizabeth tried her best to look sympathetic. Yet, one second later their eyes met, and they were doubled over in laughter.

'Well, now we've got the formalities out of the way, I wasn't sure if you were aware that I used to help out around here. And that book … you know, the one you were returning to the shelf, well it doesn't belong up in that section. It's about St Thomas. You're probably aware that he's the saint whose name once graced this building when the church was closed and sold to the earlier owner. She sought a permit to use the premises as a bookshop. But even though Thorny, bless her dear soul, renamed the place, she would have wanted you to know *The Legacy of St Thomas* is not for sale. It comes with the territory and was the first book ever to be catalogued.'

Quite without warning, Tilt then burst into sobs and wrapped her arms around Elizabeth in a bear hug that almost crushed the air from her lungs. Releasing her hold, she then stepped back to regain her composure and fumbled around inside an oversized handbag to produce a brightly patterned handkerchief gaily printed with skyrockets exploding over the Sydney Harbour Bridge. Tilt dabbed at her eyes and when attempting to discreetly blow her nose, she seemed certain to extinguish the fireworks in her effort.

Elizabeth was taken aback at this unexpected display of emotion and even more dismayed to hear her recently deceased aunt, Margaret Thornton, being referred to as Thorny.

'Gosh, I've managed to wreck my favourite Ken Done hankie,' Tilt sniffled. 'Thorny wouldn't approve of me cracking the sads and snivelling like a little kid. But here I am chattering as usual, when the real purpose of my visit is to offer my condolences, say hello and invite you out for a coffee.'

'That's very thoughtful of you, Tilt, and I'm sorry to see you so upset. I wasn't aware that my aunt … ah Thorny, that is, had an employee. So, how about we grab that coffee tomorrow morning around ten?'

Tilt's sparkle returned. 'That's fine by me, and provided the sun is shining, with a bit of luck and a good tail wind, we might even fluke a table outside Tony's Deli.' The bell tinkled once more as Tilt made her exit out through the doorway. With a couple of departing words, 'Toodles, darling', she bid farewell, and the shop reverted to its former silence.

Elizabeth cast her eyes around the books and ran a finger along the shelves where the dust had collected. There was much to be done before she spoke to an agent and arranged for the business to be put back on the market. But deciding that enough had been achieved for one day, she boiled the kettle to make a mug of tea, and her mind wandered back to the mysterious letter. She recalled the mention of an unnamed person who would make herself known. It had not taken long, as Tilt Jacobson was, almost certainly, the one about whom her aunt had been referring.

9

Coffee with Tilt

'Lizzie ... over here!' Tilt beckoned.

The main street – a hive of activity crawling with holidaymakers, posed no problem for Elizabeth when seeking out her friend. She had already spotted Tilt's colourful outfit from almost two blocks away.

Jumping to her feet in greeting, Tilt deposited a fresh air kiss on either cheek. 'Moi, Moi,' she said. 'Isn't this the most divine little place in the whole of Mariners Cove, darling? I just love sitting at a sidewalk deli breathing in the aroma of freshly brewed coffee beans and watching the passing parade. It's so deliciously European, don't you agree?'

Elizabeth's response was cut short as the two were interrupted by a hovering waiter impatient to place a tray of goodies down on the table. 'Can't complain about the service, hey, Jamie. Especially as I've brought along a new customer ... this is my friend, Liz O'Connell.'

'G'day there,' Jamie beamed, just as the sharp ding of an insistent bell caught his attention in the background. 'Sorry ladies, much as I'd like to chat, can't stop now ... duty calls.'

'Poor Jamie, he's rushed off his feet at this busy time of year. I trust you don't mind, Liz, but I've taken the liberty of ordering

47

coffee and lemon curd tarts with a dollop of cream. My treat of course!'

'You really are a sweetheart. But how on earth did you know that lemon tarts are my absolute favourite?'

'It was easy,' Tilt laughed, whipping out a business card from inside the pocket of her blouse, handing it to Elizabeth.

'Delve into your future,' Elizabeth read aloud. 'Seriously?' She raised an eyebrow and looked at Tilt. 'Renowned Psychic, Tilt Jacobson, specialising in fortune telling, tarot card readings, palmistry and astrology.'

Fanning her face with the card, 'Good God … a fortune teller! I've never known a real fortune teller. That literally blows my mind. It's insane … it's incredible.'

'Not really, darling! After all, what woman doesn't enjoy a lemon curd tart?' Tilt winked. 'Plus, you can't possibly imagine my delight when I peered into my crystal ball this morning to capture a glimpse of you happily installed behind the counter of Telltales.'

'Well, I don't mean to cast aspersions on the power of your crystal ball, Tilt, but it's a bit early for me to decide whether to re-open the shop. Besides, I have an excellent job with a publishing house in Melbourne.'

Disappointment spread across Tilt's face as she consoled herself with a delicate forkful of tart.

Noticing her companion's sudden gloom, Elizabeth continued, 'Mind you, when I do decide, you'll be the first to know of course. Because then I'll be needing someone experienced to show me the ropes and hope you might consider staying on.'

'Are you kidding? I have every finger and toenail crossed that you'll keep the bookshop open!'

'I can't deny that my aunt has made some wonderful changes to the place. It's looking most impressive.'

Tilt carefully removed a stray mint leaf from her shirtfront and wiped away a touch of cream from the corner of her mouth. 'That bookshop is not just impressive, Liz, there's something quite extraordinary about the place.'

Elizabeth raised an eyebrow. 'Really?'

'Absolutely! You see I believe it's to do with the building being a former church. The high vaulted ceiling and ecclesiastical architecture makes for a quite imposing setting, and one must never forget the true purpose of a church. I get the feeling there's something hidden within those walls that I can't clearly explain.'

In between trying to make sense of Tilt's remarks, Liz took a moment to sip her coffee. 'You've got me intrigued. Does this belief of yours involve anything that I should be concerned about?'

'Not exactly! I was drawn to the whole concept of converting a chapel into a bookstore the minute I first set eyes on it. But whenever Thorny left the shop early and I stayed behind to close up for the night, I just got a feeling in my bones that I was never quite alone.'

Removing her sunglasses Tilt's eyes glistened as the sunlight touched her face. Elizabeth giggled when noticing a white moustache had formed across the top of her friend's lip.

'It's not funny, Liz.'

'Oh sorry … I wasn't laughing about the church.'

'What … what is it then?' Tilt asked.

'It's nothing, really! Just a smidgen of froth, that's all,' Elizabeth said, discreetly pointing to the offending area on her own face. 'Yeah, a touch to the right maybe … that's it!'

'Bloody hell, darling … I always manage to get everything all over me,' Tilt declared dabbing at her mouth. 'Is that better?'

'Perfect … and normally I wouldn't worry. A moustache rather suits you actually,' Elizabeth teased as Tilt saw the funny side and chuckled in good humour while tossing a stray coffee bean in Liz's direction. Elizabeth ducked and the bean landed in the hair of a lady seated at the table behind.

'Oops!' Tilt covered her mouth when the woman looked around and glared at a customer who shrugged in innocence, unaware of why she had come under such negative scrutiny.

'Tilt, behave yourself or you'll finish up getting us both into a brawl,' Elizabeth warned while flipping her own coffee bean onto Tilt's lap.

Expressionless, she asked at the same time, 'Were you inferring the building could be haunted?'

'You really do crack me up, Liz. And you're a much better shot than me by the way. But getting back to your question, no not exactly. It's more to do with some sort of spiritual mystique.'

Leaning back in her chair and suddenly realising how much she was enjoying Tilt's company, Elizabeth was eager to learn more about her friend's background. 'Tell me, Tilt, how did you develop an interest in astrology?

'I was always the first kid in the queue at the carnival lining up outside the fortune teller's tent wanting to look into the crystal ball. Used to love dressing up in all that colourful gear and spangles.'

Not much has changed, Elizabeth thought.

'It wasn't until my marriage broke down that I packed my bags and moved to Mariners Cove, where I met a woman called Beatrice Barry who taught me everything I know.'

'Wait! Did you say Beatrice Barry? I ran into her just a couple of days ago. Strangely, she appeared from nowhere, sat down beside me and said I had no need to be afraid as I would never be alone. Can you believe that, Tilt?'

'You must have it wrong, darling. We can't possibly be talking about the same Beatrice Barry. She passed away a year ago. Can you recall what this woman looked like?'

Thoughtfully skimming the milk stain from around the wall of her coffee mug, Elizabeth peered inside as if to picture the sweet old lady. 'She was quite tiny with slightly stooped shoulders, fine white hair and … oh yes, she carried a walking stick.'

'You do realise, Lizzie, that every old person in the community looks exactly as you have described her. Were there any other unusual characteristics or distinguishing features which might separate Beaty from all the other elderly residents?'

'That's the name she told me to call her … Beaty! And now I come to think of it she did have a mole on her cheek.'

Elizabeth's mind went blank when asked if the mole was on the right or left cheek.

With a disbelieving shake of her head, Tilt said, 'My God, darling, please forgive my brutal honesty, but remind me never to call on you as a witness.'

It was at that moment that Elizabeth spotted a familiar figure approaching. She picked up the menu to hide behind.

'Lizzie, what are you doing? There's no need for theatrics. If you want another lemon curd tart just say so.'

'Don't look now, Tilt, but there's a guy walking this way and I don't want him to see me.'

Lenny Forrester pulled the menu to one side. 'Well! If it isn't Ms Elizabeth O'Connell. It must be my lucky day.'

Tilt quickly checked her mobile and excused herself. 'This might be my cue to leave, darling. Sorry, but I must away, I have an appointment in five. Nice to meet you Mr … '

'Lenny, Lenny Forrester's the name, and the pleasure is all mine, Ms … '

Placing her hand in his, 'Tilt, Tilt Jacobson. Well … toodles you two. I'll be in touch, darling.'

Elizabeth scowled at Tilt, who gave her a *two's company, three's a crowd*, knowing wink.

Casually slipping into the vacated chair, Lenny ran his fingers through a mop of dark, undisciplined curls. And as an unruly lock fell back over his forehead in a rakish sort of manner, it struck Elizabeth that this young guy was even more irritatingly handsome than she had at first admitted to herself.

'The Cove is such a small town. Not all that discriminating either. Everyone's welcome … have you noticed? Even an odd-job man.'

'Mr Forrester … are you following me by any chance?'

Lenny laughed. 'Don't flatter y'self, Ms O'Connell.'

'Well in case you haven't noticed, I was here first.'

'Really! Is that right now? And I s'pose you own the place as well?'

'Mr Forrester, if there is something more that you wish to say to me, just say it and get this over with.'

'Why do y'reckon I'd have anything further to say to you?'

A blonde woman dressed in a skin-tight mini skirt and tiny tank top emphasising the vast expanse of her bulging bosom teetered along in high heels towards the table. 'Lenny, Lenny darling, I'm so sorry I kept you waiting,' her bright red lipstick leaving an imprint as she leaned forward to graze his lips.

'No worries, Cupcake! I was just talking to this lovely lady here to pass the time.'

'A likely story, Lenny. I can't leave you alone for a minute,' she pouted. 'He's such a naughty boy you know,' she said to Elizabeth.

Gathering up her jacket and bag to leave, Elizabeth replied, 'I haven't noticed really. But I'm sure a little spanking every now and again might bring him into line. Goodbye, Mr Forrester. Have a nice day.' *I'm going to kill Tilt next time I see her*, Elizabeth thought as she wandered away.

10

A Truce

Half expecting a smack in the ear for his trouble, Lenny, like a man preparing to go into battle, stood his ground when Elizabeth conveniently stepped from the doorway of the bookshop.

Eyes blazing, she had the uncanny ability to scare the shit out of him.

'Of all the nerve, Forrester,' she reeled. 'Have you come alone? Or might I expect to see "Cupcake" any time soon?'

Lenny had watched Elizabeth hurry away from the café and turn down the laneway less than an hour earlier. He kept thinking how he wanted to ditch Cupcake and pursue this feisty person of interest who, like no other woman he'd ever met, had given him such a hard time. If only he could pluck up enough courage.

Somehow, he'd managed to slip away from Cheryl. Cheryl Canty to be exact, better known as Cupcake to all the locals who frequented the Pub. She had a reputation as being a bit of a goodtime girl and this suited Lenny who, not looking to settle down, had asked her out once or twice. But then, hadn't every other bloke at the Cove?

Elizabeth was different. More like a city girl, she was all class and quite a stunner. Normally, he was attracted to women with a bit of meat on their bones and long blonde hair. But there was something sort of eye catching about this shorter look style of hair that especially suited the shape of her high cheekbones and pert little nose.

It was difficult to accept the reason why she had taken an instant dislike to him. And equally hard to understand why he'd been foolish enough to make a third appearance so soon after their somewhat cheeky exchange at the café. What had prompted him to talk to her again and not just simply ignore her? He couldn't get her out of his mind. And now, as if he was the one at fault, he came prepared to wave an imaginary white flag and try to win her over.

Unequipped with either the right words or a flag, he instead held up the palms of his hands. 'Before you ask what I'm doing here, Elizabeth, I come in peace. It's important that we talk. Cupcake is a distant acquaintance of mine. She works behind the bar at the pub where I'm shacked up for a few nights all on account of being no longer welcome at me usual digs.'

'Who you choose to mix with is of no concern to me, Forrester. We barely know each other. So, go cry on someone else's shoulder if your digs at the pub aren't quite up to scratch.'

'Do you see a bloke crying here, Elizabeth? Truth is, it'll take a lot more than that to set me crying, I can tell ya. Losing a friend like Margaret hasn't helped, an' this has been troubling me ever since I drove off down the road. It was then that I got the feeling you should dig a little deeper into the circumstances surrounding her death. Something strikes me as not bein' quite right.'

'So, that's what this is about. Well, if you can shed some light on the matter, I'd be interested to hear what you have to say. But if you're just wasting my time, forget it.'

Considering the antagonistic nature of their last two meetings, Lenny had imagined a far more hostile reception.

'Then, provided you're not too busy of course, I was wondering whether I can interest you in takin' a stroll along the beach, so we can talk?'

Elizabeth placed a hand on her hip, and Lenny was convinced by her body language that a stroll with an odd-job man might be considered beneath her.

'Apart from listening to what you have to say about Margaret, God only knows what we could talk about, Forrester. But provided you understand I'm in no mood to do battle or be messed around, I suppose I can spare a moment or two of my time. I was about to lock up anyway.'

The cool, arrogant and smartarse attitude of this lady, who could shoot a bloke down and grind his face into the mud, was suddenly cast aside as she agreed to walk with him. Stepping back to allow her to lead the way, he thought this a heads up and allowed himself a discreet lick of his fingertip to also chalk up an imaginary "Score 1" into mid-air.

'What are you doing back there, Forrester?'

'Just checking to see which way the wind's blowing. It's certainly cooled down a notch, I reckon.'

Lenny noticed as they wandered along the street towards the beach, that for all her false bravado, walking beside Elizabeth gave him a good feeling. And he hoped that people passing by were perhaps thinking them a couple. Breaking the silence, he said, 'You know, Elizabeth, I'd like nothing better than to sort out our differences, call a truce and clear the air between us. We really did get started on the wrong foot and I'm not sure why. Maybe you can set me straight on that score.'

'Don't hold your breath, Forrester. I've agreed to join you in a walk, not sign up as friends on Facebook.'

Lenny laughed when seeing her serious expression as she truly had no idea how funny she was. And pointing to a park bench overlooking the water, he invited her to sit while he made a quick trip to his ute, which he'd deliberately parked nearby.

On his return, he plopped down beside her and produced two Kit Kats from inside his shirt pocket and offered one to Elizabeth.

'You really do have a couple of redeeming features, Forrester. But don't think for one minute that you can win me over with a melted Kit Kat,' Elizabeth warned as she accepted the chocolate bar and tore open the wrapper. 'Do you always make a habit of carrying chokies in your pocket?'

'Old truckies' trick. Always stock up on some sweet tasting travellers. A kind of sugar hit when out on the road and driftin' off at the wheel. Just grabbed a couple from me supplies on the way through.'

Elizabeth delicately bit into the biscuity finger. 'It's a wonder they didn't melt all over your shirt.'

'They've been on ice in the esky I carry around with me in the ute. Probably half frozen.'

'You seem to think of everything. What else have you got tucked away in your pockets … a salad roll? A Danish pastry or two?'

'You can't expect me to give away all me trade secrets. Let's just say, you'll never go hungry while I'm around.'

Elizabeth appeared to be loosening up, even forgetting herself and enjoying his offering. 'You polished that off pretty quickly,' he smiled. 'Have never known anyone to say no to a free Kit Kat.'

'Is that right?' Elizabeth replied brushing away the odd crumb or two. 'Who are you, Willy Wonka from the Chocolate Factory? I have a sneaking suspicion that you're setting me up and planned all of this, now expecting me to return the favour and tell you why I got so annoyed at you.'

'Well, we blokes from the bush can be a bit slow at times.'

'Slow is most definitely not a term I'd use to describe you, Forrester. But so soon after Margaret's death, I was angry to see you mowing the grass as though just another, "business-as-usual" type of day.'

'I swear I knew nothing about Margaret's death. If I had, things would a been a whole lot different.'

Elizabeth turned to look at him before asking the next question. 'Someone came into the house the other night. Was that you by any chance?'

Slow to respond, Lenny admitted, 'Margaret always left a spare key under that rock at the edge of the herb garden so that if I arrived after dark, I could let myself in, put the jug on and ease her mind about some lowlife snooping around. But after I tapped on the door, I realised she may have had someone staying over and thought it best to make myself scarce.'

'Did my aunt often have someone stay over?'

Lenny gazed out at the water. 'That's not for me to say. But there was this one time when I was chopping wood, a bloke wandered in from out of nowhere and acted like he was unhappy to see me. He looked a bit taken aback and demanded to know who I was while giving me this crazy look that you wouldn't believe. I told him I worked there, but he turned away and walked inside the house. It wasn't long after that I heard raised voices. All went quiet for a while, then he stormed out, slammed the door behind him and took off down the driveway.'

'Do you know who he was?'

'No idea! Never seen him before. I remember his face was scarred and he was quite a lot younger than Margaret. But I couldn't work out the connection.'

Elizabeth went silent, slipped off her shoes, wandered across the grass and padded through the sand to dip her toes in the ocean. How lovely she looked, Lenny thought, unable to take his eyes off her. The likeness to Margaret was incredible. Tempted to join her, he decided instead to sit and take in the view.

On her return, Elizabeth resumed her position on the park bench and looked to the horizon. 'So, do you think this stranger you just told me about may have posed a danger to my aunt?'

'Can't say for sure. But still reckon her death was very sudden.'

'Okay, Forrester, you've got yourself a deal. This information is worth thinking about. But while I wouldn't rush in and cancel your booking at the pub on the strength of all that you've told me, I'm agreeing to go along with your truce.'

Not wishing to appear too flattered by this noble gesture, Lenny played it cool. And allowing himself the satisfaction of an inner smile he produced another Kit Kat from his pocket and handed it to Elizabeth.

'This one's definitely a bit on the soft side, Forrester.'

'Well, it's the last one left. So, my advice would be to eat it quick and quit complaining.'

11

An Upsetting Discovery

After Lenny had gone on his way, Elizabeth wandered along the beach.

Reminding herself that with only a six week break before she would be expected to return to work, there was no time to waste. She needed to decide what to do for the best. And do it quickly. Of course, she could take the easy option and put the house and business on the market. But deep down a voice kept repeating, 'Hang on to it all with both hands, Liz, and don't let go!'

Margaret had always said, follow your instincts. And Elizabeth – being tempted to reopen the shop had been seriously considering it earlier that afternoon. With Tilt on board, who appeared to be a lot of fun and similar age as herself, a change of direction could be just what she needed.

Although no expert when it came to figures, a review of the accounts showed that while certain weeks business was slow, the holiday periods more than made up for the losses. So, provided this trend continued, the shop seemed a practical proposition. And, if proven correct, perhaps she could enjoy the best of both worlds and leave Tilt in charge to manage on her own, while she returned to Melbourne and kept on with her editing job at the publishing house.

Elizabeth had reneged on her promise not to speak with Gary, but she avoided discussing anything about the future, because he would be wanting to know when she was coming home.

So now, willing to give this a try and before she had a chance to change her mind, she was eager to phone Tilt with news of her decision.

Tilt's positive reaction was one of great joy and enthusiasm. 'Are you kidding me, darling … when do we start?'

'How does eight-thirty in the morning sound? Oh, and I almost forgot …' Elizabeth paused before having a playful dig at Tilt. 'Of course, you do realise you don't deserve this given your sudden departure from the café this morning when abandoning me in my hour of need.'

'You should be thanking me, darling. That Lenny Forrester looks rather scrumptious. Wherever did you find him?'

Elizabeth filled Tilt in on the details. And as though surprised to learn that Lenny had been working for Margaret, Tilt declared, 'A bit of a mystery woman at times, your aunt. A stylish lady, she could have had boyfriends all over town for all I know.'

Tilt did tend to take matters to the extreme, Elizabeth thought, as the idea of her aunt racing around town arm-in-arm with a bevy of boyfriends seemed quite absurd. 'Hardly a boyfriend, I would have thought, Tilt. He's an odd-job man.'

'Aren't they all, darling!' Tilt chuckled.

Within the week, shelves were restocked with the latest releases. 'Fingers crossed we can rake in a healthy income,' Elizabeth remarked to Tilt. It was too early to know of course, as the holiday season was in full swing. But with plenty of customers buying, sales looked promising and towards the end of the second week, the business was proving a resourceful enterprise.

'Remember not to get too carried away, Tilt. I should have mentioned I'm doing this for a trial period with a view to keeping the place open,' Elizabeth reminded her friend. 'We need to run this place at a profit, and so far, the books are looking good.'

Being her own boss and getting used to a whole new routine with the advent of change did require Elizabeth to seriously rethink her frantic pace of life at the publishing house. Then there was Gary. Although a good-looking man ever eager to spread his charm and share his winning ways, Gary's appeal seemed a touch too universal for her liking of late. But unable to overcome her strong attachment to him, she wondered if this was love or just a form of insecurity on her part.

Tilt however, who had obviously mastered the art of self-reliance, was just the opposite. Elizabeth found her to be extremely capable, and they had quickly come to share a mutual liking and respect for one another. She also loved her friend's flamboyance and playful jibes that the customers seemed to appreciate as well.

'Oh, by the way, Liz, there was a call from Philip Anderson while you were at the Post Office.'

'Do you know the man at all, Tilt?'

'Can't say I ever met the guy. He dealt with Thorny mainly and ordered books which she hand delivered to his home. Don't think he's short of a dollar mind you. But he never did come into the shop in person. Often used to think he confused this place with "Dial-a-Pizza".'

It was easy for Elizabeth to see that Tilt enjoyed being able to answer all manner of questions that might be of interest where the customers were concerned. 'This guy Philip's also got a brother I believe. Your friend Lenny Forrester doesn't happen to have a brother by any chance?' Tilt winked.

Elizabeth clicked her tongue and shook her head. 'Don't even go there, Tilt. Because believe me, one Forrester is more than I can handle.'

'Speak for yourself, Liz. You won't be the one doing the handling.'

'Please, spare me the detail.'

Tilt allowed herself a mischievous chuckle before returning to the Andersons. 'David … yeah that's his name … the brother I mean. High maintenance apparently, always unhappy. Don't you just loathe those people? I often wondered what Thorny saw in them.'

'Sounds weird. And if we weren't so keen to cash in on every sale possible, I'd let this Philip wait and get back to him when I'm good and ready. There's also the cost of petrol and time lost driving back and forth to consider. So I won't be making a habit of running after him, that's for sure.'

By the time Elizabeth arrived home that evening, she slumped down into an armchair, kicked off her shoes and gazed into the dark shadowy corners. *This place is depressing and full of doom and gloom,* she thought. Not to mention in serious need of a makeover. The first job she planned was to freshen up the place, with Margaret's bedroom being a high priority. It required a thorough clean and paint.

An incoming call on her mobile interrupted her thoughts. 'Damn it!' she cursed prior to answering.

'Hi, Elizabeth … my name's Philip Anderson. I left a message earlier at the bookshop and hope you don't mind me contacting you like this?'

'Oh yes, I'm sorry I didn't get back to you, I've hardly had a moment to spare.'

'That's quite okay. The holiday season can be a busy time at the Cove, but I was anxious to convey my deepest sympathy.

My brother, David, and I both loved Margaret and were looking forward to spending a whole lot more time together in the future.'

A little put out that her aunt might have been planning to share her future with the likes of two complete strangers who she had only known briefly, Elizabeth thought, what right do they have to declare their love? Just what sort of love was this Anderson person referring to?

Elizabeth found it difficult to disguise a shade of resentment in her voice as she thanked him.

'I'm pleased to hear you've reopened the shop. Margaret was kind enough to deliver books to my home and I'm hoping you might find the time to select a new release and drop it off to me in the coming days.'

Tilt's reference to "Dial-a-Pizza" flashed into Elizabeth's mind. 'You're most welcome to visit the shop and select from the many new titles available.'

'Unfortunately, I don't drive and have a problem walking.'

'Oh, I'm sorry to hear that. In which case, I really can't promise anything but may be able to fit in a visit on Wednesday.'

Disregarding her words that she can't promise anything, Philip Anderson acted as if Elizabeth's visit was a foregone conclusion when saying, 'That's most generous. And I'm sure you're familiar with the house at Misty Headland?'

'Yes, I know it well.'

'Good, that's settled then. I look forward to our meeting. Let's say around three-thirtyish, or thereabouts.'

'Bloody cheek!' Elizabeth exclaimed at the end of the call, stewing over this conversation that stuck in her mind even when deciding to make a start on Margaret's room. Mixed reactions about Lenny Forester, who'd left town to continue his rounds, also raced through her mind. Yet once Margaret's clothes were cleared from the wardrobe, folded and packed for delivery to the Brotherhood Shop, Elizabeth set about moving the furniture to deal with a build-up of hidden grime and sweep the carpet beneath the double bed.

A thick layer of dust was exposed as she struggled to push the heavy bed to one side and noticed that due to the excess dirt, the pattern on the carpet was no longer visible. Exhausted, she rested and ran her eyes over several dead moths, a stray hairclip, a safety pin and what looked suspiciously like a gentleman's sock. It wasn't until she began to vacuum the area that something quite bizarre registered in her mind. Once out of sight, perhaps haphazardly tossed under the bed and forgotten about, something caught her attention. She stopped, pressed her foot on the "Off" button and leaned down to retrieve the unmistakable remnants of not one, but two red and silver foil Kit Kat wrappers.

'Why in the name of God would Margaret have been eating Kit Kats in bed?' she asked.

Elizabeth could only draw one conclusion – Lenny Forrester, that rotten good for nothing liar, had been sleeping with her aunt.

12

Phyllis

Sometime past midnight, Elizabeth slid into bed, propped her back up against the pillows and carefully smoothed out the chocolate wrappers. She could barely stand to touch them. She could barely stand the sight of them – vowing never to eat a Kit Kat again.

Forrester, being a good deal younger and stronger than Margaret, must have forced himself on her aunt, Elizabeth concluded. It was unthinkable to imagine otherwise. Or to picture the pair in an act of sexual intimacy to which Margaret had willingly consented.

'Urgh!' she shuddered. This was enough to turn her stomach and Elizabeth felt deeply disturbed about having spent the first night sleeping in the same bed where this gross seduction had obviously taken place.

Well, whatever the truth, it was all the fault of that smooth talking, chocolate eating lothario who must have tricked her aunt into believing him trustworthy. And if so, what else was he lying about?

Elizabeth wrestled with these questions as she placed the wrappers inside the pages of an early edition of *Pride and Prejudice* – the silvery foil now destined to be filed away for safe keeping until she knew the full circumstances surrounding Margaret's untimely demise.

Switching off the lamp, she then turned her mind to something more within the realm of her understanding. And irrespective of any further unpleasant sightings, refurbishing the house was a big priority. With the ghastly wallpaper the first to go, quickly followed by the old-fashioned Axminster carpet, she could get stuck into whitewashing the floorboards and gradually updating the interior with a major paint job throughout. Colourful scatter rugs, throws, cushions, prints and fresh linen then being the perfect touch to complement her hard work and provide a bright and welcoming finish to her surroundings. Yes, she was excited about this project and the improvement she could make to the dark and gloomy interior.

Only then did she drift off to sleep.

The following morning, the aroma of a hearty breakfast, eggs and bacon sizzling in the pan seemed a good place to begin. Living forty minutes from town had certain benefits. But the sound of a car engine idling at the bottom of the driveway destroyed this myth and brought a silent curse to Elizabeth's lips. *So much for my bacon and eggs,* she thought.

She turned the gas jet off beneath the pan and wandered outdoors.

A woman came rushing up the pathway, 'Lizzie, it's me, Phyllis Bentley,' she gushed, reaching out to draw Elizabeth into a hug. 'Oh … you poor, dear love! Your aunt, my best friend … who would have thought.' Phyllis stepped back a pace and, taking Elizabeth's hands in her own she said, 'Just look at you! You, my dear darling heart have grown into a beauty. But then, you always were a pretty girl.'

Elizabeth couldn't say the same for Phyllis who although just short of a decade older than her aunt hadn't weathered at all well for someone aged in her early sixties. 'Mrs Bentley, how lovely to see you. Please come inside and have some tea. I'm just cooking breakfast.'

'Call me Phyllis, love, or you'll make me feel ancient,' she insisted as she made her way indoors. 'Good God, I've ruined your brekky. I'll brew us a cuppa, and start afresh,' she said while scraping the cold eggs into the bin before relighting the gas. 'Would you fancy some toast with that?'

Phyllis rolled up her sleeves. 'I do forget that not everyone rises as early as me. So, sit yourself down now and leave everything to me.'

Elizabeth remembered her aunt having often said, 'Oh no, not you again,' in jest to Phyllis's face.

'Can't keep a good woman down, Marg. Thought you might like to go into town for a counter lunch.' Phyllis would answer.

Most times Margaret had no choice in the matter. At other times she made it quite clear that she just wanted to be left alone.

'Suit yourself,' Phyllis would say and flounce off, only to reappear in good humour on the next occasion that she fancied some company.

When the breakfast was set down in front of Elizabeth, Phyllis poured the tea and seated herself opposite. 'I was sorry that I couldn't pay my last respects,' she sniffled as she withdrew a hankie and delicately dabbed at her nose. 'Margaret had many friends who would've wanted to say a proper goodbye.'

'It was her written request for a private burial, Phyllis, not mine.'

'Oh … I didn't know that! What a pity! Seemed so unlike her, that's all. She could be a real party girl when it suited, and at the very least a funeral service would have been in order.'

'The priest did say prayers at the graveside.'

'Oh, good God in heaven, as if that was enough. Whatever was she thinking? I hate to be critical, Lizzie, but you should have just gone ahead and held a proper funeral service regardless.'

Phyllis was beginning to rub Elizabeth the wrong way as she had no right to interfere. And in the hope that she would not outstay her welcome, Elizabeth sipped her tea and wondered how she might tactfully extract herself without sounding offensive.

As if reading Elizabeth's thoughts, Phyllis said, 'I won't keep you, but there is a further important reason for my visit. You're probably unaware that a couple of relative newcomers to the Cove had been taking up a lot of Margaret's time of late. So much so in fact, that the two of us had words. I warned her not to get too deeply involved, but she wouldn't listen.'

Phyllis cleared away the dishes and continued. 'You might think this none of my business, but now I want to warn you. They moved into old Mr Gentry's place. God rest his soul.' Phyllis paused to bless herself. 'And it wouldn't at all surprise me if they contact you with some sort of outlandish proposal or ongoing agenda in mind. So, just take care, love.'

Elizabeth jumped up from the table. 'Leave the dishes, Phyllis. I need to rush off shortly. But if I hear from anyone who lives at Misty Headland, I'll be sure to take your advice.'

Practically shoving Phyllis out through the doorway, Elizabeth breathed a heavy sigh when hearing the engine of the car kick over and the motor fade into the distance.

Fortified by her bacon and eggs, she opened the window to air Margaret's bedroom. She then looked through the contents of the tallboy drawers to discover a copy of Charles Dickens' *Great Expectations* slipped in between her aunt's scarves. When she removed it and opened the cover, a faded photograph fell to the floor. Retrieving the photo, Elizabeth recognised Margaret who looked no more than seventeen or eighteen. Wearing a pretty dress and silver locket, she was smiling lovingly at someone seated alongside her with an arm around her shoulder. But that side of the picture had been torn away. Elizabeth turned it over to see a handwritten inscription on the back: *Happy Birthday Darling Ma …*

Curious to read the rest of the words and see who the mystery person could be, she rummaged through the scarves in the hope of finding the missing part of the photo. Yet with no trace of a body or face to match the hand, the signed sentiments that completed the greeting had also been lost. Her aunt must have had good reason for removing any clue of the person seated beside her. 'Why?' Elizabeth kept asking herself as she emptied the tallboy and discarded the last vestiges of Margaret's clothing.

13

Stormy Weather

Elizabeth had crammed as much as she could into her one free day away from the bookshop and woke the next morning to the earthy scent of rain drifting through an open window. Minutes later a torrential downpour rolled in off the ocean, drummed on the rooftop, flooded the guttering and streamed down the windowpane. Rushing across the room to shut out the storm, she became aware of the insistent humming of her phone.

A familiar name lit up the screen. 'Can't talk now, Gary,' she answered.

'Don't give me that, Liz. What in the hell's going on? I can never catch you and all you can say is "can't talk now".'

'A huge electrical storm has hit,' she shouted. 'The noise is deafening.'

'You promised to call, and I've heard nothing. What's happening and when are you coming home?'

'Let's face it, Gary. A little time apart could be good for the both of us.'

'You've got no intention of coming home. Is that it, Elizabeth?'

Hearing his angry response, Elizabeth said, 'That's not true! I promise to get back to you, when the weather settles.' She abruptly cut him off and ended the call.

She should have felt guilty. But she'd not forgotten the time he had done the same to her. And unconcerned about hurting the man who professed to love her, she quickly showered, threw on her clothes and set off for work in the driving rain.

'Oh my God, darling,' Tilt said in greeting when confronted with a dripping Elizabeth as she burst through the doorway to make a rather undignified entrance. 'Wasn't expecting to see you today. The power's down all over town.'

'It'll take more than a storm to keep me away,' Elizabeth said, removing her jacket. 'I need to shop, go over the accounts to help make a final decision about whether to return to Melbourne, as well as pay a visit to Misty Headland. Not sure how I managed to get talked into that to be honest.'

Tilt looked uneasy. 'What's with the return to Melbourne part? I thought you'd already decided to stay.'

'No way! I'm sorry, Tilt! It's too early to say for certain. I should have made this clear at the start. But it's not so simple to just pull up stakes and move on from my other commitments. My partner, Gary, rang this morning. He's in a shitty mood because I reopened the shop and haven't been keeping in touch,' Elizabeth sighed. 'As if that isn't enough, the publishing house is on my back about how long they can hold my job open. And to top it off, Phyllis Bentley is warning me not to get involved with the Anderson brothers.'

'Good ole Phyllis. Always there when you least need her. I know she was Thorny's bestie, but she can be a real pain in the backside, darling. Since her husband died, she became extremely possessive of your aunt who couldn't step out to powder her nose without that woman dropping by and demanding to know her whereabouts.'

Scanning the new releases to choose a suitable book to satisfy the taste of a stranger, Elizabeth could well imagine all that Tilt was saying to be true. But her thoughts were interrupted by the lashing of rain and wind when the door crashed open and Constable Madden – appearing to have little control – was blown in accompanied by the jangle of the overhead bell. She jammed her body up hard against the back of the door in a bid to close it behind her.

'Lord Almighty,' she shivered, 'it's blowing a gale out there.'

Shaking the rain from her cap, she took hold of several lank strands of hair plastered to the side of her face and pinned them back behind her ear.

'Constable Madden, isn't it? Here, let me help you get out of that wet raincoat. Then you can warm yourself by the heater,' Elizabeth said.

Tilt disappeared into the former church vestry and returned with a towel, handing it to Madden. 'Here we go!' she smiled. 'I'm Eileen, by the way. But most of my friends know me better as Tilt.'

'Yeah, I've seen you around,' the constable nodded while vigorously rubbing her hair with the towel. Then warming her hands in front of the wood-burner, she turned her back to restore the circulation and toast herself on both sides. The welcome blast of heat bringing the colour back into her cheeks as she took in the surroundings. 'Nice looking set-up you've got here. All these books and a cosy fire. Who would've thought we'd need one this time of year.'

'Absolutely! That stove gets fired up at the most unexpected moments. And with the addition of a tearoom next on the list … who in their right mind would ever want to leave?' Tilt remarked while hopefully baiting Liz.

'Oh yes, and who knows, we might even open an art gallery and hang a few crystal chandeliers from the ceiling once we've sold a hundred thousand books,' Elizabeth remarked.

This sarcastic response gave cause for Madden to raise her eyes to the ceiling. Shaking her head, she replied, 'I think I'd be getting a second opinion about the chandeliers.'

Elizabeth and Tilt just looked at one another as if to say, 'Hello … is this person really serious?'

They watched the young officer then tear herself away from the potbelly stove and wander over to a shelf where she ran her hand across a row of books. 'The Classics, hey! Had to read one once. What a chore that was, if you don't mind me saying.'

'What book was it?' Tilt asked.

'Something about bondage. I remember that much. Written by a guy called Sunset Morn. A great disappointment. I was at least expecting a bit of action with a few whips and chains being involved.'

Tilt stepped forward to select a book from the shelf. 'Wasn't this one, was it?'

Madden read the title, 'Of Human Bondage, W. Somerset Maugham. Yeah, that's the one alright. Put me off reading for life it did.'

Strolling back to reach inside the pocket of her rain jacket, she handed Elizabeth an envelope. 'This is the report you requested. And you might be interested to see that your aunt did suffer a head injury. It would appear this resulted from a fall due to the heart attack.'

Elizabeth noted that Madden did not make eye contact as she mentioned the head injury.

'The deceased gashed her skull against a coffee table as she collapsed. It's not uncommon when old folk fall, break a hip and so forth.'

'My aunt wasn't old. She was only in her early fifties,' Elizabeth scoffed as she opened the damp envelope and scanned the smudged ink on the report. 'This information was withheld, and there's no mention of who found her body. I find it a little slack on the part of your department.'

Constable Madden allowed herself a chuckle. 'Excuse me, Ma'am, I don't dare jest over the serious nature of what happened to your aunt, but rather the fact that you can hardly call our place a department.'

'It is a police station I would hope, Constable? Although not an altogether efficient one,' Elizabeth frowned. 'Your senior sergeant has treated Margaret's death and my follow-up complaint about a home invasion to be of little consequence. I'd appreciate it if you'd relay my disapproval.'

'If you don't mind me saying, Ma'am …'

'Oh my God,' Elizabeth cut in. 'Would you please stop calling me Ma'am, Constable Madden.'

'Sorry, Ms O'Connell! But I think you'd be better to tell his nibs yourself about your lack of approval. He doesn't take too kindly to criticism or anything that I tell him. Which reminds me,' Madden said, checking her mobile. 'I've got to run. It's almost time to get him his coffee.'

Grabbing her raincoat and cap, the constable rushed back out into the elements leaving the door banging behind her. 'What an impudent young woman. And to think that I actually felt sorry for her on the day of our meeting.'

'Think the truth is, you scared the life out of her, darling. She wasn't prepared to stick around to answer any further questions. It's probably taken her all this time to type up the report.'

'You're so right, Tilt. Judging from what I gathered on my visit to the station, that woman spends most of her day running after that good for nothing sergeant. What an ignorant man if ever I've met one. I took an immediate dislike to him.'

<h1 style="text-align:center">14</h1>

The Anderson Brothers

Thankful that by mid-afternoon the storm clouds had vanished allowing the sun to peek through, Elizabeth reluctantly drove towards her destination at Misty Headland and wondered what might next await.

Since the discovery of the Kit Kat wrappers, the spring that had been so evident in her step had disappeared overnight. This led Elizabeth to realise that, like it or not, Lenny Forrester had played a significant role in initially lifting her spirits.

Oh yes, he was a charmer alright – him and his Kit Kats – she conceded. What a fool to believe all he had told her, while having conveniently failed to mention his own obvious shortcomings and clandestine relationship with an older woman.

As indicated to Tilt in between the visit from Phyllis Bentley, the unhappy nature of her brief conversation with Gary and the report from Constable Madden, not much was going to plan, providing yet a further reason for Elizabeth's gloomy mood. Now she must face the added inconvenience of having to go out of her way to deliver a book to this stranger who apparently had some hidden agenda she could well do without.

Reaching the crest of a steep incline on a dramatic clifftop, the remote setting of Misty Headland – both exhilarating and intriguing – came into view and jutted out into a spectacular stretch of coastline. But Elizabeth noted the gabled rooftop that once loomed in the distance, had since disappeared.

She recalled in her teenage years when the original owner, old Paddy Gentry passed away, time had caused the once imposing house to fall into disrepair. Left to lie derelict, the stately home deteriorated into a decaying and brooding mansion, boarded up to deter squatters and teenage schoolkids like herself from entering. The shadowy hallways were said to have taken on a sinister atmosphere, frightening those who dared to venture inside.

Following the winding road, she parked the car under a cypress tree and stepped outside to be greeted by the refreshing aroma of the salty sea combined with a thick layer of pine needles underfoot. Curious to make her acquaintance, a lone seagull swooped down to land at her feet.

Elizabeth could hardly believe her eyes when seeing the sweeping changes. No longer the home that her aunt used to regularly take her to visit, with nothing left of the past, the clean contemporary design of the new house had replaced the old to tastefully display a modern touch of grandeur.

Making her way to a walled entrance, she gazed through the pickets of an iron gate to spy an enchanting garden lovingly restored. Despite the often wild conditions, climbing roses and lavender flourished within the protection of the high stone enclosure and well maintained, clipped hedges. No doubt old man Gentry, once a revered horticulturist who had opened his gates to the public at the height of the blooming season, would be happy to see the grounds renewed to their former glory.

The squeaky hinges protested loudly when Elizabeth unlatched the gate to disturb someone digging at the far end of a terraced embankment. As if he was seeing a ghost, a youthful looking man wearing a brimmed hat, lifted his head from his labour and stared with an expression that was beginning to freak her out.

'Hello there!' she shouted. 'Are you Philip Anderson by any chance? I'm Elizabeth O'Connell and have come by to deliver your book.'

With not a word in reply, the man ignored her and went on with his digging.

Of all the nerve, Elizabeth bristled. Perhaps he was the hired help. Perhaps he didn't speak English. But that hardly excused his behaviour. Incensed to think he would treat her in such an offhanded manner she stepped off the pathway to approach him and lost a shoe in the process. The heel became embedded in the soft soil of the neatly trimmed lawn and now looked to be broken. Hopping on one foot she retrieved it in the hope he hadn't noticed. Then with a false air of authority, she hobbled towards him, bobbing up and down as she went with one shoe on and one shoe off.

Now at an extreme disadvantage and looking quite ridiculous, she tapped him on the shoulder.

As he turned, Elizabeth noticed the man's face was marred by a nasty scar. Yet rather than detract from his strong and compelling features, the scarring enhanced his masculine good looks. With eyes smarting, like those of a hurt child chastised by someone he loved, she guessed him to be in his mid-twenties. And for all her peg leg antics, even though he remained silent, she detected a sadness and felt an overwhelming desire to reach out and touch him.

'Good afternoon, is that you, Elizabeth?' A voice called from somewhere above. 'Please, come straight up to the study.'

Shaken, but so as not to make a further spectacle of herself, she removed her other shoe and returned to the pathway.

Brushing the stray blades of grass cuttings from the soles of her feet, she climbed the stairs and placed her shoes aside when reaching the top.

Through an open set of French doors, she stepped inside to discover a beautiful room complete with a floor to ceiling window framing a sweeping vista of the sea beyond.

A sandy-haired gentleman, who she gauged to be closer in age to herself, was seated behind a sleek timber desk. Making no attempt to stand, he too stared in surprise and then dropped his eyes to her feet. With a bemused grin, he said, 'Elizabeth, how lovely to meet you. I see you've lost your shoes.' And as though glued to the chair, he extended his hand in greeting across the desk and invited her to be seated. 'It's so good of you to come. I'm Philip, of course.'

'I don't usually make a habit of visiting someone in bare feet, but unfortunately I caught the heel of my shoe in the garden and managed to break it.'

'Well, please let me replace your shoes with a new pair. And I'm sorry for any misunderstanding out there. My brother, David, has become quite moody, suffers severe bouts of chronic depression and is generally not very good with people.'

'I'm so sorry to hear that,' Elizabeth replied, while reaching inside her bag to quickly fulfill the purpose of her visit. 'I've chosen a book and hope you haven't read it,' she said, passing it to him. 'Also, there is the matter of a small bequest of $3,000 in my aunt's Will, which payment will be transferred to you through her solicitor, Graeme Jenkins.'

'Oh, dear God,' he replied. 'I'm happy for you to hang on to it, Elizabeth. Use it toward restocking the bookshop.'

'I can't do that!'

Philip raised his hand. 'Don't worry. I'll sort it out with Jenkins. I want you to have it,' he insisted.

There was no way Elizabeth felt she could agree to this. But it did strike her as being an extremely generous gesture.

The ticking of a mantle clock and pleasant aroma of eucalyptus and woodsmoke rising from a cosy fire hung suspended in the air like an invisible curtain between the two, and heightened Elizabeth's awareness of an awkward silence. Seemingly unfazed however, Philip Anderson took his time to read a passage of the novel. And apart from the fact that he didn't rise to meet her, Elizabeth hated to admit she was finding him to be a most likeable person.

Her eyes were drawn to an eclectic collection of books and artefacts. Native spears, an oddity among the items, looked to be a mix of African and Australian Indigenous handcrafted weapons. Egyptian urns, ivory carvings and various pieces that represented differing age-old cultures were tastefully displayed so as not to distract from the ambience of the richly decorated room. A room that glowed in the afternoon light.

'You have quite a collection,' Elizabeth remarked.

Lifting his eyes from the book to gaze around him, Philip answered, 'Yes, a passion of mine. Many items have been shipped from exotic destinations.'

He then appeared to forget his manners for a moment and openly stared again at Elizabeth.

Feeling uncomfortable she asked, 'So … what do you think of the book?'

'It's incredible!' he replied. 'The likeness between you and your aunt I mean. The book looks interesting as well.'

Elizabeth recalled Jenkins saying much the same. 'Do you really think so?' she humoured him.

'Absolutely,' he nodded.

'Perhaps the likeness goes beyond the fact that my aunt raised me from an early age. You see Margaret, although younger than my mother, was often mistaken for her twin. This might better explain the strong resemblance.'

'So sorry to hear you lost your parents, Elizabeth.'

'I suppose Margaret told you. It was a long time ago,' she shrugged.

'That must have been hard on you as a child.' Philip paused to clear his throat. 'My brother and I suffered the same fate not long ago.'

Elizabeth looked up in alarm. 'No! Surely not! We both lost our parents … that's kind of unreal, don't you think?'

'I agree! David blames himself because he was driving. But it wasn't his fault. An unlicensed teenager, high on drugs, ran a red light at an excessive speed and ploughed straight into us.'

Shock registered on Elizabeth's face when Philip came from behind his desk seated in a wheelchair. Only then did she understand his lack of courtesy on her arrival. Even more surprising was that she recognised something familiar about his eyes and the shape of his mouth, He resembled someone she knew yet couldn't quite place.

'Forgive me … I had no idea that you're …'

'Incapacitated!' Philip completed the sentence to save any embarrassment. 'My legs have been useless ever since. And now that Margaret's been snatched away, it really does seem like a double blow on top of all that we've suffered.'

Elizabeth again felt angry that this man insisted on making claims on her aunt by almost inferring Margaret to be a sort of de facto replacement for his parents throughout their brief association together.

As if reading Elizabeth's mind, he asked, 'What happened to your parents, if it's not too painful to talk about?'

Her eyes glazed over as she stared through the window to a spot on the horizon. 'Reported missing, they were holidaying in Europe,' she replied. 'It was discovered they'd gone swimming and didn't make it back to shore. Their bodies were never recovered.' Elizabeth's eyes watered. 'A sad situation for each of us. But I have no other family. At least you have your brother.'

'That's debatable! I really believe he hates me. But can you be certain about having no other family?'

With an expression of despair, Elizabeth shook her head. 'There's no one!'

Returning to position himself behind his desk, Elizabeth noticed a nervous shuffling of papers and needless repositioning of pens. 'How long have you known my aunt?'

'Almost a year now, and to be honest, the reason I called on you to come here was not simply because I needed a book. There are a couple of proposals I'm anxious to discuss with you.'

Elizabeth's mind turned to Phyllis Bentley. Can this be the crazy agenda that she had warned against?

'Because David has become reclusive and scarcely speaks since the accident, I employed Margaret to read to him. She was making progress, whereas I failed miserably. The shock of her death has left him even more withdrawn, and I hope you might find time to take on this challenge.'

'Me? You can't be serious. Surely your brother can read his own books.'

'It's not about the books. More to do with companionship. Margaret helped him regain an interest in life.'

It seemed uncanny to Elizabeth that yet again her aunt had the capacity to win over another young man's affection. 'I can't help you, I'm sorry. This is not what I do and really should be on my way.'

'Please don't rush off. All I ask is that you think about it.'

Suspecting, this unlikely proposition was not ended there, Elizabeth was relieved to hear a light tap at the door. However, when the last person she expected to see entered the room armed with a tray of tea and biscuits, to say that she couldn't quite believe her eyes would be an understatement.

'Phyllis! What are you doing here?'

Philip butted in and said, 'I was forgetting the two of you already know each other. Phyllis helps around the house and is a wonderful cook.'

Avoiding Elizabeth's gaze, Phyllis placed the tray down on a coffee table.

'What a coincidence bumping into each other like this. I really had no idea you worked here, Phyllis.'

'Well, there you go, Elizabeth. I don't find it necessary to tell everyone my business.'

Philip invited Elizabeth to join him in front of the fireside where Phyllis demurely poured the tea as if some highly trained maid who had just wandered in off the set of *Downton Abbey*.

What in the heck was she up to? Elizabeth wondered. There was really no telling with Phyllis, A cagey old so 'n' so, she exchanged the necessary pleasantries but was careful to keep any conversation between the two to a minimum. Yet, for someone who had always preferred to be waited on, the title of "Phyllis the housekeeper" didn't quite sit right somehow.

Once the door closed behind her, Philip stirred his tea and raised an unexpected question. 'I've been keen to hear your thoughts about Margaret's decision to change the name of the bookshop. Do you find this in any way … maybe distressing might sound a bit over the top. But I'm sure you get my meaning.'

'Well, it doesn't keep me awake at night if that's what you're asking.'

This response appeared to disappoint Philip. 'Surely you'd agree that as the shop is housed in a church, the former name far better suits the aesthetics of the building.'

Elizabeth again shrugged. 'Perhaps Margaret simply preferred the name Telltales. She may have wanted to put her own stamp on the business. I can't see any harm in that.' But surprised by Philip's next response, Elizabeth became uneasy, thinking it high time she should be on her way.

'The harm in that in my opinion seems clear. Especially given the surroundings.' Philip's voice became passionate, and it almost seemed this was a bit of a hobbyhorse of his. 'Why convert a former church into a bookselling business only to then alter the name? The truth being that Margaret was advised to do so by a person who wielded a great deal of influence over her.'

'Give my aunt some credit, Philip. Who was this person anyway?'

'My brother.'

'Gosh, why all the fuss then.'

As though irritated by Elizabeth's continued unwillingness to side with him, Philip said, 'David did this to spite me. Filled with resentment, he openly admitted to his dislike of the name St Thomas. All Thomas's are bastards in his opinion. Particularly those professing to be a saint.'

Beginning to believe that Philip might be a little unhinged, Elizabeth got up to leave. 'Perhaps your brother's right. This whole discussion seems absurd.'

'Please finish your tea, Elizabeth. I know this might sound a strange request. But it will mean a lot to me if you'd consider reverting the name back to the St Thomas Bookshop.'

'You can't be serious. This'll create unending confusion for the customers. Not to mention a futile waste of time and expense. I inherited Telltales Bookshop and Telltales Bookshop it will remain.'

Draining his cup and replacing it on the saucer, a spoon went clattering to the floor. At the same time Philip managed to upend the biscuits. His loss of control embarrassed and angered him, especially when Elizabeth dropped to her knees to retrieve the bits and pieces.

'Leave the blasted things be, just leave them, Elizabeth. Perhaps my brother's right, awkward bastard that I am. My legs may not work, but my mind's completely intact, and I hoped you'd understand.' Philip sighed. 'I'm disappointed at the way you have so flippantly dismissed the idea.'

Elizabeth suffered a sudden pang of guilt. 'Philip, I'm sorry. I had no right to speak as I did. Please tell me why the name's so important.'

'Firstly, being well versed about the subject of architecture, the name change defeats the purpose of the bookshop being housed within the walls of the church.'

'Gosh, I had no idea. Are you an actual architect?'

'You could say that. It's not something I talk about much anymore. But believe me, Elizabeth, I know that I'm right. Secondly, I have a personal interest in ensuring the business succeeds. The third and final reason is almost like an omen, because my real name is Thomas.'

'Oh!' Elizabeth said with a look of surprise. 'Is that, Philip Thomas, or Thomas Philip?'

'Neither! Thomas Francis to be more precise.'

'Well, not to ask a silly question, but why refer to yourself as Philip if your name is really Thomas?'

Running his hands through his hair, Philip replied, 'This was a mistake. I'm sorry for keeping you so long. It's selfish of me and you must be tired.'

Touched by Philip's obvious frustration, Elizabeth said, 'You must be kidding. You can't expect me to leave now. I want you to finish what you've started.' And for the second time that afternoon, she became aware of the ticking clock and an empty stretch of silence.

'I'm not who he thought I was. But this isn't the only reason why my brother hates me. He was convinced that your aunt was in love with me.' Philip threw his head back and laughed. 'Imagine that, Elizabeth, fool that he is – enraged with jealousy. Both of us young enough to be her son for God's sake! He had no idea why she appeared to favour me.'

Philip's expression became far more serious when he revealed that Margaret changed the name of the bookshop so as not to be reminded of the son who had been taken from her at birth.

With a look of absolute shock, Elizabeth stared into the glowing embers. 'That's impossible! Margaret never would have kept something like that a secret from me. How do you know all this?'

'Because Margaret is … was … my mother. My registered name at birth is Thomas Francis Thornton – father unknown. David was right, I am a bastard. Whisked away and adopted by a childless couple who, two years later, had a son of their own. They named him David.'

'I can't believe this.' Elizabeth said shaking her head in denial.

'It's true, I swear. This is why David, who recently learned I wasn't born with the name Anderson, began to dislike me. But more importantly, you are not without family, Elizabeth. Like it or not … I am your cousin.'

15

Seeking Advice

Emerging on a sunlit morning from beneath a forested canopy of eucalypts and tree ferns, one may experience an almost Godlike moment when the light reveals the dazzling vista beyond.

Lenny Forrester had never been big on religion but could appreciate nature and welcomed this sight as he struggled to decide where the blue of the sea ended, and the sky began.

He dropped the sun-visor to shield the glare on his windscreen and thought whoever invented the rhyme, *blue and green should never be seen unless a colour is in between* had obviously never laid eyes on the approach from the upper reaches of the road that led into the township of Mariners Cove.

It was here, where from this highest point, the lush green hills rolled into the distance to meet the ocean.

Relieved to be returning, Lenny relished not only the scenery but the promise of re-visiting Elizabeth O'Connell. His reliable ute still had a way to go however, and – as the call for morning tea was long overdue – he was currently engaged in keeping one hand firmly on the steering wheel, while in the other he attacked the wrapper of a chocolate bar with his teeth.

Never likely to fall asleep at the wheel, Lenny was a great believer in keeping his energy levels up. Or was he simply a chocaholic? Whatever the answer, this was one of the last chocolates to be found in the dwindling supply of goodies stored in his esky.

Deep creases at the corners of his eyes crinkled into a smile as a vision of Elizabeth's distinctive auburn hair and fiery Irish temper flashed into his mind. 'She's a real little firecracker if ever I've met one,' he mumbled while munching on the wafer-like fingers.

His weathered good looks and easy ability to attract the ladies had never let him down in the past. But as he was unused to any form of rejection, Lenny enjoyed the thought of a challenge. Elizabeth, being obviously smitten, was playing a game of cat and mouse, he suspected, and it excited him to a point of total distraction. His desire to win her over was all he could think about. Yet he assumed that the less than friendly approach she had chosen to pursue at their first meeting had since been smoothed over and, beneath that cool exterior, she would secretly be eager to see him.

But Lenny had no idea of what he was about to walk into.

Awaiting her chance to catch up with Forrester, Elizabeth had been keeping the Kit Kat saga on hold until his return. But for now, with an entirely new set of circumstances to worry about, she hurried along to the solicitor's office.

Jenkins greeted her with a friendly welcome. 'It's good to see you again, Elizabeth. How's the bookselling business faring?'

'It's doing okay, Graeme. I'm still undecided about staying though.'

Directing her to be seated, he replied, 'That's to be expected at this early stage.'

'Something else has come up since we last spoke that's totally doing my head in. I'm eager to get your thoughts on the matter.'

'Well, that's what I'm here for. So, what's this about?'

Elizabeth pulled her chair a little closer to the desk. 'Yesterday I drove to Misty Headland to deliver a book to that Anderson guy who Margaret left that money to in her Will.'

'Was there a problem?' Graeme asked.

'You could say that. I came away feeling unsure about a certain claim that he made.'

'What was the issue, Elizabeth? Did he feel she should have left him more?'

'Well, here's the thing that didn't quite add up in my view. Who tells someone when left money in a Will, that he wanted me to have it? "You hang on to it", he said. "Margaret had earned it", he said.'

'That sounds very generous.'

'Yes, doesn't it! This being one of the things that worried me. He literally told me a lot of weird stuff that might see any normal thinking person keen to make a run for the door. Then in the middle of all this talk, he hit me with even more alarming news.'

Elizabeth noticed Jenkins move forward in his seat. 'Go on!' he said.

'If you can believe this guy, it would appear that I now have a new family member.'

'What?'

'I'm glad to see your surprise, as I had the same reaction. Imagine how shocked I felt.'

Jenkins looked puzzled but urged Elizabeth to continue.

'He claims that his birth name is Thomas, Thomas Francis Thornton to be exact. Son of Margaret who was forced to give him up at birth for adoption. So, of course, this would make him my cousin.'

'Your cousin! Good Lord … has this so-called cousin any proof of his identity?'

'I think I was in such a state, I never thought to ask. So, there's every chance he could be lying.'

'Did he say anything that might lead you to believe he may be trying to muscle in on an entitlement to a share in the house or business?'

Elizabeth thought for a moment before answering. 'He did seem interested in the bookshop but made no mention of wanting a share in it.'

'Well, I can understand why this information has made such an impact on you, Elizabeth. At the same time, I can assure you Margaret never breathed a word about having a son and to my knowledge there's been no agreements drawn up to this effect. Was she even aware of the fact, I wonder?'

'He didn't say. But this must be the secret she once spoke of.'

Elizabeth then further questioned Jenkins about any other hidden ramifications that might arise. And he seemed to think it wise to have someone check out his story if Anderson started to make any demands.

Nervously, she cleared her throat and decided to also mention the discussion they'd had about whether heart disease ran in the family. 'You should know, Graeme, that I've since received a report which says that my aunt fell and suffered a blow to the head. The senior sergeant and constable have played the matter down, but I was hoping you might investigate this on my behalf.'

Graeme laughed uneasily. 'Elizabeth, are you suggesting what I think you're suggesting? Murders are few and far between in a place like Mariners Cove.'

'I never did say the word murder, Graeme. But there seems to have been a cover up of sorts.'

Unimpressed that her request had been taken so lightly, Elizabeth, without mentioning any names, continued to relate her experience about the intruder which had added to her suspicions.

'You've been under a lot of stress, Elizabeth, and as much as I want to assist you, I'm no criminal lawyer, just a small-time conveyancing solicitor.' Graeme replied. 'If you're serious about all of this, there's a friend of mine who might agree to help. He used to be a private investigator in the city, but one day decided he couldn't stand the rat race and dropped out completely.'

Jenkins searched through the top drawer of his desk and then jotted something down on a notepad. 'I'd have to say, Elizabeth, that this does seem a bit far-fetched. But if you wish to ease your mind, I can give you this bloke's name and number.'

Tearing the note from the pad he handed the details to Elizabeth. Her face went pale when she read the words: Lenny J. Forrester, phone no. …

16

The Men in her Life

Tilt dropped what she was doing to openly admire a male customer who entered the bookshop.

Overjoyed, she offered up a silent prayer – please God, let him be single.

'G'day there, lovely,' he warmly greeted with a smile that could melt the heart of a hardened harlot. 'You surely can't be, Pisa, the Leaning Tower?' he asked, extending his hand. 'I was expecting an old biddy with a walking stick.'

'Oh darling, you are a comedian. Have you ever met an Italian with red hair and freckles? My friends call me Tilt, short for Eileen. But I'm prepared to answer to anything.'

The stranger held her hand a little longer than necessary. 'Eileen!' he repeated.

Tilt's once much maligned name suddenly sounded like a finely tuned note plucked straight from the pages of a Rachmaninoff concerto. Even more pleasing – no wedding ring, she noted. I love him already.

'Eileen's a cool name,' the stranger assured her. 'Mine's Gary … Gary Cartwright. You've probably heard of me.'

'Not really, darling. Did you win the Gold Logie or something?' Tilt teased. 'Don't tell me you're a famous author?'

'Me, famous!' Gary laughed. 'Now, who's the comedian? My main claim to fame is Liz O'Connell. Thought she may have mentioned me given that I'm the love of her life.'

'Oh, you're that Gary!' Tilt replied with a little less ardour. 'Liz did mention a Gary once. But she's been pretty snowed under of late what with the Anderson brothers to worry about as well as getting the shop back up and running.'

'The Anderson brothers? Let me guess … they must be the star attraction at the local karaoke night.'

'Just the opposite,' Tilt laughed. 'They're a couple of reclusive bachelors who've taken quite a shine to your girlfriend.'

Seemingly unperturbed, 'Can't say I blame them,' Gary said, as he thumbed through a couple of the latest releases.

Replacing the books on the shelf, he paced about the shop before returning to Tilt with an ultimatum of sorts. 'Okay! I give up … where have you got her hidden, or have the Andy brothers abducted her?'

Eager to keep Gary to herself, Tilt asked, 'Was she expecting you?'

'Are you for real, lovely! Do I need an appointment?'

Unable to keep from laughing, Tilt finally cracked. Her prayer had gone unanswered, and although tempted, all the bells and whistles were sounding in her head. Gary was strictly off limits. She would never make a move on Liz's boyfriend. Playful but disappointed, she decided to put him out of his misery telling him where he could find the love of his life.

'You're an angel,' Gary said as he pecked her on the cheek and was suddenly gone.

The story of my life, Tilt thought.

Crossing the busy street, Elizabeth, being lucky enough to find an empty park bench along the foreshore, sat to make a note in her contacts list of the number that she'd only recently deleted. *What a joke*, she thought. It was almost laughable really that she should employ Lenny Forrester, the most obvious suspect, to investigate her aunt's death.

Hands encircled her eyes from behind and someone planted a kiss on her head. *It's not possible*, she thought. Gary was one of the few who wore that distinctive Armani aftershave. Pulling his hands from her face she asked, 'What on earth are you doing here?'

Elizabeth's heart soared when she saw how cute he looked. Athletic and tanned, with his close-cropped hair, trendy unshaven stubble and expensive dark shades, he could easily be mistaken for a movie star.

'God, I've missed you,' he said, taking her in his arms. 'Drove from Melbourne, called into the bookshop and the leaning lady steered me in the right direction. But then this pretty woman caught my eye. Just happened to spot her from across a crowded street sitting here all alone. Rushed over in the hope that she might agree to marry me. What's the verdict, Liz?'

'Gary, I wish you'd told me you were coming.'

'Then it wouldn't have been a surprise. We've got the whole weekend … you and me. I thought you'd be happy to see me.'

'Of course, I am. It's just that it's Tilt's weekend off and the shop doesn't run itself.'

'Don't worry, sweetheart, the leaning tower has agreed to cover for you.'

'I'm going to text her right now just to be sure.'

In between his marriage proposal and expecting Elizabeth to spend the weekend with him, Gary's glance was momentarily distracted as he moved his sunnies up on his forehead to check out a couple of scantily clad women wandering along the beach. 'Wow!' he said, as he openly appraised them while Elizabeth was messaging Tilt.

She'd become used to Gary's ability to multitask. He could have a disjointed conversation with her and at the same time ogle every female that happened by. She also felt incensed that he'd already spoken to Tilt and was now referring to her friend as the leaning tower. A compulsive flirt, he had a habit of reorganising her life. Just two reasons why marriage to a pilot seemed like an invitation to disaster.

Gary sat beside Elizabeth, looked over her shoulder and asked, 'What's the verdict?'

'A thumb's up! "No problem", she said.'

'There you go! That wasn't so hard. Tilt's a great lady,' Gary said.

'I think I know that better than you. But I feel bad about this. Tilt would never say no and will have to work two weekends in a row.'

Gary scoffed, 'You worry too much, babe. You'd do the same for her,' he said slapping his knees and jumping to his feet. 'So now that's sorted, how about we make a raid on the Fisherman's Co-Op, then swing by the bottle shop. I'll put a match to the fire, cook up a storm and tomorrow we'll walk along the beach and dine at that expensive restaurant overlooking the ocean. Your shout,' he laughed.

Lenny Forrester pulled into a parking bay just in time to see an unexpected sight. Elizabeth, the woman of his dreams, strolled by hand in hand with a tall, tanned and irritatingly fit looking stranger who appeared to have taken ownership of her. Lenny's heart sank as he slid down beneath the dashboard in the hope that he hadn't been spotted.

17

The Onlookers

Phyllis Bentley scoffed, 'Just like her aunt,' when seeing Elizabeth in the company of a fancy young gentleman friend who looked for all the world to be cast in the mould of Mr Universe.

Like a sun goddess, her head thrown back in laughter, Elizabeth clung to his arm. How confident they appeared, Phyllis thought, as the pair stood out like a beacon, turning heads in the main street.

'That one's a hussy for sure,' Phyllis made an on-the-spot decision based on the fact Elizabeth had been back at the Cove for only a matter of weeks and already an all too familiar pattern was emerging.

There was a time when Phyllis Bentley would have considered Margaret Thornton to be her best friend. There was a time when Phyllis Bentley would have looked upon Elizabeth like her own niece and done anything for her. But times change and friendships flag. Phyllis was not fooled by the less than lukewarm reception she had received when calling in to welcome Elizabeth. Nor the look of surprise on the hussy's face when seeing Phyllis serving tea at Misty Headland.

Margaret had brought her fate on herself, Phyllis thought. As indeed might Elizabeth who had wasted no time in defying her advice to stay away from the Andersons. One man was never enough for women like Margaret and now her niece, who obviously craved the admiration of all.

When Phyllis had started to work for the Andersons, she was happy. But Margaret had to spoil what little joy she had in her life and destroy all that by endearing herself to both brothers. She craved their affection and set one against the other.

Margaret could do no wrong in the eyes of Phyllis's husband, Jack. 'Fool that he was – he couldn't see past her either,' Phyllis muttered. When he rolled the tractor and lost his life in that horrific accident, Phyllis was prepared to forgive and forget in the hope that herself and Margaret would become closer. But Margaret seemed determined to push her away in favour of her numerous male acquaintances.

Phyllis shuddered as she thought back to the last time she had spoken to Margaret. It was just prior to her death. They'd argued, and Phyllis had lashed out at her friend. It was unfortunate that Margaret had died not long after. But the way she had been conducting her affairs sleeping around with considerably younger lovers, it was little wonder that her heart failed.

'I tried to reason with her, but she wouldn't listen,' Phyllis sniffled.

Senior Sergeant Ian Henderson had his own battle to fight as he pushed his way out through the crowded doorway of the bakery. He pulled a gourmet steak and mushroom pie part way out of a paper bag. It smelt delicious and when he bit into the pastry, steam rose in front of his face, tomato sauce dribbled down his chin and the piping hot meat spilt from his mouth causing gravy to congeal on the front of his uniform. 'I'll be damned,' he swore as he brushed away a mushroom caught around a button on his shirt.

It was only after he gulped down the rest of the pie, screwed up the bag, tossed it into the bin and wandered back to the station, that he noticed that snooty niece who had given him a hard time over some cock and bull story about an intruder. But even more concerning was the fact that she was suspicious about the death of Margaret Thornton. *Good riddance,* he thought as he never was too keen on that aunt of hers who had always shunned his advances.

She thought she was too good, that one, for the likes of a senior sergeant. Uppity so 'n' so that she was. Truth be known she was little better than a lowly shop girl. He'd always had a hankering to set her straight, he sneered and recalled the day that he'd gone out to see her about a spate of break-ins around the area. She had treated him so offhandedly.

He'd disliked her ever since. And was glad that she had got her comeuppance. She deserved to die.

But like her aunt before her, there was no denying that the niece was a good looker alright. *Shame about her being such a high 'n' mighty know-it-all who it seemed was moving back to stay.* He'd never seen the bloke she was with. Yet if this Elizabeth person insisted on stirring up trouble, there would be a duty for him in his role as the keeper-of-the-law to set her right. *I'd like nothing better than to teach her a little respect,* he thought.

Graeme Jenkins had stepped out of his office to grab a coffee. He saw Elizabeth in the distance with a rather handsome young fellow. The two appeared to be close and were laughing. *Must be her boyfriend*, he assumed. His thoughts turned to her visit just one hour earlier with the news of a cousin and questions that could prove difficult to answer.

Not many people were aware that he had known Margaret a whole lot better than purely on a business level. But then Margaret was the sort of woman who could convince the devil himself to enter the seminary if she so desired.

Graeme chuckled to himself at even contemplating the idea that Margaret would be likely to urge any man to consider entering the priesthood. And although he had chosen to remain single, like most men, he was partial to a bit of female company from time to time, and Margaret had on several occasions been only too willing to invite him home for a candlelit dinner.

Careful to stay hidden, one further onlooker watched the progress of Elizabeth and her male companion. He rarely visited the town, but his curiosity had been aroused. *Margaret's niece was even more compelling than her aunt*, he thought.

Running his finger gently along the scar on his face, David Anderson looked forward to a second meeting with Elizabeth as he wasn't at all happy with the way he'd been left speechless at the sight of her on the day of her visit. Meanwhile, he made a quick visit to the seaside cemetery where he placed a long-stemmed rose from his garden at Margaret's gravesite.

18

She Loves Him – She Loves Him Not

In the early days of their partnership, Elizabeth had adored being seen with Gary. But as they strolled along the busy stretch of shops and cafes at Mariners Cove, she wondered if she was fooling herself and others with her outward display of affection.

Following her sudden departure from Melbourne and in the brief period that they had been apart, she'd been having serious doubts about their relationship. But short of pulling petals from a daisy to figure out the answer, Elizabeth remained unsure.

Many men had an eye for the ladies but perhaps were a touch more discreet than Gary. She felt this trait downright rude and insensitive when in his company. Then came the moments like the present, when she was happy and any thought of ending their partnership was cast aside and all but forgotten.

'Don't you just love the smell of fresh seafood, sweetheart?' Gary asked when they approached the entrance to the pier-side Fishermen's Co-Op.

'Well, if given a choice, I much prefer Chanel No.5,' Elizabeth laughed, as she untangled herself from the multi-coloured plastic strips hanging across the open doorway.

Wiping each hand on a grubby apron, a balding middle-aged man behind the counter greeted them. 'G'day folks … what can I get you on this lovely sunny afternoon?'

Gary focused his attention on the ice-covered trays laden with the deep-sea catch of the day. Elizabeth could only feel sorry for the poor lifeless creatures. She'd always hated to see their struggle when flapping and gasping in their last dying moments.

Undeterred by the glazed eyes staring back at him, Gary opted for a couple of lobster tails to add to a brimming bag of calamari, scallops and prawn marinara mix.

Taking hold of the goodies, he courteously pulled aside the door flaps for Elizabeth then fell into step beside her and lovingly squeezed her hand. She smiled, suddenly looking forward to the evening ahead.

There was a great deal of truth in the saying that absence makes the heart grow fonder. And following their arrival home, Gary hurried from the car as if eager to let Elizabeth know just how much he'd missed her.

Once indoors, feeling powerless to resist his advances, Elizabeth did her best to curtail his enthusiasm with the excuse that they needed to refrigerate the seafood and collect the shopping bags. 'Why don't you make yourself useful and pour us a drink, Gary, while I unpack the groceries.'

There weren't too many times that Gary wasn't interested in pouring a drink, but this was one of them. Dinner could wait it seemed as he scooped Elizabeth up in his arms and like the proverbial caveman, strode towards the bedroom.

Her earlier resolve to end everything vanished. Willingly she surrendered and welcomed his impatience to familiarise and take ownership of every part of her body. His eagerness to satisfy his hunger reflected in a frantic need to disrobe and smother her body in kisses.

Elizabeth moaned at the sensation of his touch. Her longing for him was aroused. How she had missed the gentle caresses, lips tenderly tracing each curve of her perfumed body as his tongue probed deeper to seek out the hidden valleys of her being. They wrapped themselves around each other, legs entwined, and when neither one could wait to fulfil the urgency of their lovemaking, he rolled on top of her. She clung to him as he entered her, and tears spilled from her eyes when finally, she cried out in elation.

Night had fallen by the time Elizabeth finally sipped her wine and watched Gary find his way around the kitchen. *Most women would kill to call this man their lover*, she thought. She'd almost forgotten how skilled he was at making her forget all else as he manipulated and moulded her to suit his every desire. This was the hold he had over her. Yet wasn't this the very reason for her moments of discontent?

In between preparing a salad, he put a match to the fire. 'I want you to sit back and relax,' he ordered while topping up Elizabeth's glass, plying her with soft music and the promise of a romantic candlelit feast to follow.

The aroma of seafood, garlic and crusty herb bread was enough to ensure that she would relish the mouth-watering flavours when time to sample the meal which, as Gary had predicted was to exceed all expectations. And when dinner was ended, aware of a pleasantly sated and tipsy feeling, Elizabeth responded warmly to his continued attentiveness. It was as if he'd cast a spell over her as they polished off a second bottle of Pinot. She knew that alcohol was her undoing as her head swam, but she would have married Gary right there on the spot had there been a minister handy.

However, Elizabeth wasn't too far gone to recognise how tense she'd allowed herself to become lately. So now she savoured the indulgent and relaxing release of her own undoing and more than anything wanted Gary to not merely make love to her again, but to wildly ravish her until she, this time, cried out for mercy.

Elizabeth languidly stretched and yawned when she woke the next morning. The world appeared to have taken on a rosy complexion even though she was feeling a little fragile. She could hear Gary up and about preparing breakfast. 'Okay, little lady, wakey, wakey,' he shouted.

A lazy day filled with clear blue skies and sunshine perfect for a dip in the ocean, a picnic on the beach and a walk along the sandy shore made for a lovely diversion from all that had been happening since the death of her aunt. And later that evening when she showered and changed into one of her favourite dresses in readiness for dinner, she felt refreshed and invigorated. 'Gary's visit has been just what I needed,' she smiled.

Seated at the best table in the house, the stunning clifftop view and soothing motion of the surf enhanced the ambience of an exceedingly stylish restaurant. Champagne corks popped and the food tasted exquisite. At her happiest when dessert was placed in front of her, Elizabeth picked up her spoon and wondered why Gary watched on so closely as she delved into several strategically placed mint leaves. Her mouth dropped open in disbelief. 'Gary … what in the world …'

'Open it, sweetheart. I can hardly wait.'

Hesitantly, Elizabeth lifted the lid of a tiny jewel box. A solitaire diamond sparkled in the candlelight.

Gary got up out of his chair and traditionally went down on bended knee. 'Will you marry me, Liz?'

'I don't know what to say,' she stammered.

'Just say yes. It's as simple as that.'

'Gary, please sit down.' She reached out across the table to take his hand. 'This is such a surprise, and I don't want to sound … well … it's just that marriage is a big step. I need to think this through.'

A look of sheer devastation and disappointment spread across Gary's face. 'You can't be serious! This has been the most perfect two days in my life, and I thought after last night …are you turning me down?'

Without waiting for an answer, he caught the eye of the waiter who nodded in the direction of the kitchen, a complementary cupcake mounted with a fiery sparkler was delivered to the table. 'Congratulations to you both,' he smiled.

Shaking uncontrollably, Gary fumbled with his wallet to withdraw a bundle of fifty-dollar notes which he slammed down on the table. He then stormed off in a fit of rage.

Shocked, Elizabeth lowered her eyes and stared at the offending ring, all the while the sparkler sparkled on in a profusion of endless gaiety.

19

A Confronting Accusation

Tilt looked surprised when Elizabeth turned up at the bookshop on Sunday. 'What happened to Gary?' she asked.

Even though her mind was focused on the events of the previous night – quick to roll up her sleeves and get to work – Elizabeth knew there was no time to talk as several customers were waiting for assistance.

When she'd been unable to get a hold of Gary on the phone after he walked out of the restaurant, the head waiter had kindly arranged for a female member of staff to drive her home.

The place was in darkness when she arrived with no sign of Gary or his car. He'd vanished, leaving his overnight bag. A chilling emptiness pervaded the house. Shivering, Elizabeth had wrapped a woolly cardigan tightly around her shoulders. She then closed the curtains, switched on every light and waited. Only then did she place the ring on the bedside table and asked herself, 'What have I done?'

Daylight brought no further news. So now, at the bookshop, the sound of an incoming call caused her to drop all she was doing in her haste to answer.

Recognising the voice, Elizabeth said, 'Oh … it's only you!'

'Sorry to disappoint, but George Clooney was busy this morning.'

'I'm in no mood and haven't got time for this right now, Forrester. What's the problem?'

'Judging by your obvious excitement to hear from me, I suppose there's no point in asking if you would consider joining me for a drink sometime.'

'Normally the answer would be no. But as it happens, there's a little matter to do with Kit Kats that I've been eager to discuss since last we met.'

'Kit Kats, hey? You wouldn't be pulling a bloke's leg by any chance?' Lenny laughed.

'No chance of that I can assure you.'

'Well, now you've got my full attention, how does this evening suit? Say around six in the cocktail lounge at The Cove?'

'A lemon, lime & bitters might be all I can manage. I've got to drive home remember.'

'Right! Lemon, lime & bitters it is.'

Elizabeth pressed end and turned to Tilt. 'Can you believe I just had a call from that despicable Lenny Forrester?'

'Gosh what's so despicable about him, darling? Rather yummy I thought.'

'Depends on how much you like Kit Kats,' Elizabeth scowled. 'I think he must have shares in the chocolate factory.'

Tilt looked puzzled. 'No need to explain, I can see you're not yourself this morning. By the way, what happened with Philip Anderson?'

'Oh my God, that's a whole different story in amongst many I'll need to tell you whenever I get a minute.'

'How about a coffee after work then?'

'Can't, Tilt, I'm sorry. I've got a bit of important business to sort out with Forrester.'

Tilt raised an eyebrow. 'Geez, darling, you don't mess around. You've got them all lined up and waiting.'

Lenny was already saddled up at the bar when Elizabeth entered the pub.

Dressed in a smart shirt and a tie, his eyes lit up when he saw her. But in his haste to greet her, he managed to get his foot tangled in the leg of the stool which caused him to stumble. With nothing more than his pride being shaken, Elizabeth imagined, he was quick to recover and keep his balance.

'Nice save on your part, Forrester. It was a bit touch and go there for a minute.'

'Needs tossing out on the scrap heap. Got a wonky leg on it I reckon.'

Leading her to a quiet booth, he shouted, 'Make that a Carlton Draught and a lemon lime & bitters for the lady, will you, Joe.'

'Comin' up,' the bartender replied, and gave Lenny a knowing nod.

'You're looking even lovelier than I remember and I'm not sure what I've done to deserve this honour,' Lenny complimented Elizabeth.

'Drop the sweet talk, Forrester. And don't go fooling yourself. This is not a social get together.' Elizabeth slid into the booth and removed her jacket. Then without any form of preamble she blurted out the question that had been nagging her. 'I need you to tell me just how well you knew my aunt.'

A little shell shocked, Lenny remained silent until Joe, who arrived at that inopportune moment with the drinks, had placed them down and returned to the bar.

Lenny picked up his beer and offering Elizabeth a glass clinking cheers he watched her take a reluctant sip through the straw. 'There's nothing quite like a bit of polite conversation to get off to a friendly start I reckon, Elizabeth. You could go with something like it's so nice to see you, Lenny – how's your day been?'

'Forgive me if I skip the small talk and insist you answer the question.'

'What is this exactly? I've already told you about my arrangement with Margaret.'

'A little matter of discarded Kit Kat wrappers, that's what this is, Forrester. Lies by omission.'

'Kit Kat wrappers! What is it with you?'

Elizabeth glared at Lenny. 'Me? Don't twist this around to me. You're a two-faced liar, Lenny Forrester. Admit it. You were sleeping with my aunt.'

'Never let up, do you? Even if it was true, what business is it of yours?'

Elizabeth bristled, 'So now you're admitting it. I can see it in your eyes. How old are you, Forrester … thirty-seven, thirty-eight maybe? My aunt was fifty-two. Twelve years your senior when she died. Or was she murdered? I wonder!'

Lenny's eyes widened. 'You think I murdered your aunt? Is that what you're implying? You've got the gall to sit there and accuse me of being a murderer over a Kit Kat wrapper.'

'Nice one, Forrester! But you're not fooling me for a minute. You never once admitted it was you that came into the house that first night I arrived.'

Enraged, Lenny shook his head and looked away. 'It was me! What's the big deal? I've already told you I used to let Margaret know before I bunked down in the cottage. You're a crazy person, do you know that? I've just about had enough. Either apologise or leave.'

'Right! Suit yourself. Because unless you tell me the truth, I'm planning to inform the police of incriminating evidence that implicates you in a possible murder investigation.' Elizabeth grabbed her jacket and purse and without a backward glance, flounced out through the doorway. But in her haste, she realised her mobile was missing and she turned to see the bartender wander over to Lenny's table.

She quickly slipped back out of sight and heard him collecting the glasses. 'That didn't go too well,' he chuckled. 'Got a better offer, did she?'

'Wipe that grin off your face, Joe. Or I might have to wipe it off for you.'

'Hey, keep y' shirt on, Forrester. Can't you take a joke?'

Elizabeth then heard Lenny get up to leave. She moved further into the shadows and waited for a few moments until he headed up the stairs. The room now sounded quiet as she rushed to the table and searched for her phone.

When finding it under the seat, the barman who had briefly disappeared, suddenly returned and as if surprised to see her, he said, 'Mr Forrester has just left.'

'That's okay, it wasn't Mr Forrester I was looking for. But then again, I'm sure you may already know that.'

Saying nothing, the barman gathered up a tray of dirty glasses and scurried away out through the swinging door into the kitchen.

20

A Kiss is Just a Kiss

Although inconvenient, the drive to Misty Headland was hardly a chore. The scenery along this fertile stretch of coastline provided a feast for the eyes with its rolling hills, peaceful farmland and shady forests. Yet, when Elizabeth traversed the country laneways and glimpsed the ocean, her mind was elsewhere. How had she managed to alienate two men in less than a matter of days?

Lenny Forrester, it seemed, had come from the school of thought that the best form of defence was attack, judging by the way he had lashed out at her. She hadn't seen that coming. But for all she cared, he could take his unending supply of Kit Kat wrappers and paper the walls of his jail cell with them.

To top it off, she'd received a call from the airline. Gary hadn't arrived for his scheduled flight to Los Angeles, and his failure to check in might provide reason for him to be suspended. Elizabeth believed he'd had good reason to be upset, but it was unfair of him to run off and refuse to answer her calls.

Prior to meeting with Philip, time alone was what she needed. So, close to her destination, she parked the car out of sight and walked a short distance to hook up with the track that led down steep steps to the beach below. The overgrown vegetation proved slippery in places, and not wanting to lose her footing, she grabbed hold of a prickly tea tree which spiked her hand and offered little in the way of support. Twigs snapped beneath her feet and although she could hear the sea, it wasn't until arriving at the base of the cliff that the ocean came fully into view.

Elizabeth shielded her eyes from the glare and delighted in the smell of the ocean. Waves washed onto the shore, slapping the sand and receding to leave a trail of bubbly white foam, tiny shells and clumps of seaweed in their wake. Her gaze followed the curve of the smooth wet surface and came to rest on the one sight she hadn't expected.

A lone figure standing before an easel looked her way and shouted, 'Didn't you read the sign? Unless you have a permit, this is a private beach … which I happen to own by the way.'

'Good for you!' Elizabeth's voice carried on the breeze as she defiantly padded across the sand and stood before the artist with her hands on her hips.

'So, it's you,' he said. 'Well, if you've come here to insult me, you can turn around and head back the way you came.'

Recognising the scar-faced brother from the garden, Elizabeth said, 'To think I actually felt sorry for you, believing you to be both deaf … and dumb. Now I think it only fair to tell you I was a friend of the former owner, old Mr Gentry. I've been coming here since I was a kid and left my footprints in this sand long before you arrived.'

'Is that right? If only I'd been forewarned prior to investing the family's life savings into this place,' he said. 'I had hoped to escape the rat-race and spend some time alone. But maybe I should think about setting up hire boats and the entire community of holiday campers could join me for a friendly dip.'

'With your anti-social disposition, I doubt you'd get many takers,' Elizabeth replied.

David Anderson stepped away from the canvas. 'I can see that I'm wasting my breath here. Short of me physically removing you, why not make yourself useful and tell me what you think of my painting.'

Elizabeth turned her head on either side, then picked up a pencil. Holding it upright with her thumb along the shaft, she closed one eye and peered down the length of her outstretched arm with the other. She wasn't sure why artists did this, but at least he was not to know any different. 'I think your composition a little pedestrian if you want an honest opinion.'

'A little pedestrian?'

'Well, yes. Anyone can see that you need to place something in the foreground. Perhaps the hull of a boat or something, to make it interesting,'

'Really?'

'Yes really.'

'Thanks for the advice. But there doesn't appear to be the hull of a boat anywhere in sight.'

'Use your imagination and take a bit of artistic licence.'

David rinsed his brushes and abruptly changed the subject. 'Tell me … what did my big brother discuss with you today?'

'I haven't spoken to him yet.'

'What's he on about anyway making you drive out here twice in one week? I'm guessing he's already told you his real name is Thomas?'

'Is it true?' Elizabeth asked.

Sitting on the sand, David patted the spot beside him. 'Here, seeing that I can't get rid of you, come and sit with me and let's not talk about my brother. I'm not sure why I mentioned him in the first place.'

Hesitant, Elizabeth accepted his offer but was unprepared for what came next. Aware that he was staring at her, he then reached out and placed his finger beneath her chin. Guiding her face towards him, she assumed he was making a study of her features with a view to sketching her. Instead, he unexpectedly leaned forward and kissed her.

Shoving him away she exclaimed, 'Just what do you think you're doing?'

He fell back and propped himself up on his elbows. 'It seemed pretty obvious to me. Don't tell me you've never been kissed before.'

'Most people don't go around kissing total strangers.'

'That's true. But then, you're so much like her, I can hardly think of you as a stranger. And should you be completely honest, I believe you'd enjoy nothing better than for me to kiss you again.'

Elizabeth jumped to her feet and prudishly readjusted her shirt as if at any moment she might expect to be relieved of it. 'Oh yes, right! I'm just hanging out to be kissed by an egotistical chauvinist who happens to own a beach, and I've known for less than twenty minutes. Go right ahead and help yourself. But the fact is I'm not my aunt and never will be.'

David Anderson caught her by the wrist. 'There's no need to get so upset.'

'Only moments ago, you were ordering me off the beach. Well, I've got news for you … this is not the way I do things.' Elizabeth released his fingers from her wrist and realised she could now carve a third notch on her belt, having alienated yet another man from her life.

'I knew it! I just knew it!' Phyllis repeated in a low voice so as not to be overheard. 'That bold and shameless hussy is now intent on seducing the brothers. First one, then the other, no doubt. She has indeed inherited the somewhat questionable behaviour of her aunt.'

In the habit of talking to herself, Phyllis Bentley was lying on her tummy hidden behind a clump of bracken on the clifftop. With binoculars focused on Elizabeth, she'd discovered her to be currently engaged in an enthusiastic exchange of kisses with the likelihood of more intimate moments to follow.

Phyllis really did see herself as looking to be quite foolish should she be discovered. She could say she was birdwatching, which wouldn't be a lie. But the truth was that birds were a little less offensive in their coupling than those who should know better than to flaunt their passion in public. Fornicators, in Phyllis's opinion, were an impulsive lot who should control their lust for the privacy of the bedroom.

She had checked Philip's diary on her arrival that morning to see he had another appointment with Elizabeth. And although she'd been listening for the car engine, it was quite by accident that she happened to look up from the sink while rinsing dishes to spot a movement in the bushes. It was then that she clearly saw someone making their way down to the beach.

Now convinced that she'd seen enough, she hurried away from her vantage point and – in the hope that Philip had not yet entered the study – replaced the borrowed binoculars.

'Good morning, Phyllis,' Philip greeted as he wheeled his chair through the open doorway.

Phyllis jumped in alarm. 'Morning, Mr Anderson. I was just tidying up your desk and doing a bit of dusting. I'll leave you now to enjoy your solitude.'

'Phyllis, when are you going to drop that Mr Anderson nonsense? And there's no rush. Solitude is something I get plenty of since moving to Misty Headland. Although I'm expecting that young friend of yours to be along any moment. How long have the two of you known each other?'

'I've known Elizabeth since she was a child. But if you don't mind me saying, I think her to be … well … a little flighty and even a bit above her station since she went off to live in the city. So, if you're thinking of instigating any dealings with her of a business nature, just take care, Mr Anderson.'

Philip laughed. 'I'll keep that in mind, Phyllis. But it's not such a bad thing. I feel certain Elizabeth is extremely competent and knows her mind. Also, I'm keen for my brother to get out and about a little more. He needs to mix with people his own age.'

'I think the same could be said for you.'

Turning to stare out the window, Philip said, 'Being tied to this confounded chair, I wouldn't want to inflict myself on anyone.'

'That's not right at all. I know it's easy for me to say, but you shouldn't allow that to stop you from enjoying your life.'

'Let's not talk about my problem, Phyllis. And I'll say it again. I think it high time for you to address me as Philip. I'm still only a young buck you know.'

A smile broke out on Phyllis's lips as she coyly nodded in agreement.

'Right, that's settled then,' Philip said as she made her way out the door.

Later, when Elizabeth gently tapped and entered the room, Philip said, 'Have you been rushing, Elizabeth? You look quite red in the face.'

'No, no, not at all.'

'Well, sit yourself down. And I'm sorry to call on you so soon after we met. It's just that there are a few things I didn't get to touch on when I last saw you.'

For some reason, Elizabeth had an unsettling feeling. It had little to do with whatever Philip wanted to discuss but everything to do with Phyllis. 'Would it be okay if I grab a glass of water before we get started?'

'Of course. I'll get Phyllis on the job.'

'Don't worry. I'd welcome the chance to talk to her alone for a moment if you don't mind waiting.'

'Go ahead. You'll find her in the kitchen, I think. Take your time. I've got some paperwork to catch up on.'

Elizabeth wasn't sure where the kitchen could be found until hearing the clatter of dishes. So, she made her way along a wide corridor towards the direction of the noise.

'Hello, Phyllis. I hope you don't mind, but I've come in search of water.'

'Oh, Elizabeth.' Phyllis turned away and reached for a glass. 'Here, help yourself.'

Elizabeth filled the glass from the tap and said, 'Is there anything wrong? You seem a little upset.'

'Wrong? What could possibly be wrong?'

Detecting the coolness in Phyllis's voice, 'Well, you don't seem quite yourself lately. You used to always call me Liz or Lizzie, never Elizabeth.'

'I suppose I've come to realise you're no longer that sweet, innocent little girl I once knew.'

Sensing there was a lot more to this than Phyllis was admitting, Elizabeth lowered her voice and said, 'Look Phyllis, we both know I haven't been a little girl for a long time. I'm not quite sure what's bugging you. You did warn me not to get involved with the Andersons, but it really was beyond my control.'

The sour expression on Phyllis's face, said it all.

'I swear that Philip chased me up, not the other way round. And if it comes to that, why all the cloak and dagger secrecy about you working here?'

'I didn't want you here, that's why,' Phyllis snapped. 'When the Andersons moved in, they advertised for a housekeeper. Jack was gone and I needed work. So, I applied for the position and got it. And for the first occasion in a very long time, I was happy.'

'Well, that's a good thing, isn't it?'

'I certainly thought so. But shortly after, Margaret started sticking her nose in and the next thing I knew, she was coming here on a regular basis. Ruined everything, she did, and began taking over, working her charm on both Philip and David. It was disgraceful the way a woman of her age was acting.'

'What are you saying? The two of you used to be such good friends.'

Phyllis scoffed and stopped what she was doing to glare at Elizabeth. 'Used to be is probably more to the point, because once you left things began to change. I know it's wrong to speak ill of the dead, but Margaret's attention became more focused on her male friends. I would hate to see that happen to you, Elizabeth.'

Annoyed with this statement, Elizabeth began to get angry. 'Put that damned tea towel down for a minute and let's get something straight here, Phyllis. I'm twenty-seven years old and just split up with my partner. I can hardly be accused of having a lot of male companions.' Elizabeth rinsed her glass and circled the kitchen. 'Are you sure you aren't being overly critical of my aunt? She was a good person and may have been lonely. There's no law to say she must remain unattached for the rest of her days. What proof do you have that she was engaged in anything that might be seen as unladylike?'

'Give me some credit. I'm no fool, Elizabeth. I do have eyes and ears you know. And she had Jack on her list as well.'

'That's a terrible thing to say.' Elizabeth replied, shocked.

Phyllis pulled a tissue from a box on the bench and loudly blew her nose. 'Terrible is not nearly a strong enough word to describe how she treated me–her best friend.'

Elizabeth plopped into a chair and sat at the table. 'I'm sure you are mistaken and allowing your imagination to get the better of you. Losing both your husband and best friend has been so upsetting.'

Phyllis, who appeared unwilling to be pacified, shook her head.

'What's really going on here?' Elizabeth urged. 'Because it's one thing for you to have been upset with Margaret, but what's caused you to turn your dislike on me?'

'I saw you earlier today kissing David Anderson.'

'You saw me? How could you possibly see me?'

'There's not too much that escapes my notice, let me tell you. But that's not the point, is it?'

'You're jumping to the wrong conclusion. You know nothing, Phyllis. David Anderson kissed me without my okay. And no matter what you saw or believe you saw, we are two young people who could quite simply be attracted to one another and have every right to kiss.'

'Don't give me that, young lady … you barely know one another, and I don't want to see you upsetting Philip.'

'Why would I be upsetting Philip?'

'I suppose it hasn't occurred to you that he may well be wanting to kiss you himself.'

'Stop this right now and get your facts right before you go around making false assumptions.' Elizabeth got to her feet, pushed the chair in under the table and when reaching the doorway she turned and said, 'Next time you want to spy on me, don't go skulking around behind bushes. Come right out in the open and face me.'

21

Fear

Something bad was about to happen. Elizabeth could feel it in her bones.

Since driving home from Misty Headland after the run in with Phyllis, she was beginning to wonder who would be next – because at this rate, she would have no friends. At least she had felt a sense of relief when returning to the study to speak with Philip, who on this occasion wanted nothing from her other than her friendship.

Still unable to contact Gary, life had progressively gone from bad to worse. Home alone, she jumped at the sound of every noise and when preparing for bed, Elizabeth swallowed a sleeping tablet before switching off the lamp.

She woke with a start – her head groggy. *Oh no, not again,* she thought. *This can't be possible.*

'Is that you, Forrester? Because if it is, I swear that you'll regret this.'

'Sorry to disappoint, lady. I dunno who Forrester is, but I'm not him,' a figure clothed in black, his face distorted, answered in a muffled voice. He leaned over her, his breath sour as he clamped a hand over her mouth and pinned her head to the pillow.

'Don't struggle,' he warned.

Elizabeth mumbled behind his hand, her eyes wide with fear as he shone a small flashlight onto her face. 'Look at me!' he said, his voice low and raspy. He held the light under his chin, and she squirmed as she caught sight of his disfiguring garb; his nose squashed and hideously flattened against his face. A stocking, he had a stocking pulled over his head like she had seen bank robbers wear in movies. A guttural sob escaped from her throat.

Smothering her mouth, she felt like she was suffocating. He was hurting her, but there was something about him that didn't quite fit the mould, when he said, 'Stay quiet and I won't harm you. Nod if you agree.' He shone the torch back on her as she moved her head up and down. Slowly withdrawing his hand, he relieved the pressure. She gasped and took a deep breath. 'I'm not here to hurt you,' he repeated. 'I've come for what's mine and nothing more.'

Helpless and trembling, Elizabeth couldn't speak. Who was this? What did he want? Why was this happening? Please God don't let him hurt me. She huddled in a ball, trying to make herself smaller.

He removed himself from the bed, paced around the room, ransacked the drawers and shone his flashlight from one spot to another in his fruitless search. 'The money. That's what I've come for. The money she cheated me out of. Where is it? I know it's hidden here in this house.'

Elizabeth kept shaking her head.

'Speak, damn you. Speak!'

Her voice quivered as he dragged her from the bed.

'I swear, I don't know about any money!' she cried.

He shoved her back down on the quilt and continued to pace the floor while rambling on about her aunt. 'It was for the bookshop, she said. She needed it, she said. But then she said a whole lot of things, but really couldn't be trusted. Find it, or next time I won't be nearly so understanding. This is just a warning,' he said as he picked up a box from the top of the bedside table and flipped the lid open. 'I'll be taking this with me when I leave. Call it a little down payment if you like.'

'No! Please take anything. Don't take that, it's worthless,' Elizabeth pleaded.

'Shut y'face an' find the money.'

'I will,' Elizabeth's voice cracked. She begged him, 'Take anything except the ring. Please, I promise if the money's here, I'll find it.'

'That's more like it,' he said as he pocketed the ring and stepped back into the shadows. 'I'll be in touch. Have the money waiting or you can kiss your precious diamond goodbye.'

Parked along the dark country backroad, Gary anxiously watched and waited for his accomplice in this charade to return. At last, he could see him in the rearview mirror running towards the car.

'Did you get it?' Gary asked as his panting friend, Tony, opened the door, jumped into the passenger seat and handed him the box.

'A piece of cake, mate. It was sitting right there in open sight on the nightstand begging to be taken. I could have picked it up and been out of there. But, like you said, the whole idea was to make her believe I wasn't after the ring and just scare her a little.'

'So, it was on the nightstand, you said. What's a nightstand?'

'You know, the table next to the bed that you put a lamp on. Me mum used to always call it a nightstand.'

'Was she scared? You didn't hurt her, did you?'

'Me mum? No, course not. She could be pretty trying at times but …'

'No, you fool, Liz I mean. You swear you didn't hurt her?'

'What do you take me for? A thug? There's no need to worry. It all went smoothly, and she fell for the story about the aunt, and the money and all.'

'I owe you one, mate. Thanks for that. I've got to get the refund on this ring. That was the terms of the agreement. A full refund within ten days if the proposal wasn't accepted. That diamond cost a packet, but I wouldn't lower myself to ask Liz for it back even though I'm broke.'

'No point beating yourself up about it. I totally get it. When my ex left me, I was like a man on the way out. Now you need to get your life back on track.'

'Truth is I can't live without her.' Gary's voice cracked. 'If it wasn't for you helping me out, I never would have made it.'

'Look at it this way, mate! She's done you a favour. You're better off without her.' Tony sounded fully convinced as he dropped Gary's spare house key back in the glovebox. 'Now, let's get out of here. I've got to be back in Melbourne in time for work in the morning.'

At that moment. Gary wasn't feeling proud of himself and secretly wanted to knock on Liz's door, take her in his arms and say that there was no need to be afraid anymore. That it wasn't safe for a woman on her own to live out here in the sticks and he was there to protect her. He hoped that tonight would bring her to her senses.

Instead, he turned on the engine and switched the headlights to low beam. Like a couple of hardened criminals in their getaway car, the two snuck quietly up the road, out of the bushland and followed the signposts to Melbourne.

Deeply disturbed and threatened by the frightening episode, Elizabeth switched all the lights on, checked the windows were closed and sat up for the rest of the night feeling terrified in case this horrible person returned. She had no idea how he'd got in. She waited till sunrise before packing a bag and locking the door behind her.

Her first instinct made little sense. Particularly given her recent adverse history with Lenny Forrester. But she didn't stop to question why he of all people was the one she should run to. Instead, she drove directly to The Cove Hotel, pulled into a parking bay, bolted up the steps and raced through the lobby. It was still early, but at the entrance to the dining room, she stopped and peered inside.

There were few people about at this hour apart from a waiter. 'Good morning, Ma'am,' he greeted. He then picked up a menu and issued a cheery invitation. 'Come right this way.'

'Oh no, I'm not a guest,' Elizabeth stammered. 'I'm looking for a Lenny Forester. Do you know him?'

'Everyone knows Mr Forrester. He should be down at any moment. If you follow me, he usually sits at Table 9.'

Twenty minutes later, Lenny appeared with a newspaper tucked under his arm. A look of dismay was evident when he spotted her and without waiting to be escorted across the room, he at once strode to the table and sat in the seat opposite. 'What's happened?' he asked checking his watch. 'Don't tell me there's been another murder. And, let me guess, I'm the most likely suspect.'

Apart from a tell-tale crack in her voice, Elizabeth managed to hold herself together. 'I deserved that, Forrester, and I'm sorry. I really am. I realise that if you were sleeping with my aunt, it doesn't make you guilty of murder. I had no right to speak to you the way I did.'

'Would you mind repeating that, Elizabeth? I'm not sure I heard right. Has this supposed murderer of yours suddenly 'fessed up? Cos if you think you can come crawling back and win me over with whatever sob story you're about to spin, you'd be sadly mistaken.'

Elizabeth's dislike of the term crawling would have normally brought a negative reaction. But her stoic resolve had deserted her as she picked up a napkin from the side plate and discreetly dabbed at her nose. 'Please stop, Forrester. I've suffered enough. Can't you see I've come to you for help?'

'Bit late for that, I reckon.'

'Well, until last night, I had reason to jump to the wrong conclusion. But now that reason has become a whole lot less valid. So, there's no need to rub my nose in it … I've already said I'm sorry.' Elizabeth's voice grew shaky as she went on to relate the terror to which she'd been subjected.

Lenny remained silent. He turned side on, casually crossed one knee over the other and opened his newspaper.

'Did you hear what I just said, Forrester? I thought this guy was going to rape me or worse. Are you just planning to sit there pretending to read your paper and ignore me?'

Seemingly unmoved, 'Shame about that!' Lenny replied. 'But you're a big girl, Elizabeth. You've proven that on more than one occasion. Why would you now come running to me?' he asked with an air of disinterest.

Unwilling to provoke him with her usual haughty response, Elizabeth struggled to fight back tears. 'Forrester, I thought you cared about me.'

'Try putting y'self in my shoes, is all I can say. Have you ever stopped to consider how ridiculous you sounded when accusing me of murdering your aunt over nothing more relevant than a couple of flimsy chocolate wrappers? I've got t'feel sorry for that poor misguided bastard wearing the stockin' over his head. He was prob'ly more frightened of you than you were of him.'

Lenny's lack of sympathy seemed surprisingly callous to Elizabeth. 'Do you think this a joke? How can you be so cruel? I was terrified last night, and you haven't the decency to ask if I'm okay. I apologised to you.'

'That makes everything all right, I s'pose. Give 's a break. I'm just expected to forgive 'n' forget you could believe me capable of such an evil act. What is it with you, Elizabeth?'

'We all make mistakes,' Elizabeth shrugged. 'I came here in good faith to offer you the chance to come back and live in the cottage for a couple of weeks. This hotel must be costing a great deal of unnecessary expense.'

'That's a load of bulldust and you know it, Elizabeth. 'Specially as this unnecessary expense didn't seem t'worry you in the past,' Lenny pointed out while folding the paper as the waiter approached and placed a serving of bacon and eggs down before him.

Elizabeth's mouth watered as she watched Lenny eagerly salt and pepper his breakfast and douse the plate with a generous lashing of Worcestershire sauce. Her tummy rumbled as she breathed in the bacon and secretly held out the hope that he might invite her to join him in a slice of buttered toast.

Yet demolishing every morsel, the best that Lenny could come up with in between gulping down mouthfuls of strong black tea, was that Elizabeth should report this break-in to the police.

'Forrester, I've no faith in that idiot Henderson who runs the local station. Stop giving me a hard time and tell me you'll do this,' Elizabeth pleaded while impatiently checking the time on her phone. 'I need to get on my way to deal with a personal matter in Melbourne. Here's the key and there's no shortage of jobs to keep you busy. I'll pay you well for your trouble.'

Lenny pushed the key back across the table. 'If y'want my advice, move int' town for your own protection because this is never gunna work between us.'

'I'm not asking you to marry me, Forrester, and there's no way I'll be leaving home, even if I have to install iron bars on the doors and windows.'

'That's your call of course, but the answer's still no. It's not gunna happen. I thought I would forgive you for anything. But no one questions my reputation or accuses me of being a murderer. Not even you, Elizabeth.'

<h1 style="text-align: center;">22</h1>

<h1 style="text-align: center;">Lenny's Strategy</h1>

It was all a lie – his lack of sympathy, his outward display of disinterest.

Nothing that had just occurred reflected his true feelings. And as Lenny left the hotel dining room and stepped outdoors, he knew that even though he had managed to fool Elizabeth, he had certainly not fooled himself.

This woman had a permanent hold over him.

In the past, not only had she remained distant, disapproving and rejected him at every turn, but now expected her outrageous allegation of murder to instantly bounce right off him and be forgiven.

Was she for real? Lenny shook his head. He was desperate to ask if she'd been harmed. But until Elizabeth realised that she may no longer be his favourite person and acknowledged the hurt inflicted, he was not prepared to let her see how worried he was for her safety.

He strolled toward the water's edge, then turned in the direction of the cemetery. Along the way, he helped himself to a handful of stray geraniums trailing over a fence. Seeking out Margaret's burial site he filled a container with water and placed the flowers on her grave.

Apart from the departed and a big black crow squawking on an overhead bough, the place was deserted; the morning cloudless and still. He breathed in the salty tang of the seaside and heard the gravel crunch underfoot, along with the lapping water washing in on the tide. Sadly, Lenny thought of his friend and confidante, the woman he so fondly remembered. 'What's it like, Marg … on the other side?' he asked. A sudden gust of wind ruffled his hair, and he took this as a sign. 'I'll look out for her, I promise.'

His mind shifted to the good-looking city boyfriend he'd seen Elizabeth walking hand in hand with. It had left him with a bitter taste, seeing her laughing and enjoying herself the way she rarely did whenever he was in her company. Consumed by envy, he thought of Elizabeth's assistant who worked at the bookshop. Maybe she could enlighten him.

An overwhelming sadness had swept over Elizabeth when she watched Lenny walk away, just as Gary had walked away before him. Tears pricked her eyes blurring her vision. She rushed from the table and locked herself inside a cubicle in the ladies' powder room where no one would see her, no one would hear her. She gave in to her tears and the despair of her loneliness.

How could he be so uncaring? It was so unlike him, so out of character. This was not the Lenny Forrester she had come to know. This was not the easy-going, Kit Kat eating Romeo who – desperate to befriend her – had walked her along the beach and wooed her with his cheeky grin.

Lenny was lying, she was sure of it. He had wanted to teach her a lesson. That's what this was about. It all made sense now.

Deep down she knew he was worried; she knew he would protect her. Yes, it was all a lie, his disinterest, his lack of sympathy because she had accused him of murder and then expected him to roll over like an obedient puppy.

Blowing her nose, she opened the door and rinsed her face at the sink. She needed to go after him.

Sighting Lenny in the distance, Elizabeth hurried towards him. 'What's going on?' he said. 'Thought you'd be halfway to Melbourne by now.'

'Melbourne can wait. But the way you treated me back there at the hotel … well, that can't wait. What was that, Forrester? You, eating breakfast in front of me, acting like an unfeeling moron pretending to read your newspaper.'

'I s'pose y'reckon I was tough on you? And you're probably right.'

'Truth is, Forrester, like I already said, I don't blame you … not anymore. That day I accused you of murder, I wanted to lash out at you. It was irrational and unkind. I can see that now. But what you don't understand is, it was hard for me imagining the two of you together. Margaret, being so much older. So hard in fact, that the thought was literally doing my head in.'

'Why beat yourself up about it?' Lenny asked. 'Because she was older, or because she was sleeping with an odd jobs' man? Margaret was a good looking lady. We were friends, I was fond of her and occasionally we shared a bed together … end of story.'

'It's too much, Forrester. What were you thinking? But if someone did kill her, it's important to know if Margaret shared that same bed with others?'

'Never asked and wouldn't wanna know,' Lenny shrugged.

'It's easy for you. But she was like a mother to me, and no one likes to imagine their mum to be …'

'Sleeping around,' Lenny finished the sentence. 'What if she was? Would y'deny her that? Would y'be labelling her a woman with no morals? This is the twenty-first century, Elizabeth.' Lenny paused and turned towards her. 'Now … tell me that that no-hoper didn't harm you. Coz if he did, I'll catch up with the bastard and can guarantee he won't be in any fit state to be payin' you a second visit.'

Elizabeth smiled, 'You do have a heart, Forrester. I just knew it! As for me, I'll survive. His main interest was in retrieving money he claimed to have lent Margaret.'

'Dunno about any money. Only thing that matters is you're not hurt. And seeing as how I didn't buy y'breakfast, how 'bout I shout you a toasted sandwich before you head off?'

'That's okay. I've got to run. Should mention though, the fact that you're an odd-job man has never been an issue for me … or my aunt by the sound of it. I'm not nearly so stuck-up as you seem to think,' Elizabeth assured Lenny, and then stepped forward to peck him on the cheek. 'Thanks, Forrester, I knew you would never stay mad at me.'

23

Tilt's Tips

In two minds about whether to enter the bookshop, Lenny Forrester poked his head around the open door. Relieved to see there were no customers, he hesitated for a moment before stepping inside.

The place had undergone changes. Yet, preferring the outdoors and being a man of simple needs when it came time to down tools at the end of each day – apart from the bookshelves – he would be hard-pressed to describe just what these changes involved exactly. Never a church goer, he'd only visited the interior of St Thomas's on a couple of occasions when best man at a mate's wedding.

'Hi there! How can I help?' Tilt's head popped up like a magical Jack in the box from beneath the counter.

Apart from buying the necessities of life, shopping was not Lenny's idea of a fun day out. Awkward and ill at ease in such environments, he deliberately struck a nonchalant air and strolled across to speak with Tilt. 'G'day, I'm Lenny Forrester,' he said offering a firm handshake. 'We met once at the coffee shop.'

'Yes, darling, you're Liz's friend … I remember you well.'

'Yeah, gotta make the most of it … the friendship, I mean,' Lenny laughed. 'Could be back in the bad books as early as tomorra.'

'Oh dear, I have heard chocolate can have a weird effect on people.'

Lenny didn't understand what this woman was on about. *Hey, hang on, who said anything about chocolate?* he thought. *Did I miss something here?*

'Far be it for me to enlarge on the ramifications involved,' Tilt continued. 'But not to worry, Lizzie's visiting Melbourne today. Maybe I can steer you towards a particular book, Roald Dahl, perhaps?'

Lenny looked at her blankly. *Does she call everyone darl?* he thought.

'You know … *Charlie and the Chocolate Factory*!' Tilt giggled.

Thinking he had made a big mistake coming here, Lenny was now convinced this woman had a serious problem. 'That's ah … really quite hilarious, Tilt,' he replied, believing it best to humour her. 'But I'm not much of a reader, and was wondering if I could ask a small favour?'

Tilt's face lit up. 'Reminds me of another conversation I had recently with Gary, one of Liz's other boyfriends. He wasn't much interested in books either.'

Other boyfriends … how many does she have? 'Can't claim to be a boyfriend. But reckon there's no time for reading books in my line of work. Lotta jobs at the Thornton place before, well … y' know …' Lenny struggled to say the words.

'Thorny, God bless her soul. She always did have a keen eye for a handsome man.'

Nothing wrong with Tilt's eyesight. Lenny smiled. Perhaps she wasn't so deranged after all. 'Handsome, you reckon? Blokes at the pub would fall over laughin'.'

'Take no notice, darling. A few beers under their belt and they'd have you believe that Mr Bean is the classiest looking guy they've ever seen,' Tilt said, as she withdrew a stack of receipts from under the counter. 'Round these parts, you've got to remember most are looking at sheep all day. The rest are out fishing. So, best not to store too much faith in their judgment.'

'Nice of y'to say, Tilt.'

'Well for what it's worth, I stick by my original assessment. But can't stand around all day debating the pros and cons of your physical attributes. I need to catch up on some paperwork and am happy to multi-task while we're talking. So, what's this favour you're wanting?'

Lenny hesitated. 'It's about that boyfriend y' just mentioned. City fella, I reckon. Looks a lot like one of them movie stars.'

'Isn't he divine, darling?' Tilt said, suddenly looking a little starstruck.

'That's one word to describe him, I s'pose. And I'm sure the boys at the pub wouldn't disagree. But he's not my type really.'

Tilt took time out to place her elbows on the counter, lean her chin on her knuckles and stare dreamily into space. 'Just thinking about him makes me go all weak at the knees,' she sighed.

'Kinda scary, Tilt. But the thing is, are the two of 'em, serious about each other?'

Snapping out of her reverie, 'You don't beat about the bush, do you? But your guess is as good as mine. I got the feeling he's really keen on her. Yet not so sure she feels the same about him.'

'Why's that do y'reckon?'

'Lenny Forrester, you're not fooling me for one minute. And if you're looking to impress Liz, the only favour I'll be providing is a little free advice.'

'Wha'd'ya recommend?'

'Updating your profile for starters. Beers with the boys at the pub, not a good look. Odd jobs tripping around the countryside, a big thumbs down.'

'Hey, hang on! That's me one most enjoyable social outlet you've just eliminated, along with me workaday livelihood.'

'You did ask, darling!' Tilt reminded him as she returned to her paperwork and tapped in some figures on a calculator. 'You're a Taurus, aren't you?'

'I dunno! Why? Is that lookin' bad for me?'

'You don't know your own star sign?'

'Come t'think of it, I'm a bull, I reckon.'

'I knew it! Liz has been pushing you away. Feels she must do battle. Am I right?'

Lenny nodded in agreement.

'Deep down,' Tilt continued, 'she struggles to admit you hold some sort of power over her which she's determined not to acknowledge.'

'Other way round … the power bit,' Lenny corrected.

'Trust me, darling, I'm rarely mistaken. You do hold a certain degree of power over her. Be sure to make use of it. Now's the time to act and provide a strong shoulder for her to lean on.'

'Thanks for the Tilt tip. Ah, tip, Tilt. Owe y'one, I reckon.'

With a wild look in her eye, Tilt grabbed hold of Lenny's sleeve. 'Before you dash away, the third and final factor I'd suggest you take the most serious. Because, in my estimation this could be the absolute clincher,' Tilt paused. 'The Kit Kats!' she warned.

Lenny now understood what the earlier references to chocolate were about – news of the wrappers under Margaret's bed must have gotten out and preceded him. 'What about the Kit Kats?' he said.

'Think we both know the answer to that, darling!'

24

Caught Out

Leaving Mariners Cove and driving inland along the winding road, Elizabeth tried, without success, to ignore the persistent questions that hammered away inside her.

Why had she allowed herself to become so agitated over Forrester's intimacy with her aunt? Was he as obliging to other lonely ladies when travelling on his rounds? Elizabeth found this second scenario – to which she might never know the answer – almost as distasteful as the first. And it was true she had accused him of murder to simply convey her disapproval and make him suffer.

Just listen to yourself, Elizabeth, uttered an inner voice of reason. *You didn't even know the man until a few weeks ago. And even if he is sleeping with the entire membership of the Country Women's Association, what right have you to judge him?*

Reaching the turn off onto the multi-laned highway to Melbourne, Elizabeth adjusted her speed and locked it on cruise control. With time to further reflect, she hated to admit that Forrester had captured her interest from day one. Tanned by his days of labour in the sun, a hardworking and capable man, he displayed a charm impossible to resist.

Nearing her destination, Elizabeth turned her attention to Gary. She became increasingly worried about what might eventuate. How would he react? What would he say about the stolen ring? Would he blame her? Would he even believe her? Should she offer to repay him? Should she have reported the theft? These questions ticked over in her mind when she pulled up outside their suburban home.

The first thing Elizabeth noticed was the small patch of garden which had a tired and neglected appearance. Browning and wilted pot plants on the porch led her to ask a further question – had someone, other than her aunt, recently died? She unlocked the front door and stepped from the warm sunlight into the gloomy darkness. The stale air almost made her gag. Blinds drawn, windows bolted, the temperature so chilly and uninviting that the house felt like a tomb.

Rotting food and discarded packets littered the benchtops. Congealed spillages had hardened on cupboard doors. Unwashed dishes soaked in greasy sink water and grimy glasses, cups and saucepans covered every available surface in the kitchen.

In the adjoining room, rumpled sheets left in disarray on the unmade bed and jocks hanging over the lampshades made for an interesting accompaniment to the soiled clothing draped across chairs and strewn on the floorboards.

Elizabeth, desperate to use the bathroom, was unable to salvage even a measly scrap of soap to wash her hands. She searched the shelves of the mirrored wall cabinet and checked the cupboard beneath the vanity basin. But, apart from a couple of lonely toilet rolls, plus the usual tubes, bottles and various pharmaceutical products, there was nothing that came close to looking like a bar of soap or liquid dispenser. Grabbing a perfume atomiser, together with rubber gloves, she raced around squirting each of the rooms, raising the blinds and throwing open the windows.

Frantically, she scraped every food scrap into a garbage bag and dumped it in the outside bin. She stacked the dishes, wiped the benchtops then gathered the clothing and dropped the bundle into the laundry basket.

Now that the smell was a little less offensive, Elizabeth returned to continue her search in the bathroom. Shifting everything aside, she reached into the rear of the cupboard as something ran along her arm. She slapped at it in fright. A daddy long legs dropped to the floor and scurried away. She then got down on her hands and knees to see more clearly into the bottom shelf. 'That's strange,' she said, spotting a tiny box hidden away in the corner. It looked familiar, and at once grabbed her attention.

Removing the item out from the shadows, Elizabeth placed it down unopened in front of her. She stared at an exact replica of the jewellery box that had held the engagement ring. Baffled, she asked herself if this could hold a matching wedding ring. *Hardly*, she thought. *Gary wouldn't be that organised surely.* But anything was possible as this seemed a most unusual place to hide something.

In two minds about whether she should look inside, Elizabeth took the box to the light of the bedroom window where curiosity got the better of her. She lifted the lid.

Shocked, 'Oh my God!' she cried. Fitted snugly into the tiny satin slot, rested the dazzling solitaire diamond engagement ring, last seen being pocketed by the stocking-faced intruder when leaving her bedroom the previous night. How on earth did it finish up here in Melbourne under the bathroom sink?

It would seem the timing couldn't be worse for the one person who could answer this very question as she heard the lock turn in the door and recognised Gary's cough when he entered the house. A surprisingly gaunt figure of the man she once considered spending the rest of her life with, now stood framed in the doorway. 'What in the hell are you doing here, Liz?'

Elizabeth could see a momentary glimmer of hope light up his eyes, only to quickly fade as his skin turned a paler shade of white once catching sight of the box in her hand. None of the usual witty banter or smart remarks that he normally used to make her laugh passed his lips – only an expression of undeniable guilt.

What were the chances, the realisation and enormity of being caught out, Elizabeth imagined him thinking.

Barely able to control her anger, 'How did you get this?' she asked.

A moment of silence. 'I can explain,' he stammered.

'Really … you can explain,' she repeated. 'You can explain.' Her voice now bordering on hysteria as she threw the box at him, stepped forward and pummelled her fists into his chest.

Gary stood unmoving, his face drawn, as he succumbed to the punishment and humiliation that he so deserved. Elizabeth belted him as if he was a punching bag and she in training for the lightweight championship of the world. It being easy to see her opponent a beaten man when making no effort to stop her.

Exhausted she fell to her knees, her breathing laboured, her hair in disarray. She peered up through loose strands and asked, 'Have you any idea how afraid I was? Answer me! Have you?'

'It was a bad decision, babe.'

'You bet it was a bad decision. And don't even think about calling me babe. Did you deliberately set this up because you honestly thought I wouldn't return the ring? And what was with that hideous stocking-faced lunatic and the talk of hidden money?'

'It was all a lie. There never was any money. Tony won't be back, I promise.' Gary dug his hands deep inside his pockets. He looked at the walls. He looked at the floor. He walked to the window. 'I didn't know what else to do. It was never my intention to hurt you. I just wanted to frighten you a little, so you'd know how dangerous it is to live in that house alone.' Gary then reached out to help her up from the floor. 'Liz, I'm sorry.'

Elizabeth pulled away and shouted, 'No … don't sorry me. Don't you dare sorry me. What have you done? What were you thinking? You could have just knocked on the door and asked for the ring.'

'Forgive me,' Gary pleaded as he dropped to his knees and tried to embrace her.

Elizabeth raised her hands. 'Don't touch me. I never want to see you again. Never! Neither you nor your crazy friend.'

Gary slumped against the side of the bed, rested his head back and stared at the ceiling. 'Liz, you're tired and upset. It'll be okay. You don't mean that. Let me help you up onto the bed where you can rest. I'll make you a cup of tea then we can talk when you're a bit more rational.'

'When I'm a bit more rational? That's a joke coming from a man who has just attempted to scare the shit out of me. And as for finding a clean cup in this hellhole … well, good luck with that. I've just wasted an hour of my life trying to put this pigsty into some sort of order.'

'I'll wash the dishes.'

'That must be another joke, because there's not even a smidgen of soap or dishwashing detergent to be found in the place. I just want you to get out of my sight.'

'You know you don't mean that, Liz.'

'I'm warning you. Get out of my sight or I'll call the police and tell them what you did.'

Again, begging Elizabeth to hear him out, she insisted that it was no use. She could never forgive him for disappearing the way he did, then needlessly putting her through this whole drama and scaring her so badly that she felt her heart might stop beating. 'I'm moving out Gary. I'll pack whatever I can fit in the car, and I'd be grateful if you could deliver the rest of my belongings to the bookshop.'

Gary sat on the bed with his head in his hands. 'How will I survive without you? You've got to understand how upset I was. I went completely off the rails and would've done myself in if not for Tony. He came to my rescue when I wasn't well, my bank account overdrawn, and I received notice of my temporary suspension from flying.'

Elizabeth finally pulled herself up onto the bed and could see the box still laying open on the floor. 'That's a very sad situation, Gary, and all you had to do was pick up the phone and I'm sure we could have sorted this out. Instead, what you did last night was the act of a madman. And your friend Tony needs to take a good hard look at himself. You need help, the both of you.'

'I'll do anything if you'll just give me a chance to make this up to you.'

'It's too late for that. The other night at the restaurant you never gave me a chance. I didn't say no. And if you'd just allowed me to speak instead of rushing off like that things may have been different. There was a time I wanted to marry you. Now that time has passed.'

Elizabeth went on to say she wouldn't be returning and that she'd decided to toss her job in at the publishing house and stay at Mariners Cove. 'No one is sadder than me to think we have reached a stage where we must go our separate ways.'

Defeated, a tear rolled down Gary's cheek. Elizabeth remained defiant even though moved as she thought him incapable of tears and had never seen him cry. He reluctantly agreed to leave and allow her time to gather her things. His rounded shoulders spoke volumes as he sorrowfully made his way to the door. 'One of these days when you're not so upset, perhaps you might forgive me, Liz, and hopefully change your mind. Because I'll be waiting, no matter how long it takes.'

Unreceptive, Elizabeth continued to sit in silence as he disappeared, and the door closed behind him. It had taken all of her courage when seeing him so broken not to rush to his side and throw her arms around him in forgiveness. But something was stopping her, and instead she picked up the ring, slipped it back in the box and placed it on his pillow. Only then did she set about the difficult task of bundling up anything she could carry, and, once the car was full, left without a backward glance.

Before heading out of Melbourne, Elizabeth decided to call into the publishing house and speak to her boss, Bernie Blackwell. A middle-aged, tall stamp of a man, he was someone who had come up the hard way and considered by most to be street smart. Elizabeth had developed a close bond with him and being always prepared to listen when he offered advice, she looked on him as a father figure and mentor.

Pleased to see her, he took time out to offer his thoughts after she confided in him. 'Well, Liz, I'd be unhappy to lose you,' he said. 'You are going through tough times following the loss of your aunt, and now a split with your partner. Maybe you should consider extending your leave to three months.'

'That's very generous of you, Bernie. It's a tempting offer and a more sensible option as opposed to resigning at a period when my life is at an all-time low.'

'It's not the usual practice of course. But because of your valued contribution in the past, if you're prepared to take this extra time with unpaid leave, I think this a wise decision. Plus, on a more personal note, and I know it's none of my business, but this pilot of yours … sure he's done something stupid, but don't we all mess up from time to time?' Bernie paused. 'Don't be too hard on him, Liz. Because if my best girl had turned me down after I proposed, I wouldn't have been too happy either. Try putting yourself in his shoes.'

Elizabeth said her goodbyes and thanked Bernie for the benefit of his wisdom and lending a shoulder to cry on. She'd miss him if deciding to permanently move to Mariners Cove and owed it to him and herself to at least consider his suggestion.

Returning to the car and knowing there was nothing more to fear, Elizabeth looked forward to sleeping in her own bed. It had been a big day, but she was anxious to beat the peak hour traffic out of town and head towards home.

As the kilometres clicked over, and the evening grew dark, Elizabeth pulled into a service centre, topped up the tank and ordered herself a small bucket of chicken nuggets as she realised she hadn't eaten for twenty-four hours.

She wolfed down the food before continuing her journey and spared a thought for Gary. Perhaps Bernie was right. Had she shown no compassion and completely overreacted? The poor guy! She still had feelings for him, that was true and had blamed him for everything. But then Lenny's face flashed before her eyes. No doubt he was the most irritating of men and they seemed constantly at each other's throats. Why then, could she never get him out of her mind? And what of David Anderson and that sensual kiss on the beach? He had stirred up a quite unexpected feeling of emotional turmoil.

Elizabeth had dated a few boyfriends along the way but never experienced a serious relationship with anyone prior to living with Gary. How she could be attracted to all three men at the same time seemed confusing and downright inconvenient if nothing else.

'Oh God,' she sighed. This was impossible.

A huge yawn was telling her she hadn't slept in two days as she thankfully approached the front gate hours later. The biggest surprise being a light burning in the cottage and Lenny's ute parked outside.

He'd come to her rescue.

Elizabeth drove up the driveway and turned off the engine. She had never felt so weary, both physically and emotionally drained; the energy having been completely sapped out of her.

She rested her head on the steering wheel, and for the second time that day, openly wept.

25

It's All Happening

The persistent squawking of a lone magpie woke Elizabeth with a start at ten minutes past nine the following morning. She scrambled out from beneath the sheets, headed straight to the shower and rushing to leave for work, drove off down the driveway.

Spotting Lenny seated on the steps of the cottage, she pulled on the handbrake and hurried out of the car to release the chain from the gate. Shielding her eyes from the blinding sunlight, 'Morning, Forrester,' she shouted. 'Thanks for changing your mind. I owe you one.'

'Who's counting!' he shrugged. 'Gutters needed cleaning, but I didn't want t'wake you.'

'Wish you had. I've slept in and got to run.'

'No worries, I'll get the gate,' Lenny waved her off.

'Thanks, catch you later.' Elizabeth raced back to the car and lowering the window she called, 'Hey, Forrester, maybe I could throw an extra chop in the pan tonight if you feel like joining me?'

Lenny gave her a thumbs up as she slipped the car into drive and set out along the dusty track with a friendly beep of the horn.

'It's great for some,' Tilt teased when checking her watch as Elizabeth came crashing through the doorway.

'Sorry, Tilt … what would I do without you to open up?'

'It's easy for me, darling, I'm only five minutes around the corner.'

Elizabeth removed her jacket and started clearing paperwork off the counter.

'Hey slow down … stop!' Tilt ordered. 'How about you get your breath while I pop the kettle on before the rush hour starts?'

Minutes later Tilt returned from the vestry kitchen with two steaming mugs of tea. 'How was Melbourne? Did you catch up with Gary?'

'It's over! Gary and I are finished, and I've moved out.'

'No way!' Tilt's mouth fell open in an exaggerated moment of disbelief. 'That guy is drop dead gorgeous, not to mention totally divine, sublime and as funny as they come. Had me in stitches when he called in at the shop. Please, tell me you're not serious,' Tilt pleaded.

'Well, he may be all those things,' Elizabeth admitted, 'but it's still over.'

This news caused Tilt to gulp the hot liquid down so fast that she clutched her throat in a coughing fit. Elizabeth whacked her on the back as Tilt went red in the face and her eyes watered.

Alarmed, Elizabeth asked, 'Are you okay?'

Struggling to release the rasping words, 'Do I look okay to you, darling? Bloody hell that was like a near death experience and it's all your fault the tea went down the wrong way,' she spluttered. 'Why would you do that?'

'You were choking. What else could I do?'

'Not the backslapping for God's sake. Why would you break up with someone as cute as Gary?'

'There's no point me cracking the sads or holding endless post-mortems about the whys and wherefores of the state of my love life, especially as it's all so fresh in my mind. I'm over it right now so let's move on, shall we?'

When Tilt didn't answer, Elizabeth apologised. 'I'm sorry, Tilt. That remark was unkind. I know you are looking out for my best interests, and the truth is you and I make a good team. I've been thinking if we're ever to get that coffee shop up and running, we need to boost the sales.'

'You're full of surprises today. What's with the sudden talk of a coffee shop? I thought we agreed on a tearoom.'

'Coffee shop, tearoom, it's all the same to me. And I think you'll be pleased to hear I've now got three months unpaid leave at the publishing house. But, and it's a big but, I'm seriously considering tossing the job in and staying permanently.'

Tilt's expression was one of sheer delight. 'Wow! Are you for real?' Tilt laughed and threw her arms around Elizabeth, crushing her in a bear hug just as Phyllis Bentley walked through the doorway.

'Oh, my Lord!' Phyllis blessed herself in shock. 'Perhaps I should have knocked. Either that or walk back out and come back in again. Don't tell me you two are a couple now?' she sniped as she looked the pair up and down in disgust.

'Yes! You're the first to know. But please remember this building is no longer a place of prayer, Phyllis. We're just about to go public with an official announcement of our engagement,' Tilt winked at Elizabeth. 'So, we probably won't need to worry now as news does have a habit of travelling fast around the Cove.'

Phyllis harumphed, 'Elizabeth O'Connell, never in a month of Sundays did I think it would come to this. How terribly disappointing. And from what I've seen of late, you have completely lost the plot. Now a lesbian no less. Is your betrothed aware of your flighty ways?'

'Flighty ways?' Tilt looked puzzled.

'Go on, tell her, Elizabeth. Tell her about that scandalous kiss you exchanged on the beach with David Anderson. Tell her about that other young man of yours. And what of that odd jobs' fellow who is always stuffing himself with chocolate?'

Elizabeth took Tilt by the hand and tried to keep a straight face. 'Don't listen to her, sweetheart. There was nothing going on, I swear.'

Tilt looked lovingly into Elizabeth's eyes. 'I know you would never lie to me. I trust you, darling.'

'Don't say I didn't warn you, young lady,' Phyllis snapped at Tilt as she turned on her heels and rushed out through the doorway.

Elizabeth and Tilt burst into laughter. 'You're hilarious, Tilt. Did you see the look of horror on her face? How could you mislead the poor woman like that?'

'Believe me, it was easy, darling. She's such a busybody it's made my day to have a laugh at her expense.'

In a heightened state of anxiety, Phyllis hurried away from the bookshop.

Suspecting that her heart palpitations and blood pressure count had risen at an alarming rate, she felt it necessary to delay her plans to spend the morning shopping. Yet, the enormity of being the first to pass on this highly contentious news was an opportunity she would hate to forego.

So, she battled on to simply settle for a quick stop at the pharmacy where she had a script filled for her anti-depressant medication. This visit availed her the perfect excuse to mention the latest gossip to Flossy Bowman, who served behind the counter.

'No! That can't be right, surely?' Flossy insisted.

Feeling far too poorly to argue, Phyllis thought it best to save her energy and drop by the newsagency to pick up a copy of *New Idea*. In doing so, she mustered enough strength to pass on the "have you heard" news of the impending engagement to locals along the way. Only then did she head straight home to take a Panadol Rapid and lay her head on the pillow.

Behind closed doors, Phyllis recalled various scenes that left not the slightest doubt that Elizabeth's morals were sadly lacking and her multiple choice of partners an utter disgrace. Cosying up to that odd-job man who'd been sleeping with Margaret – even though some fifteen or more years her aunt's junior – was the first in a list of disconcerting incidents.

Days later, the two-timing hussy brazenly strutted hand in hand with another young stranger along the main street. This episode quickly followed by a visit to Misty Headland where she snuck off to the beach to share a steamy kiss with David Anderson.

As if this wasn't enough, now embraced in the arms of a woman in plain sight of the customers, she was planning to wed her shop assistant. *What next?* Phyllis thought. The evidence being clearly abundant that in her determination to play the field, Elizabeth had indeed inherited her aunt's genes.

Resting in the darkened room, a damp face washer on her brow, Phyllis had drawn the blinds and pulled the quilt up under her chin.

Troubled memories continued to haunt her. Especially those of her one-time best friend who had more or less – and there were no other words to describe it – dumped her. Yes, Phyllis sobbed – dumped her.

It was pitiful when they'd grown up together having lived on neighbouring properties.

Phyllis had long suspected something unsavoury in Margaret's past that saw her scurrying back from the city to again live in her childhood home.

The two renewed their friendship while Margaret cared for her ailing parents who never recovered following the tragic drowning of their eldest daughter and son-in-law. Margaret then took charge of her niece. But once Elizabeth left school she was determined to live and work in the city. Margaret's parents eventually both passed away and she then invested her inheritance into the bookshop and began to move in different circles, including mixing with certain business owners in town.

Pushing Phyllis away, Margaret became secretive about her activities. Even so, Phyllis's husband, Jack, was often called on to fix a leaky tap or mend the fences. These demands became more frequent, and Phyllis was reminded of how unhappy she felt about this arrangement. It was then that Jack started to disappear from the marital bed in the dead of night and out into the darkness, claiming insomnia. When Phyllis pretended to be sleeping, he would tuck the blankets around her and administer a token peck on the cheek – the Judas kiss of betrayal – as he crept away to be with Margaret.

Phyllis's sorrow was fully compounded when fate stepped in, and Jack's tractor rolled over on top of him while at work in the paddock. After his death, it was obvious to Phyllis that Margaret began entertaining various male associates who often stayed late into the night along with the odd-job man who visited regularly and supposedly slept in the cottage.

Meanwhile, Phyllis applied for the Andersons' housekeeping job and settled in nicely until Margaret – not content with the male friends already accumulated – set her sights on the brothers. This situation proved unbearable to Phyllis and when confronting Margaret, a heated argument ensued. That being the last she was to see of her former best friend.

A knock at the door hours later disturbed Phyllis from her nap. She rushed down the passageway, stopping to fix her hair at the hallstand mirror.

'Oh, it's you, Graeme. My appointment! I completely forgot.'

The solicitor stepped in through the open flywire screen. 'I tried calling, but you must have had your phone on silent.'

'It's good of you to come so far out of your way,' Phyllis said leading him into the kitchen. Then, as soon as he sat at the table, she began to relate the reason why she'd had to return home.

'Goodness, I've had several dealings with Elizabeth and find it surprising that she's partnered up with Eileen Jacobson. I thought she'd get engaged to that young man from Melbourne.'

Phyllis clucked her tongue. 'She never breathed a word to me about any young man in Melbourne. I had no idea.'

Withdrawing papers from his briefcase, Graeme said, 'When you get a moment, I'll just need a signature and then we'll be in business.'

'Yes, I've been eager to lease that paddock ever since Jack died. It holds bad memories, and now the sheep are gone there's no way I can keep the grass down, so this will guarantee me a little extra income. Thanks for taking care of the paperwork. It's a load off my mind.' Phyllis took a seat at the table and picked up the pen. 'Where do I sign?'

Graeme Jenkins pointed to the dotted line and the pencilled X marked at the bottom. 'You'll need to date it as well,' he said reeling off the day and the month. 'Now I'll just put this back in the folder, and we're all done.'

Phyllis was quick to remove a couple of mugs from the shelf and fill the kettle. 'You'll stay for a cuppa, won't you? Because the other thing I forgot to mention about Elizabeth was ...'

26

Dinner with Elizabeth

Lenny, being in no hurry to rush away, lingered at the table over coffee feeling pleased to be back in Elizabeth's favour as she again thanked him for changing his plans.

The meal was one of simple fare, but he wasn't complaining as after a day's work in the outdoors, he rarely knocked back an invitation to dinner, especially when the invitation had been issued by Elizabeth.

'I won't forget this in a hurry, Forrester,' she smiled, refilling his cup.

A fleeting fragrance of wildflowers accompanied her every move, together with the tinkle of a bracelet. These simple feminine pleasures were not lost on Lenny or the fact that Elizabeth had let her hair grow, and he fought to control an overpowering urge to admit there was no place he'd rather be than right here beside her. Instead, he lowered his eyes and stirred the sugar a little longer than necessary.

It was clear that she now trusted him enough to open up about the reason behind her visit to Melbourne, followed by a detailed account of her past relationship with Gary. Her concluding statement being, 'Any chance of us getting back together ended when I stumbled on the truth.'

Lenny leaned back in the chair and placed his hands behind his head as he thoughtfully considered all he'd been told. 'That's a crazy thing he did. I've gotta feel sorry for the guy.'

'Why? Why would you feel sorry for him, Forrester?'

'Dunno!' Lenny shook his head. 'But I'm thinking for someone who's always been used t'landing smack bang in the middle of the runway, his behaviour seems a bit off the grid.'

'Well, he's not used to rejection, and my reaction to his proposal appeared to tip him over the edge.'

Lenny sat forward, paused to drink a mouthful of coffee and placed his cup back down on the saucer. 'I saw him once with you at the Cove. Struck me as a larger than life kinda fella. Someone who'd be in complete control under pressure. Part of his training I would a thought.'

'You wouldn't say that if you'd seen him yesterday. It was as if all the vitality had been sapped out of him. He's lost weight and doesn't look well. But after scaring me the way he did, you can see why I couldn't continue our relationship. So, I've moved out and told him it's over.'

'Sounds pretty final. Are y'sure you're doing the right thing?'

'Why does everyone ask me that? My boss, Tilt and now you. It's as if all of this is my fault. Maybe you're right and there is something else going on that he hasn't told me about.'

Lenny wished he'd kept his mouth shut as he didn't want Elizabeth to be changing her mind. 'I could be wrong of course,' he said, in a bid to erase the thought he'd so foolishly planted in her mind.

'Whatever!' Elizabeth shrugged. 'The good thing is Gary's mate won't be back and I'm not expecting any further trouble. You know you're welcome to stay for a bit. But, apart from the jobs that need doing, I no longer have an excuse to keep you here.'

You don't need an excuse, Lenny thought. 'Best for me to stick around a few days I reckon and let the dust settle.'

Elizabeth sounded relieved. 'I'd like that, Forrester.'

'Tell me if I'm out of line here, but why did you turn Gary down?'

Gazing intently into her wine, 'That's a tricky question,' she said. 'And I didn't actually turn him down, I just didn't say yes. I needed to think about it.'

'Fair enough,' Lenny replied.

'Forrester, let's not talk about Gary anymore. There's something far more important I'd like to discuss.'

Retaining a poker face, Lenny hoped the something important might be about him.

'If you're not in a hurry to get away let's move to the loungeroom, I'll pack the dishwasher later as I'd really like to talk about a matter that I know will come as a surprise.'

Lenny took his cup to the sink and did as he was instructed when seating himself down into a cushiony armchair beside the fire.

Elizabeth then began to tell him about the reason why she was planning to stay on at the Cove. 'It's all to do with Margaret as I know so little about …'

The rest of the sentence faded into obscurity as Lenny switched off when disappointed to hear this had nothing to do with Elizabeth's feelings towards him. The constant reference to her aunt was becoming tedious. She had laboured the subject once too often for his liking and he was on the verge of saying he needed to call it a night. Then something she said captured his attention.

'… claims to be her son?'

'Son?' Lenny snapped out of his dazed state. 'Whose son did you say?'

'Margaret's, Forrester! Margaret's! What's up with you? You look like you're a million miles away.'

'Who said this again?'

'Philip Anderson, one of the brothers who lives at Misty Headland. I know it's a shock; I couldn't believe it either.'

'Geez, Elizabeth. Is he sure?'

'He seems to think so.'

'Now that you've mentioned this, when those two guys moved in, that friend of hers, Phyllis, got really pissed off about Margaret spending too much time there. I remember Jenko saying …'

'Who the hell is Jenko?' Elizabeth cut in.

'The solicitor, Graeme Jenkins. A good bloke,' Lenny added. 'Seems Phyllis started driving him mad. Kept finding reasons to drop by his office and ask his advice.'

'What about, for God's sake?'

'If she should report Margaret to the police. Claimed she was stealin' from the Andersons. Jenko put all this down to Phyllis losing the plot since her husband died.'

Elizabeth rested her head back and looked to the ceiling. 'I don't believe it! On top of all the other accusations, Phyllis accused Margaret of stealing. What's going on with that woman?'

As the night progressed and the fire began to burn low, Lenny, thinking that Elizabeth looked tired, yawned and made a move to leave. 'If you're sure you don't need a hand with the dishes, I might make tracks 'n' turn in for the night. It's been a big day one way 'n' another and I could use some rest.'

'You and me both. I won't be long out of bed that's for sure,' Elizabeth said, leading Lenny out through the back doorway. 'Wait a sec and I'll grab you the torch.' She walked across to the kitchen bench. 'Here it is, hiding behind the bread box.' She flicked the switch on to satisfy herself that it was working.

Lenny, thinking the faint glimmer to be of little value said, 'I won't be needing a torch to cover that short distance.'

Stepping outdoors, the damp night air penetrated his clothing. He cupped his hands together and blew into them, 'Bit brisk for this time of year. Stay inside, outta the cold, Elizabeth, 'n' thanks again for cooking dinner. I'll have t'return the favour and whip up a Forrester specialty. Wha'd'ya reckon about baked beans on toast?'

'I've eaten worse,' Elizabeth laughed. 'But here – you might as well use this now I've found it. The batteries could be a bit flat, but it still does the job, and I'll never forgive myself if you trip over.'

'Night, Elizabeth. Sleep tight,' Lenny said as he took hold of the flashlight, turned up his collar, and shoved his other hand inside his pocket. He shone the weak yellow beam down the hillside and staggered off in the direction of the cottage.

The night was still and remarkably clear given the chill that touched his bones. And a distinct feeling of being watched caused him to shiver just as he caught sight of two glassy eyes staring back at him in the distance. A startled rabbit dazzled by the barely visible glow remained frozen like a garden ornament before scampering off into the shrubbery.

Lenny dispensed with the torch and lifted his gaze to the sky – a vast expanse aglow with a sea of starlight. A sight that could rarely be seen in the grey confines of the city. This being precisely why he'd chosen to live and work in the countryside. Yet, when a second hauntingly beautiful vision took shape in his mind, he had to admit this reason in isolation was not entirely true.

A sadness re-awakened. Lenny thought it strange how he could never quite let go of this picture he carried inside him. Rosalie Reynolds, an old flame was a sight to behold as hundreds of jewelled crystals glittered within the layered folds of her midnight blue gown. Until now, he had thought no star had ever shone so brightly as Rosie did on that evening he had partnered her to the dance.

Lenny, a dashing hero that novels were made of, had escorted her into the foyer. Just a young bloke, he'd thought to conquer the world when all polished and turned out in his formal attire with Rosie on his arm. She'd certainly turned heads as they entered the grand townhall, and he suspected himself the envy of every man.

Rosie lit up the dancefloor. He'd never forgotten the pride he felt when the music stopped, and she was officially declared the belle of the ball.

Believing himself in love, life was never better until Lenny – considered an unworthy prospect by her parents – discovered that Rosie was to be snatched away and forbidden to see him again. Lenny being just one of many hopeful suiters who had been victim to this same harsh treatment.

Women had come and gone in his life since Rosalie agreed to wed Gerald Stanley, a partner in a Collins Street law firm. The hurt had stayed with him, and Lenny turned his back on the city promising himself that no other woman would ever get close enough for this to happen again.

Now no longer the insecure boy he had once been, his promise mattered no more. Elizabeth O'Connell had no need of a bejewelled gown to take his breath away. She had only to place her hand in his and he would willingly stay forever.

As Lenny approached the tiny two room cottage, the ocean thundered, and the earth vibrated beneath him.

Entering the cold impersonal interior, he became aware of the sparse emptiness of his temporary abode. His solitary existence living in unheated bungalows and out of an overnight bag suddenly seemed of no significance. He owned nothing of value.

Loneliness can sometimes cause a man to seek companionship in unexpected places, and although he strongly believed in no wrongdoing caused by his intimate sojourns with Margaret, the idea of his meaningless dalliances was no longer appealing. He trusted that this period of Elizabeth looking on him as a guilt-ridden gadabout had passed.

Yes, he thought, as he slipped inside his sleeping bag, dining together and chatting without the usual animosity had been an important breakthrough, and he was more than happy to stay longer to accommodate her wishes. Although unsure what to make of the surprising news, Lenny felt relieved that the city boyfriend was out of the picture, and he could understand why the poor guy was so dejected. He knew he wasn't in the same league as a pilot, but to hell with that. The pilot struck him as having given in too easily, having shown a weakness that he should have never revealed.

Pulling the zip fastener up close beneath his chin, Lenny switched off the lamp, burrowed his head down into the pillow and imagined he could smell the wildflowers in Elizabeth's hair as she slept peacefully beside him.

27

A Delivery

Two weeks slipped by, and Elizabeth had had no further contact with Gary.

It was then that Jovial George – as Tilt referred to the local delivery man – arrived at the bookshop with a large carton in tow.

Fortunately Tilt – who was not in the least bit fond of the man – was enjoying a day off. But that didn't prevent Elizabeth from imagining a whisper in her ear. 'Oh no, don't tell me it's Jovial George again – Mr Misery Guts himself.' Because Jovial George was of course anything but jovial according to Tilt, who reckoned he was either born with a permanent scowl on his face or had been hit over the head one time too many with the unhappiness stick.

With that, Tilt would make herself scarce claiming she needed to powder her nose so as not to have to deal with the man. 'There are few things in life that I just can't tolerate, darling, Jovial George being one of them.'

It was also clear that the delivery man had thoughts of his own when it came to Tilt. He never failed to ask her whereabouts and once satisfied that she was out of earshot he'd lean in close to Elizabeth and say, 'Thinks she is it 'n' a bit that one ... you mark my words.'

And today – like every other day – George, a middle aged, red-faced balding man, carrying a beer belly paunch, wasn't about to disappoint. Life was such a challenge it would seem as he was currently employed in a mammoth struggle to get the delivery in through the doorway. Awkwardly manoeuvring the box balanced on a trolley up over the step, he moaned and groaned. The matter being made worse once catching sight of Elizabeth nibbling a biscuit and sipping a cup of tea. 'Okay for certain people, I see. But no, no,' he raised one hand, 'there's no need to concern y'self. Good ol' George'll fix it.'

'Sorry, George. I don't like to interfere.'

'Yeah, that'd be right! You do realise don't you that I'm employed to deliver the post and light weight packages only? This one weighs a ton 'n' I'll be having something to say about it when I speak t'the boss later.'

Choosing to ignore his complaints, Elizabeth brushed a crumb from her shirt. 'Can I offer you a cuppa, or glass of water perhaps?'

'No time for smoko in my line of work.'

'Well then providing it's not too much trouble would you be a darling and unload that box down beneath the choir loft?'

Judging by the black look that George bestowed on Elizabeth, she might as well have asked for the delivery to be transported to the moon. Her one saving grace being that she had taken a leaf out of Tilt's book and referred to George as 'a darling'.

Noisily he trundled the trolley along the floorboards and shouted, 'Where's that other lazy assistant of yours today? Never around when y'need 'er that one.'

Wiping his brow and stretching his back on his return, 'Right-o,' he said. 'Just be needin' an autograph an' I'll be on me way. No rest for the wicked.'

'And a cite less for the righteous,' Elizabeth added as she dashed off a signature and watched him leave, his shoulders slumped as if the weight of the world and her carton were the ongoing cause of his misery.

She turned the Open sign around to Closed on the door behind him and raced down to the storage area to check the name of the sender.

Seeing Gary's return address, she wondered if this signified that he'd accepted their separation to be final. She'd been thinking of him recently and kept recalling her boss Bernie Blackwell's advice about not being too hard on the man. Perhaps later she should call to thank Gary for sending this on. Meanwhile, Elizabeth thought to make a start on sorting the contents.

Slitting the tape and opening back the cardboard flaps, Elizabeth, thinking she'd heard a noise, stopped to listen. It sounded as if it had come from inside the sacristy or vestry which was where the church altar was once situated. Making her way from what would have been the rear seating area to the front section of the building, she glanced between each of the bookcases. 'Is that you, George?' she shouted.

But how and why would George have snuck back in without her seeing him?

'Is anyone there?' she again asked.

Feeling uneasy, Elizabeth approached the room. The door stood slightly ajar. She positioned herself up against the sidelong crack and peered through the tiny slit. Seeing nothing unusual she gingerly pushed the door inward. It protested with a haunting creak, and she could not summon the courage to step inside.

Late afternoon shadows had settled in the corners but there were no hidden recesses or places to hide as the sacristy was a tiny space lit by a small window and single light bulb. Now used as a tearoom, beneath the window a kitchen bench, sink and cupboard covered the lower half of the wall opposite. Next to the sink a second door led outside to a toilet and washbasin. A table and two chairs sat to the right, with storage shelving and an open closet that had once held the priest's vestments tucked away against the back wall. The fourth wall being home to a speckled mirror and crucifix.

Relieved to find the room empty, Elizabeth's shoulders relaxed and breathing a sigh, she poked her head around the doorway. Stepping forward her leg went from beneath her as she slipped on something underfoot. Careering across the floor she skidded and landed on her back. Badly shaken and expecting the worst, she groaned and rolled her head to one side.

Elizabeth then saw something that scared the hell out of her.

A rat – a dirty big rat. She froze.

Nose twitching, it sniffed the air and watched her lying motionless on the floor. Elizabeth imagined herself a giant Gulliver in comparison. Perhaps hoping her dead, it would start gnawing at her flesh. Only then did she think to thump the floorboards and wave her arms about. 'Get away, get away,' she squealed.

The whiskery rodent, little realising the terror its presence inflicted on the angry giant, ran in fright to disappear beneath the shelving.

But rats weren't known to spit and hiss, and an unmistakable guttural sound alerted her that something far more sinister was lurking overhead. She looked up just as a furry creature sprang from above and landed on top of her. Screaming, she tried to hurl it off as sharp claws dug in to pierce her clothing. Seizing the moment, the animal wasted no time when a strong gust of wind blew the door wide open to provide a welcome escape route.

Relieved to see a bushy tail disappearing out and up into a tree trunk, 'Thank God,' a shaken Elizabeth cried.

Her heart still pounding, she rolled over to clutch the table leg. Dragging her knees up under her, she pulled herself to her feet feeling fortunate not to have suffered a serious injury. Scouring the floor, she noticed the offending object that had caused her to fall. 'Would you believe it. Nothing more than a stray button,' she said to herself.

The wind whipped up the dust and leaves outside and with what little strength she could muster, Elizabeth hobbled over to close the door. She shoved the bolt firmly into position, shuddering to think the animal might be nesting in a wall and would almost certainly reappear. A rat running loose was bad enough, but a possum trapped indoors could create havoc.

Elizabeth released a sigh and assessing her bruised ankle, staggered back to the storeroom. Returning to place blocks of bait under the shelving, she used the cane of a feather duster to poke the poison back against the wall. A clump of accumulated hair and fluff along with a metal object clung to the tip of the handle when she withdrew it.

Entangled amid the grime, a small key attached to a ring bearing a religious medallion gave Elizabeth cause to wonder. Never having seen it before, she shrugged and dropped the key into her pocket alongside the button, deciding it time to continue what she had started.

The content of the carton was a bit like a lucky dip that she knew consisted of books and various other forgotten belongings.

Yet, instead of delving deeper, she chose to select a wrapped parcel resting right on the top.

Discarding a piece of bubble wrap, Elizabeth discovered a further item that she didn't recognise. With a look of surprise she said, 'A button, a key and now a leatherbound bible,' as a note floated to the floor.

She unfolded it and read Gary's handwritten message: *Found this among my things. Thought about that Anderson guy you told me about, who claims to be your cousin and says his name is Thomas. Because he wants you to call the bookshop by the former name of the church, maybe this might help you decide. Hope you can find answers and hope you can forgive me. … Missing you,*

Gary.

Elizabeth felt a pang of guilt together with a tug at her heartstrings. After all that had happened, for Gary to even remotely care about the bookshop, let alone a stranger and the question surrounding a name, it showed a thoughtful side to his nature that had once been lacking. She was touched by this gesture, especially given that the death of her aunt and subsequent responsibility of taking over the bookshop had ultimately triggered the demise of their relationship.

A ribboned marker attached to the spine gave cause for the book to fall open at the right page. Scanning the scripture, Elizabeth – being mindful of Philip's request – found her eyes drawn to the account that followed Christ's death and resurrection. It was then the Apostle earned the title of "Doubting Thomas" due to his refusal to believe news of the risen Christ unless he could see and touch the inflicted wounds that had resulted from his crucifixion. Which proof, it was written, he reached eight days later.

Elizabeth also recalled the name of a learned and prolific writer, Thomas Aquinas, a Dominican and great theologian and for a short time it was unclear which saint was the rightful namesake of the former church. The solution seemed conclusive when she was to later discover the Apostle to be the patron saint of architects, carpenters and builders.

Philip Anderson claimed his mother had registered his birth name as Thomas before the adoption. With no knowledge of the saint, he'd attained a degree in architecture and in between his studies was employed as a part time builder in his father's business. He later developed an interest in collecting artefacts which of course included a collection of spears – a weapon attributed to causing the death of the saint.

Prior to coming in search of Margaret, he said she changed the name of the shop to "Telltales", so as not to be constantly reminded of the son she had been forced to give up at birth. Elizabeth suspected Philip then developed more than a passing interest in the business and may have even become a silent partner and contributed financially. This could then explain why Margaret had added a codicil to the Will.

Elizabeth, being better able to understand why Philip would be influenced by these coincidental twists of fate, thought even though the building now housed books, nothing could disguise the fact that this was once a house of prayer. Philip was right. Using the history of the building to promote the business suddenly made sense. So, she decided right then and there to reinstate the original name and contact Graeme Jenkins in the coming days to arrange the legal requirement.

Once the paperwork was completed, she would surprise Philip and invite him to share in the grand vision she had mapped out in her mind for the future.

28

A Grand Plan

Dreaming big, Elizabeth asked Tilt at the end of the following workday to stay behind and pop the kettle on.

'What's going on, darling? I'm not getting my marching orders I hope.'

'Not likely, Tilt! Just because the delivery man has got you in the gun, that's not my problem,' Elizabeth laughed. 'No, this little meeting has to do with my vision for the future, beginning with the reinstatement of the original business name, the St Thomas Bookshop.'

'That's fine by me.' Tilt shrugged. 'As long as you don't expect me to get the old rosary beads out and say ten Hail Marys every morning.'

'Well, it's not part of your job description, but a Hail Mary here and there could do no harm,' Elizabeth smiled, as she watched her friend dunk the teabags in hot water. Tilt lifted them out and with the aid of a spoon wrapped the string around each bag to squeeze the excess liquid back into the mug before dropping the sachets into the pedal bin.

'That's one of the many things I like about you, Tilt. Quite often I've seen people use their fingers to ring out the teabag.'

'Don't worry. Whenever you're not looking, I often do the same and am even tempted to dip my big toe in those cups of tea I make for people like Jovial George.'

Elizabeth screwed up her nose in disgust. 'Hope you clean your toenails before you do that.'

'That'd spoil the fun,' Tilt chuckled as she placed the mugs on the table and plopped down on the chair.

'I hesitate to ruin your sense of the ridiculous, Tilt, but I've got a bit of a twinge in my ankle,' Elizabeth said as she placed one leg over the other and rubbed at a tender spot while relating her ordeal with the rat and the possum.

Tilt shuddered and propped her feet up on the rung of the chair. 'Good grief … you poor darling! And here I was trying not to draw attention to the fact that you were limping. I just put it down to your dicky knee.'

'The toe in the tea I can tolerate, Tilt, but since when have I ever complained of a dicky knee? That's not even remotely funny.'

'My … aren't you the grumpy one today?'

Elizabeth winced in pain as she lowered her foot to the floor. 'Well, it's no joking matter as I did bruise my ankle and my backside,' she frowned as she pulled the button from her pocket. 'Oh, and that reminds me … did you happen to lose this?'

'Sorry about your fall, darling. I really am. But nope not guilty, I know nothing about the button. A customer did ask to use the loo on my last shift. Maybe that could account for it.'

Resurrecting the key and dangling it from her finger, Elizabeth asked, 'How about this?'

'Can't recall seeing that before either.'

Elizabeth paused to sip her tea. 'Not to worry, as the real reason I wanted to talk has nothing to do with the button or the key. It's about the coffeeshop we've been planning. You'll probably think me crazy, but I've come up with a grand proposal.'

Tilt raised an eyebrow, 'Really?'

'Yes really. You see, I'm thinking about putting this place on the map with a bold extension that will attract not just book buyers but the passing tourist trade. The kind of addition no one will be able to resist once they catch sight of it.'

Munching a biscuit, Tilt waved the remainder of a Malt-o-Milk around in the air and mumbled with her mouth full. 'Forgive me if I go with the much-overused exclamation – WOW! I'm impressed and beginning to warm to this.' She washed down the biscuit remnants before broaching the all-important question. 'But how do you propose financing this project? Are you hoping to sell off the family jewels and make a killing at Cash Converters?'

'No, smarty pants. The way I see it, I have a few options. Don't forget I now own a property I could use to raise collateral. Failing which, once I have the plan drawn up, it could rouse the interest of local investors.'

Reaching for another biscuit, Tilt asked, 'What sort of look do you have in mind?'

'Eye-catching! A multi-purpose glass gallery construction to reflect oodles of light and space not just for coffee but author talks, exhibitions and classes. The stock would be expanded to include an array of stylish products stamped with our logo to enhance the overall reading experience.'

Tilt looked thoughtful, 'What like, for instance?'

'Endless possibilities spring to mind. Bookends, to name just one, plus a unique choice of designer bookmarks exclusive to St Thomas's. I'm not talking the norm here. I'm talking in terms of a wide range of valuable collectibles monogrammed in gold, along with hand crafted and painted pieces to be presented like precious gems displayed in purpose built glass lit showcases. Nowhere in the world has anyone specialised in beautiful bookmarks to my knowledge.'

'Cool!' Tilt nodded. 'I really like that idea. But getting back to the gallery … would council and the Mariners Cove residents and traders object to such a progressive structure in a small seaside village?'

'They may take convincing. But given the right architect, a mix of contemporary and old could complement each other to produce a winning drawcard. Just think about it, Tilt, the town's crying out for something like this that would in no way detract from its historical appeal.'

'Who would you get to design it?'

'The Andersons! Because Philip, believe it or not, says he's an architect, and I've seen what David can do in the garden. They're capable of working on this sort of project. So as soon as I get the paperwork on the change of name completed, I'm seriously thinking about asking them if they'd be interested.'

Tilt seemed a bit hesitant. 'Are you sure about all of this?'

'Yep! I reckon this place would be transformed. It's a big risk, but one I'd be willing to take.'

29

A Terrible Misfortune

Low-lying rain clouds masked the horizon.

Puddles – from an earlier downpour – filled the potholes and splashed beneath the tyres as Elizabeth journeyed the slippery roadway to Misty Headland.

Prior to this adverse change in the weather, she had felt pleased with her decision. But now the gloomy outlook dampened her enthusiasm and dashed her spirit. She shivered as a foreboding entity dressed in a hooded cloak took shape inside her mind. Wearing heavy boots, the sinister intruder tramped across the plains of her heart to enter uninvited into the depths of her soul. Unable to dispel an intuitive fear, her body grew tense, her shoulders hunched as she passed a flat swampy expanse separating the sand dunes from the narrow stretch beyond – the boggy wetland threatening to swallow all who dared set foot on its murky surface.

Elizabeth, with a sense of relief, noticed a handful of cows huddled on higher ground where they wisely sheltered beneath a clump of cypress trees.

Was she getting ahead of herself with her grand ideas? Whatever the answer, it was important to remember this bleak turn in the weather was only a passing phase. The necessary paperwork had been drawn up and it was as though St Thomas himself had reached out to lend a guiding hand.

Daylight dimmed to a dark brooding shade of grey. The storm, fast approaching, swept across her path. Muddied droplets spattered the windscreen, and the heavens burst open. The rain hammered against the rooftop and hampered her vision – its damp aroma drifting in unseen between the shuttered air vents creating a draught beneath the dashboard. Normally Elizabeth welcomed the refreshing smell of rain, but not today.

Distracted, she switched the headlights on and flicked the wipers to high. The car jolted, shuddered and bounced. A split second being all it took to misjudge a curve and hit a rocky outcrop. The vehicle careered out of control, skidding across the empty path on the wrong side of the road. It spun full circle before skating along the icy bitumen, cutting out and coming to a standstill. She sat dazed and unmoving in total shock.

A spritely old man dressed in a dripping, misshapen Akubra hat, gumboots and well-worn Driza-Bone jacket came hurrying out from a farm gate. His face at the window, he tapped frantically and shouted, 'Are you okay, girly? Are you okay?'

Elizabeth gazed straight ahead not quite sure where she was. The man pulled on the door handle, but finding it locked, rapped harder on the window. 'Speak to me, girly … are you okay?'

Her words seemed leaden. 'A little shaken,' being all she could muster when opening the divide between them.

'You're bloody lucky! You could a been killed,' he said with a look of concern. 'Are you able to kick the engine over? If not, I can rope 'er up to the tractor.'

'I'll try,' Elizabeth sighed, her head feeling quite wooden. 'Please let it start,' she implored, turning the key in the ignition.

After a couple of clicks and familiar shake, the motor came to life, and she revved the accelerator offering a thumbs up to her kindly rescuer. Steering the vehicle back into the left lane, she pulled over to park on the gravel, leaving the engine to idle while resting her racing heart.

'Well done, girly!'

The farmer checked beneath the bonnet and wandered around the car. 'Couple of your tyres are lookin' a bit bald,' he shouted. 'Wouldn't hurt to swap 'em over for some newies if you're planning to drive these roads in the rain. Everythin' else looks pretty much in order.'

Returning to the window he introduced himself. 'Tom Moody's the name.'

Reaching out to shake the weathered hand on offer, 'I'm Elizabeth and can't thank you enough for your help.'

The leathery faced gentleman had the look of a man getting up in years. His craggy features hidden behind a bushy beard, moustache, sideburns and prominent eyebrows. 'You sure you're alright to drive? Cause the missus, Molly, is cookin' a batch of scones. You're more than welcome to come up to the house for a cuppa.'

'That's very kind. But Misty Headland is just up the road a bit.'

'Misty Headland hey!' The farmer leaned his arm against the roof above the window and despite the weather seemed keen to prolong Elizabeth's stay. 'They don't get too many house callers there. Hope you have more luck with those two fellas than I've ever had. Strange pair. Keep to 'emselves and make no secret of the fact that visitors aren't welcome.'

When Elizabeth didn't respond, he asked, 'Friends of yours, are they?'

'I just drop off some books now and again.'

'Are they for the bloke in a wheelchair?' Moody paused. 'Damnedest thing I've ever heard! Cause I could swear I've seen two different fellas out 'n' about at times.'

'You must be mistaken. Philip's unable to walk.'

'Is that right?' he nodded. 'Well, sure hope they're paying you for your trouble, cause they're certainly not short of a quid. That old Gentry place must've cost 'em a packet to rebuild.'

Seemingly disappointed at Elizabeth's reluctance to provide additional information, the farmer stepped back a pace, tipped the brim of his soaking hat and bid her farewell. 'Safe travel 'n' take your time now, girly. And if you want my advice, I'd be keeping those blokes at arm's length.'

Continuing at a slower pace, Elizabeth was aware that a headachy feeling of nausea worsened when pulling into the Andersons' driveway. It was what she saw in the distance that really put the fear of the devil into her. Stepping out from the woodshed, boots squelching in the mud, the shadowy figure that had plagued her thoughts right before she almost ran off the roadway, magically materialised. Whose face was it hidden beneath the hooded cloak? Elizabeth couldn't be sure … until …

A wild gust of wind whipped away the cover to reveal the answer.

'Phyllis!'

Why of course it was only Phyllis. *Who else would it be?* Elizabeth thought. The woman works here for God's sake, and in this rain, it was perfectly normal to wear boots and a hooded coat. But wasn't Thursday her day off? This being the reason Elizabeth had chosen to visit.

The housekeeper's arms were laden with logs, and she didn't look Elizabeth's way. A feeling of dread and a graveyard shiver coursed through Elizabeth's body as she believed the woman's presence too much of a coincidence. Nothing could be kept secret without Phyllis knowing about it. She was a snoop and had made it clear that Elizabeth wasn't to come here.

Phyllis had no right to do so, and avoiding the front entrance, Elizabeth walked up through the dripping garden to tap on the glass panelled doors of Philip's study.

Philip looked up from his desk and beckoned her to enter.

The crackling glow of the embers, the wood panelled walls, books, cabinets and collectibles never failed to captivate Elizabeth – her eyes drawn to the glint of the shiny weaponry. These artefacts stood out as among the most curious objects in the room.

'Elizabeth, I really wasn't expecting you to drive out here in this weather. You're as white as a sheet.' Philip came around from behind the desk to greet her. 'Phyllis will be along shortly with morning tea.'

Saying nothing of her embarrassing mishap, Elizabeth could do without the company of Phyllis and also so easily forego the tea on offer preferring to be left alone. But she made light of the fact that she felt unwell. 'I'm okay. Just tired, that's all.'

'What's this about then? It must be important.'

'A subject I'm eager to discuss with you about reconfiguring disused churches. But first things first,' Elizabeth said. 'You might as well know I've broken up with my partner in Melbourne and plan to resign from my job. So, it looks like I'm here to stay.'

'Well let me say I'm sorry about your boyfriend … Gary, wasn't it? But, naturally overjoyed with the news that you've decided to stay. Are you sure about this?'

With a sigh of resignation about breaking up with Gary, Elizabeth nodded. 'It's been a difficult decision, but one that allows me the freedom to determine my future. You see I'm considering extending the bookshop. And as luck would have it, I happen to know of a well-qualified architect who I hope might be interested in taking on the design process.'

Philip's response was left hanging as David popped his head around the door. 'Sorry to interrupt, but now the rain has cleared, I'm about to gather my gear and head to the beach. If you have time to come down before you leave, Elizabeth, I'd be interested to hear your thoughts about my latest painting.'

'I was under the impression that visitors aren't welcome on your private beach, David.'

'What! What's this nonsense you're talking, Elizabeth … visitors not welcome?' Philip asked.

David laughed. 'Well, there is some truth to it, but I've decided to make an exception where you're concerned.'

'All I can say is don't hold your breath. I've got a bookshop to run and need to get back to work.'

'That's a shame … all work and no play. But if you change your mind, you know where to find me.'

Philip grumbled when the door closed behind his brother. 'What the hell is he on about and who in their right mind would paint outdoors after the storm we've had? He can be such a pain when he wants to make life difficult, but at least he seems to have changed his attitude towards you. I wonder why?'

Not wanting to get into too much detail, Elizabeth pulled up a chair beside Philip. 'Don't worry about it. He was a little put out after getting off to a bad start at our first meeting. You remember! It had something to do with the fact that I looked so much like Margaret. He didn't know how to handle that and during a second meeting ordered me off the beach.'

'Well, he seems to have had a sudden change of heart.'

Elizabeth didn't dare mention what else had taken place on that day at the beach except to say, 'I offered him an opinion about his painting, so perhaps that has broken the ice. But, how about we leave this discussion for another day because I have something that I can't wait to show you,' she said, thrusting a manilla envelope under his nose.

Philip's eyes lit up when he pulled the "Change of Name" document from the envelope. Overcome with emotion he reached out to take her hands in his and drew her towards him in a hug.

Right on cue there came a light tap at the door and Phyllis, whose timing was impeccable and who had the uncanny ability to capture Elizabeth in what she so often misconstrued as being a gesture of far more complex intimacy than intended – burst in with the tray of morning tea.

Her expression held a look of shock, obvious disapproval and utter contempt. However, unlike the day at the bookshop, something inside her snapped and she appeared to lose complete control of her sense when she lashed out in anger. 'Get your grubby little hands off him!' she shouted as the tray and teapot of steaming hot liquid clattered to the floor.

Elizabeth and Philip broke apart in dismay, both astonished and unprepared to see Phyllis with a manic look in her eyes rush across the room and yank a spear from the collection on the wall. She charged towards them, a demented woman determined to ram the razor sharp blade clear through Elizabeth's body and out the other side.

The foreboding figure in Elizabeth's premonition was real and the deadly implications were being played out so fast that Phyllis managed to catch her foot on the edge of the rug. She stumbled, causing a dire twist of fate that led her to completely miss the mark and bury the point of the spearhead into Philip's shoulder.

Realising her mistake, she watched on in horror, her hands clasped over her mouth as blood gushed from the wound.

30

Assault with a Deadly Weapon

Hysterical, Phyllis ran from the room screaming.

Elizabeth rushed to Philip's aid as David, hearing the commotion, raced back through the open doorway. A look of fear took hold of him when seeing his brother awkwardly slumped forward in his chair, his face contorted, hands clutching the imbedded spear as if in a vain attempt to withdraw it. Blood seeped through his shirtfront and saturated his sleeve. 'Call triple zero, quick, Elizabeth!' David shouted.

Philip's breathing was shallow, his skin clammy. Too weak to speak, he momentarily raised his eyes in an imploring plea for help but struggled to hold his head up. David knew enough not to move him and placed a cushion on one side in the hope his brother could rest against it. He then removed his own shirt and packed it around the wound in a bid to stem the flow. But by this time Philip had gone into shock and was now unconscious.

Weak at the knees and expecting she might pass out herself, Elizabeth trembled violently as she held the phone to her ear. A man who identified himself as Michael asked her name and address. 'Okay Elizabeth, I want you to take a deep breath and try to stay calm. Do you have someone with you?'

Her voice still shaky, Elizabeth did her best to explain what had happened and let him know that David, the victim's brother, was trying to stop the bleeding.

Michael instructed Elizabeth to put the phone on speaker so he could talk David through what needed to be done until help arrived. By this stage Philip's face was grey and the situation looked dire. 'You're doing well, mate,' Michael assured David. 'Hang in there … an air ambulance is on the way.'

'Oh God, tell them to hurry, he's so pale,' David pleaded. 'I don't know what to do about this fucking spear! He looks so uncomfortable.'

'Don't attempt to move it,' Michael advised before again repeating help was only minutes away, wished them well and said he was about to sign off.

The intervening minutes however seemed like hours as they anxiously awaited the vibrating sound of the circling helicopter now hovering overhead. The noise of the rotor blades cut through the air penetrating the ceiling as the chopper could be heard settling on a nearby patch of open ground. Paramedics came rushing into the house to take control. 'Thank God he can't see what's going on right now,' David said, still in shock.

Tending to Philip's immediate needs, the uniformed aides wasted little time in assessing his worsening condition as they carefully cut away the upper part of the spear. They then strapped him into a gurney and at lightning speed wheeled him out through the doorway with David trailing closely behind.

Elizabeth followed and could see that David, unable to be with Philip during the airlift to hospital, was prevented from entering as the deafening whir of the helicopter whipped up the wind and muddied clumps of dirt around him. His face ashen and hair dishevelled, he watched them leave and sank to his knees in despair. Elizabeth rushed forward to console him.

When they later entered the kitchen, Phyllis was tightly huddled on a chair in the corner, as if trying to make herself look smaller, staring into space, eyes glazed. Appearing to be in a trance, she rocked back and forth humming a tuneless rhyme. She then slowly got to her feet and like a sleepwalker moved to the stove. 'I think I'll pop the kettle on, and we'll all have a nice cup of tea.' Setting out four cups, she said, 'Philip likes a drop of milk in his.'

The police arrived in a blaze of sirens led by Elizabeth's least favourite person. Senior Sergeant Ian Henderson appeared to be in his element as he inspected the scene and scribbled on his notepad amid the bloodied surrounds. A gloved Constable Madden was bullishly reprimanded when carefully picking up the blood splattered shaft of the spear and dropping it into a plastic bag. 'Not sure you should be taking charge of that, Madden, without specific orders from police headquarters.'

When he questioned Phyllis, her zombie like state of passive stupor changed dramatically to one of rage. She began to rant and point the finger at Elizabeth. 'It's all the fault of that hussy who's just like her aunt. Someone had to stop her.'

Elizabeth could read the senior sergeant like an open book as he appeared barely able to stifle an expression of satisfaction due to this outburst; the implication that she was the sole source of incitement for this terrible incident. An immediate air of pompous superiority took possession of the man. 'Phyllis

Bentley, assault with a deadly weapon is a serious offence. And it would appear from the evidence provided, you acted with malicious criminal intent to inflict grievous bodily harm on one, Philip Anderson. It is my duty to inform you of your legal rights,' he advised before placing her under arrest. 'You will be held in custody pending further enquiries.'

Handcuffed and escorted to the waiting divi van, Phyllis remained silent as she was led away past a lone reporter accompanied by a photographer from the local press.

Amid a flash of lights, 'Can you tell us what happened?' The two hounded Elizabeth when seeing her at the open doorway. 'Is the victim still alive?' the reporter asked.

'I have nothing to say.' Elizabeth closed the door behind her while pondering how this attempt on her life had gone so terribly wrong. Less than ten minutes had elapsed between her breaking the news about the name change of the bookshop and the extraordinary assault that may well have placed Philip's life in jeopardy. What was the likelihood of anyone in this day and age, being attacked with such an antiquated weapon? St Thomas had been killed with a spear.

Elizabeth prayed that history was not about to be repeated.

Waiting to meet with the surgeon, Elizabeth grew apprehensive as David paced the floor.

Doctor Ben Beaumont finally appeared and introduced himself. A relatively youthful looking man, his regular features and deep-set blue eyes harboured an intelligence Elizabeth imagined would never fail to afford a trust in his ability. 'Your brother is resting comfortably, Mr Anderson,' he assured David with a convincing degree of confidence in his voice. The doctor then turned to include Elizabeth, 'He's a lucky man! His injury could have proved far more serious, even fatal, should the razor sharp blade have severed an artery. The delicate task of removing the spearhead and repairing a minimal amount of internal damage should see him come through this without too much of a problem.'

David's hunched shoulders visibly relaxed when hearing this positive news.

Dr Beaumont went on to add, 'Philip may feel weak for a few days. But that's to be expected. The worst is over and now he just needs to rest, mend and regain his strength. Also, the police have confiscated the blade to be withheld as evidence.'

At the mention of the weapon, David looked at him in horror and shuddered. 'To be honest Dr Beaumont, I'd prefer never to set eyes on it again.'

'I mean no offence, Mr Anderson, or to make light of your brother's suffering, it's just that I've removed many grisly body parts along with other oddities at times that patients like to hang on to as some sort of souvenir trophy. But never a spear!'

Feeling that they owed their gratitude to the good doctor who had just come from the operating theatre in his scrubs after saving Philip's life, Elizabeth graciously stepped in to say, 'I'm sure I can speak for all three of us when I say with a great sense of relief that we thank you for what you have done to ensure Philip's recovery.'

The patient, although pale and groggy, joked with them both when they arrived at his bedside the following day. 'Not too many can boast they've been attacked with a spear,' he managed a smile. 'Did you get a decent shot of that thing, Dave?'

'Afraid not, mate! I was a bit tied up at the time trying to stop you from bleeding all over my favourite shirt. And, judging by the way you pegged out, a selfie was out of the question.'

'By God, all I can recall was seeing that woman charging like a wounded rhino. What the hell got her so fired up in the first place do you think, Elizabeth?'

'I strongly believe, had she not tripped over the rug, it should be me lying in that bed, not you, Philip. Phyllis misinterpreted an innocent act of affection as something far more unacceptable and presumed me to be in the throes of having my way with you.'

'You're kidding me?' Philip replied.

Elizabeth shook her head. 'I've never been more serious. She looked devastated when she realised her mistake and it was you she had harmed, not me. Especially when convinced that I've inherited the genes of a loose living, red light harlot. No, Philip, there's not a doubt in my mind that she was setting out to protect you until it all went so horribly wrong.'

Resting his head back on the pillow, Philip suddenly seemed wearied by the conversation, and as if having heard enough for one day he complained that his bandaged shoulder was giving him a lot of pain. Elizabeth suggested he press the bedside button and alert the nurse. She then gently kissed his forehead and tiptoed from the room leaving David alone with his brother.

31

Significant Revelations

News of Phyllis Bentley's arrest was met with mixed emotions by the people of Mariners Cove. Perhaps none more so than Graeme Jenkins from whom Elizabeth received a call, asking her to meet with him in his office.

On her arrival, he took her hand in his and sighed. 'This upsetting business with Phyllis has left me feeling terribly troubled. I should have seen this coming and am relieved to read in the newspaper that Philip Anderson's condition is stable.'

'He did lose a lot of blood but fortunately the blade didn't penetrate an artery,' Elizabeth assured him.

'Thank God!' Jenkins replied. 'Phyllis is a client of mine, and I could see that things were starting to get on top of her. In recent years she's suffered a great deal of disappointment which has affected her health and obvious mental stability. This in no way can justify her actions but could be of paramount importance when her medical history is revealed at the hearing.'

Jenkins paused and fiddled with a pile of paperwork on his desk. 'The fact that Phyllis has been denied bail and is being held in remand has prompted me to share with you certain matters of a personal nature. What with the sad circumstances of our first meeting, I didn't think it the right time to mention I grew up in Mariners Cove and was in the same grade at school as your mother, Helen.' Jenkins cleared his throat and wiped his brow as if a little guilty about keeping this information from Elizabeth. 'Before I left to study law in Melbourne, she and I were inseparable and secretly agreed to become engaged as soon as we were both employed and able to start saving for the future.'

'You and my mother were planning to marry?' Elizabeth repeated in surprise.

'Does that sound so crazy?'

'It's just hard to imagine her with anyone other than my father. And I'm a little disappointed that you didn't tell me about this before.'

'Yes, I can understand why. Even more surprising is the fact that your father was my best mate at uni. And when your mother came to live and work in Melbourne, the three of us shared a house together. The rest is history! Your dad stole my girl away from me.'

With a note of concern, Elizabeth replied, 'Goodness, how very mean of my father, but fortunate for me I suppose.'

Jenkin's smiled. 'That's one way of looking at it I guess. But it took a long time for me to get over losing Helen and after all these decades there seemed no reason to think it necessary to burden you further with this information.'

'Well, I still wish you'd told me.'

'The reason I am telling you now, is to explain why I also knew your mother's younger sister Margaret and her best friend, Phyllis. Because Margaret, being far from perfect, like all of us, had on one occasion upset her sister so badly that Helen wrote about it in her diary. In later years when we were dating, Helen mentioned how scared she had felt, and tore the pages out so I could read what happened.'

Graeme picked up the papers he had been fiddling with on the desk in front of him. 'I never did destroy them,' he said, handing Elizabeth the faded pages. 'This entry is an account of a childhood incident and proof of a jealous rivalry.'

Elizabeth looked down at the handwriting and browning edges of the paper. 'I'm not sure I want to read this to be honest. I'd find it hard to believe anything derogatory about Margaret even though my mother wrote these words. Sibling rivalry is not in the least unusual, and let's face it, kids are mean; kids are nasty. It's also likely Margaret may have had an altogether different version of the same incident.'

'Fair enough, Elizabeth. I'm not sure why I even kept these pages. Toss them away if you like. It's up to you.' Jenkins sounded agitated. 'But I should add that once Margaret completed her schooling, she applied for a job in Melbourne.'

'How do you know all this?'

'The day I moved out of our shared accommodation, Margaret moved in.'

'She lived with my parents before they were married?'

'And for some time after they married, I believe. So, naturally I assumed that what you now see written in the pages of the diary may have been long forgotten, forgiven and totally irrelevant.'

Elizabeth looked questioningly at Jenkins and wondered why the need to bring this up right now. His lost love being one thing, but his willingness to cast aspersions on Margaret's character didn't sit well with her. 'What does all this have to do with Phyllis?' she asked.

'Very little, apart from the fact that I wanted you to understand. You see it wasn't just Phyllis that Margaret hurt, even though your mother must have put aside any ill feelings from childhood once her younger sister arrived looking to find a new home in the city.'

'Okay,' Elizabeth said. 'Now we have established that, Graeme, tell me what happened exactly between Margaret and Phyllis?'

'It seems that before finding her husband's mangled body pinned beneath his tractor, he had been spending an unusual amount of his time in the company of Margaret. Phyllis became suspicious and arrived at your aunt's house one day to discover the two in an illicit act of betrayal.'

Elizabeth shuddered and tried to erase an ugly image of Jack's khaki work overalls draped in a crumpled heap around his ankles.

'Lord knows I'm no saint, and it's not my intention to judge or denigrate either one of them,' Jenkins insisted. 'But after Jack's tragic death, Phyllis confronted her with damning accusations when believing her to be intimately involved with different male companions.'

Should this be true, Elizabeth's loyalty to her aunt made her want to protest and ask why Jenkins would take the word of someone like Phyllis. Poor Jack wouldn't be the first to stray and was probably so under the thumb he must have welcomed such a romantic distraction.

'I feel certain Jack's name would have been right at the centre of this heated exchange,' Jenkins continued. 'But it was Margaret's close association with the newly arrived brothers that was the latest bone of contention. Then – given your return – perhaps preferring to think of you as being cast in the same mould, Phyllis's imagination began to work overtime.'

Attempting to process this information, none of which portrayed Margaret in a good light, Elizabeth said, 'No matter the excuses you are intent on making for Phyllis, the trauma she has undergone cannot either excuse or lessen the gravity of her actions. I don't think I can ever forgive her.'

'That's to be expected, Elizabeth. Yet I felt obligated to tell you all that I know so you might better understand why Phyllis had become so bitter and resentful.'

'We each experience hurt in our lifetime, Graeme. Nevertheless, Phyllis's judgment is in the hands of the justice system … not mine!'

This senseless affair that Phyllis had created, marked the beginning of a series of events that would see Elizabeth struggle to navigate her life in a way she would have otherwise preferred.

Her first mistake being brought about when choosing to divide her time between the bookshop and the Andersons. And now she rushed back to the shop on a whistlestop check in with Tilt before visiting the hospital.

'How's this new work schedule suiting you, Tilt?' she asked.

'Don't worry, darling. All's well at this end. And apart from us both being on different shifts and unable to enjoy each other's company, I'm thinking this arrangement might give me more time on my days off to make some much needed trips to the city.'

'Well, it won't be forever, I hope. I'm looking forward to things returning to normal.'

'What's going to happen to Phyllis, do you think? Or is it too early to say?'

'Your guess is as good as mine! But I'd be surprised if she doesn't get a prison sentence. Attempted murder is not to be taken lightly.'

Tilt wiped at a speckle on the counter with the tip of her finger. 'Gosh I can't imagine a woman like her amongst all those hard-nosed criminals.'

'It's difficult for me to feel sorry for her, because if she hadn't tripped on that rug, I'd probably be pushing up daisies right now.'

'Oh, dear God in heaven … that'll teach us never to pretend we were planning to be wed in front of her. I didn't realise she was such a loose cannon.'

Elizabeth looked at the time and threw her bag across her shoulder. 'I don't think any of us did. But got to go, Tilt, I'm sorry!'

Running out through the doorway, Elizabeth felt relieved to know her friend was happy about their new alternating arrangement of four days on and three days off. Also, before leaving home that morning, she'd made certain that Lenny Forrester was prepared to stay for a while and start the paintwork she had originally planned to do herself. Naturally he, like everyone, was surprised about the news that seemed all anyone could talk about at the Cove.

The one thing that she couldn't help but feel irritated about was the self-important Senior Sergeant, who had acted like he was joined at the hip with Detective Frank Norton in charge of the investigation. Individual statements had already been taken, while forensic evidence was gathered from the ribboned off scene of the crime – an area which remained off limits for two days. But as Philip's stay in hospital was expected to be brief, Elizabeth was keen to help David in every way possible, including cleaning the study in readiness for his brother's homecoming.

32

Beneath the Stairs

Thinking back on her recent meeting with Jenkins, Elizabeth had certainly been both surprised and enlightened by his admission of having had a romantic relationship with her mother during their youth. And now, she was especially curious to read the unsettling childhood account from the diary but didn't want Jenkins knowing that. Particularly when he'd felt it necessary to show a side to Margaret about which Elizabeth had no knowledge. And not a very pretty side at that.

There had been no time to stop and read, however, in between rushing back to the bookshop and meeting with David to visit the hospital, then returning to Misty Headland to help clear out Philip's study.

Her time seemed no longer her own as life became centred around the Andersons. She began to lose track of everything else when David appeared desperate to keep her to himself, insisting she stay for an early dinner. 'It gets very quiet being here on my own and you'll still have time to drive home before dark,' he promised.

'Okay,' Elizabeth agreed. 'But only if I'm out of here by seven.'

'Right! Well, how about you go and relax in the living room while I rustle up a bowl of pasta. I'll pour you a glass of wine.'

'Just the one, or I won't be able to drive. And if you're sure you don't need a hand, there's something Graeme Jenkins gave me to read recently. It'll only take ten minutes.'

Elizabeth left David to his cooking in the kitchen.

The living room, like the study, looked out over a beautiful vista of the ocean. She sank down into a plush mulberry coloured sofa and kicking off her shoes, breathed in that luxurious aroma of newness that still lingered in the material nature of her surroundings.

Withdrawing the brittle, yellowing pages of the diary from a folder that she'd placed in her oversized handbag, Elizabeth realised she needed to handle them with care. There was something almost sacred about seeing the handwriting and touching the same paper her mother had once touched. And as she tried to picture her mother's tear-stained face on that day they had last waved goodbye, only then did Elizabeth begin to read.

The writing turned out to be a challenge, as in between the spelling mistakes, smudges, crossed out lines and jumbled sentences, the words were difficult to decipher.

Having worked in editing, Elizabeth used her skill to unravel certain words and re-write the content of the story so she might better understand it. She put it aside when David called the pasta was ready and they should hop into it while it was hot.

Later when she arrived home, Elizabeth settled back in bed to re-read the story. There was little doubt it left her feeling unsettled. But then sisterly love often soured in moments of rivalry, whether due to attention seeking or jealousy. Kids do horrible things to one another. And unable to believe anything unkind about her aunt, Elizabeth looked upon the incident as a misplaced childhood prank or that Margaret, being so young, had no knowledge of the serious nature of what she had done.

'No peeking!' I warned my sister.

Hands over her eyes, Margaret turned her face to the wall and slowly started to count.

I scrambled out of the room and into the closet beneath the stairs where I hid behind a large cardboard box.

' … nine, ten. Coming, ready or not!' Margaret's feet pattered along the hallway in the opposite direction. 'Am I warm?' her voice echoed in the distance.

'You're colder than an Eskimo's nose in a blizzard,' I shouted.

Minutes passed before I heard her approaching. 'Come out, Helly … please come out,' she pleaded. 'I don't want to play hidey anymore.'

Always a sooky la-la, this was just so typical of my sister.

'Ouch,' I cried as I crawled out from behind the carton. Something had dug into my kneecap but in my haste to squeeze between suitcases and storage crates, it was too dark to see what I had scraped my leg against. Then I bumped my head on the base of an overhead step.

I pushed the door open to find Margaret sitting at the bottom of the stairs. 'You're such a cry-baby and spoil every game by giving up so easily.' A disgusting trail of snot ran down her nose into her mouth.

Using the back of her sleeve, she wiped away her tears.

'Ugh, you look gross. Where's your hankie?'

'It's not fair, Helen,' she blubbered. 'You're bigger than me, but you always make me look for you, and never take turns to let me hide. You cheated as well. So, I'm telling on you because Mummy said we're not allowed to play in that closet.'

'You're nothing but a snivelling scaredy cat, Margaret. Scaredy cat, scaredy cat,' I chanted, while placing the tip of a finger inside each end of my mouth. Stretching my lips out to their widest, I made a face at her and poked out my tongue.

Margaret leapt up from the step and stamped her feet. 'Stop it, Helen, stop it, I hate it when you do that. One day the wind will change, and your face will stay that way forever and ever and I'll be glad and say I told you so.'

Mum's head appeared from around the kitchen doorway. 'Margaret, Helen, what on earth is going on here?'

'Helen went into the closet under the stairs, Mummy.'

'Tattle tale,' I whispered.

'Is this true, young lady?' With an angry look on her face my mother walked towards me. 'Well, I'm waiting, what have you got to say for yourself?'

'I didn't do anything,' I lied.

'You disobeyed me, Helen. Go to your room this minute. There'll be no dinner tonight and you will not step one foot outside your door until the morning. Is that understood?'

Unable to sleep, my tummy rumbled. I waited until the house was silent then crept down the stairs and into the kitchen to raid the biscuit tin and help myself to a glass of milk. I found a torch in the drawer and shone the light up at the clock. It was ten past midnight. A lightning flash lit up *the room and I nearly jumped out of my skin. Rain began to pound on the roof.*

Tiptoeing out into the hallway I noticed the door was open beneath the stairs. I was surprised to see a dim shaft of light shining from inside the closet. When I reached the doorway, I saw that much of the clutter had been cleared away and I realised the light was coming from a gaping hole in the floorboards. Then I knew how I had grazed my knee.

A small trapdoor fitted with a metal clasp lay open to expose a storage area under the floor. I had never noticed it before as it was always hidden from view. No wonder Mother hadn't wanted Margaret and I playing in here.

A cold draught crept up my pyjama pants as I stepped forward and peered into the hole. The light flickered and dimmed but I could see there was a ladder leading down into a basement.

Curious to know what was down there, I swung my legs over the side and placed my feet on the top rung. There was a sudden scampering that sounded like a mouse. Then I heard a rustling noise. Focusing the torch into the gloomy unknown, I called out, 'Who's there? Is that you, Daddy?' But then I wondered what my father would be doing so late at night.

There was no answer and even though I knew that if Mummy found out I would be in far worse trouble than I was already, I plucked up courage, placed the torch to one side and began my descent. Reaching the ground level, the flickering light bulb fizzled and sputtered. Everything went black. My heart thumped so loudly that I felt it might jump right out of my chest.

I'd left the torch turned on up on the floor of the closet. It gave off a tiny glow as my eyes adjusted to the darkness.

The chill in the air made me shiver and brushing away a cobweb I had a sudden change of heart. Eager to get back to the safety of my bed, I was planning to return upstairs as quickly as possible.

It was with this comforting thought of my bed when suddenly I froze in terror. The hairs on the back of my neck stood on end, as I heard someone or something breathing right behind me. Two bright eyes stared back at me only to scurry away disappearing out through a tiny cavity in the wall. But when I was about to make my escape, a ghostly figure stepped out from the shadows. I choked back a scream.

'Oh my God, you scared the daylights out of me! What're you doing down here?'

Dressed in a thin cotton nightgown, Margaret didn't appear to notice me. She stared ahead as if in a trance, glided past me and stood at the foot of the ladder. I stepped back and waited as she climbed, anxious to see her safely to the top. Only then did I follow. But before I reached the opening, my sister replaced the lid and fastened the clasp. I heard her close the door of the closet behind her and walk away. The stairs creaked overhead.

I was to later discover that a clap of thunder and the click of Margaret's bedroom door handle woke my mother, who in turn woke my father. 'What was that?' she'd asked when realising Margaret had been sleepwalking again. 'I hope she wasn't anywhere near the stairway closet. I'm worried she might fall into the cellar.'

Dad told mum to go back to sleep, and he would put a lock on the door the next day.

No one heard my cry over the storm. Huddled in the corner, dressed in my flimsy pyjamas I could not believe my fate. It felt like being in a nightmare as the whistling wind circled the walls, and I prayed to wake up. Cold and scared in the darkness, I spent the night in that awful cellar and felt certain I would freeze to death.

When my bed was found empty in the morning, my parents didn't need to look very far. Struggling to pull my body up the ladder, I hammered against the trapdoor and shouted. I was so relieved to see my father and clung to him when he rescued me from my prison.

Shivering and white-faced, I was sitting in front of the fireplace wrapped in a blanket to recover from my frightening ordeal. Mother explained that after she had ordered me to my room, she decided to get rid of the clutter under the stairs. 'That was obviously a bad idea,' she said.

Having acted in my younger sister's best interest, knowing never to wake her when sleepwalking, Margaret denied any memory of her movements claiming no knowledge of the cellar.

Later when alone together, she sidled up to me, cupped her hands around my ear and secretly mimicked the teasing chant that I had taunted her with only one day earlier. 'Scaredy cat, scaredy cat.'

I never thought it possible, but these few harmless words sent a far deadlier chill up and down my spine than what I had experienced in the cellar, and – for the first time – an element of doubt entered my mind. Had Margaret really been asleep, or had she locked me in the cellar on purpose?

I stared into my sister's eyes and wondered.

33

Preparing for a Homecoming

In a contemplative mood, Elizabeth sat sipping a mug of coffee in Philip's study, while, whenever unobserved, she'd cast an admiring glance in David's direction. She wondered how little it had taken for the two of them to have reached a stage where they could barely keep their hands off one another.

It was Phyllis's fault, she thought, not her own.

What else could she have done? There seemed no doubt her closeness to David had grown out of the situation brought on as a direct result of the attack. And because the spear had been meant for her, Elizabeth felt obligated not to abandon either of the brothers in their hour of need. But the hours turned into days and eventually weeks, and in between dealings with the police and visits to the hospital, the two were constantly thrown together.

Emotionally invested and hopelessly caught up in their welfare, Elizabeth simply expected Forrester to take care of everything that needed doing on the home front in her absence, and Tilt to cover for her at the bookshop even though a whole new roster had been put in place.

Four days had slipped by following Philip's hospitalisation when Dr Beaumont called with news that a few complications had arisen. Philip had an infection. He needed further medical supervision and would not be released from hospital as initially planned. The promising prognosis had suddenly turned to a worrisome period of uncertainty as his condition worsened.

The pressure began to build. 'I'm going to kill that woman with my bare hands if anything happens to Philip,' David had said.

Increasingly reliant on Elizabeth, he pleaded with her to stay overnight. A dangerous proposition. But given their mutual concern, she didn't take much convincing when agreeing to make up a bed in the spare room. David, looking a whole lot brighter, poured them both a drink. 'A nightcap,' he'd said. 'It'll help us sleep.' Then they got talking and he topped up the glasses pouring out another and another.

Yes, it was David's fault, she thought, *not hers.*

Ever since they had kissed on the beach, their relationship seemed like a ticking time bomb that could explode at any moment. So, why was Elizabeth not surprised when around two that morning, she'd woken to see him standing beside the bed. She had switched on the lamp and noticed his eyes were red and he was shivering.

Anger had turned to sadness, and in a moment of vulnerability his distress caused Elizabeth to let her guard down. Weakening, she threw back the doona and invited him to slide in beside her.

'I promise I won't touch you, Liz. I just need to get some rest.'

But as their bodies lay side by side and eventually brushed up against each other the feeling was electric.

Elizabeth had held her breath as he broke his promise and reached out to place his hand on her shoulder. When she didn't object, he'd then moved forward and moulded his body into her back. She turned to face him, and seeing his eyes filled with longing, 'I don't think this is a good idea,' she'd said as he looked to silence her and covered her mouth with his own. And seeking some much-needed emotional release, the two found refuge in each other's arms. The heartbreak having stirred up their desire to find comfort and solace in a bid to alleviate the depth of their despair through a passionate night of lovemaking.

Elizabeth woke to question her actions as Forrester's face flashed before her. Yet his feelings had been left unspoken and since that kiss between herself and David on the beach, perhaps she had subconsciously longed for him to take this infatuation further.

Yes, it was Lenny Forrester's fault, she'd thought, *not hers.*

Why had he never expressed any feelings for her? If he had – this may never have happened. And now her reasoning suddenly abandoned her because all she wanted was someone to cure her ills and provide the pent-up release that she had hungered for. David had made her feel wanted and cared about, unlike Gary.

Yes, it was Gary's fault, she thought, *not hers.*

To put it bluntly, Gary could never be trusted and had expected her to bow to his wishes.

Whereas Elizabeth had wanted David to kiss her. She had wanted David to take this further, to which he willingly obliged. But strangely he had called her Margaret, which she couldn't stop thinking about.

Yes, it was Philip's fault, she thought, *not her own.*

Was he really her aunt's son?

Elizabeth had drawn the conclusion that she had been the only one who was totally blameless.

'Are you okay, sweetheart?' David cut in on her thoughts as he took the mug from her hand and placed it on the bar in the study. 'You looked to be a million miles away.'

'Just thinking that's all.'

'About me, I hope!'

Should she broach the subject that had been nagging her ever since that first day they met? She had not forgotten how he had looked at her with such shock and dislike in his eyes. It was like he was seeing the ghost of Margaret reincarnated.

'Fire away!'

'You and my aunt were lovers … weren't you?'

David sighed and ran his hands through his hair. 'Fuck, Elizabeth … why bring this up now? Well don't answer that because I can tell you for a fact, yes, we were lovers, and I've never tried to hide that.'

Shocked, Elizabeth felt violated in some way, and she now thought her instinct to be right. He'd been struck dumb by her unexpected appearance on that day they first met, and it was all to do with the likeness between herself and Margaret. He'd resented her being alive, while her aunt was dead.

'You mean to tell me that you actually had sex with my aunt even though you were half her age, and when knowing your own stepbrother claimed to be her son?'

David let out what sounded to Elizabeth like a fake fit of laughter. 'Her son, did you say? Is that what he told you?'

'That's exactly what he told me. He also told me that you were jealous because you foolishly thought she was fonder of him than she was of you.'

David shook his head as if to say it was nothing less than pure fantasy. 'Why do we have to talk about Margaret right now just when you and I have something special happening?'

'Sounds to me like it was special with Margaret.'

'Now who's the jealous one.' David said as he gave Elizabeth a blistering look of pure hatred in that moment. 'Leave it alone, Liz. Don't go there. Margaret's dead and you can't be jealous of a dead woman; that's all in the past. It's you and I now and that's all that matters. Don't spoil things.'

Elizabeth was relieved she had not mentioned that he called her Margaret during their lovemaking. In some ways it felt like less hassle because she wanted whatever it was that they had right now just as much as he did.

Two months had passed since Philip had been carried from the house. And perhaps without accepting something in her mood had shifted, Elizabeth continued to help pack the dangerous weaponry in crates to be stored away. Yet, all the while in her silence, her mind kept working.

Sure, he had slept with her aunt. But then, so had Lenny Forrester. And she was supposed to believe it wasn't a big deal. That was the thing about men, they would later excuse themselves by saying sleeping with someone other than the person they loved, meant nothing.

Somehow, she had forgiven Forrester. But when learning David had been guilty of doing the same, she felt a sense of shame about having given herself so willingly to him. So why hadn't she immediately put an end to this intimacy? Instead, she was encouraging their relationship. The whole thing was sick. *I am sick*, she thought in disgust as she kept stealing a sneaky look at a man she barely knew, let alone the man she could be in love with.

The truth was, he knew how to press all the right buttons.

She was weak and like putty in his hands. Gary used to do the same, which gave him a controlling power over her. And now as she looked at David dressed in jeans and a t-shirt, he no longer seemed self-conscious about the scarring on his face. This distinctive marking enhanced his otherwise regular features, magnetic eyes and overall physical appeal. Elizabeth would be lying if she denied how much his physical appeal had attracted her. She had wallowed in the warmth of his body when she slid between the sheets and snuggled in beside him. But what Elizabeth did worry about was how Philip would react on his return. Would he approve?

Then, there was Forrester. He haunted her dreams, and it didn't seem to matter how often she slept with David, Lenny Forrester was never far from her mind, looking on in abject disapproval.

Elizabeth couldn't see she needed to take a step back, go home and give herself a chance to work out what she really wanted. Instead, she jumped to her feet and threw her arms around David from behind while burying her nose into his back.

'What's going on?' he asked.

'Let's get married,' she said on a wild whim.

Now it was David's turn to look shocked, 'Woah there, Liz … did you say married? A minute ago you were giving me the silent treatment.'

Elizabeth pulled away. 'Of course, I'm mad. I'm crazy mad, furious and totally pissed off. Just wanted to see what you'd say.'

'Phew, you had me worried. Maybe somewhere down the track we could get a place in town.'

'It's just that … I can't do this in front of Philip. You and me I mean. Somehow it doesn't seem right.'

'We're both adults. What's so wrong about it?' David asked. 'We need to take this slowly. But I'm not letting you go just because my brother may not approve.'

'I don't want you to get the wrong impression about me. I'm not the sort of person who sleeps around. That is what Phyllis accused me of. Exactly that!'

'That's rubbish. Why would you listen to that weirdo after what she's done? You're just tired, Liz. We've all been through a lot.'

'Yep, perhaps you're right,' Elizabeth sighed. But deep down she knew this wasn't right. Their brief flirtation that had come about for all the wrong reasons had been tainted, whether she wanted to deny it or not.

The two continued clearing Philip's study when Elizabeth found something of interest. 'What's this?' she asked with a change of subject.

David looked up from wrapping and taping. 'I haven't seen that for years,' he said, taking hold of a framed measuring device and wiping the dust off the glass with his sleeve. 'It's Philip's builders' square. Our parents had it mounted and framed to present to him on the day he graduated in architecture. He was a builder as well, you know. Learnt from Dad!'

'We should hang this in a prominent position,' she said.

'Absolutely!' David agreed. 'And you know, Liz, whether adopted or otherwise, Philip, Thomas, call him by any name he chooses, he'll always be my brother, and I never knew until now how much I needed him to survive.'

'Sometimes it takes something bad to happen before any of

us realise what someone we take for granted can really mean to us.'

'You're not wrong. I didn't think things could get any worse. But seeing him slumped over that spear brought me to my senses. The way he's battled through this has made me wake up to how self-absorbed I've been. If not for you, I doubt I could have coped.'

'We needed each other at a time when we've both been feeling vulnerable. Maybe now that need might change.'

'Nothing's going to change, Liz. Get that thought out of your mind.'

Elizabeth's mind right at that moment was centred on Philip's struggle with the golden staph infection and how he'd fought to make a full recovery. It was what happened next that had created the biggest impact and caused excited rejoicing.

Philip had regained a little feeling in his legs. This extraordinary development baffled the doctors and for weeks he'd been undergoing an intensive physical rehabilitation program to help him walk again. This unexpected outcome prompted Elizabeth to ask, 'David, do you know the farmer who lives just down the road?'

'That'd be old Tom Moody. A bit of a fruitcake that bloke. I try to avoid him.'

'Well, he did invite me in for a cup of tea with his wife some time back. I had trouble with the car, and he helped me out.'

With a look of concern, 'What? I hope you didn't agree, to the tea I mean?' David said. 'He's delusional, that bloke. And as for his wife ... apparently, she died several years ago. Who knows where you might have ended. Maybe buried in a ditch somewhere.'

'Really? That surprises me, because he couldn't have been nicer when I met him. But that could explain why he told me he'd seen Philip out walking.'

'Philip out walking! That's ridiculous. That old-timer's really lost the plot.'

'Now Philip's got some feeling back in his legs, it doesn't sound all that crazy. What if he already had some inkling the strength was coming back in his legs but didn't want to raise any false hope. He could have been trying to walk without telling anyone.'

'Why would he do that?' David asked.

'I have no idea. But don't you find it strange that this old bloke told me he'd seen him out and about?'

'That old geezer wouldn't know shit from clay. Could've been anyone he saw.'

Being able to understand why Tom Moody had thought the Andersons unfriendly and perhaps imagined seeing Philip out walking, Elizabeth felt the old man hadn't given her any reason to distrust him. Yet hadn't she experienced an unsettling hostility in David's treatment toward her right from the word go? She'd also suspected him to be the man who ran away at the cemetery. Even a crazy person wouldn't have to be too crazy to notice the odd way that he'd acted back then.

Now there was also his attachment to Margaret that kept bugging her.

Elizabeth suggested they stop what they were doing for a lunchbreak. David followed her into the kitchen and as they prepared a salad sandwich and seated themselves at the island bar, the discussion turned back to Philip. 'What do you think Philip will do now he has some independence?' Elizabeth asked.

'I doubt this'll change much even if he doesn't need that wheelchair.'

'Do you think he'd be interested in drawing up plans for an extension to the church?'

'What?'

'Yes, a coffee shop and gallery type affair.'

David whistled. 'You're talking big bickies there. How are you planning to pull this off?'

'I've got my ways. But it's a matter I am planning to again ask him about when he comes home.'

The following afternoon, Elizabeth closed the shop and arrived early to find David busy pruning. 'Shouldn't you get ready to go and pick Philip up?'

'No there's plenty of time. Let's sit for a few minutes and enjoy the garden.'

'Old Mr Gentry would have loved how you've brought this place back to life.'

'Glad you like it. And why don't you take a little peek up there behind you.'

Elizabeth turned to see Philip, with the aid of his sticks, standing at the top of the stairs with the broadest grin on his face.

'What's a bloke got to do around here to get a bit of attention?' he shouted.

'Well, aren't you the show off,' Elizabeth smiled as she raced up the stairs, two at a time, in her haste to throw her arms around him.

'Don't go getting too carried away,' he laughed.

'Sit down in that wicker chair,' Elizabeth said. 'I have some unfinished business to discuss with you.'

'Well before you do that, Elizabeth, I would like you and David to get busy unpacking those crates in the cellar and putting all my collectibles back where they belong. Is that understood?'

34

A Secret Rendezvous

Tilt Jacobson completed her tour of the floral display housed in the Conservatory and stepped out into the open to the sound of church bells peeling from the soaring spire of St Patrick's Cathedral. She seated herself on a park bench at the edge of a leafy avenue in the Fitzroy Gardens and thought of Elizabeth's ex-boyfriend, Gary, who had made a lasting impression on her during his brief visit to the bookshop.

The Phyllis fiasco had created a situation that allowed Tilt sufficient days to travel to Melbourne. She was careful not to mention a word about the real reason she was doing this to Liz, as the last thing she wanted was to risk ruining their friendship.

Surprisingly, Gary had agreed to meet, perhaps in the hope that Liz may have sent her as some sort of mediator with news that she had forgiven him and wanted to get back together.

Never a person to become ruffled in times of uncertainty, Tilt tried to relax and ignore the nagging tremor in her knees. 'Breathe,' she told herself. 'Deep breath in, deep breath out.'

This surge of anxiety was due to her bold decision to contact him in the first place. *What was I thinking?* Tilt wondered, lifting her face to the sky to soak up the warmth of the sunlight.

'Ah, if it isn't the wonderful Leaner,' Gary greeted with a fleeting brush of his lips to her cheek. 'It's good to see you, Eileen.'

Confronted with that cheeky grin and stray lock of hair that fell forward on his forehead, 'You too, my darling,' Tilt smiled. 'But surely you must know that in European culture it's customary for such kisses to be administered on both sides of the face.'

'Got to admit they're smart people those Europeans, even if we are in East Melbourne.' Gary happily obliged with a second kiss to the opposite cheek. Only then did he plop down on the seat beside her.

'And what's with the Eileen? Call me Tilt, darling … everybody does.'

'Wouldn't want to start the revolution, but I kind of like Eileen.'

Tilt was normally no shrinking violet, but with her tremor already forgotten, she marvelled at how alive and completely at ease he'd made her feel. And now being more than prepared to give him a bit of stick and engage in some innocent banter she replied, 'The way that you say my name, darling, I could kind of get to like it myself, I think.'

'Okay, that's settled then, Eileen it is,' Gary smiled. 'But before you go handing out further instructions, I should mention I've reserved a table at a classy little eatery nearby.'

'Oh, you really shouldn't have,' Tilt gushed. 'But you'll get no complaint from me, darling.'

'Good! At least I got one thing right because complaints will not be tolerated,' Gary laughed. 'Outstanding organisational skills are a specialty of mine. Planning ahead being one of them. And while no expert on European culture, in Aussie culture it is customary that as you invited me today, that must make it your shout.'

'True!' Tilt agreed, detecting a glimmer of the old sparkle in his eyes. 'But if it's my shout, darling, we may have to settle for a cheeseburger and chips at Macca's.'

With a look of despair, 'Would that be the "Drive Thru" you prefer, or maybe a table beside the playground?' he teased, and held his elbow out in invitation for Tilt to place her arm through his. 'Allow me my good Lady Eileen … let us depart,' he said in a toffy voice, 'and let us have no more talk of Macca's.'

Walking so closely beside this the handsomest of men, Tilt savoured the distinctive cedar and spice fragrance of his soapy aroma.

'Hold your horses there Eileen, as my old mum used to say,' Gary insisted when coming to a halt. With a furtive glance in each direction, he plucked a forbidden flower from a garden bed reserved solely for the viewing of the public. Managing to extract the entire plant, roots and all, 'Oops … hope the curator's not watching,' he chuckled. Then hastily snapping it apart and returning the lower section back into the hole, he stamped the dirt back in place with the sole of his shoe and thread the stem through Tilt's hair. 'How about a selfie of us both in front of Captain Cook's Cottage,' he said as he whipped his phone from his shirt pocket.

The restaurant – a cosy and intimate space lined with rustic brick walls and large windows – opened out to an inviting courtyard surrounded by a green oasis of potted plants and vines complete with a trickling fountain.

Dodging between tables, the waiter ushered them to a quiet corner and once settled, Gary removed a leafy frond away from his ear and gazed over the top of his menu. 'This is nice, isn't it? And you know what, Eileen,' he added, 'I reckon it's all the nicer because you're here.'

Tilt, who was a bit young to be having a hot flush, realised she must be blushing. 'What a lovely thing to say, darling.'

'It's true! And the last time anyone called me darling was when I slipped on a banana peel and skinned both my kneecaps. I was about six at the time.'

'Don't believe a word of it,' Tilt laughed. 'Someone like you must have been called darling a million times. Surely Liz would have used endearments?'

'Endearments!' Gary scoffed. 'Nope, can't say endearments were high on her list,' he admitted with a note of sadness in his voice. 'Speaking of which, how is Liz? Don't tell me she's sent you here to beg me to take her back?'

'Not at all. This was my own idea. Liz knows nothing about it. All this drama surrounding Phyllis Bentley is the only thing anyone can talk about at Mariners Cove, and it's had a huge impact on her. Liz believes it was her who Phyllis was trying to kill, and she now feels compelled to spend most of her time at Misty Headland.'

'How can she afford to do that?'

'We divide the week's work between us. It's a short-term arrangement but suits us both and gives me the chance to get away for a change.'

Gary picked up a knife from the side plate and buttered a bread roll. 'The one good thing to come out of all this is that the two of us have been able to meet. But, getting back to the Bentley woman, is it true that she was suffering a bipolar episode?'

'According to her lawyer, she didn't take her medication for several weeks prior to the attack, so I think it's likely they'll go easy on her when handing down the sentence. You know the sort of thing … she was not in control of her thoughts or responsible for her actions.'

In between taking bites of his bread roll, the conversation was interrupted by the waiter. Once Gary had placed the order he responded to Tilt's earlier comment. 'We all get pushed to the edge at times. I can vouch for that and understand why in a moment of madness Phyllis might have wanted to kill Liz. Because for one crazy moment on the night I asked Liz to marry me, I felt I could have strangled her myself.'

Shocked, Tilt said, 'Darling, I can't believe you just said that. Whatever went wrong between the two of you?'

Tilt noticed Gary's hand grow unsteady as he took a swig of wine and then gazed thoughtfully into the glass. 'I'm fooling no one, Eileen. You don't need to be too smart to work that out,' he said, before draining the rest of his drink. 'When Liz got all fired up at our last meeting, it was a real kick in the guts, I can tell you. And the way I was feeling, I would've been carried off the ground on a stretcher had I been playing footy.'

'Really!' Eileen said in surprise. 'You do look a little thinner in the face. But I took you for a guy who'd be in complete control of your destiny.'

'Not where Liz is concerned,' Gary sighed. 'I found it impossible to cope with the reality of losing her.'

'When we met at the bookshop you struck me as a confident guy with a great personality, good looks, a bucketload of charm and a job that sees you travelling the world. So, it's hard to imagine that life could get the better of you.'

'That's a glowing report, Eileen, but one that's obviously not shared by Liz.'

Tilt, now tucking into the meal placed down before her, wondered if she should back off and allow Gary to enjoy his lunch or continue to pry into the rift between himself and Liz. He did seem as if he wanted to confide in her. So, she decided to pursue the matter. 'Well, I'm yet to learn the full story, of course. But to hear you speak of Liz in such harsh terms does seem kind of tragic in a way.'

A lull came over the conversation as the waiter stepped in to top up the glasses and enquire whether the food was to their liking. Gary nodded and they were left to themselves to pick up where they'd left off.

'You're right, Eileen. Absolutely right. It was all my fault … is that what you'd rather hear?'

Tilt shook her head as the light-hearted mood they had been previously experiencing shifted and the expression on Gary's face had become a whole lot more subdued. 'Forgive me, darling, but when someone talks of strangling the person they love, alarm bells start ringing and my nervous system gets a bit out of whack.'

'Come off it, Eileen. Haven't you ever been guilty of saying you could kill someone?'

'You might be right! I used to think I could strangle my brother whenever that little tattle tale dobbed me in for weeing on Dad's Brussel sprouts.'

'You pissed on your dad's veggie patch?' Gary laughed.

'Well, he was hardly eating them with his roast at the time. But if he had been, I'd be in trouble unless I demolished every disgusting sprout on my plate. Those leaves killed our canary you know.'

'Shouldn't laugh, but I'm never sure what you're going to come out with next.'

Relieved to see Gary's mood swing, 'It's good to hear you laugh,' Tilt said. 'I thought I'd lost you there for a minute.'

'You can't get rid of me that easily … it's your shout remember,' Gary teased. 'And if you've got a bit of time up your sleeve, we should return to the Gardens, and I'll fill you in about the rest of the story.'

Tilt's curiosity was aroused and when Gary later insisted on paying for lunch; he said, 'It'll be your shout next time.'

Was there going to be a next time? she wondered as they returned to find a vacant bench alongside a pretty duck pond.

When they were seated, 'What made you decide to contact me, Eileen?' Gary asked.

'I've been worried about you, darling. Both you and Liz.'

'You're a good person … do you know that? But I don't think there's a chance in hell that Liz will take me back.'

'She'd be mad not to if you ask me,' Tilt replied.

Leaning forward, Gary stared into the water. 'Thanks for the vote of confidence. But the truth is she doesn't trust me and has no idea that I had a secret which started out innocently when my mate Tony became a part owner in a racehorse. I began placing small bets at first and then had a couple of collects. These winnings lured me into increasing the kitty.' Gary paused and tossed a couple of pebbles in the water. 'I got sucked in and started to invest heavily in multiple bets not just in Melbourne but during flight stopovers.'

Tilt remained silent in the hope that Gary would enlarge on what had happened from there.

'When Liz left for Mariners Cove, I took the plunge and placed three thousand dollars on a twenty to one tip. The horse won by a nose. I couldn't wait to rush out and buy her a solitaire diamond engagement ring. It cost a packet I can tell you.'

Tilt placed her hand on his arm. 'Keep going,' she said.

'I was on a high that weekend we met at the bookshop. Little knowing that high was about to turn to an all-time low. You see, Eileen, I couldn't believe the look on Liz's face when she opened that fancy box and sat there in that classy restaurant saying nothing. It might as well have been a plastic trinket that she'd found inside a Christmas cracker given her reaction.'

Lowering his head into his hands, he rubbed his fingertips up and down his forehead. 'To say I was disappointed would be an understatement. I hated her at that moment. Really hated her. She embarrassed me in front of everyone, and I could feel myself losing control. I wanted to shake her because she'd hurt me so badly.'

'I understand,' Tilt nodded, saying nothing of her own failed marriage.

'I left her sitting there, staggered out into the darkness and took off in the car until I could go no further. Wearing the crumpled clothes that I'd slept in, the next day I went on a binge to a country race meeting.'

Tilt watched as Gary walked to the edge of the pond and stood with his back to her. She knew at that moment she had strong feelings for him and never should have come to Melbourne.

'I blew every cent of what was left of my savings. So, I begged Tony to break into Liz's house and get the ring back in the hope I could retrieve the money.'

'Why didn't you just speak to her about it?'

Thrusting his hands into his pockets, he kicked his toe at a tuft of grass. 'Couldn't face her. Then she found the ring on the day she came to Melbourne. And it was ended.'

Tilt's heart went out to Gary as she stepped over to his side and reached out to touch his hand. 'I'm sorry! I'm so very sorry.'

Tilt's trips to Melbourne were to become more frequent over the coming months and Gary, who she now knew had hit rock bottom after the split with Liz, responded to her belief in him. Willingly, she gave him the support he needed and was there to see him turn the corner and begin the difficult climb back out of the big black hole he'd dug for himself.

Then came an emotional moment. 'Remember when I simply knew you as Tilt, the leaning tower? Well, never did I think we'd become great friends, and you'd play such an important role in my life, dearest Eileen. Thank you!' he said and kissed her on both cheeks.

It took all of Tilt's willpower not to respond with a much more meaningful kiss. But she resisted and secretly held out the hope that one day Gary would, of his own free will, fulfil her wish and indulge her with the love he'd once felt for Liz.

35

Moving On

'Christmas dinner at the pub again, Lenny?' Fred, the local newsagent, quizzed his long- time friend and customer.

'Nope! Other plans this year, mate,' Lenny replied placing a swag of tinsel, fairy lights and colourful baubles on the counter, together with the *Herald Sun*.

'What's going on?' Fred asked. 'Tinsel and fairy lights! You'll be asking me to save you a copy of the *Women's Weekly* next. Not to worry, your secret's safe with me,' Fred winked hoping to prise a bit of saucy information from this confirmed bachelor as to why he was buying all this festive ware.

Lenny moved in a little closer and lowered his voice. 'I'm sure I can count on you, Fred … but wouldn't want anyone in town getting the wrong idea, if you get me drift.'

'Come off it, mate! I'm a wake-up to you after all these years. Anyone I know, is she?' Fred asked with a knowing grin as he tallied up the damage.

'Truth is, I'm having myself a private little celebration of sorts. A bit of seasonal cheer never hurt anyone.' Lenny returned Fred's wink as he collected his change and wished the shopkeeper a happy Christmas before rushing away, impatient to get back and cut down a pine tree.

Fred shouted, 'Merry Christmas, Forrester, and let me know how the party turns out.'

Wanting to surprise Elizabeth, Lenny set about stringing up lights and assembling the tree on his return to the house. He then stood back to admire his handiwork and whistled, "It's beginning to look a lot like Christmas".

This gesture seemed especially important given that Phyllis had gone off the rails and Elizabeth, who was rarely home, had been under a heap of pressure. Prepared to give her space, he felt confident she would return to celebrate this one special day of the year. It was then – perhaps over a takeaway chicken and supermarket plum pudding – that he was planning to make his feelings known.

But Elizabeth never appeared. Lenny knew that Philip Anderson had been released from hospital over a month ago, yet she continued to spend so much time there and never once mentioned she wasn't planning to be home on Christmas Day.

Nursing a heavy heart, Lenny watched and waited. Christmas came and went, and in a sorry state, he finally dismantled the lights and tossed the tree on the garden scrap heap ready for mulching. What a romantic fool he'd been. Time to be on his way. Tempted to leave without a word, he decided to seek satisfaction in telling her when she returned home.

'I'll be movin' on in the morning,' he'd repeatedly rehearsed in a lacklustre couldn't-give-a-damn-kind of voice.

But after thinking things through, Lenny stuck around and worked on the house and garden for months before finally telling Elizabeth that he would be moving on.

Expecting her to beg him to stay, with a look of surprise, she simply replied, 'I'll be sad to see you go, Forrester.'

Really … Is that it? Is that the best she can do? he thought. By God this woman runs hot and cold.

Was Elizabeth just a tease sending him mixed messages of hope one minute and the next he could please himself?

With his presence no longer in great demand, it suddenly seemed that any inconvenience caused due to his absence could so easily be overcome. Also, with the threat of spears being aimed in her direction and multiple break-ins obviously behind her, he had become completely redundant.

The likelihood that David Anderson, not Gary, being the all-important player in Elizabeth's life, was to become blatantly clear when Lenny's hopes were dashed when he recognised the same angry stranger who had exchanged heated words on a long ago visit to Margaret.

Working in a distant corner of the garden, Lenny was not so distant as to be left in any doubt about the familiar way Elizabeth greeted this bloke when he turned up at the house one day. The two embraced and held each other close for far longer than considered neighbourly – the kind of hello that Lenny longed to take place between himself and Elizabeth–but the kind that never occurred.

Confronted with the easy comradery between the two, an inconsolable jealousy engulfed him. An emotion he certainly didn't need in his life. And one that caused a shift inside him when suddenly having gone from a sense of finally belonging to now being no more than a rank outsider.

Lenny's disappointment when seeing Elizabeth cosy up to someone who didn't rate highly in his estimation was more than he could handle. Couldn't she see through his slick, shallow persona? He turned away in disgust, not wanting to think of history repeating itself. Not wanting to recall the raised voices he'd heard between this man and Margaret, knowing it was due to his jealous disapproval about an odd-job man bunking down in the cottage. And what of the claim his brother, Philip, was making about being Margaret's son?

Elizabeth hadn't even thought enough of him to mention her arrangement with Tilt to work alternating shifts so she could spend more time at Misty Headland. Lenny had learnt about the change of shifts by accident when bumping into Tilt on a visit to town. And what started as an overnight stay turned into her practically moving in. Well, she was entitled to make her own decisions. But Lenny was no convenient babysitter called on to keep her safe when it suited.

Yes, it was time alright – way past time to pack his bag. Moving on was what he did best and while he would have liked to be around to support Elizabeth during the upcoming trial, Mariners Cove was the last place he was planning to return. He had outstayed his welcome and been a fool to think Elizabeth needed him.

When it was clear that the brothers could manage without her, only then did Elizabeth realise the full extent of the hole Lenny Forrester's absence left in her heart. Unbeknown to him, she was terribly upset by his departure. She'd hoped he might stay permanently but felt unwilling to speak out, as he seemed so impatient to leave.

Fond as she was of calling him Forrester, in her mind she referred to him as Lenny – dependable and someone she could count on. And suddenly an overwhelming emptiness and sense of despair swept over her no matter how hard she tried to convince herself she was in love with David. She longed to hear Lenny's voice and confide in him. She needed to speak to him urgently as soon as she could manage to get hold of him. Elizabeth was reminded of how Gary had disappeared for days, but Lenny wasn't like Gary. His decision being typical of his unwillingness to be tied down in the one place for too long, Elizabeth thought, without once admitting that her own actions may have contributed to his urgent desire to leave. Slow to blame herself, deep down a guilt existed that she refused to recognise.

So, she turned to David who scooped her up in his arms whenever he saw her, without knowing that she often cried herself to sleep at night thinking about Forrester. But now when they were together, she became restless and aware that while her and David connected on many levels, his admission about his relationship with her aunt had never sat well with her.

Meanwhile, Philip's recovery program seemed nothing short of miraculous, now able to get around without the aid of the wheelchair. His shoulder had healed, and he spent part of his day eagerly drawing up plans and consulting with Elizabeth about the gallery extension.

The days and weeks slipped by with no sign of Forrester. His visits to the Cove ceased. And whenever Elizabeth tried to contact him, his phone just rang out. It was as if he had vanished.

Yet perhaps the biggest surprise had crept up on her without much fanfare. It had to do with Tilt, who, since they'd started working different shifts, had been regularly driving out of town or jumping aboard a train on her days off while insisting that the city lights and a change of scenery might do her good.

'I reckon you've got a lover tucked away somewhere,' Elizabeth had teased.

'Do you really think so, darling?' Tilt responded with an innocent grin.

36

The Sentence

'Will the defendant please rise!'

Phyllis flinched as she heard this clear proclamation resound from the mouth of the judge. Yet never did she imagine these familiar words would be directed at her, of all people. How did she get here? How could she have allowed this to happen?

Sure, she had seen dozens of courtroom dramas on television, but now it was real and now there existed her mug shots and fingerprints on every police record. She was right at centre stage – the actual perpetrator of a crime – at this trial conducted within the historical building of a bluestone courthouse. A place where even the bare timber floorboards, whitewashed walls and vaulted ceiling seemed to close in around her in a cold and calculating manner.

Phyllis recalled shaking uncontrollably when the verdict had been handed down.

'We the jury, find the defendant, Phyllis Jane Bentley, guilty,' decreed the appointed spokesperson and head juror, who really had no idea as to Phyllis's disciplined character. How dare she. *This must be a mistake,* Phyllis thought, because she knew herself to be a good churchgoing and respectable woman. Didn't this woman know how freely she had given of her time to work on the hospital charity board and volunteer to help the sick and needy? Didn't this count for something? A person makes one mistake to then be ostracised and treated so harshly.

But now ashamed and humiliated, she had stolen a quick glance at Graeme Jenkins and was also aware of the presence of Elizabeth and Philip, who, during the hearing, had been summoned to give evidence. Her knees trembled and feeling shaky on her feet, she relied on her barrister to aid her to stand in readiness for Judge Keane to deliver the sentence.

A hush came over the courtroom.

'Phyllis Jane Bentley,' the judge began as he gazed sternly over the top of his half-moon reading glasses. 'You have committed a grave and serious offence that could have resulted in death. However, throughout this trial you have displayed a deep remorse when claiming that at no stage did you willingly foster any malicious intent to harm your employer, Mr Philip Anderson.'

Phyllis remembered in this fleeting moment how Graeme Jenkins had so confidently assured her of his optimism when told that Justice Colin Keane would be presiding over the hearing.

'And in addition,' the judge continued, 'since the accidental death of your husband, you have suffered severe bouts of distressing mental trauma and as a result cannot be held fully responsible for your actions.' He paused. 'While I in no way trivialise the horrendous nature of the attack, I do take these factors into account. Also, given you have no prior convictions, and have been portrayed in the past as an exemplary member of society, I hereby sentence you to eighteen months imprisonment whereby you will undergo weekly counselling sessions and be duly reassessed before your release back into the community.'

Phyllis let out a sob when handcuffed like a common criminal and led out of the courtroom.

A relieved Graeme Jenkins felt the tension in his shoulders relax. Who would have believed he could've pulled this off, he thought. His support for Phyllis after she was denied bail and remanded in custody while awaiting trial had been unwavering, and he quietly raised his eyes and gave thanks that she had fluked Justice Keane. The leniency of the sentence being a far better outcome than he dared hope. And with three months already served, Phyllis had only to grit her teeth and tough it out for fifteen of the months imposed.

Did she appreciate just how fortunate she'd been, he wondered, as he quietly congratulated himself for recommending a close friend and criminal lawyer, Andy Roberts, to represent her. Jenkins recalled how he'd strongly advised Phyllis to alert Roberts that her husband, Jack, had – before his death – been a much respected Worshipful Master in the Freemasons Society.

Roberts then, in turn, briefed the barrister to ensure that Jack's infidelity and tragic death would draw attention to the reason why this important factor had contributed to Phyllis's erratic behaviour.

The barrister had put forward a convincing case when calling a leading mental health physician to testify on behalf of the defendant. His opinion being that when Phyllis neglected to take antidepressant medication prior to the attack, she likely suffered an extreme bipolar disorder episode – the severity of the condition giving cause to create an imbalance in her brain.

It was a long shot, but as luck would have it, Justice Colin Keane – who didn't own up to having known Jack, was also a member of this same society and a likely contender when on the regional circuit to preside over this trial. Of course, he would never have allowed the fact that they were freemasons to influence any decision making when it came to ruling so kindly in favour of the defendant – but then again one may never know for certain.

Jenkins tapped Elizabeth on the shoulder as she and Philip Anderson, who leaned heavily over a walking stick, were leaving at the close of the trial.

Elizabeth, making no secret of her disappointment, lowered her voice to a whisper. 'I find it outrageous, Graeme, that the judge would rule so favourably on the side of Phyllis.'

She then took a moment to introduce Philip.

'We've spoken on the phone a few times, but it's good to meet you in person,' Jenkins said as he held out his hand.

But, with a clumsy movement in reciprocation, Philip almost overbalanced.

Jenkins grabbed him by the arm. 'Careful there, mate. You need to keep a firm grip on that stick I see.'

'Yep, I'm getting a bit too cocky and probably should have an *L* plate on my back. Yet I have Phyllis to thank for being able to leave that wheelchair behind.'

Elizabeth scoffed. 'That's ridiculous, Phil. How could a wound to your shoulder have anything remotely to do with restoring the feeling in your legs?'

'It's a mystery, I know. But if that hadn't happened, I never would have met Doc Beaumont. He's the one I should really be thanking.'

Jenkins cut in. 'Well, whatever the reason, I'm pleased to see you on the mend.' Then directing his next words to Elizabeth, he said, 'In Phyllis's defence, you'd have to agree she wasn't herself when inflicting that injury. People do terrible things when their mind is affected.'

'Stop making excuses for her, Graeme. Eighteen months is absolute bullshit, excuse the language. I can't understand what some of these judges are thinking. Phyllis deserved the law to come down hard on her.'

Philip clearly disagreed and shaking his head he said, 'She looked so frail standing there in court. I kind of felt sorry for her.'

Elizabeth threw her hands in the air. 'Seriously? Phyllis could have killed you, and all you can say is that you felt sorry for her?'

Turning her attention back to Jenkins, she looked to him for even the tiniest ounce of support, but he chose to make no further comment.

'Well, that's just great! The two of you prefer to stick up for the guilty party here, while I'm expected to say, "that's quite okay, Phyllis, all's forgiven. You can throw a spear at me anytime, and I'll totally understand."' Elizabeth looked up at the sky in despair.

37

The Walking Wounded

As Jenkins hurried away, Elizabeth – still stewing over how Phyllis had gotten off so lightly – was not just bewildered by Philip's willingness to side with Graeme, but his remarkable ability to walk again. So, as she helped him into the car and pulled out along the road, her thoughts were focused on this question.

'Philip, I hope you don't mind me asking but tell me what happened exactly when you first noticed something was different about your legs.'

Looking tired, he didn't seem happy. 'Let's not do this right now, Elizabeth. It's been a long day.'

'Please, Philip, you never have told me the full story. Did you have a stroke do you think … is this why you couldn't walk? But why wouldn't they have picked up on it?'

'What's with the sudden need to interrogate me, Elizabeth? Can't you just be happy for me? After all, I'm as much in the dark as you are.'

The grey sky darkened as if to match his words. Rain began to drizzle and trickle down the windscreen. So too the mood inside the car turned a little gloomy. The squeak of the wipers and gush of warm air flowing through the vents when Elizabeth switched on the heating sounded more pronounced due to the stillness of their voices. Surprised by Philip's reaction, Elizabeth broke the silence. 'Gosh, I didn't mean to upset you, Phil, and I can't believe you'd even ask that question about me being happy for you.'

'Well, I'm sorry, Elizabeth. Maybe I sounded a little abrupt. But if you were in my position, you might be a little short yourself. All I know is, Beaumont patched me up well and I had faith in him, especially when feeling a tingling sensation in my right leg. He took an immediate interest and threw back the covers right then and there to examine me.'

'You never said a thing about that before.'

'I didn't want to raise any false hopes. But Beaumont brought in a specialist to investigate and although he couldn't be certain, he suggested it would be well worth undergoing an intensive physical rehabilitation program.'

Gazing straight ahead, Philip looked to be concentrating on the road. 'I can hear your mind ticking over, Elizabeth. What more do you need to know?'

'I'm just interested, that's all,' Elizabeth replied but was thinking that even the doctors seemed baffled when claiming his earlier diagnosis had been inconclusive and he'd suffered a temporary form of paralysis, likely due to an abnormality in his brain brought about by a head injury.

'The only other thing I can tell you,' Philip said, 'is, according to my medical records, I suffered certain trauma and damage to my spine. Nothing was mentioned about a knock to the head.'

Confused, Elizabeth chewed this information over in her mind as Philip emphasised that the specialist advised there were no guarantees he would walk again.

It had taken months of treatment. But Elizabeth couldn't help recalling Tom Moody's words about having seen Philip out walking at a time when he was supposedly bound to the wheelchair. Why would he say that if it wasn't true?

David seemed to think the man quite crazy, and she had taken his word on the matter. Yet this nagging suspicion took hold of her. What if Philip was able to walk all along? But what possible motive would he have had to pretend otherwise? This whole assertion seemed ridiculous. Unless to prey on Margaret's sympathy. Yet even this sounded extreme.

Any possible reason to doubt him appeared to be more of a failing on her own part.

'I've never mentioned this, Philip, but there's an elderly farmer who lives down the road from you. I met him that day Phyllis attacked you.'

'Yeah, I know who you mean. Silly old bugger that bloke Moody.'

'Well, that's what David said. But I lost control of the car that morning and he came to my rescue.'

'Good God! You weren't hurt, were you?'

'A bit shaken that's all. Suppose my pride was hurt more than anything else. Maybe Moody was having a lucid moment because he appeared to know exactly what he was doing. We later got talking and he made a comment about having seen you out walking.'

Philip scoffed and reacted as though this remark was not worthy of an answer. 'Then to top it all off the day really went downhill from there.'

Elizabeth agreed and waited in the hope that Philip might address Moody's claim. But he made no further mention of the matter as they pulled into the driveway, and he unbuckled his seatbelt.

By this stage, the rain was bucketing down, and the ocean was a white out.

'Let's wait until this storm passes,' Elizabeth suggested. 'It's dangerous underfoot and I'm afraid you might slip over.'

Philip nodded and the conversation turned to Phyllis. The two again discussed how Justice Keane seemed to ignore the harsh reality of her irrational behaviour, having almost gone out of his way to make certain she would not suffer one minute longer than necessary.

'Well, I'm glad it's over,' Philip sighed.

'Me too!' Elizabeth replied and noting a lull in the wet weather made a move to hop out of the car.

Philip placed his hand on her arm. 'Before we go, I wasn't planning on giving that interfering old geezer Moody any air space, but instead of making outrageous assumptions, first up he should take some time out to get his eyes checked.' Philip paused. 'And, if you bump into him again, you can tell him I said so.'

Elizabeth's thoughts on the matter were that both David and Philip seemed a bit hard on the poor guy. After all, they might be old themselves one day and she felt certain he had meant no harm.

38

A Ghostly Encounter

Now that the excitement had died down and that old nark, Phyllis Bentley, was safely locked away, Senior Sergeant Ian Henderson stood in the darkness at the foot of Margaret Thornton's grave.

Weary of his lazy, overweight wife Maxine, who had failed to produce any children and always had a drink and cigarette in her hand, he had slammed the door behind him and walked away in anger.

Somewhere a clock struck twelve and the witching hours were upon him.

Bitterly cold, his teeth chattered. His legs felt like lead. Freshly turned soil caked the soles of his boots as he squelched in the mud underfoot. Turning up the collar of his jacket, he shoved his frozen hands deep inside his pockets and flinched at the sound of a howling dog.

The cemetery appeared to be filled with ghostly spectres. A thick fog rolled in off the ocean. The misty white veil curled around his ankles and slowly rose to cloak the headstones. The hound kept wailing in the distance and the senior sergeant thought it would take more than this eerie atmosphere to scare him.

Yet as he stood there in his aloneness, a sudden phantom-like formation began to take shape in his fuddled mind. He reeled back in fear as it appeared to float up from beyond the surface of the grave and manifest itself into a shimmering figure of a woman. Or was it the devil?

Shielding his face in fright, the senior sergeant's earlier sense of bravado vanished.

The apparition enshrouded him. Henderson felt trapped. He clutched his throat and gasping for air, he struggled to breathe. Choking, his face reddened, and in a frantic bid to escape this deadly wraith, he fell to the ground believing his fate to be doomed.

Reaching inside his coat for his whisky flask, he took a generous swig. The burning liquid warmed and calmed him. The deathly wraith quickly dissipated, and the vital necessity of life again started to flow. In relief, he laughed to think his mind had been playing tricks on him. Or maybe he'd had a panic attack. After all, Margaret Thornton could no longer hurt him. Now no more than an empty shell, she lay stiff, lifeless and decomposing beneath the earth. Yes, his eyes had deceived him. It was only the fog.

Slumped against the grave his thoughts turned to a time in his youth when he had relentlessly pursued her. Rejection had caused him to grow bitter. And since recently spotting that snooty niece of hers with Mr Pretty Boy from the city, nothing would have given him more pleasure than to see Elizabeth O'Connell fall flat on her face. She needed to come a cropper that one.

'Remember when I first asked you out, Marg?' he said. 'With your looks, you were the envy of every girl in the Cove and had a teasing way of flicking y'hair back out of your eyes and pointing your nose in the air. "Forget it Henderson", you'd say.

'Attitude! Yeah, you had plenty of attitude alright. Didn't give a toss when I said you'd be begging me to take you out once I joined the force. It's too late now!' he cried.

Drowning his sorrows in the last of his whisky, Ian Henderson welcomed the silence. The hound had stopped wailing. Muttering a curse to himself, he staggered to his feet, kicked a clump of mud up against the gravesite and quickly disappeared into the thick blanket of fog, leaving behind nothing more than a track of heavy footprints.

39

How Time Flies

The months had slipped by in a heartbeat following Phyllis's confinement in prison and life had long returned to normal at the bookshop. Almost a year and a half, Elizabeth thought, as she navigated the scenic route towards the Cove. It was hard to believe.

Matters of the heart had also seen her prolong her relationship with David Anderson. And in her moments of need, she'd put aside any doubts and allowed him to take complete possession of her in the privacy of the bedroom. Yet her confusion persisted as she continued to crave the company of Lenny Forrester and wondered if he would ever return.

Reaching the main street, she pulled into a carpark and looked forward to a much overdue lunch with Tilt to hopefully take her mind off the matters that had plagued her along the way.

Quick to exchange hellos and place their order, Elizabeth and Tilt settled back to discuss the latest gossip that somehow managed to lead into the topic she had promised herself to avoid. 'Do you realise, Tilt, that Phyllis is due to be released shortly?'

'No! Where has that time gone, for God's sake?'

'Exactly!'

'Don't worry, darling! I suspect that senior sergeant what's his name, will keep an eye on her.'

'Please don't wish that on me,' Elizabeth shuddered. 'That guy's an absolute joke – a smug opinionated excuse for a man. How he ever rose to the rank of senior sergeant is beyond me.'

Tilt raised an eyebrow.

'Sorry, Tilt, I know you're only trying to be helpful. But that suggestion brings me small comfort.'

'You've made your dislike of that guy clear on more than one occasion. I should have thought of that before opening my big mouth,' Tilt replied. 'It's obvious he carries a gigantic chip on his shoulder.'

'More like a boulder if I'm any judge.'

'You crack me up sometimes, Liz,' Tilt chuckled as she sank her fork into a slice of carrot cake and moved on from the senior sergeant. 'What's happening with the gallery? It seems like an eternity since you organised to have the plans drawn up.'

'I've put them on hold.'

'Why would you do that?'

Elizabeth sighed. 'There's been opposition to the idea. One guess who the troublemaker is. Mr Big Shot himself, of course.'

'Geez, it's a bit like we can't talk about anything without the senior sergeant's name popping up. He's got a finger in every pie it seems.'

'Including local council,' Elizabeth sighed. 'I heard on the grapevine he's raised an objection to the proposal before I've even lodged the plans.'

'All the more reason to get on with it, Liz. He's just one lone voice in all of this.'

Leaning forward in her chair, Elizabeth pushed her cup aside and rested an elbow on the table. 'That's not the only problem. I've got cold feet about the extension.'

'I didn't know that.'

'Don't get me wrong. Between the two of us, we're keeping our head above water as far as sales are concerned. It's just that I'll need to sell the house.'

'That's difficult, I understand. But no matter what you decide, council approval can take months, so I wouldn't delay getting the plan out there. Then you'll at least set the wheels in motion and know where you stand.'

Aware of how keen Tilt felt about the project, Elizabeth weighed up the risk. 'I'll think about it,' she said. 'But tell me, what's been going on with you, Tilt? All this tripping off to the city has got me intrigued.'

As always, Tilt shrugged the matter off. 'It's nothing really!'

'Aw, come on now, Tilt, it's me you're talking to. I'll never forgive you if you've got some guy stashed away in Melbourne and haven't bothered to tell me. Who is this mystery man?'

'You've had your head inside too many of those mushy books, darling. Just thought a change of scenery and a bit of retail therapy might do me good, that's all.'

Aware there was something Tilt was holding back, Elizabeth said, 'Hope you haven't got plans to bail out on me. This is your project as much as mine you know. And I don't want to go ahead if you're not serious about sticking around.'

Tilt laughed. 'No need to worry about that. I know when I'm on a good wicket and I'm not going anywhere.' She then paused before raising the matter of Elizabeth's current situation. 'Speaking of which, where's that Kit Kat man of yours? And what's with you and that Anderson guy? This must mean it's completely over with Gary?'

Elizabeth's shoulders slumped and she clucked her tongue.

'Wow … is it that bad?' Tilt asked.

'I'm in a bit of a bind, if you must know, Tilt. I know you're not fond of David. We just kind of got thrown together because of the Phyllis affair. It's nothing serious.'

'You don't sound too convincing. Does he feel the same?'

'I can't answer that question. But I can tell you there never has been anything of a romantic nature going on between Forrester and me. So, this situation with David kind of crept up on me and developed a life of its own. As for Gary, well, I think I'll always have feelings for him.'

Tilt looked uneasy and tucked a hair behind her ear. 'It's none of my business, but you do sound half-hearted. I think Lenny Forrester was really hoping the two of you might get together.'

'What gave you that idea?'

'I've got eyes, darling. And if you really want to know, he came into the shop once to more-or-less suss out whether he might have a chance with you.'

'That's news to me, Tilt. Why didn't you ever mention this?'

'Sorry, Liz. I didn't think it important once seeing you so caught up in life at Misty Headland.' Tilt's expression changed however at the sound of raised voices amid a commotion outside the café.

40

A Twist of Fate

'What's going on?' Elizabeth asked.

Jovial George, the delivery man from the post office, raced into the deli waving his arms in panic. 'Come quick!' he shouted. The look on his face and fear in his words being enough to generate alarm among the customers and staff.

'A bomb!' someone cried. 'Let's get out of here,' came the voice of another.

A bomb in Mariners Cove. *Not likely*, Elizabeth thought.

In their haste to vacate the premises, a frantic scramble broke out. Chairs scraped against the hard wooden boards and were haphazardly shoved to the floor, left upturned, adding to the sudden chaos and confusion. So – without knowing what the excitement was about – Elizabeth and Tilt rushed from the table, slipping dangerously on spilt drinks and abandoned food scraps.

People gathered in a huddle outdoors and fighting their way through the crowd, Elizabeth asked, 'Has there been an accident?' just as a blast of sirens sounded in the distance.

The traffic pulled off to the side of the road and came to a standstill. Beachgoers lined the grassy foreshore and shopkeepers drifted out into the street. The deafening noise drawing closer reached a high pitch as fire engines screamed by in a flash. The sky darkened, and an irritating smell of acrid smoke curled its way up inside Elizabeth's nose and caught at the back of her throat.

Tilt grabbed Elizabeth's hand and the two ran as fast as they could to keep up with George who was last seen dashing away in the direction of the bookstore.

'Oh no! Flames, I can see flames! It's not the bookshop is it, Tilt? Please God don't let it be the bookshop.'

George looked back over his shoulder and called, 'Hurry!'

The church came into view and Elizabeth's fears were realised. Shouting and noise gripped the busy scene. Firefighters aimed their powerful hoses towards the former altar area at the rear of the building where water gushed directly into the burning wreckage.

'Oh my God, the books will be ruined.' Elizabeth charged past Senior Sergeant Henderson and Constable Madden who were doing their best to redirect the traffic and control the swelling crowd.

Stumbling through the back laneway Elizabeth mentally took stock of what she needed to save. A fallen gum tree had smashed its way through a section of the roof. Flames licked up the gaping hole and a sea of rubble along with cracked stonework lay strewn around a collapsed wall.

The heat became unbearable. Yet Elizabeth shielded her face and stormed the vestry door determined to kick her way through. Scorched embers rained down on her and a man in a helmet cried, 'Hey, lady, get back, get back!'

A fiery rafter came crashing from above. 'Look out!' he warned, taking a giant leap towards her.

Inhaling an enormous intake of smoke, Elizabeth couldn't stop coughing as he pulled her aside to safety. Singed hair fizzled, and her none too happy rescuer patted her head with his gloves. Removing his jacket, he smothered the lit particles on her clothing, and seeming relieved when he spotted Tilt, he shouted. 'Please help this lady out of here.'

Joe Gresham, the local hardware store owner and regular customer at the bookshop, raced across to where Elizabeth and Tilt joined the onlookers congregated at the end of the side street. 'Don't worry!' he said. 'Those guys know what they're doing and will soon bring the fire under control. You're lucky you weren't inside.'

Equipped with a camping chair under each arm he thoughtfully offered them a place to sit and handed them bottled water that he pulled from his trouser pocket. 'George will be along in a minute with tea.'

'Oi! What do you think you're doing there, Joe?' Constable Madden demanded. 'This is no place for a picnic unless you're planning a spit roast. Be on your way and the rest of you lot move on as well.'

'Sorry,' Joe replied. 'Come on, ladies, let's wait in my office.'

George appeared carrying a paper cup in each hand. 'Good man!' Joe said slapping him on the back. 'You're a hero, mate! Because of your quick thinking, the damage has been confined to one end of the church.'

Looking pleased with himself, 'It was nothin' really,' George said. 'I was making a delivery when I heard this almighty crack, and down she came,' he whistled. 'The earth shook under me feet 'n' I thought the ground was gunna give way as the roof caved in and somethin' exploded. Stuff went flyin' everywhere. Then seein' the flames spark up from outta nowhere, I whipped out me phone t'report what happened.'

'Thanks, George,' Elizabeth said, lifting the lid off her tea but secretly thinking a cold beer would have gone down so much better.

'No worries, luv! The folks 'round 'ere 'll chip in t'give a hand, 'n' Joe can lend a tarp t'keep the weather out.'

Even Tilt felt compelled to shake the delivery man's hand.

George tipped his cap as Joe led the way up a metal staircase to his office tucked in under the iron sheeting above the hardware store.

'What now, Tilt?' Elizabeth asked when Joe disappeared out through the door.

'Look at it this way, Liz. That damage has been done right where the gallery is to be added. So, by the time these guys get through, it will be a smouldering mess and all the less for the builders to dismantle. The good news being that Thorny had the church insured and I reckon this whole nasty business might well work in our favour.'

'You're not serious, are you?'

'Yes, I'm deadly serious, darling.'

Elizabeth's face brightened as they drew closer to the window and continued to watch the drama play out.

41

The Aftermath

Once the fire was brought under control, Elizabeth turned from the window to see a weary Constable Madden step through the doorway of Joe's office and remove her hat.

'Wanted to let you ladies know the senior sergeant asked me to keep a constant surveillance on the church overnight.'

Madden picked up a ragged towel hanging over a wash basin and wiped her brow. 'Sorry to say, even though the flames didn't destroy the entire building, most of the books that haven't been incinerated are either buckled or waterlogged. The internal fittings will need replacing as well. Oh … and not forgetting the roof, of course.'

'Don't mean to sound disrespectful, Constable, but a whole lot more than the fittings and roof will need replacing. As for the books, that was to be expected. You really should go home and rest,' Elizabeth replied.

'Can't leave the place unattended. Could still be things of value in the church,' Madden said.

'Have you heard what caused the fire?' Tilt asked.

'A power line seems the obvious answer. It's unlikely there's any foul play involved. Arson is not something we might expect in this town. Firelighters have more chance of going unseen in the bush. Meanwhile, the senior sergeant and I will inspect the scene to rule out any doubt.'

Moving from one foot to the other and nervously fingering her hat, Madden stammered, 'Sorry about all this, Elizabeth. A crying shame, really. Kind of got used to seeing you around and hope you'll be able to rebuild, as does everyone at the Cove.'

Elizabeth stepped forward and placed a hand on Madden's arm to thank her. 'That's kind of you to say.'

Madden, keeping a stiff upper lip, placed her hand over Elizabeths and added, 'I'm sure you'll come through this, and it might be an idea to tee up an insurance assessor first thing in the morning.' She then turned to leave and paused to say, 'If there's anything else I can do, don't hesitate to ask.'

'Well, that's a bit of a turn up wouldn't you say, Liz?' Tilt remarked once Madden had gone on her way. 'People are batting for you, including Jovial George along with Madden who seems a bit of a softie at heart. But I'm thinking we'd better get out of here and leave Joe to his office.'

'Yes, Madden did seem quite touched about the sorry state of the church. And yes. You're right again, I've had enough excitement for one day.'

'Come on, kiddo. I'll take you home and rustle up some food. Then you can rest at my place, and we'll worry about this tomorrow.'

Hoping not to disturb Tilt, early the following morning Elizabeth pulled on her clothes and crept out through the kitchen.

She passed Madden's van and suspecting she was asleep, quietly picked her way through the smouldering debris. Relieved to see the greater section of the outer building remained intact, she followed the strewn path leading to the main entry door.

Inside Elizabeth gazed at the charred remains, then sifted through the ashes to discover certain books lay blackened or badly damaged. With little reason why certain novels had survived, she felt overjoyed to pull from an untouched shelf housed near the choir loft, the little volume she had discovered on the floor when she first arrived – the long forgotten *Legacy of St. Thomas*. As if old friends, she fondled it lovingly and clutched the book to her breast.

Continuing to navigate her way through unrecognisable bits and pieces, she walked a short distance along what had once represented the central aisle for a closer look at where the focal point of the disaster had occurred. Skeletal remnants of the tree trunk hung precariously suspended from the jagged surrounds of the open rooftop where it appeared no longer safe to walk and had in fact been taped off.

Elizabeth placed the precious account attributed to St Thomas aside and pulled her mobile from her pocket.

'You have reached Philip Anderson. I'm unable to take your call right now … Elizabeth,' Philip intercepted the recording and spoke in a groggy voice. 'Is everything okay? What time is it?'

'Don't tell me you haven't heard?'

'Heard what? Where are you?'

Fighting back tears, she swallowed and could barely speak – her mind brimming with the reality of it all. She'd lost everything – her parents, her aunt, Gary, Forrester, the books, the church, her job at the publishing house and life as she'd known it. In desperation she had called a man who claimed to be her cousin and the architect of her vision for the future that now involved a burnt-out bookstore. Philip's voice was not the one she longed to hear. It wasn't David's either. What alternative did she have?

'Philip, I need your help. I'm at … at what's left of the bookstore.'

'I don't understand.'

'A tree fell on the church along with a power line it would seem, and … well … don't ask! I just need you to come and see for yourself.'

'Don't move a muscle. I'll be there before you know it.'

Huddled on the edge of the gutter, Elizabeth watched as his car zoomed around the corner and into the street. Brakes squealed when coming to a halt. The door flung open and true to his word he had arrived in record time. His first words, 'What the hell …'

Hair uncombed, the legs and sleeves of his pyjamas sticking out under tracksuit pants and a lightweight hoodie, it was obvious he'd dressed in a hurry. His face filled with an expression of disbelief. He stood back for a moment and clasped his hands together on top of his head. He then turned a full circle in the middle of the road after which he somehow managed to ease himself down alongside Elizabeth. She thought this no mean feat for a man once unable to walk. Shaking his head, he reached for her hand. She leaned against his shoulder and for the first time was glad she had a cousin.

'We can fix this, Elizabeth. It might take a while, but we can fix this. I can promise you that.'

'It'll cost the earth.'

'Don't worry. The important thing to remember is we can fix this.'

Elizabeth spotted Madden coming towards them.

'Would you mind helping us up please, Officer?' Philip asked.

Offering a hand to each, Madden said, 'See any smoke in your vicinity yesterday, Mr Anderson?'

'None at all. I had a shocking migraine and spent the afternoon tucked up in bed with the blinds down.'

'And your brother?'

'He's away, unfortunately.'

'Well, I'm surprised you didn't smell the smoke even if you were in bed. Otherwise, you would have been here … right?' Madden wasn't letting Philip off the hook.

'There's no way I would have left Elizabeth to cope with this on her own.'

'Glad to hear it. But just one other thing, Mr Anderson. She wasn't on her own!'

Aware of an awkward silence, Elizabeth looked from one to the other and said, 'Don't know about anyone else, but I'm in serious need of a coffee. Can I get you one, Constable Madden?'

<h1 style="text-align:center">42</h1>

Doing Time – Claremont Prison

Serving the final week of an eighteen month prison sentence, Phyllis Bentley spent her days preparing and dishing up meals in a women's low security correctional facility. Keeping her distance from anyone who might want to pick a fight, she now sat in silence at a stark table in the common room and looked all around to make certain the Snatcher was nowhere to be seen.

Valerie Thatcher, a low life, better known as the "Snatcher", preyed on the weak and grabbed anything that wasn't nailed down. Petty theft, the law called it, and somehow this bullying inmate had managed to escape the hardship of being locked away in a maximum security prison where Phyllis believed the woman truly belonged.

From day one, the Snatcher had singled Phyllis out as a person of particular interest and seemed hellbent on making life a misery for her. Following numerous nasty run-ins, she had purposely bumped Phyllis when carrying a large pot of boiling soup.

'Oops,' the Snatcher said, as the liquid splashed down Phyllis's arm, scalding her so badly that she was rushed to the infirmary and confined for several days.

Now, well over a year later, being satisfied that no one apart from Simmonds the guard – who drifted in and out – was watching, Phyllis withdrew an envelope from beneath her clothing. For the umpteenth time she scanned the handwritten address before slowly turning it over to study the name of the sender. A cold draught skirted around the grey sterile walls surrounding her and the soulless room seemed almost as barren as her heart.

Lifting the flap, she pulled out a single sheet of paper and laid it flat in front of her.

Able to recite every word by heart, Phyllis preferred to read the letter each day as it filled her with hope and held her ticket back to a life that had been suddenly snatched away.

Phyllis,

I have recently spoken with Graeme Jenkins who has passed on your message of genuine concern, regret and heartfelt sorrow for your actions. I understand and respect the leniency of the court ruling when handing down your sentence and consider the unfortunate incident brought about by circumstances beyond your control deeply affected your state of mind and ultimately led you to perform a violent act of aggression. An act that I, along with your friend, Graeme, believe would have otherwise been abhorrent to you and completely out of character.

There's no denying you made a grave mistake, but in times of adversity everyone is worthy of a second chance. So, as you continue with an ongoing program to rehabilitate your health with the aid of the prison counsellor, once you have had a chance to get settled following your release, I would like to reinstate your services as housekeeper at Misty Headland.

Please do not look on this offer as an act of charity, but rather one of forgiveness and faith in a lady who has undergone countless personal hardships. Should you choose to return, I am confident you will prove my decision the right one.

Philip Anderson.

Even after all these months, Phyllis was still in a state of disbelief since having almost killed her employer who she would never have intentionally harmed. Each day she prayed for his survival and felt profoundly moved by his willingness to forgive her. She vowed to never let him down again and faithfully serve him for the rest of her days as his grand gesture was a true mark of a man she had always admired and strived to protect.

Carefully she refolded the sheet and inserted it back into the envelope.

'What's that y'got? Give it 'ere,' the Snatcher demanded, grabbing the envelope from Phyllis's hand.

Noticing Simmonds was never around when needed, Phyllis reached out to retrieve the letter as the Snatcher took delight in taunting her while dancing and dodging from side-to-side.

'Give that back,' Phyllis pleaded.

'Say, *pretty please!* And if you're extra nice, I might consider returning it. But then again, I might just tear it up right now,' the Snatcher smirked while ripping the envelope into dozens of little pieces and scattering them on the floor like confetti.

Phyllis grew angry when the Snatcher – in a show of satisfaction at having rid herself of something she considered of little worth – defiantly wiped her hands together as if to say a job well done.

Normally meek and mild mannered around any of the bossier inmates, Phyllis surprised herself and did something she'd been itching to do ever since her badly scarred arm had been unbandaged. She eyeballed the Snatcher, walked to within an inch of her nose, shoved her in the ribs and smacked her squarely on the jaw.

Clutching her chin, the Snatcher reeled back and slumped to the floor with a look of utter dismay. Phyllis slapped her hands together mimicking a job well done.

Never hearing another word out of the Snatcher until the day when Phyllis packed her few belongings, Valerie Thatcher sidled up to her and with an expression of renewed respect handed her a small and rather tatty cardboard box tied with string.

Once safely outside the gate and breathing the air in a land of the free that would never again be taken for granted, expecting the box might hold a dead rat, Phyllis gingerly lifted the lid. Inside she discovered – like the pieces of a jigsaw puzzle – every remnant of Philip's letter tediously glued back together.

Unless having seen this with her own eyes, Phyllis would never have believed the Snatcher capable of performing such a humane act. Was it possible they had both grown into better people due to their time spent at Claremont Prison?

Being more than content and forever left to wonder, Phyllis could vouch for herself, of course, but wasn't about to stick around to find out about the Snatcher who was probably already in the throes of sussing out her latest victim.

43

Constant Surveillance

Fire. Fire, sent to fry her … Elizabeth woke from an alarming flame-coloured dream filled with visions of devils and pitchforks. She'd forgotten to turn the electric blanket off – her body was roasting and covered in sweat.

Now familiar with Tilt's spare bedroom, she turned off the switch, threw the doona aside and rolled onto her back to stare at the ceiling. Even in the half-light she could define a patchy area where the paintwork was peeling, possibly due to the heat that had risen straight from the bowels of her hellish nightmare. However, the main thought that popped into her mind had little bearing on the state of the ceiling.

Elizabeth knew something wasn't right. It had nothing whatsoever to do with the fire, but everything to do with the questions that had plagued her since returning to Mariners Cove. The more she dwelt on the subject, the more inclined she was to connect this disturbing feeling with the infuriating behaviour of the senior sergeant.

She sprang from the bed, rushed to the window and lifted the edge of the blind away from the framework. Sure enough, there he was parked outside the house next door in an unmarked police car. Appearing to have a coffee in hand and munching on a muffin, he looked in her direction and had the audacity to wave.

As if zapped by a stun gun, Elizabeth leapt back out of sight. 'Far out!' she said. 'That idiot's doing my head in.'

The cold contrast of the bathroom tiles caused her to shiver as she then stepped into the shower, turned the taps on and tried to push her anger aside to instead concentrate on the overwhelming support shown by the local community. Not only did the business owners volunteer to get their hands dirty and remove the excess rubble – they also chipped in to fund the erection of a high cyclone fence to hopefully deter souvenir hunters and vagrants from entering the premises.

Grateful to see so many willing hands rally around with the promise of raising further funds to help restore the church, even this positive response could not shake the feeling that something of a sinister nature was bubbling to the surface and about to explode. It was not Phyllis she needed to fear, but more so the unwanted attention of Senior Sergeant Henderson who saw himself the heroic leader through all of this.

He openly boasted his frequent visits were a necessary consequence of the disaster and his detailed investigation had put an end to any suggestion of human intervention. 'There's no need to thank me,' he'd said. 'But what I can say is this information has directly influenced the insurance assessor's recommendation and will result in a generous payout in compensation.'

Elizabeth believed this an exaggerated distortion of the truth when seeing the company representative devote the greater part of an afternoon on site to make an independent report of his own findings.

Unwilling to let the matter rest, the senior sergeant had then appointed himself Elizabeth's personal bodyguard. 'Don't want to alarm you, Elizabeth, but there's a need for vigilance following Phyllis's release from prison and I'm fully intending to keep a watch on the situation.'

'That really isn't necessary,' she insisted.

'Morning, Liz … sleep well?' Tilt asked when Elizabeth entered the kitchen.

Sitting on a stool at the island bar, she tipped cereal into a bowl and said, 'Don't ask. Would you believe he's out there right now as we speak? Why this incessant obsession to follow me?'

'Got the hots for you I reckon, darling. And I don't think it's at all healthy. Let's see what today brings and if this harassment continues, I'm going to have a quiet word in Constable Madden's ear.'

'Not sure I can put up with this for another day, Tilt. I've had a gutful and am close to marching out there and telling him to go take a hike.'

Gulping down her breakfast, Elizabeth rinsed the bowl before packing it into the dishwasher. 'Wish me luck,' she said, as the door slammed behind her, and she made her way across the damp grass to knock on the car window.

Henderson lowered it midway. 'Elizabeth … you're up!' he said.

'Senior Sergeant Henderson, the time I get up of a morning is really none of your business. I find your behaviour a direct violation of my privacy and want you to leave.'

Unblinking, Henderson stared straight ahead and only when Elizabeth hurried away, did he lower the window right down and shout, 'Please yourself of course. But at the first sign of trouble, it'll be me you'll come running to.'

Not a chance in hell, she thought.

The weeks slipped by following Phyllis's release, and it seemed she had since laid low and kept to herself. This fact was lost on the senior sergeant however, who still appeared to have little else to do apart from keeping track of Elizabeth, who on this occasion had somehow managed to outsmart him.

Enjoying lunch with the Andersons, she discussed the proposed plan for the rebuilding of the church. All was well until Philip mentioned over coffee that Phyllis was due to start back in her former position as housekeeper.

Elizabeth jumped in fright when David angrily thumped his fist down on the polished surface of the table and the crockery clattered. 'What in the devil were you thinking, inviting that woman back into our house, Phil? You know how strongly I feel about this. Sometimes I wonder if you've completely lost it.'

'Settle down, Dave. There's no need to raise your voice. You know better than most how depression can affect a person, and I'm sure Phyllis has changed since serving her time in prison.'

'It's you who has changed! Did you ever stop to think how Elizabeth might feel when knowing it was her who Phyllis wanted dead?'

Philip looked at Elizabeth, and said, 'Well no, I didn't.'

'For God's sake, say something, Liz,' David said.

'It's not really for me to be telling either one of you what to do.'

With a look of disappointment, David frowned. 'Come on now, back me up. You must have something to say about Phyllis working here again.'

'This is not my house, David. But I am surprised about your decision, Philip. Then again, good on you for doing her a great kindness.'

Saying nothing, Philip – who appeared slightly embarrassed by this remark – shifted uncomfortably in his chair.

'So, is that a yes or a no, Liz?' David asked.

'Neither I suppose. Yet, while I'm not so willing to forgive, before the hearing, Graeme Jenkins opened my eyes to certain disturbing matters that were later raised in court. He's also since told me that Phyllis is keen to make amends.'

'I'll bet she is!' David chipped in. 'She'll be shunned by everyone at the Cove.'

'That's something she'll have to contend with,' Elizabeth replied. 'But I do know she thinks highly of you both and, from all reports, seems sorry for the suffering she caused. So … and I never thought I would say this, I'm willing to stick my neck out and trust in Jenkin's judgment. Because if the locals see you are prepared to trust her, they may be happy to do the same.'

David jumped to his feet and paced back and forth shaking his head. 'The two of you have gone completely off the rails. I can't believe what I'm hearing.' He stopped and gazed from one to the other. 'How could you even consider letting this woman back in the same room as you? I just don't get it!'

'Maybe you're right and we're wrong, David. But you asked my opinion, and suddenly I have talked myself into believing Phyllis deserves a second chance.'

Phyllis's return, of course, not only caused an argument between the brothers, but also prompted the senior sergeant to now step up the vigilant regularity of dropping by Elizabeth's house under the pretext of checking up on her safety while bailing her up at the door. He repeatedly made no secret of the fact that he was unhappy about the leniency of the sentence, while suggesting Phyllis must have had friends in high places to have pulled this off.

Elizabeth, trying to convince him she was busy, could never get the message across. He just kept talking, she knew, in the hope that he could get a foot in the door.

'That woman's completely unstable,' he insisted, 'and I can't understand why she's walking the streets or employed in the house of the man she almost killed. Who knows what mischief she might get up to.'

'What do you mean by that?' Elizabeth asked.

'Well, it wouldn't at all surprise me if she did away with your aunt.'

'What! You have certainly changed your tune since I read that report,' Elizabeth replied.

'Yeah … but it's now common knowledge that your aunt and Phyllis's husband, Jack, were getting up to a bit of no good on the side, I'm beginning to wonder if she could have done away with 'em both. It's easy to tinker with a tractor you know.'

'That's outrageous!'

'Too right it is. But you've seen what she's capable of. I wouldn't trust a woman like her as far as I could throw 'er, and reckon them two brothers may not be so lucky next time round. But I'll be looking out for you, so there's no need to worry.'

Elizabeth hated to agree on anything that came out of Henderson's mouth. And as Phyllis was already fulfilling her promise to have changed her ways, this would have meant she was either a good liar or as guilty as the senior sergeant was making her out to be. But none of this helped when trying to rid herself of this nuisance who had appointed himself her personal protector. She could no longer stand the sight of him and decided to make it very clear. 'Stop harassing me. Stop coming to the house. I'm in no danger … go away and leave me alone.'

'Allow me to be the judge of that, my girl,' he said, determined to needle his way into her good books.

Then it happened – the evening when Henderson decided to visit after dark.

44

The Senior Sergeant

Elizabeth pulled the curtain aside and cleared a patch of fog from the window. Peering out into the darkness she recognised the familiar outline of the senior sergeant. 'That bastard will not take no for an answer,' she sighed.

His clothes dripping from the rain bucketing down, she could hear him rapping loudly on the backdoor. Hardly able to turn him away on a night like this, reluctantly she unlatched the lock. He didn't wait for an invitation, but with a sense of urgency pushed past her in his muddied boots claiming he had stepped in a puddle and needed to dry his socks.

Elizabeth reeled back at the smell of alcohol on his breath, along with a cheap cologne that did nothing to disguise the sour stench of unwashed body odour when he removed his drenched rain jacket and threw it over the back of a chair. He then reached inside a pocket and withdrew a silver flask, unscrewed the lid and took a generous swig.

Sensing trouble, Elizabeth glanced around in search of her phone.

Henderson appeared to read her mind. 'Think you'll find that mobile of yours about as useless as tits on a rocking horse, Lizzie. There's no signal!' he sneered. 'And let's face it, even on a good day out here in the sticks, I don't like y'chances.'

'I wasn't looking for my phone,' she lied. 'And what are you doing here anyway?'

'Patrol duty! Got a tip off that some crazy woman had been let out of prison. But then the engine seized up, and as I was in the neighbourhood, thought you might appreciate a bit of company. Then again, if anything bad was to happen, you can relax. I'm here to protect you.'

'In this foul weather?' Elizabeth shook her head. 'We both know who you are talking about, and your obsession to save me from Phyllis is no longer needed. I've already made that clear.'

Pulling back a chair and seating himself alongside the kitchen table, Henderson pounded his fist into the pine surface. 'I'm in charge here and you don't get to make anything clear. Do you hear me, Elizabeth? That storm out there provides the exact sort of conditions that anyone up to no good might use to settle a score,' he shouted.

Shocked, Elizabeth became even more alarmed about his angry outburst and seriously unstable behaviour.

Kicking off his boots with no thought of the mess he was making on the floor, he peeled his socks away to expose his ugly white feet and blackened toenails. 'Here,' he said, thrusting them towards her. 'Make yourself useful and hang these up to dry.'

This was a command, not a request.

The stench of the wet wool, coupled with a cheesy smell of dirty feet, was enough to turn her stomach as she took hold of each sock between the tips of her thumb and first finger. As if contaminated pieces of dogshit, careful to avoid any contact with her body she held them out at arms' length and turned her head to the side. She then hurried to the back door, thinking this her chance to escape as an almighty gust of wind released the catch and swung the hinges wide open. Sheets of rain swept into the room and with her hair lashed to her face she stepped out into the wild.

The senior sergeant called, 'Oi! Where do you think you're going?' The door crashed and banged as she looked back to see him hobble to the doorway just in time to see his socks being dropped into a pool of sludgy rainwater only metres from where he was standing.

The wind howled and lightning lit up the sky. Elizabeth then heard a loud crack like the sound of a gunshot at very close range as something whizzed by her head. Terrified she froze and felt that her feet were nailed to the spot.

'Don't even think about taking off, Lizzie, or next time I'll aim a bullet right between those two pretty ears of yours. Now, fish them socks out of the mud and get your arse back in here.'

Elizabeth willed her legs to move as she slowly turned to see him framed in the open doorway with a gun in his hand.

He fired at her. He'd actually aimed that weapon right at her head. He could have killed her. Henderson was even madder than she had given him credit for. And while she didn't fancy getting her head blown off, in that fleeting moment, she weighed up whether she was able to run.

'Don't make me come out there and get you, Lizzie, or I'm going to be mighty pissed off.'

Shivering, Elizabeth felt she had little choice and decided to do as she was told. Then when making her way back into the kitchen, she let go of the sloppy, mud-ridden socks and they slapped to the floor.

'Pick 'em up right now! Right now! Do you hear me? Soak them in the sink.'

Too afraid to move, Elizabeth tossed each sock across into the sink from where she was standing and the stinking water splattered around the room.

Henderson's fists clenched and he looked like he might kill her right there on the spot. 'Find me a towel,' he shouted, wiping a streaky clump from his face.

Wringing wet, her teeth chattering, the one room she didn't want him to enter was the laundry where she had left the door unlocked and knew it was her only escape route.

'I'm warning you, Lizzie, treat me like a fool and you'll pay. Be nice. I came here to keep you safe, not just from Phyllis, but also that nasty intruder you filed a complaint about. Thought you'd be pleased to see me and this is all the thanks I get.'

Elizabeth stammered, 'Most people who visit don't pull a gun on me.'

'Just letting you know who's boss. If I wanted to shoot you, I would a done it by now. I had no intention of killing you. Not yet anyway. But I'm tellin' ya to get out of them wet clothes. So, hurry up about it and lead the way.'

When they entered the bathroom, Henderson pulled a tracksuit from a hook behind the door and shoved it up against Elizabeth's chest. He grabbed a towel from the rail and said, 'I'll give you ten seconds to slip that tracksuit on while I dry myself down.'

Elizabeth could see the hungry look in his eyes as she turned away and hurried to whip the top over her wet shirt and pull the pants on under her skirt she then discarded.

Henderson tossed the towel at her feet. 'Time's up!' he said as Elizabeth picked it up and rubbed at her hair as best she could.

'Take that wet shirt off like I told ya.'

He grabbed hold of her wrist and led her into the nearest bedroom, opened the wardrobe door and pulled a fleecy plaid work shirt from a hanger. 'Here. Think yourself lucky that I'm being so nice to ya.'

Elizabeth cowered into a corner shaking her head.

'Do as I tell ya!'

She turned her back to him and trembling violently, struggled to perform this simple act and get the shirt buttons done up when frightened he would pounce on her and wrestle her to the bed. Instead, he sat quietly and watched in the darkness.

'Find me some warm socks,' he demanded.

She led the way into the living room where she handed him a pair of knitted pink, one size fits all, padded sole variety which she'd left lying on the couch.

'Is this the best you can do?' Henderson scowled and produced a pocketknife from somewhere around his hip to slice off the fluffy bobbles attached to the end of the cords.

He warmed himself with another swig from the flask and ordered Elizabeth to pull the socks on his feet.

'What are you looking at?' he sneered. 'Gutsy little bitch, I'll say that for ya.'

'Why are you doing this to me?'

'We both know why, Lizzie, and there's no point in screaming because we're all alone. I want us to be friends. It's kind of cosy don't you think? Just the two of us.'

Panicking, Elizabeth made another dash for the door. But it was clear that Henderson, a seasoned drinker, could hold his grog and was still strong enough to grab hold of her before she could escape. She kicked like a wildcat yet was no match for him as he flung her down on the couch.

Not wanting to provoke what was shaping up to be a volatile situation, she moved as far away from him as possible and huddled against the armrest while wondering what grisly plan he had in store for her.

'That old cow Phyllis may be ten cents short of a dollar, but she was right about one thing. You're just like your aunt,' he sniggered. 'A little tease … am I right?'

Nothing riled Elizabeth more, and she longed to smash his ugly face in when hearing these words, "just like your aunt".

A tired and much maligned phrase, it ricocheted around in her mind as if to imply Margaret was the most wicked individual who had ever walked the streets of Mariners Cove. What an absolute joke, when coming from the mouth of her crazed captor who appeared completely unhinged.

'Picked it the first day you came into the station grandstanding and believing you were too smart for the likes of me. Who do you think you were fooling, Lizzie? Answer me, girl.'

Spittle showered her face as he shouted, 'Not so cocky now, I see. Yet I've seen first-hand how happy you are to kowtow to them highflyers around town. Just like that Thornton bitch.'

Surprisingly, the power hadn't cut out even though the persistent noise of the rain drumming down on the roof couldn't drown out the snide remarks or sudden decision on his part to switch on the TV. Seeming fascinated by Michael Jackson moonwalking across the screen, Henderson removed his gun and placed it down on top of a cabinet. He then launched himself into the dance routine and almost overbalanced as he staggered backwards in a futile effort to mimic the movement himself.

Taking another gulp from his flask, he loudly burped and with the back of his hand carelessly wiped away the excess liquid dribbling down his chin. He then placed the flat of his hand over the crotch of his pants and thrust his flabby hips forward and back in a pathetic attempt to imitate another of Jackson's suggestive dance moves.

How totally bizarre, unrelated and almost laughable his behaviour was given her predicament, Elizabeth thought, feeling as though she was close to throwing up all over the carpet. 'I think I'm going to be sick,' she said.

'Sick my arse. You're just plain scared. That's all that's wrong with ya. Pull yourself together, you're trembling all over like a frightened puppy.' Henderson snarled and flicked off the TV.

'The smart thing for you to do, is to be a bit more accommodating an' invite an officer of the law t'bed down here for the night. Keep each other warm, hey, Lizzie. You'd like that, wouldn't ya?'

Waves of nausea washed over her. Elizabeth staggered to her feet not knowing which way to turn. She fell to her knees and began to retch yet coughed up nothing more than a dribble of bile. In a cold sweat, she knew that Henderson was right.

He pulled her up by the hair and shoved her back on the couch.

She raised her hands in front of her and pleaded. 'Leave me … don't touch me.'

'We can't have that, Lizzie. It would spoil all the fun and more-or-less sums up what that stuck up *Margee* might a said under similar circumstances. But I'm looking forward t'just the two of us being shacked up here with no one out-n-about to disturb us.'

Henderson cast a lascivious eye over Elizabeth as if appraising a piece of juicy meat into which he was itching to sink his teeth. Shuddering, she concluded by the sound of his heavy breathing that he was becoming aroused at the prospect of indulging in an act of such a lewd nature that she couldn't bear to contemplate.

A shiver went down her spine when he upended the flask and shaking the empty container, chucked it across the room so forcefully that it became embedded in the plaster. Seizing a whisky decanter, he poured the liquid into two glasses and handed one to Elizabeth demanding that she drink it down to rinse out her mouth. Then, perhaps hoping to entice her with an added incentive to take part in his disgusting proposal, he reached inside his trouser pocket and withdrew a roll of one-hundred-dollar notes held together in a rubber band. 'There's ten here, Lizzie,' he said flicking through the stack and fanning them out right under her nose. 'A cool thousand for an hour of y'time.'

He slapped the cash into her palm and curled her fingers around the money. 'Think of this as a contribution of sorts. A down payment on the reconstruction of that burnt out church of yours. An' let's not forget that coffee shop I keep hearin' about.'

As much as Elizabeth detested the thought of drinking whisky in her wretched state, it warmed and calmed her momentarily as Henderson went on to say, 'I'm a man who wields considerable influence. Especially when it comes to gettin' things off the ground at council … like a buildin' permit for instance. On the other hand, I could put a stop to the entire project.'

Bleary-eyed and slurring his words, white foamy spital had attached itself to the corners of his mouth. 'Think of it, Lizzie. No one'll ever know about our little arrangement. It's just the beginnin'. The first in a series of little cash donations. There's plenty more where that came from – a whole succession of the slippery bastards in exchange for y'services.'

Placing his glass on the coffee table, he staggered towards her. He picked up the discarded money and pulling her to her feet, he stuffed it down the front of her shirt – his stinking breath right in her face. His fingers lingering inside her damp bra cup. 'That seems fair wouldn't you say, darlin'? You should be happy that I'm willin' t'reimburse ya. Let's start with a friendly kiss. C'mon now, there's a good girl. We both know how much you want this.'

Incensed, Elizabeth struggled to escape the touch and taste of his slobbering lips from connecting with her skin. She broke free and threw the money back in his face, 'Get off me! Get off me!' she became hysterical and screamed. 'You're drunk, Senior Sergeant. I'm not some cheap whore. Even if I was to agree to your vulgar suggestion, I doubt you could fulfil your end of the bargain. Besides, what would your wife think? Maxine, isn't it?'

Elizabeth knew she had taken an enormous risk, because this attack on his manliness brought with it an immediate reaction. The sergeant's already ruddy face turned a brighter shade of red. 'Ungrateful little wretch,' he spat, as he whacked Elizabeth with an almighty crack across the jaw, sending her sprawling to the floor. 'Mention my wife's name again an' this little game might get a whole lot rougher.'

Elizabeth's eyes smarted. She fought to stop from crying and dragged herself to her feet. 'Your career in the force will be finished when I report you to your superiors,' she warned.

Henderson's bloodshot eyes took on an expression of delight as he broke into a belly roll of laughter, while at the same time releasing a barrage of wind. 'Go ahead, darlin'. Be my guest! Your word against mine will never stand up. No one'll believe it. That teasin' floozy you called y'aunt treated me bad just like you. Ordered me out she did, as if I was no better than a pile of sheep shit beneath her feet.'

Elizabeth's intense fear turned to absolute horror when waiting to hear where this admission was going.

'No one speaks to Senior Sergeant Ian Henderson like that an' gets away with it. No one, do you hear me, Lizzie?' he said, shoving a finger into her chest to make his point. 'You know what happened to her, Lizzie? She died, darlin'. It was what she deserved.'

Elizabeth's hand went to her mouth as she backed away. 'What? What are you saying?'

'I'm saying, Ms high 'n' bloody mighty, that I was here with 'er at the time. Just like I'm here with you now. The stupid bitch took fright, tripped over a fuckin' doorstop, fell an' hit her head. A heart attack, I reckon. Her own fault for threatenin' me, an officer of the law with a carvin' knife. Had no alternative but t'defend meself. Funny how history can have a habit of sometimes repeatin' itself, don't y'think, Lizzie?'

With no longer even a small element of doubt, Elizabeth became frantic knowing the man to be a lunatic for sure. 'Are you sure that was the way it happened?'

'Are you calling me a liar?' Henderson chuckled as he could see how scared she was.

Elizabeth put her hands over her ears and kept shaking her head in denial. Tears streamed down her face, 'You sick bastard! You killed her! You killed my aunt! You murdering hypocrite, masquerading as an upholder of the law. I don't believe Margaret had a heart attack.'

'Believe what you like. An unfortunate accident, I'd call it. But if you don't do exactly what I tell ya, who knows what could go wrong.' Henderson laughed as he dragged Elizabeth into the middle of the room and ordered her to stand in front of him while he grabbed his gun and slumped back down on the couch. He placed it close beside him. 'One wrong move 'n' you're a dead woman. So don't go gettin' any ideas, coz now we've sorted out who's in charge here, we're gunna have ourselves a little strip show. So first up, get that top off.'

Henderson flicked the TV back onto a music channel. 'There'll be no more blubbering or stallin' around. I've been patient with you, Lizzie. Unbutton your shirt nice an' easy like 'n' wiggle that sexy arse of yours. I wanna be entertained with a bit of erotic dancing.'

At that precise moment, Elizabeth caught sight of a movement in the shadows of the darkened hallway. Constable Madden had a finger pressed to her lips and what looked to be a gun in her hand.

'What's the bloody hold-up, girl? Get on with it or I'll rip that fuckin' shirt off ya meself.' But when Elizabeth made no move, he impatiently staggered to his feet and yanked at the shirt with an almighty tug, causing the buttons to pop and spill to the floor.

Constable Madden crept up from behind and held a pistol to the back of his head. 'That's enough, Senior Sergeant. It's over!'

Recognising Madden's voice, Henderson froze when feeling the cold metal barrel at his head, and quick-thinking Elizabeth snatched up his gun from the couch.

'Raise your hands in the air and don't try anything smart. I'm placing you under arrest for attempted rape and the suspected murder of Margaret Thornton. Elizabeth, slide that gun under the cabinet out of reach.' She then tossed her a set of handcuffs. 'I want you to lock them on his wrists. Do you think you can do that, Elizabeth?'

Her shirt hanging in tatters, 'With pleasure,' Elizabeth replied.

'Okay, Henderson,' Madden said, 'hands behind your back and turn around slowly.'

Quick as a flash, Henderson lurched forward to whip the handcuffs out of Elizabeth's hands and swung round to whack Madden across the head before she knew what hit her.

Elizabeth dived on Madden's pistol when seeing the constable slumped against the wall, blood oozing from her head. Henderson landed on Elizabeth's back, twisted her arm up behind her and grinded her face into the boards beneath her. He shouted in her ear as she kicked and screamed, 'If you wanna play dirty, I'm all for it, Lizzie.' He dangled the handcuffs over her shoulder. 'Now nice 'n' easy, put these on that good for nothin' bitch and make sure you do it properly.'

Madden was out cold, and Elizabeth said, 'She's not dead, is she?'

'She'll survive. Here,' he pulled his tie from the pocket of his trouser pants and ordered Elizabeth to bind Madden's ankles. He retrieved his gun and while pointing it in the direction of Elizabeth, he laid his holster and Madden's pistol right next to him on the side table.

A great clap of thunder boomed across the night sky and several streaks of lightning lit up the house. The lights flickered and dimmed. The TV cut out and he ordered Elizabeth to put a match to a couple of oil lanterns before pushing her back to the centre of the room. He then returned to the couch and demanded that she continue to undress.

Elizabeth didn't think it possible to feel any more afraid than she had already. But now the crunch was coming she found it difficult to breath when threatened by the likely outcome that Henderson was planning to rape and murder her. He appeared to have drunk himself sober as he demanded that she disrobe. She slowly stripped to her underwear. She stood shivering, crying and hugging her chest. Every vestige of hope and decency gone. Henderson looked on with a satisfied grin. Even in the shadowy half-light, his leering expression was unmistakably that of a greedy lecher anxious to devour her like a succulent meal set before him.

He again staggered from the sofa, pulled the straps of her bra down over her shoulders and ripped the clasp asunder. Like a crazed animal eager to demolish its prey, he grabbed at each breast and squeezed with such force that Elizabeth whimpered in pain. Slobbering all over her, he then reached a hand up between her legs.

At close range, the capillaries on his bulbous nose appeared to multiply like dozens of eroded craters. His face flushed to a brilliant red etched with purplish veins and broken blood vessels that squiggled across his cheeks – the tissue beneath his skin appeared riddled with thread worms that feasted and festered on the internal decay within. Elizabeth felt disgust at the sound of his frenzied breathing like a lusting animal on heat, and the distressing humiliation of this hideous act of violation. Turning her head away at the touch of his probing fingers inside her, the smell of his fetid breath and the revolting awareness of his filthy tongue as he took hold of her hair, yanked her head back, and like a deranged bloodsucking vampire, sank his teeth into her neck.

A heavy lump of a man, Elizabeth felt that her fate was sealed as she fought to release herself from his grip when he ripped away her last and most precious item of clothing to completely expose her nakedness. Unzipping his trousers and dropping his pants, Henderson clearly didn't know what hit him as he buckled over in pain when a shadow shot out from the darkness and yelled in angry retribution before striking him with a karate chop to the side of his neck. A svelte figure dressed all in black swiftly swung in a circle kicking the sergeant's feet from under him causing the sleazy lecher to land on the floor with an almighty thud.

Dazed and disorientated. Elizabeth's aggressor floundered and fumbled blindly for the guns. But they were gone and his attacker—with arms outstretched—held a pistol professionally clutched in both hands and pointed the weapon directly at his head. 'Stay right where you are and don't move a muscle or I swear that I'll blow your brains out and serve them up on a platter to the devil himself for breakfast.'

'Tilt, what the hell!' Elizabeth couldn't believe her eyes. 'Where on earth did you learn to do that?'

'Never mind that now. Are you okay?' she asked. 'And what about Constable Madden?'

Elizabeth reached for her tracksuit top to cover herself and Constable Madden moaned in the background when Elizabeth untied her feet and told Tilt she needed the key to unlock the handcuffs.

Tilt, never taking an eye off Henderson said, 'You heard the lady. Hand it over.'

Once her hands were free, with the help of Elizabeth, Madden, badly cut and bruised, managed to get to her feet and this time made certain that Henderson's hands were safely locked out of harm's way. 'Step outside, Senior Sergeant,' she said grabbing the shoulder of his shirt and giving him a shove.

'Get your hands off me, Madden. You'll live to regret this,'

'We'll see about that Senior Sergeant, as I just happened to get a nice little recording of all you confessed to Elizabeth and it's going to make for compelling evidence.'

'Never did like you, Madden! You can't even make a decent coffee. Are you sure you had that device switched on properly?'

Madden answered with a smile on her face. 'I'm happy to report that's the last time you will ever put me down, Senior Sergeant Henderson. Now you can march yourself right into the back of the van and shut the fuck up.'

Elizabeth's body collapsed to the floor in a crumpled heap. She gratefully felt the warmth of a blanket being thrown around her and the comfort of her friend Tilt holding her close.

Elizabeth sobbed.

45

Badly Shaken

Drained of energy, eyes swollen and red, Elizabeth thought she might spend the rest of her days crying and never emerge from beneath the warmth of the blanket and Tilt's comforting arms.

She kept thanking her over and over for rescuing her. 'I need to shower! I need to wash away that creep's slimy saliva.'

'Sorry, darling, but Madden gave me strict instructions not to let you wash away any evidence. You will need to throw on something warm and I'm to drive you to the nearest hospital for a full examination before reporting back to the station.'

'No! Elizabeth cried. 'You can't make me. I'm not going! That's so easy for Madden to say. She wasn't the one being pawed all over. I'm having a shower to clean the filthy slime of that evil bastard. I hate him! I hate him! I hope he dies and goes straight to hell. I'm not going anywhere, Tilt.'

'But there's photos and a statement to be taken,' Tilt said.

'I don't care. That can wait. The bruising will look worse in the morning and thanks to you, he didn't get the chance to ...' Elizabeth, being unwilling to say the words out loud, shuddered and ran her hands along her arms.

'Fair enough, Liz. Nobody is going to force you to do anything. It does seem like madness to drive in this weather,

270

and Henderson won't have a hope in hell of clearing his name in court. Do you feel strong enough to get to the shower?' Tilt asked as she helped her to her feet. 'Here, lean on me and I'll go with you just to make sure.'

Elizabeth asked Tilt to leave the bathroom once she began to soak herself beneath the running water. 'I think I'll be able to manage now. I'd like to be alone for a while.'

'Okay, I'll make you a hot drink and then maybe you should get into bed.'

Once Tilt left the bathroom, Elizabeth again burst into tears and began to lather soap all over her body. She scrubbed her skin till it was red and washed her hair so vigorously that it seemed she might never stop. The water ran for so long that Tilt rapped on the door and asked if she was okay.

Elizabeth turned off the taps and assured Tilt she would be out in a moment. And after she doused herself in body lotion and pulled on her fleecy pj's, robe and slippers, she bundled up every piece of clothing she had been wearing both before and after the ordeal to be thrown in the rubbish bin. Soiled or unsoiled, she could never stand to let anything he had touched near her again.

Stepping into the kitchen, her skinned glowed in the lamplight.

With her hair wrapped in a towel she placed her hands around a warm mug of tea while Tilt unravelled the towel and vigorously rubbed away the dampness.

'When you've finished your tea, you should take a couple of painkillers and try to get some rest.'

'I doubt I'll be able to sleep,' Elizabeth said, jumping at a clap of thunder that boomed directly overhead. 'After surviving two break-ins and now tonight's …' She looked away. 'I can't stand the thought of living on my own in this house anymore. As much as I hate the idea of letting go of this place. It doesn't feel right to be here. I'll be glad of your company tonight, Tilt.'

'You won't catch me heading off in a hurry. Especially since my car is parked back down the road so as not to alert Henderson of my arrival. But I agree! It would be a wise move to set yourself up in a smaller place somewhere in town.'

'Yes, I should plan to put the property on the market as soon as I get a moment to talk to an agent. I might even call Gary and head back to Melbourne. Not sure I'm cut out for all this excitement.'

Tilt looked horrified. 'Oh no! What about all your plans for the bookshop? Please don't make any rash decision. You've just undergone what could have evolved into something far worse. Wait until you've had a chance to think this through.'

'I'm over it, Tilt! All the dramas … all the sniping innuendos about Margaret, the senseless threats on my life, the fire and now this. I've got to find enough capital to restock the entire shop. Life wasn't perfect in Melbourne, but at least I had a good job, and Gary I'm certain – for all his imperfections – did genuinely care for me.'

'But do you love him, Liz?'

'I used to think so,' Elizabeth sighed. 'But now … well, I'm not totally sure anymore.'

Elizabeth thought the look of devastation on Tilt's face was disconcerting. But why would Tilt be opposed to the idea of her getting back with Gary? She barely knew him as they'd only briefly met once.

'I know your thoughts about David, but don't you like Gary either, Tilt?'

'It's not that I don't like him, Liz. It's more about you giving up and returning to live in Melbourne. And yes, it's selfish I understand that.'

'Oh, enough about me, Tilt … and Gary for that matter. What I would like to know is how you knew to come to my aid. Where exactly did you learn that fancy kickboxing and blackbelt karate chop?'

'It's a bit of a long story. I knew there was no love lost between Madden and the senior sergeant. So, after I raised the alarm about him following you around, when all the time insisting that he was performing a legitimate police duty, Madden hopped right on board. She agreed to more closely observe his movements and keep me posted.'

'I'm lucky to be blessed with such a caring friend as you, Tilt. You still haven't answered my question though.'

'Oh, darling, you do make me blush. I'm only sorry I didn't get here earlier. It was Madden who told me to stay put when she contacted me,' Tilt said. 'Apparently, she'd been working back on the late shift and saw Henderson drive away in the direction of your place. She was planning to follow him. But when I didn't hear back, I suspected something had gone wrong and decided to investigate.'

Yet perhaps the biggest surprise for Elizabeth was Tilt's admission that she had taken up self-defence lessons to stave off the regular physical abuse administered by her ex-husband both prior to and after their divorce. And finding that she enjoyed the martial arts, Tilt continued to improve her skills and had regularly attended training sessions.

Since the trauma created by Phyllis, the last thing Elizabeth had expected was that lightning would strike twice in the same place, causing her to again have to undergo all the police requirements necessary following Henderson's arrest.

It didn't take long for a black emptiness that had not been present before Elizabeth underwent the fearful incident at the hands of Ian Henderson, to catch her off guard, having crept up and robbed her of any sort of joy in her life. And now even though Henderson was stripped of his badge and safely behind bars, Elizabeth shut down and no longer allowed anyone, including David, to get close to her in an intimate sense. Her body was suddenly off limits and as gentle and understanding as David could be, the sexual nature of their relationship ceased.

Elizabeth withdrew into a completely celibate world where she felt content in the knowledge that no one could ever again accuse her of being just like her aunt. Because all her troubles began with her comparison to her aunt. Yet every now and then when tucked up in bed, she dreamt of Lenny Forrester.

Longing for his return, she woke one night to the sound of her own moaning response to the sublime touch of his imaginary caress. He was back and suddenly the emptiness disappeared until her eyes adjusted to the darkness, and she saw it was not Lenny who caressed her.

David had entered her bed uninvited, and she turned on him in anger.

'Liz, please don't be mad. I let myself in just like I used to. I didn't think you'd mind, because all I wanted was to hold you. Remember how much you used to enjoy that?'

Elizabeth pounded his head with the pillow. 'Get out, get out … I can't do this, David. Go home.'

David grabbed her hands. 'Settle down, Liz. You're not yourself and I think you should speak to a doctor about all that has happened. Promise me you'll do that.'

Elizabeth despairingly turned her head towards the wall and rolled up in a ball.

46

Wise Advice

Elizabeth's melancholy state persisted. Ravaged, humiliated and unable to deal with the torment to which she'd been subjected, she took to her bed, stopped eating and lost interest in everything.

Tilt delivered meals to the house along with news about anything that might cheer her friend. But, preferring to be alone, Elizabeth no longer cared. Never bothering to dress, she laid about moping. 'Let me work my way through this at my own pace, Tilt. I've lost interest,' she said.

Strangely, it was Phyllis Bentley who was to give the brooding Elizabeth a bit of a much needed shake-up when she stormed into the bedroom unannounced, threw back the covers and pulled Elizabeth from her bed.

'I could have you arrested for this, Phyllis! How did you get in?'

Phyllis dangled a key between her fingertips. 'Think this might have belonged to Jack at one time.'

'Let's not go there right now if you don't mind. I have enough to contend with.'

'Yes, and that's why I'm here,' Phyllis said pinching her nose in disgust. 'It smells like something has died in this room. When was the last time you showered?'

'A lecture from you of all people is the last thing I need,' Elizabeth shouted as she dived back into bed and pulled the doona over her head.

Phyllis dragged it off again. 'Look, Liz, a bit of advice,' she said seating herself on the edge of the bed. 'If you want to feel sorry for yourself and hide away for the rest of your days, go right ahead. But, if you don't want to finish up like I did, then do yourself a favour. Don't allow this unpleasant business to eat away at you and turn you into a nasty old nark like I became.'

'To be honest, Phyllis, you are scaring the shit out of me right now. I'm not sure whether you might be armed with a carving knife tucked under your shirt or more likely a Watusi spear.'

'No need to freak out,' Phyllis calmly responded whipping the pillow from under Elizabeth's head and tugging at the sheets. 'Lunch'll be ready in fifteen, and I'll expect to see you sitting at the table.'

'Who do you think you are, my mother for God's sake?' Elizabeth scoffed as she flounced off the bed and slammed the door of the bathroom behind her.

A small vase of wildflowers adorned the centre of the table set up on the front veranda. Salmon salad along with a glass of white wine awaited Elizabeth as she took her place opposite Phyllis. 'Why are you doing this, Phyllis?'

'I consider myself lucky not to be sitting in a jail cell right now. The truth is, I thought I hated you because I came to dislike Margaret so much. Not only did she seduce my husband. She wrecked our friendship.' Phyllis flicked out a folded serviette and placed it on her lap. 'You need to understand how this tore me apart. She could be cruel, your aunt. Then when Jack had the accident, I became bitter and blamed her for it all.'

'Yes, yes, I've heard this all before, remember. And while I can understand how this must have hurt you, why hold me responsible for my aunt's actions?'

Phyllis's eyes watered. 'I was wrong, Elizabeth. I know now that Philip Anderson is Margaret's son. I know now that you and Eileen Jacobson were just having a cruel little joke at my expense. I know now that you are entitled to spend time with whoever you please. And I know now how it feels to hit rock bottom. So, like it or not, I'm here to help.'

'I don't need any help from you, Phyllis. You're a maniac and about as unstable as a tin roof in a tornado.'

'I've made a full recovery. I can promise you that.'

'Glad to hear it, but I haven't. You can't really expect me to just bounce back and put this all behind me as though it never happened,' Elizabeth said while peering down suspiciously at a lettuce leaf. 'And you're not serious about me eating one mouthful of this salad that you probably rinsed in a mix of undiluted Ratsak?'

'Suit yourself about the salad, Liz. I know I don't deserve your trust,' Phyllis said reaching over to help herself to the piece of rejected lettuce from Elizabeth's plate. 'But I refuse to stand back and watch you make yourself ill. Believe me I know, because I allowed myself to become consumed with negative thoughts due to a betrayal by the two people I most trusted. That obsession almost destroyed me and everyone around me.'

'Can I believe you have changed, Phyllis?'

'Elizabeth, a certain princess once told the world there were three people in her marriage. "It was a bit crowded" she said. We all felt sorry for her.' Phyllis dabbed at each eye with her napkin. 'But what about all those living in the real world who discover their marriages are a bit crowded? Does anybody else really give a damn? No! The one betrayed has just got to grieve alone and get through the best way they can.'

Pausing to take a sip of wine, Phyllis placed the glass down and continued. 'Unfortunately, many don't cope, and I was one of them. My gradual decline brought about my mental illness.'

The unfairness of it all only now began to seriously resonate with Elizabeth and in that moment, she completely understood where Phyllis was coming from. 'You must miss Jack terribly,' she said in the first outward sign of compassion.

'I've had a lot of time to think, Liz, and not a day goes by when I don't miss them both. People we trust and love make mistakes, hurtful mistakes. It is one of the greatest disappointments in life. And not easy to accept. But forgiving them will set you free.'

Phyllis reached out to Elizabeth. 'Ian Henderson has done a dreadful thing and I'm not suggesting you forgive him. But I do know that you were involved in a conversation with the Andersons and agreed with Philip that I deserved a second chance. That act of kindness hasn't gone unnoticed. And now I think I owe you one.' Phyllis spoke with an empathy that Elizabeth had never heard coming from her mouth before. 'I beg you, Elizabeth, please don't hand Ian Henderson the power to mess up your life.'

'I think you really do mean that, Phyllis.'

47

Good News

In a sudden light bulb moment, the key flashed into Elizabeth's memory.

Jack's spare key, Phyllis had said.

'Just how many keys were out there do you suppose? Six, eight, twelve, distributed among the disillusioned husbands of Mariners Cove?' Elizabeth asked as she insisted Phyllis return that which she had used to enter the house at her own discretion. 'It would almost appear that keys had been handed to all like a bag of lollies judging by the highly offensive and sordid implication of Margaret's scandalous involvement with multiple male companions.'

'Sarcasm will get you nowhere,' Phyllis replied.

But both Phyllis and Graeme Jenkins wanted her to believe Margaret had no scruples. And while Elizabeth couldn't deny her aunt may have been capable of entering into an affair with Jack Bentley – and even the odd flirtation – as for the rest, the whole idea sounded absurd. Nothing and nobody could ever dim the respect and love she had for her aunt.

Sweeping this matter aside, Elizabeth was prepared to admit Phyllis had put forward a persuasive argument about not allowing this shocking assault to get the better of her. But Elizabeth – being not quite ready to go back out into the world

– thought to humour her visitor into believing she'd taken note of her advice. Which wasn't entirely untrue. Yet the minute Phyllis left, Elizabeth, breathing a heavy sigh, stood with her back against the locked door and raised her eyes to the ceiling.

Beating a quick path back to bed, it almost seemed a necessary procedure to freely wallow in her state of self-pity as opposed to suppressing her emotions and getting on with life as though nothing had happened. Was it too much to ask that she be left alone to weep or gnash her teeth in anger at the unfairness of it all? Apparently so, according to her advisor. Yet had it not been for the tireless persistence of Phyllis who several days later again returned to rattle the chains, Elizabeth may have reverted permanently into the safety of her cocoon, never to re-emerge.

'Don't tell me you're back in bed, Liz?' Phyllis rapped on the window. 'Get out of there this minute or I swear I'll break the door down with my bare hands.'

This is too much, and I thought she had a key, Elizabeth reminded herself as she stormed across the room and raised the window to shout. 'Enough is enough, Phyllis. Get out of my garden.'

'My God, just look at you, Elizabeth! You're as thin as a whippet and still sulking in that bed after all we talked about. If you keep this up and refuse to answer your calls, I can promise you'll have a whole lot more than just me arriving on your doorstep.'

'Go home, Phyllis. You've made your point.'

'Don't you dare speak to me in that tone, young lady!' Phyllis implored, waving what appeared to be a letter in the air. 'Do you think I enjoy coming here and getting abused?'

'You really don't get it do you, Phyllis? Because whatever you've got there, even if it's your last Will and Testament and you've come to inform me that I'm the sole beneficiary, I couldn't be less excited.'

Phyllis scoffed 'You're such a smart alec at times, Elizabeth. Well, sorry to disappoint, but I'm planning on living a long life and can assure you that in your current state, I wouldn't be leaving you so much as the sniff of an oily rag in my Will. And if not for Philip asking me to drop by before you so rudely ordered me out, you might wish to read what I'm holding in my hand.'

'The tension is killing me. Let's get this over with Elizabeth replied.

'Here, see for yourself,' Phyllis said thrusting the paperwork through the window.

When realising what was in front of her, Elizabeth unintentionally released a little squeal of delight. 'What?! Council approval for the planned extension.' Her eyes lit up when reading the official permit.

'There's only one problem,' Phyllis said. 'And after the way you have treated me, I don't even know why I would bother to mention it. But Philip needs you to okay the project so the rebuilding and the gallery can get underway.'

Convinced that nothing could ever make her smile again, Elizabeth now needed no further prompting. This news had brought with it the desired motivation to get back out there and do whatever it might take to fulfil her once so strongly held dream. 'Stay right where you are, Phyllis. There's something I never thought I'd be needing to do.'

Elizabeth raced through the hallway, threw back the door and ran in her bare feet across the grass to throw her arms around Phyllis. Crushing her in a bear hug she planted a kiss on both cheeks.

'What's this for?' Phyllis laughed.

'Well, yes, on second thoughts this might be an overreaction,' Elizabeth joined in the laughter and suggested, 'How about I pop the kettle on?'

A million jobs needed sorting, and Elizabeth wasted no time setting up appointments with the bank manager, plus a local real estate agent. Within the week the house went on the market and any thought of ever returning to live in Melbourne became yesterday's news.

Ian Henderson posed no further threat safely behind bars. Yet Elizabeth still felt jittery about now living on her own so far from town and was keen to find a buyer. She needed to raise some revenue, and if she could manage to get a good price for the place, she planned to downsize and would hopefully be left with a healthy sum outstanding. A large insurance payment would take care of restocking the shop and the bank had also agreed to grant her a loan. She was sitting pretty and now in a position to raise enough capital to begin the development without the aid of outside investors.

Once more fully absorbed in the future, Elizabeth's recent woes gradually faded, and she was eager to make a fresh start.

48

An Unlikely Attachment

Seated alone at a coffee shop opposite the Fitzroy Gardens, Lenny Forrester – having temporarily migrated back to the city – thought he recognised an attractive redhead in the distance.

If not mistaken, she looked a whole lot like that friend of Elizabeth's. 'Tilt! Yeah, that's her for sure. But what's she doing in Melbourne?'

About to rush across the road to speak to her, he noticed a guy wander up from behind. Taking hold of her hand, he threaded her arm through his in a proprietorial manner. Unable to get a clear view of his face, Lenny recognised something familiar about him.

He tapped his fingers on the table and racked his brain for an answer. 'Who is that? I've seen him before … I'm certain.'

The two began to walk in his direction. The answer became glaringly obvious as they got closer. Lenny had a clear picture in his head of the day he'd first seen Elizabeth hand in hand with her good-looking boyfriend – Mr Universe, he had nicknamed him. Jealous as a schoolboy dumped by his first love, Lenny also recalled how they almost stopped the traffic. Heads had turned to check out their movie star-like quality as they walked along the main street. Yet, less than a week later, Elizabeth had broken up with him.

When unexpectedly confronted with what he was now seeing, this development raised an eyebrow. But that was it. His brow dropped back into place very quickly. Eileen Jacobson – better known as Tilt – seemed like a lovely woman and what she did in her spare time was coincidental to a bloke like Lenny. He'd seen it all before and Elizabeth had made her feelings known. Yet, if being totally honest, he would like to spend a bit of time in Gary's company as he was curious to learn his side of the story. What had caused the break up between him and Elizabeth?

Lowering his newspaper, once the couple exited the gardens to reach the street, he watched them turn away and walk as far as the corner.

Lenny, not wanting to lose sight of them, drained the last of his coffee. He then made a mad dash to catch up and follow them along Flinders Street. It was here where they parted with a friendly kiss at the intersection of Swanston Street.

Tilt appeared to be heading towards the station. Mr Universe crossed at the lights and entered Young & Jacksons pub.

Breathing in the stale aroma of spilt beer, 'How's it goin'?' Lenny asked as he sidled up beside Elizabeth's ex-boyfriend at the bar. Sliding onto a stool he ordered himself a VB from the bearded gentleman behind the counter.

With his drink in hand, he then swung around and offered a convivial *Cheers* to the few unknown customers seated around the tables. 'Bloody hell!' he said in surprise. 'Gary, isn't it? Reckon I've seen you around, mate.'

Gary looked at Lenny with a bewildered expression.

'Forrester's the name ... Lenny Forrester.'

'Sorry, buddy!' Gary replied. 'Not sure how you know my name, but I haven't a clue where we met.'

'No worries, mate. Understand the confusion, coz we've never been formally introduced. Spotted you once at Mariners Cove with a friend of mine.' Lenny paused. 'Goes by the name of O'Connell.'

Gary almost choked on his beer, and Lenny, having at once grabbed his attention, could see he was now all ears.

'You must have a good memory for faces, pal,' Gary said.

'Could say that! Did a bit of private investigating in a former life before takin' up a spot of general maintenance and handyman jobs around country Victoria. Worked for Elizabeth's aunt, Margaret Thornton, on a regular basis. That's how I met up with her niece.'

'Hope you had more luck than I did. She fucking broke my heart!'

'Yeah, news kind a gets around at the Cove. One of the reasons why I'm wondering if you'd be willing t'have a little conversation of sorts.'

'Why would I want to do that? I've moved on ... and if you want my advice, I'd suggest you do the same, buddy.'

Lenny swilled the last drop of his beer around in the bottom of the glass.

'Spotted you a while back with a friend of Elizabeth's who works in the bookshop.'

Gary didn't look happy, and the hackles rose. 'What the hell is this? Have you been following me around? Did Elizabeth put you up to this?'

Forrester, aware that he had crossed the line, said, 'No way, mate! Whatever's going on between you and Tilt, stays between you and Tilt. A pure accident that I happened to see you. But I wanna be completely up front because,' Lenny felt he was sticking his neck out here, 'you and I have had more than a passing interest in Elizabeth.'

None too pleased judging by the sound of his voice, 'Is that right?' Gary sneered.

'Afraid so, mate. But seems she's given us both the flick in favour of a couple of shifty bastards who I wouldn't let loose with my eighty-year-old maiden aunt.'

'Don't know them!' Gary shook his head. 'Don't want to know them … or I'd probably kick their ugly teeth in along with yours while I'm at it.'

Lenny put the flat of his hands up. 'Fair enough! I deserved that. But before you head off, at least let me shout you another beer.'

One beer led to another, and a little worse for wear, Lenny and Gary spent the rest of the afternoon and evening together on a pub crawl before finishing up at Crown Casino where the pair were irreverently tossed out at 3 am. But having got what he came for, Lenny felt a genuine affinity for Gary's plight. Elizabeth had been hard on the poor bastard. The two had put their arm around each other's shoulder and wept into their beer. And by the time they parted, they both knew each other's life history and were the best of mates. Lenny couldn't be sure how he got home that morning but nursed a hell of a hangover for the rest of the week.

49

A Double Whammy

With the loss of Lenny Forrester from her life and tradesmen constantly coming and going, Elizabeth's refurbishment program leading up to the sale of the house was in full swing.

'Seems a shame to sell a place like this,' Harvey, the house painter, remarked as he finished the final touches on the windowsill and stood back to appraise his work. 'Wouldn't mind putting in an offer myself. The missus has always loved this house.'

Imagining Harvey's wife in her aunt's kitchen left Elizabeth secretly questioning her sanity. And she was relieved when a call came through on her mobile.

'Hi, Tilt!'

'Have you heard the news, Liz? Henderson's dead!'

'What? The senior sergeant? Are you sure?'

'Absolutely! What other scumbag who goes by the name of Henderson do you know? Seems he died of natural causes. Or so they're saying. Heartbreaking, isn't it?' Tilt couldn't keep the sarcasm from her voice.

'That is … bizarre and so … sudden,' Elizabeth stammered.

'Isn't it just!' Tilt sniggered. 'And while I hate to speak ill of the dead, in this case what's happened would be well justified, wouldn't you think?'

'There's no talk of suicide, is there? That might have made more sense.'

'Apparently, he'd been undergoing treatment and taking medication for an undisclosed condition which was not mentioned in the news report. Mental derangement, sexual deviate tendencies perhaps being two afflictions that spring to mind.'

'Gosh, Tilt, who would have thought? But you're right. I'm shocked … yet can hardly feel sorry for the bastard. It sounds callous I know, but at least that's one less thing to worry about.'

'Kind of expected you might say that. Poetic justice, I'd call it. Also, be grateful you don't have to face up to another trial so close on the heels of the Phyllis saga. Neither one of us, including Constable Madden will regret that.'

'You're not wrong there, Tilt. He certainly gave Madden a rough time. But this information will give me even more incentive to try and move on, because I've been literally run ragged getting this place in order before it goes under the hammer.'

'Not regretting your decision, I hope?'

'Oh, come on, Tilt. You know how I hate the thought of selling. I'd be lying if I said otherwise. But then, I think of how this venture is going to put us on the map. It's super exciting.'

The mobile went silent for a moment and Elizabeth thought they'd been disconnected. But then Tilt said, 'I do have a further piece of news I've been keen to talk about. It's nothing on the scale of what I've just told you, of course. But I'd prefer not to tell you over the phone, Liz.'

'Sounds serious, just the same. You're kind of scaring me.'

'Oh, to hell with it! You're always busy, and I can't put this off any longer,' Tilt said. 'It's to do with a person you so often accused me of meeting on my trips away.'

'Bout time you came clean. So … what's this guy's name?

And please don't tell me you're pregnant or getting married. I couldn't stand it.'

Quick to reassure Elizabeth, 'No, no!' Tilt said. 'There's no way I'd leave the Cove and miss out on setting up the gallery and coffee shop. I've been down the marriage path before and that didn't work too well.'

'Well then, what's the big deal and why all the mystery?' Elizabeth asked.

'Last thing I want is for this to cause a rift between us.'

'Don't be so dramatic, Tilt. There's nothing or nobody who could ever break up our friendship … you know that.'

'I certainly hope that's true Liz, because his name is … Oh hell! His name is Gary – Gary Cartwright.'

Shock, anger, betrayal, touched with a pang of bitter resentment coursed through Elizabeth's bloodstream. She couldn't trust herself to speak. Instead, her immediate reaction was to firmly press end and switch her mobile to silent.

'What just happened?' Tilt feared the worst and was left in no doubt this would result in not just the end of a phone call, but the end of a beautiful friendship – a situation she had been so desperate to avoid.

Grabbing her car keys and driving off in a mad dash to face Elizabeth, Tilt became concerned on her arrival to find the place deserted.

She drove to the beach in the hope that Elizabeth, following her normal pattern, may have gone for a walk. Sure enough, she spotted the parked car and pulled in alongside. Cutting through the track surrounded by low growing vegetation, she reached the top of the grassy dune. Confronted with the sight on the other side, she took in the stretch of white sand, the vast expanse of the sky and thundering intensity of the ocean. And there in the distance she saw a solitary figure. 'Lizzie, wait!' she frantically waved and shouted. But only the nesting plovers seemed aroused by the sound of her voice, as Elizabeth, who had her back to Tilt, just kept walking.

The treacherous surf rose fearfully high, reminding Tilt why the shipwreck coast was so named. A dangerous place to swim, warnings were signposted in the nearby camping area and intermittently along the beach – the foam-crested breakers providing a dramatic seascape to match the uncertain mood. Salty air filled her lungs and left a stinging sensation on her skin. Tilt removed her shoes and chased down the side of the dune, her feet sinking deep into the sand. The biting wind whipped wildly in her face, and she sensed the rumbling earth beneath her as the waves washed in and pounded the shore.

Something ominous nagged at her gut. A feeling of unease intensified when she noticed Elizabeth way ahead having already crossed a rivulet and fast approaching a rocky outcrop that cut her passage off where the steep cliffs curved inward to meet the sea.

A mist blocked out the horizon, but at the edge of her vision Tilt got the fright of her life to see a wall of water looming towards the direction in which Elizabeth now bent to investigate the rockpools. 'Oh my God!' she cried when realising the gigantic wave threatened to engulf Elizabeth. There was no time to warn her.

Catching her completely off guard, the almighty volume of water swept over the rocks and smashed into the base of the cliff face to knock Elizabeth off her feet and swallow up everything in its path. The noise roared in Tilt's ears as spray erupted into the air.

The following seconds seemed like an eternity before the wave died down and receded to expose the shoreline once more.

Tilt tossed her jacket aside and ran as fast as she could. Clambering between the slippery surface of the rocks. A clump of slimy kelp snagged itself around her arm, and with the smell of floating seaweed in her nostrils she waded and splashed through waist deep pools calling, 'Hang on, Liz … I'm coming, I'm coming!'

Her clothing clinging to her body and dragging her down, Elizabeth floundered as Tilt arrived to help her. 'Take hold of my arm. I've got you,' she shouted.

Struggling to pull her free to safety, the two eventually came to rest on a stretch of wet sand. 'You're not hurt, are you?' Tilt asked.

Elizabeth, pale and shivering, coughed and spluttered, her body heaving up water. Fearing for her friend, Tilt rushed back down the beach to retrieve her jacket and returned to place it around Elizabeth's trembling shoulders.

'Stop it! Stop it, Tilt!' Elizabeth shrugged the jacket off.

'Stop what?' Tilt asked.

'Treating me like a mother hen, for God's sake.'

Detecting the unmistakeable bitterness behind Elizabeth's tone, Tilt said, 'Look, Liz, I know you hate me right now, but your teeth are chattering. Put the jacket back on. I'm not asking, I'm telling.' Tilt demanded as she pulled the coat back around her and jammed Elizabeths arms into the sleeves. 'You've had a fright and you're lucky you're not hurt. You could have been washed out to sea. We need to get you home and out of that wet clothing.'

'I'm quite capable of getting myself home.'

'It's not a matter of what you're capable of. I'm not exactly warm myself and not prepared to argue. So come on, lean on me and we'll head back to the car.'

Elizabeth pulled away as if her saviour had something catching. She then stubbornly stumbled along unaided until slowing down on the uphill climb to reach the carpark. Tilt grabbed her hand to help her and when finally on even ground, she said, 'I'll drive, Liz. We can come back later to collect your car.'

'Don't be ridiculous. I'm perfectly able to drive. I'm just a bit wet, that's all.'

'Just listen to yourself, Liz! I never knew you could be so pigheaded. And only now have I noticed that you're bleeding. Here, let me see that.'

'Oh my God, you never let up. I grazed my skin on the rocks. No big deal. It's only a scratch.'

Tilt reached a point where she'd had enough, and her composure finally left her. 'What a pompous and ungrateful person you are, Elizabeth O'Connell. Suit yourself. But you'll not get rid of me so easily. I'll be following you up the road. Then after you've had a chance to shower and climb into something warm, the two of us are going to talk.'

50

A Fiery Exchange

When reaching the house. Tilt marched Elizabeth to the bathroom and later bathed and dressed herself in a borrowed tracksuit and cosy socks. She then lit the fire and cranked up the coffee machine.

Elizabeth sank back into the cushions of a comfortable armchair and arranged a throw rug over her legs. 'Looks like you've settled in for the night,' she said when Tilt returned from the kitchen and placed two mugs on the coffee table. 'I can't recall inviting you to stay.'

'Well, get used to it, as this is where I'm intending to stay until I can be certain you're alright and agree to have that talk.' She then fixed her eyes on Elizabeth's legs and said, 'I hope you've put some antiseptic on those scratches.'

'Forget about the scratches, if a talk is what you really want, then that's exactly what you're going to get. But don't expect me to just roll over and go easy on you because of what happened today.'

Elizabeth's face coloured as she appeared to be winding up for an all-out battle.

'And another thing … your timing stinks, Tilt. Here I am in the middle of risking everything, selling the house to rebuild the business while believing you to be the one friend I could truly trust and rely on.'

'Good God, Elizabeth … are you for real? This is the second time I've come to your rescue in a matter of months, and all you can say is …'

Elizabeth raised her hand to silence Tilt. 'Allow me to finish,' she insisted. 'None of this would have mattered so much if I didn't give a stuff about you. That's the real cruncher in all of this! But before being so rudely interrupted, I was about to say, when everything else was going so horribly wrong, it was you who made everything seem possible again. It was you who lifted my spirits and made me laugh. It was you who encouraged me to stay. And it was you, Tilt, who saved me from Ian Henderson and pulled me out of the drink today.'

Even after saying this, Elizabeth pulled away as Tilt tried to place a hand on her arm in a token of gratitude to make amends.

'Don't touch me! Don't say a word! I don't want to know. I don't want to hear it. And yes, you have every right to meet Gary, but don't expect me to be happy about it.'

'My, that's a whole lot of don'ts, Liz. I drove out here to tell you I have no excuse for my actions. Our friendship is all important to me.'

'You should have thought of that before rushing off to meet my ex. Was it at his invitation?'

'No way! That guy was so in love with you, and probably still is. I just wanted to talk to him to see if your differences could be sorted.'

Elizabeth scoffed. 'Who put you in charge? Plus, I doubt you're being completely truthful about the real reason you arranged to meet. At least be honest about your motive.'

'Okay, I admit feeling sorry for Gary and really do like the guy.'

Tilt's admission appeared to stir up a streak of jealousy in Elizabeth. 'Why go behind my back?' she asked.

'A poor decision on my part and I didn't think I'd need your permission. After all, you insisted it was over between the two of you. Then I got wind of you and David Anderson becoming very close and assumed any thought of Gary was far behind you.'

'You assumed, did you?'

'Yes, and I really think you are kidding yourself, Liz.'

'Why on earth would I now care what you think, Tilt?'

Feeling these words cut right through her, Tilt felt a real need to assert herself. 'That statement's so very hurtful, Liz, and not at all like you. Especially since you answered that question just a moment ago. And it seems obvious to me that the reason you knocked back Gary's proposal had nothing to do with his so-called roving eye and everything to do with your attachment to Lenny Forrester.'

Elizabeth raised an eyebrow. 'You think yourself such an expert on these matters. But in case you haven't noticed, given your brief friendship with Gary, he does have a liking for the ladies which can be quite off-putting. As for Forrester, he's possibly spreading his charm as we speak, having left when I most needed him.'

Now standing with her back to the fire, and not wanting to be accused of scorching the seat of Elizabeth's borrowed tracksuit pants, 'Could you really blame the poor guy?' Tilt said, returning to her armchair. 'All I could see was you treating him like he was never quite good enough. And just as you did to Gary, you gave Lenny the flick. You also accused him of murdering your aunt and used him whenever convenient.' Tilt shook her head in disgust. 'I hate to say it, Liz, but it needs to be said because first chance you got, you cosied up to that Anderson loser. A person I find difficult to warm to.'

'Wow! Don't hold back, Tilt. What else has been pissing you off?'

'If you really want to know, it's the way all these good-looking guys keep coming back for more.' Tilt fired up. 'And if true friends can't say what's on their mind, there's no point in being friends. Sure, it may not always be what we want to hear, but I'm wise enough to admit, you're the dearest friend I've ever had. No man is going to change that.'

Elizabeth stared straight ahead, unmoving. Tilt could see the reflection of the flames flickering in her eyes and swallowed hard when feeling tears pricking her own eyes. She gulped before repeating, 'When it comes to losing what we have, Liz, it would break my heart. Please don't let this spoil everything. I couldn't stand not sharing in the redevelopment of the bookstore. Especially when we've been so focused on doing this together.'

'To hell with you, Tilt! But without you, this whole enterprise means nothing. And even though I'm bloody mad at you, you're spot on about Lenny Forrester and my selfish interest in three men. You've got the points on the board and have every right to keep meeting him.'

Tilt reached out and squeezed Elizabeth's hand. 'If you still love Gary, you should tell him,' Tilt said. 'Yet, it seems to me that you've been in denial about Forrester from day one.'

'Look, Tilt, I know I'm being unreasonable and can't quite put my finger on why the thought of you being with Gary is so upsetting to me. It just is, that's all and is going to take a bit of getting used to. Yet with you being a clairvoyant, perhaps you're right about Forrester. But don't go thinking you can just squeeze my hand and all's forgiven.'

Tilt laughed. 'Here, come and give me a hug.'

'Give me a break, I'm not that desperate. Whatever would Phyllis say?'

'God, you drive a hard bargain. And not sure about you, but I'm absolutely famished How about we grab a toasted sandwich and crack open some wine. Then I'll make up the spare bed … I must be due for a sleepover.'

51

Lenny's Warning

Seated over coffee at his favourite deli, Lenny Forrester turned the page of the *Herald* and *Weekly Times* to check out the real estate section. 'What!' he said out loud. 'I don't believe it.'

'Got a problem, mate?' the waiter asked as he stepped outdoors to clear away cups and wipe down the empty tables.

'Aw … it's nothing major, really, Maurie. Just noticed a property on the market that belongs to a friend of mine.'

'Maybe it's time to think about settling down, Lenny. Life's too short, as they say in the classics.'

Lenny folded the newspaper and tucked it under his arm. 'Not wrong there. I never did like the city,' he said as he got to his feet and threw a couple of coins on the table.

'Appreciate it, mate,' the waiter responded. 'Soon as I get enough cash together, I'm out of here. You should do the same I reckon.'

Lenny nodded and hurried away while all the time wondering why Elizabeth was selling.

Maybe she's closing the shop and leaving the Cove, he thought. *Either that or, desperate to raise money, she's gone an' gotten herself in too deep with the Andersons.* He checked his mobile and a news item flashed on the screen. "Ian Henderson found dead in prison cell." Once again Lenny couldn't believe his eyes.

"… former senior sergeant and head of Mariners Cove police station, charged with the alleged assault and attempted rape of Elizabeth O'Çonnell …'

'Bloody Hell!' How could he have missed this? He needed to pack his belongings and get back to the Cove. No wonder she was selling. That mongrel copper never was any good, and Lenny would have killed him with his bare hands if the job wasn't already done.

Unlike that smooth talking Anderson guy, he'd not suspected Henderson a threat, and now had to warn her about those Misty Headland bastards – the shady dealings and people who signed over their life savings to invest in a new home. They never were going to get past the planning stages before the shonky construction company went bust and left dozens stranded.

Lenny lowered the car window and breathed in the fresh sea air as he cruised along the main road of Mariners Cove. Suddenly catching a glimpse of the church, he stepped on the brakes and made an unexpected U turn in front of the oncoming traffic. 'What the hell!' No more than an empty shell, the bookstore was practically gutted at one end and all that remained standing was the external section that housed the entry porch, the choir loft and perhaps three quarters of what would have once been the seating area.

He leapt out of the car and questioned an old guy walking his dog down the street. 'What happened here, mate?'

'Tree fell on the roof and brought down the wires. Set one end of the building alight.'

'Geez! Is the lady and her friend who ran the bookstore okay, do you know?'

'Believe so. Luckily, no one was inside at the time. But the good news is, the whole thing is going to be rebuilt I hear.'

'Is that right?'

'Yep. Some of the locals aren't too happy about the design. Nothing better to think about if you ask me. What do you reckon, young fella?'

'Me … aw, I happen to know the lady who took over the place, and she wouldn't be putting her money into anything she didn't believe to be good for the Cove.'

The man nodded in agreement. 'Yeah, she's a nice young woman, that Elizabeth. Good looker, feisty and was just getting her foot in the door. It's a bloody shame this happened, and you can tell her from me that I wish her well.'

Lenny stopped off at the pub, freshened up and was on his way. Elizabeth might even kick him out seeing as how he'd never bothered to contact her. There didn't seem much point when she was so wrapped up in those blokes at Misty Headland.

But Lenny had smelt a rat and his decision to move back to the city and take up his old investigating job led him to better understand why the brothers were laying low.

The information he gathered revealed their fraudulent activities began after a serious car accident. David Anderson was at the wheel and the parents died at the scene. Philip suffered what was thought to be a temporary paralysis in his legs. This much was true. The family construction company was in debt and their father had borrowed against the house to keep the business afloat.

Philip somehow managed to organise written confirmation that his condition was long term as opposed to temporary. This ensured him of receiving government-funded payments for the rest of his days.

Equally as cunning, David took on a bit of gardening for vulnerable widows and was known to spin a sob story about needing money to support his disabled brother. On top of his wages, lonely heart contributors regularly handed over gifted cash credits in exchange for a promise of romance and the mere pleasure of his company.

The most worrying concern was that Philip's claim to be Margaret Thornton's son checked out. Yet, the motive for seeking out his birth mother remained unclear. Had the brothers decided to quit while ahead? Lenny wondered. They'd been clever alright and had sufficient funds secretly stashed away to quietly retire to the seaside backwater. But now when hearing from this guy in the street about the plans to rebuild the bookstore, Lenny grew suspicious about Elizabeth being duped.

Driving up to the house, he thought of the first time they'd met and the animosity Elizabeth had shown towards him. Then he saw her as she opened the back door and stepped outside. He felt his heart doing flip flops inside his chest when he turned off the motor and slid from behind the wheel to stand just metres apart.

'Well, well, Forrester, it's been a while. I'd almost forgotten what you look like. What's brought you back?'

'You did, Elizabeth. You brought me back, like always.'

'Bit late isn't it considering all that's happened? Not sure you would have heard about all that on your travels.'

'Elizabeth, do y'think I enjoyed seeing you get caught up with that Anderson guy?' Lenny shook his head. 'I haven't come to argue. I just wanna warn you. They can't be trusted. Believe me I know. And I hate to see you sell this place only to be taken for a ride.' Lenny moved a few steps closer. 'I only just found out about that bastard, Henderson.'

'Forrester, you mean to say you've come back here to tell me the Andersons are nothing better than a couple of crooks? I don't believe it. I think you're desperate to turn me against them and I'm not sure why. Just come right out and say so if that's the case, instead of making accusations. I've had enough of your talk. Where were you when I needed you?'

'That's just it, Elizabeth … you didn't need me.'

'Of course I needed you!' Elizabeth burst into tears. 'Let's not talk about the Andersons or Henderson right now, Forrester. Please just hold me for a second. I just need you to hold me.'

52

A Question & Answer

Was it something he'd said?

Had he caused her to cry?

Lenny found it most confusing that Elizabeth, who had greeted him with her usual cool reception and hadn't bothered to invite him in, would then ask him to hold her.

A complicated woman, he thought. And Lenny didn't understand complicated.

Between the mixed messages and unending contradictions, he was happy to accommodate her, but not at all certain if her request an invitation to take the matter further, or like some big brother, just simply comfort her whenever bad news struck. He held her close, closed his eyes and breathed in her wildflower perfume – his head swimming. With every manly instinct on the verge of overtaking him, disappointment set in as Elizabeth's tears dried up and she abruptly shoved him away.

She now looked deflated, and even mad at him.

He'd missed his chance. Was she thinking the same? Why did he keep tiptoeing around this issue instead of coming right out and declaring his feelings. God only knows, it was not for the lack of experience. He'd never been bashful when it came to the ladies. But where Elizabeth was concerned, he looked on her as having a touch more class than many of his former flames who he treated as a passing interest. Elizabeth was different, and he didn't want to cross any boundaries for fear of misreading her.

'Sorry about that, Forrester. I thought I'd recovered from the memory of that lecher's slimy tongue. But the mention of his name still makes my skin crawl,' Elizabeth shuddered.

'He's gone, Elizabeth. No need to worry. But y'do look like you could use some rest. Why don't you go 'n' lay down. I'll rustle up a cup of tea. I think I can remember where everything is.'

'Well … I guess I could use some company. Come in. I'll take some Panadol with that cup of tea.'

Lenny rolled his sleeves up and remembering where everything was, didn't take long to get the tea together. He tapped on the bedroom door minutes later. Elizabeth's face still looked pale as he placed the cup down on the side table.

'Black with one sugar,' he said.

'You remembered. That's impressive, Forrester.'

'Good t'know I can still do something right. Cos if I didn't know any better, I reckon you seem kind of mad at me.'

'You got that one right. Of course I'm mad at you. What do you expect after all this time? It's almost like you have a diploma in pushing me away.' Elizabeth scoffed. 'You sometimes treat me like a little girl that needs to be wrapped in cottonwool. And in case you haven't noticed, I'm all grown-up.'

Lenny raised his eyes to the ceiling, 'Yeah, I've noticed.'

'Do you find me attractive, Forrester?'

'Dunno really!' he teased. 'Depends, doesn't it?'

'On what? Elizabeth asked. 'Isn't this the sort of thing you either know, or you don't know. Supposing … and this is just supposition … I said you could kiss me right now. What would you say?'

'Fair go! I'm not the sort of guy who goes round kissin' just anyone.'

'That's not the impression I've been getting. I take it you don't find me in the least bit appealing. Is that what you're trying to say?'

'You are kind of bossy. Damn right difficult in fact,' Lenny said rubbing his chin. 'Reasonably good looking in a fairly, non-descript sort of a way. Not everyone's cuppa tea … if you get me drift.'

'Well, thanks for the glowing report.' Elizabeth's expression changed into a sullen pout as she pondered his words.

'Bloody hell, are you tryin' to seduce me, Elizabeth? I thought you weren't feeling great.'

'The truth is, Forrester, you're beginning to give me a complex. The way in which you held me, out there. It was almost like you were frightened of catching a chest cold or something even worse,' Elizabeth sighed. 'Why don't you unbutton my shirt, purely for the sake of seeing if you have any sort of adverse reaction.'

'Are you sure about this, Elizabeth? I always got the impression it was only me Kit Kats you were interested in.'

'Just shut up for a moment and do as I say.'

Not wanting to seem too eager in his happiness to oblige, he slowly fiddled with the buttons and slipped the shirt away from her shoulders.

'Well?' Elizabeth asked, 'Anything? Anything at all?'

Lenny didn't answer as his eyes took in the beauty of her perfectly formed figure.

'I'm waiting, Forrester. Put me out of my misery. What's the verdict?'

'I reckon a kiss might give me a better idea.'

'Okay, just do it.'

Slowly Lenny took her face in his hands and drew his mouth to her lips for the long-awaited kiss he had only ever dreamt about. Neither one could disguise the hunger they felt for each other as Lenny climbed on top of Elizabeth and their passion intensified. The springs beneath them creaked, the bed started to shift and shake and for a moment he thought this seemed perfectly normal until a bout of uncontrollable tremors began to erupt.

Crack. Lenny looked up to catch a glimpse of an uprooted gumtree flash past the window.

It crashed to the ground with an almighty thud.

'What the hell!' Elizabeth looked at him in fear. The entire house began to sway.

Books fell from the shelves. The cup rattled and tea slopped onto the saucer.

'An earthquake, Elizabeth! Quick, we need to get out of here,' Lenny said grabbing her hand.

With a sense of sheer panic, the shaking sent them running in fear, not knowing if the house and contents were about to be swallowed. 'Look out!' Lenny shouted as a table lamp crashed to the floor and a picture fell from the wall just missing Elizabeth's bare toes.

The Gods of nature had failed to account for the fact that the timing of this quake interfered with their longing to fulfil a long denied frustration as they ran from the verandah only to realise that as suddenly as it had started, once outdoors, all became silent and still. 'Listen!' Lenny said as he looked around in wonderment. 'Nothing! Just you and me. Not even the sound of a bird. It almost feels like the whole world has stopped turning.'

They looked at the fallen tree and the cracks that had opened on the surface of the ground. Then they gazed at each other.

Now was not the time for Lenny to be concerned about a mere earthquake. Should this be the end of the world, he had unfinished business that urgently needed attending to, and this time round he wasn't waiting for an invitation.

The following morning Elizabeth woke to the sound of plates crashing and banging in the kitchen. She stretched like a contented kitten and recalled the last time she had awoken to a similar situation after Gary had made love to her. But this was different somehow. She was different. Forrester was not Gary. Forrester was not David. Forrester was Forrester, just as she had imagined him.

Irrespective of a possible further quaking floor, she had never felt more secure. The profound physical aftershock of their lovemaking had brought with it something unseen, something deep inside her that she couldn't explain if someone had asked her, why Forrester? The question would have been impossible to answer. She just knew in her heart that he was the one. With Forrester by her side, she would fear nothing.

Feeling better than she could ever remember after sleeping in his arms, Elizabeth wasted little time stepping into her slippers and wrapping herself in a robe. She wandered down the passageway to the door of the kitchen. 'How long has this been going on, Forrester? Something smells so good.'

Two glasses of orange juice awaited and when Lenny had dished up crispy rashers of bacon on toast with lashings of butter and vegemite, the two sat at the table like an old married couple.

'Can you believe, Forrester, the earth literally moved?'

'You can say that again,' Lenny laughed.

'This is a special day. The builders are due to start the church and that means two good things have happened. Although I will have to get the tree removed and fix a few cracks in the plaster.'

'Elizabeth, it is a good day, and I don't want to spoil it. But I just need you to listen.'

'Oh my God, I don't want to hear any more about the Andersons please, Forrester.'

Lenny took hold of Elizabeth's hand and said, 'Once I've told you of all the information I've gathered, you'll be in a better position to decide whether you want to risk this house for the sake of the bookshop.'

Elizabeth sighed. 'Okay, you win. I'm listening.'

Lenny didn't hold back and was obviously intent about impressing how important it was for her to understand the Andersons' shady dealings in the past. And when he finished, Elizabeth said, 'I've had a gutful, Forrester. This is the absolute pits, and the work is only minutes away from getting started. Are you one hundred percent certain this is true?'

'It's true alright,' Lenny assured her. 'An' I can appreciate that with this guy Philip being y'cousin, it makes this news doubly disappointing. Truth is, I'm worried about you and wondered why you were crying yesterday.'

'Don't ask. It's a long story, and sometimes I wonder myself why I'm crying and whether I'm doing the right thing selling the family home. Now on top of everything that's happened, after hearing this I get the feeling that the parting of me from my money may not be the only issue I will be needing to sort out. Maybe I should chuck it all in and head back to the city.'

'I've been kind a hoping y'might stick around. I've missed you, Elizabeth, 'n' after last night, well … '

'Not as much as I've missed you, Forrester. But I'm mature enough to know that one night of lovemaking does not for a summer make, as the saying goes. The fact that you travel all over the countryside for work would make any long-term commitment between us impossible.'

Lenny never offered a word of reassurance about chucking in his work to be with Elizabeth as she went on to say, 'I can't live here alone anymore. Besides I've got a potential buyer who has put in a generous offer, and I'd be a fool not to take it.'

Lenny stared into his coffee mug and said, 'I can't imagine this place in anyone else's hands. Margaret would've been sad to see it go. I hate to think about it.'

Elizabeth's eyes glistened as she looked away, 'You and me both, Forrester.'

'Would you like me to come to Misty Headland with you?'

'God no. It's enough that you are here. And I'm happy for you to stay until I need to move out. But I think I might take a trip into the Cove first and see how much progress these builders have made before confronting Philip.'

53

Out of the Ashes

Pleased to see the building site a hive of activity, the noise of power tools and diggers sounded like music to Elizabeth's ears as she picked her way around a pile of splintered timber, rusty nails and shredded sheets of plasterboard.

Lenny's warnings got pushed to the back of her mind when seeing labourers busy pulling up what was left of the flooring and dismantling the storage section beneath the choir loft. Other workers were making steady progress pegging out the area for the new extension that looked almost in readiness to pour the foundations.

Jack Cooper, the builder in charge, shouted, 'Elizabeth, watch your step there.' Downing tools, he wiped his hands with a rag and hurried across to meet her. 'You're just the person I wanted to speak with.'

'Oh! Should I be worried?' Elizabeth frowned.

'No need!' he laughed. 'You're the boss remember. But you might be interested to hear that while the boys have been taking the old boards up, they came across a second storage space beneath the floor.' Distracted for a moment, he yelled at a boy named Caleb to load the damaged planks into the hire bin.

'Sorry about that. Caleb's first day on the job. I was just about to say that luckily the blaze was brought under control way before it came anywhere near where we found a metal box that looks to be completely intact.'

'I never knew of any area under the flooring and thought I'd pretty much cleared everything away,' Elizabeth said.

'Thing is, if you didn't know about it, the entrance not much bigger than a manhole, could have easily gone unnoticed when hidden beneath some empty crates.'

'Oh yes. I remember now. Those crates weighed a ton, and I couldn't budge them. But tell me, how large is this box?'

'Just a small container like someone might use to keep important documents. Come and you can see for yourself.'

Elizabeth followed Jack to a pile of discarded building material.

'The boys have wiped off the dust. But as you can see, it's padlocked. Would you like me to jemmy it open?'

Elizabeth suddenly recalled the key she had found in the vestry during that awful episode with the rat but agreed to take advantage of Jack's offer.

He prized the lock open with little effort. 'There you go, all done. Let's hope it's filled with hundred dollar notes,' he chuckled.

'Thanks, Jack,' Elizabeth said as he handed her the container with the open padlock left swinging in the clasp. 'A few extra dollars would come in very handy right now,' she laughed. 'I'll put it in the car and go through it later.'

Elizabeth then thought to ask Jack if the St Thomas foundation plate could be resurrected and restored to its former glory, as she was keen for it to be placed in a prominent position.

'Yep, Phil Anderson mentioned that same matter and picked it up when he dropped by first thing this morning. He was eager to see the job get started.'

'Pleased to hear it!' Elizabeth inwardly shuddered at the thought of confronting Philip about his past unlawful activities.

'I'm planning to meet with him later. But before I go, I'd like to take a further look around if that's okay.'

'Go right ahead,' Jack said. 'I'll tell Caleb to get you a hardhat and vest out of the truck.'

This seemed a bit extreme Elizabeth thought, and she felt a little embarrassed when aware of the workers staring as she self-consciously paced out the size of the extra floor space. She then tried to picture the high vaulted ceilings to be included in the new wings on either side of the once existing altar and checked the width of a huge expanse of glass panelling planned to replace the mid-section of the wall. The landscaped courtyard, she also thought, would provide the perfect focal point where a modern sculpture of St Thomas holding an open book was to be positioned.

The successful bringing together of the old with the new required great daring and Elizabeth couldn't wait to become involved in the fitting out of the interior. 'Okay, Jack,' she waved. 'I'll leave you to it and hopefully see if I can make some sense of what's inside the mysterious box.'

'Right-e-o, Elizabeth. But don't go spending all those notes on a crateload of champagne just yet. Save them for the opening.'

A lot of self-discipline was required by Elizabeth not to peek inside the box before driving to the far end of town where she parked alongside the cemetery and found a seat near her aunt's grave.

She placed the box on her lap, and taking a deep breath lifted the lid.

A jagged photograph lay on top of a yellowing document and what looked to be a pile of letters tied with a ribbon. Seeing the heat had caused the outer and slightly browning edges to curl over, Elizabeth lifted the photo out carefully. It almost certainly looked to be the missing half of the torn picture she had found in her aunt's drawer. A sign of recognition took hold of her when studying the faded image. Shocked, she brought a hand to her mouth and felt she might be physically ill as her tummy lurched. 'No! No! There must be some mistake. This isn't possible.'

But her hopes were dashed when opening the document to discover it was the birth certificate of Thomas Francis Thornton. And as she scanned the page, she noted *Father Unknown* penned in an inky script beneath her aunt's name. *No wonder Margaret had hidden the truth, she* thought when next withdrawing a silver heart-shaped locket and chain. A scrolled etching traced the border. And when she turned it over, the inscription read – *Love Always* followed by initials that left her in no doubt as to the giver. A declaration of love and signature was written on the back of the photo and each of the letters she suspected. Devastated, Elizabeth opened the locket to discover a picture of a youthful Margaret on one side and the same handsome man she had instantly recognised on the other. The locket fell from her fingers, and she slammed the lid down.

Her face went white as she approached the graveside and openly cursed her aunt. 'I've dismissed those who have tried to tell me what a wicked person you were. But now I know the truth. I hate you!'

Disillusioned with life itself, Elizabeth walked away in disgust.

54

Past Misdeeds

In her present state of mind – afraid she might be tempted to finish what Phyllis had started and murder Philip – Elizabeth decided to return home. She planned to delay their meeting until she could trust herself to drive to Misty Headland.

With Forrester already come and gone to deal with a job he had teed up, there was no one to discuss this latest matter with. Unable to think of anything other than the contents of the box and alarming news about the Andersons, Elizabeth felt determined to make her position clear.

A restless night followed. But anxious to face the day, at first light the next morning she got out of bed and waited for the clock to tick round to 8:30 before setting off to do battle.

'Elizabeth!' Philip's eyes lit up in surprise as he looked up from his desk. 'What are you doing here so early? Don't tell me something's gone wrong already.'

'It certainly looks that way, Philip,' she said.

Rummaging around in her handbag and withdrawing the torn photographs, she slapped them down in front of him. 'Anyone you know?' she asked.

'Look, Elizabeth, I'm not sure why you seem so pissed off. I'd much prefer if you'd come straight out and tell me.'

'Take a look at the photos, Philip. That might give you a clue.'

Philip sighed and picked up the one on his right. 'This looks to be an early picture of Margaret.' He then glanced at the second image. 'Not sure who the other guy is. Why do you ask?'

'Take a good hard look, Philip, and join the two together. You'll see it's like they are a couple. You'll also see a great resemblance between you and the man in the picture.'

Checking the photo again, Philip began to shake his head in denial. 'Where did you find these?'

'It doesn't matter where I found them. What does matter is that the man in the picture is in fact my father.'

Still confused, Philip looked up at Elizabeth and shrugged.

'Don't you understand what I'm saying?' Elizabeth hammered the desk with her fist. 'You need to go and get your eyes tested if you can't see that the two of you look identical. And the point I am trying to make, is that this guy in the photo is not just my father … he's your bloody father as well, Philip!'

'What!' Philip's mouth dropped open. 'That can't be right, surely.' He picked up a magnifying glass and studied the facial features closer. 'By God, I think you're right! No wonder you're here so early. We're not just cousins, you're my sister, Elizabeth!' Philip appeared so overjoyed he jumped up out of the chair and shouted, 'Where's that brother of mine? This news calls for a celebration. Is it too early to pull the bung out of a bottle of Moet?'

Elizabeth, having since moved to the opposite side of the desk, stared at him in disgust.

'I take it this isn't good news?' he said.

'You're damn right it isn't, you insensitive bastard. No sooner do I discover that I've inherited a brother … albeit a half one, thank God, after having just found out what a lying, two faced, despicable scoundrel you really are, Philip Anderson.'

With a thump, Philip flopped back into his chair. 'Why blame me? I'm the innocent party in all of this. And how can you be sure there weren't other boyfriends?'

'Are you kidding? Apart from the fact that the two of you look so alike, there are letters to prove as much.'

Elizabeth got to her feet and wandered across to the window. An eerie whistle of wind circled the walls and pressed against the windowpane.

With her back to Philip, she wondered at his silence. 'My biggest disappointment in all of this doesn't just stem from the fact that my own father betrayed my mother and had his way with her sister, but that you … yes you, Philip, feel the need to celebrate.' Elizabeth turned to face him. 'Oh yes, let's throw a party shall we and invite the whole of Mariners Cove along.'

'Okay, okay!' Philip swivelled around in his chair. 'That's enough, Elizabeth. So, I stuffed up. Haven't you ever stuffed up? There's no need to be so sarcastic. It doesn't suit you.'

'Doesn't suit me, hey! I'll tell you exactly what doesn't suit me. Because even sadder is the fact that your mother had the misfortune to conceive and give birth to a person devoid of any common decency,' Elizabeth scoffed. 'You are a dishonest man, Philip, who, along with that bullshit artist you call your brother, has betrayed my trust.'

Philip threw his hands in the air. 'What's gotten into you, Elizabeth?'

Her anger simmering at boiling point, 'The game's over, Philip, I know who you really are. And to think of all that crap you handed me about St Thomas. What a fool I was, while all along you've been planning to take me for every cent I inherited.'

Pacing up and down, hands going everywhere, her voice raised, 'How could you?' she shouted. 'Living the pretentious life of a gentleman unable to walk who stooped so low as to steal from those who trusted you so that you might live in this luxurious house and collect your precious antiques. How could you?' Elizabeth repeated. 'My dream of the bookshop and gallery has ended. I am done with you, Philip.'

Intent on making a quick exit, Elizabeth hesitated when Philip said, 'You really don't mean what you're saying. You think you do … but you don't.'

With her hand on the doorknob, Elizabeth felt uneasy about losing faith in everyone around her. Life was falling apart. So, she made a snap decision to give Philip the benefit of the doubt and releasing her hold on the handle she replied, 'Okay, I'm listening.'

'It's true that Dave and I lost our way for a while and needed to get out of Melbourne. Construction businesses were going bust all around us. Meanwhile, it seemed a good time to find my birth mother, and Misty Headland proved a likely place to start afresh.'

Elizabeth stepped forward and taking in the lavish surroundings threw her hands in the air. 'If you were so deeply in debt, how could you afford this?'

'Don't be fooled, Elizabeth, it's all owned by the bank.'

He then encouraged her to return and suggested they would be more comfortable in front of the fireplace. She begrudgingly agreed and the two sat down opposite each other.

'Times were tough. We took the easy path and got it wrong.' Philip said as he removed a cushion from behind his back and threw it to the floor as if it was somehow responsible for his past mistakes and present discomfort. 'I'm not proud of my actions, but Dave and I had to survive, and yes I admit, we did build ourselves a little undeclared nest egg which we socked away.'

Resting his elbows on either side of the chair, he clasped his hands together. 'Everything has changed however since Phyllis plunged that bloody spear into my shoulder. I wasn't sure if I was on the way out.'

Feeling no bigger than Thumbelina, Elizabeth sank deeper into the leathery confines of the chair and could have made good use of the discarded cushion but wasn't about to ask for it. She breathed in the masculine aroma of the tanned hide, and with arms outstretched along the padded armrests, watched Philip restlessly rise and step across to the mantle to reach for a box of Redheads. He removed a match, struck it and then put a flame to the perfectly laid fire stack. Once satisfied that the kindling had caught alight, only then did he continue.

'When you asked me to draw up the plans for the gallery extension, I realised how I enjoyed working again. David felt the same about his gardening. We planned to make amends, as has Phyllis. That's why I was keen to give her a second chance.' He rubbed his hands and cupping them together, blew into them. 'I'm confident if you see this through, Elizabeth, you won't regret it. This is the best work I've ever produced, and David and I are prepared to put our heart and soul into it.'

The fire sizzled and crackled as Elizabeth looked questioningly into Philip's eyes. 'That sounds all very well, but I'm not one for gambling. How can I trust you to be telling the truth and not planning to take off with the money I've already paid you up front?'

'What? And leave this house!' Philip laughed. 'If you don't believe me, make a detour on your way home and drive into town to see for yourself. The materials are being delivered on site as we speak, and I can promise to oversee the entire job at no cost to you. The reason being, I believe tourists and day trippers alike will come in droves just to visit the St Thomas Bookshop & Gallery.'

'What about the people you've ripped off and the payments you've been receiving illegally from the government? Moody was right! You've been able to walk all the time!'

'I'll let you be the judge of that. But the truth is, Dave and I have been working our butts off to repay some of what we owe, and I spend most of my days drawing plans for a confidential client who sells high-end designer homes for the rich Asian market.'

Squaring up for any wrongdoing, Philip seemed to have an answer for everything which sounded all too good to be true to Elizabeth. 'So, tell me about the money you received in Margaret's Will.'

'Didn't want it! The shop was struggling, and I donated a gift. There was never a need for me to be a beneficiary. Margaret always insisted it to be a loan, and I never stole a cent from her.'

Still unconvinced, Elizabeth touched on the matter of why the police hadn't caught up with them.

'Like I said before … just a case of we're not the only builders to go under.'

'What about David and his lady friends?' Elizabeth asked.

Philip remained silent for a moment. 'You really missed your calling, Elizabeth. This is like the bloody Inquisition. All I can say is we've put that all behind us and are looking to the future. You just wait and see. When the church is completed, you'll know I'm telling the truth.'

The door opened. 'Nice of you to wake me. But what's with all the chatter?' David asked as he made a beeline across the room to kiss Elizabeth who deliberately turned her head away.

With no prior knowledge about what had happened between Elizabeth and Philip, David looked from one to the other and asked, 'Will someone please tell me what's going on here?'

Elizabeth snatched up her bag and placing it over her shoulder pushed past him. She again resumed her position at the door where she turned and said, 'Your change of heart all sounds very encouraging, Philip, but I think it might be best if this whole project is scrapped, and we sever our ties.'

Philip raced after her as she disappeared through the doorway. 'The job will be going ahead Elizabeth no matter what you say,' he shouted. 'You're my sister and I'm not going to let you down. Do you hear me? The job will be going ahead even if I have to build that bloody church with my bare hands.'

55

Phyllis Cops it Sweet

Unable to catch her breath, Elizabeth wondered if she was about to have a heart attack. The lies, the hurt she had endured at being misled by the Andersons seemed like the final blow in a constant stream of unrest.

Desperate to block out the sound of Philip's false promises, she needed to get away, be by herself for a while and settle her nerves. But no, she should have known better. Because, whenever life was about to go off the rails, Phyllis Bentley was never more than a few steps away and had just pulled her car in beside Elizabeth's in time to hear the shouting.

With a look of shock on her face, she was propped squarely beside her front passenger door blocking Elizabeth's entry into her own car. 'Liz, whatever's going on? Are you okay?' she asked.

'No … I'm not okay, Phyllis.' Elizabeth's voice trembled and her hand shook when pressing the unlock button on her keypad.

'Wait! You don't look at all well and shouldn't be driving. Tell me what's happened.'

'Can't talk right now. Please step aside, Phyllis, I need to get away from here and maybe you should too.'

'How come?'

'You were right. I never should have become involved with the Andersons. Why do you keep working here? Are they even paying you a proper wage?'

'This is a sudden change of heart. Why would you ask such a question?'

Still inconveniently positioned between Elizabeth and her car door, Phyllis continued to prevent Elizabeth from leaving.

'Excuse me, Phyllis. I've already said I don't want to talk right now, and you're blocking my way.'

'Listen to me, young lady, I don't know what's going on exactly, but I thought you and I were friends since that business with that horrible senior sergeant. Whatever the Andersons have done, I've changed my opinion and think they are trying to move on. Just like I am. Why not give them the benefit of the doubt, Lizzie.'

'Please let me by, Phyllis. You are not my mother, and I am not a young lady who needs to be lectured by you every time something goes wrong. Let me pass so I can get into my car.'

Phyllis stood her ground. 'No, I'm not moving! You'll have to physically remove me if you want me out of the way.'

Elizabeth sighed and shook her head. 'I'm warning you, Phyllis. I've had a gutful of the lot of you. What is it they put in the water at Mariners Cove? Because everyone in this town seems determined to create a problem for me. And yes, like you, Phyllis, I thought we had agreed to rise above all this nonsense,' Elizabeth said clenching her fist. 'But if you don't move your arse right now, I could do something we might both regret.'

'Good heavens. You're acting like a spoilt brat. What is it with you, Elizabeth? You're always so obnoxious and unhappy.'

'Four times I've asked you to move and I'm literally sick of it, Phyllis. I've had enough.'

Elizabeth's face broke into a sweat. Tossing her keys in her bag, a long held bitterness bubbled away just beneath the surface and a great eruption of pent-up anger she had held in check since childhood threatened to rise to the surface and spill over. Suddenly, eight years old and shaking her head – no, no. She didn't want to think about it, not now, not ever. She didn't want to believe her parents would never be returning. They'd promised to come home. She'd wanted to throw a tantrum and hit out at everyone given the unfairness of it all. But no, Aunt Margaret and Grandpa had cuddled her, wiped away her tears and there was an end to it.

Why had God made her suffer? She didn't deserve this. Wanting to scream, she had given fair warning and was now about to explode – Phyllis standing right in the firing line to deliberately test her just one time too many. But Elizabeth wasn't seeing Phyllis whose body had taken on the form of whoever responsible for drowning her parents. The blame needed to be finally addressed and Elizabeth, seeming incapable of understanding how the devil himself had taken her over, lost complete control, hit out and socked her wicked antagonist smack, right in the eye.

Phyllis reeled back with a look of absolute disbelief and Elizabeth acted as if what she had done didn't even register. She had administered a long overdue punishment and when settling in behind the driver's seat, she revved up the engine then screamed off down the road like an entrant in the Grand Prix, never once looking back.

Phyllis, of course, hadn't expected Elizabeth would carry out her threat. 'I had it coming!' she assured Philip and David as they rushed to her aid and helped her inside. Taking an icepack from the freezer David asked, 'Would you like to lie down for a bit while Philip makes a cup of tea?'

'Good gracious, no! That won't be necessary.'

Hardened by the odd assault in the lock-up, Phyllis decided to cop it sweet and say nothing adverse, knowing something major must have happened for Elizabeth to resort to physical abuse. 'I don't blame the girl,' she admitted. 'She wasn't herself, poor soul.'

'You may not feel so forgiving when you wake up in the morning,' Philip laughed. The brothers however remained silent on the matter of what had led to this outburst.

But Phyllis could swear she'd heard Philip shout something about a sister. The lack of information was almost killing her, and it was this terrible longing to always stick her nose in where it wasn't wanted that had paid out on her. Phyllis understood perfectly why she was wearing a shiner, and whenever asked in the following days what happened, she used the oldest excuse in the book, claiming she had accidentally walked into a door.

56

A Pep Talk from Tilt

During the off-peak season, the wide coastal backstreets of Mariners Cove seemed far easier to navigate. And – when brushing aside her woes – Elizabeth felt a deep seated love for this, her childhood community.

With the paths less trodden and the bitumen laid bare due to the absence of traffic, scattered pine needles had spread underfoot, and tufts of greenery sprouted through the eroded surface cracks. Mossy mounds padded the muddied laneways and shrubbery spilled over the paling fences.

Generations had come and gone. Yet, smoke billowed from chimney stacks set above iron clad rooftops of houses left standing from a long-ago era. The weathered cottages – lovingly restored – still survived and exuded a humble dignity and charm that often got lost amid the bustling crowd when city dwellers invaded the township in droves to set up camp and laze in the afternoon sun.

Elizabeth considered these surrounds as she'd driven along Wild Dog Road and onwards to the building site. The thought of returning to the rat race of suburbia weighed heavily on her mind as she slowed the car and scanned the church grounds.

Unable to face the builders and tell them to down tools as the job wouldn't be going ahead, Elizabeth's detour had at least clarified the materials had been delivered, as Philip had promised. Given this small degree of comfort, she decided against acting on her hasty decision and instead, sent an urgent text message to Tilt asking if it would be okay to drop by.

Coffee machine is fired up and ready to go. Tilt's response ended with a smiley emoji.

The whitewashed fisherman's cottage, a renovated relic surrounded by an established garden, never failed to lift Elizabeth's spirits. An abundance of camelias hanging in clusters on the glossy leafed bushes swayed on the breeze and carpeted the ground beneath her feet. But, when she tapped on the door and entered the kitchen, Elizabeth was quickly reminded of why she had come. 'What happened to you for God's sake?' Tilt asked, with a look of concern.

Self-consciously tucking a few strands of stray hair behind her ears, 'If you reckon I look bad … you should see Phyllis. I just smacked her in the eye.'

'No way! Whatever happened to that polite young woman I met staring down at me from the top of the ladder?'

'It's true! Nearing thirty, I've gone feral in my old age, Tilt. Although I never set out to hurt Phyllis, it just kind of happened. The worst part being I now realise I've been hanging out to sit her on her bum ever since my return to the Cove.'

'Geez, darling, I would have loved to see the look on her face,' Tilt chuckled. 'And wouldn't you know, I've just this minute dropped a capsule into the coffee maker. But you look like you could use a stiff drink.'

'Actually, I'd kill for a coffee, Tilt.'

'Bloody hell, Liz! I wouldn't mention the word kill if I was you. Maybe you should choose your words more carefully.'

'You're right! But anything stronger and I'm likely to have a mega meltdown and murder all three of them at Misty Headland,' Elizabeth admitted.

With coffee mugs in hand, Elizabeth spent the next half hour updating Tilt.

'No wonder you're in such a state,' Tilt sympathised. 'Yet, you can't let this latest setback influence your decision. It would be crazy to wreck your plans now. Besides, I've just received a carton of the bookmarks we ordered.'

Elizabeth raised a hand. 'Don't show me. We might have to sell them at the Sunday Market and that would break my heart.'

'No market will be grand enough for these babies. Because as bookmarks go, these are the crème d'la crème.'

'I'd rather not know right now.'

'Okay, if that's the way you feel,' Tilt said, jumping to her feet, 'it must be time to make a sandwich.' Buttering the bread and slapping slices of ham, cheese and tomato in between, she set it down in front of Elizabeth. 'Eat!' she insisted. 'And don't worry. We are going to get through this just like we've got through all the other problems.'

Not realising how hungry she was, Elizabeth gratefully demolished every last crumb.

'Good to hear Lenny's back,' Tilt added. 'That's got to be a positive sign, doesn't it?'

Elizabeth purposely neglected to enlarge on the more personal details concerning Forrester.

'Uh huh, I know that look,' Tilt said. 'Come on, Liz, 'fess up. He's staying with you … isn't he? Has he … you know?'

'Maybe we should save this for another day.'

'If you insist. But remember what they say about all work and no play. Fortunately, I'm happy to report that most mornings I wander over to the church to watch the progress and check out the talent.' Tilt winked. 'Never could resist those tradies in their singlets and super short shorts without a second glance.'

'God, you crack me up, Tilt. You're not serious, are you?'

'Never been more serious in my life, darling. Spot on about the crack, as it happens. Coz boy, when those guys bend over, phew,' pausing to fan her face, 'I've needed to rush home and take a cold shower.'

Elizabeth laughed as Tilt dismissed any talk of shutting down. 'I couldn't stand to think of the deprivation such a callous act would cause if you were to destroy the joy of seeing those muscle-bound men at work.'

With a sudden change of subject, Elizabeth asked, 'Do you mind if I make myself another sandwich, Tilt?'

'How can you think of food when I'm discussing the livelihood of these builders?' Tilt scoffed. 'Where's your compassion?'

Feeling guilty, Elizabeth sheepishly helped herself to the bread from the packet. 'If I can't pay their wages, you can forget about compassion.'

'Well, in your present state, don't point that knife at me, darling. You need to play this game smartly when it comes to dealing with the Andersons, and don't underestimate the fact that I've got a few aces up my sleeve to help deal with the matter.'

57

Keeping her Cool

At Forrester's urging, Elizabeth paid a visit to the doctor, who recommended she cut down on the stress levels. 'You're far too young to be experiencing high blood pressure,' he said.

Elizabeth also suspected that her empty threats would not be taken seriously with it being too late to back out and start a life again in Melbourne. It almost killed her to distance herself from the proceedings and remain in the background. But to avoid further clashes with Philip, she never visited the site unless first ensuring no one was around. The weeks passed and work on the church progressed at a steady pace. Updates from Tilt confirmed he had kept his word.

This plan had worked in her favour until, with the completion date fast approaching, it came time to make her presence felt and she openly walked back on site with every good intention of remaining calm.

It was clear that Philip had contributed his time to save on expenses, having done a huge amount of the work himself. Elizabeth also felt he deserved full marks for the creative ingenuity of the design. He had not only managed to restore the church to its former glory, but had improved on it, and she sensed an almost spiritual enchantment generate from the light reflected through the soaring window at the centre of the extension.

So now she dropped the pretext of having no further interest when eager to discuss the positioning of the all-important sculpted statue of St Thomas.

David, dressed in jeans, a t-shirt and heavy boots, was hard at work on the layout of the landscaping when she approached him. He stopped, and – leaning on the handle of his shovel – was quick to dismiss any thought that he needed to be told what to do.

'I'm familiar with the layout, Liz, as we planned it together … remember!' He instead appeared more interested in broaching the subject of Philip, who, having delivered on his promise, had hesitated to ask for more funding.

'You'll get your money, David. Every cent that's owing. And yes, he has kept his promise, and I couldn't be happier.'

'It might be good to tell him that,' David said.

'I'm prepared to admit he's done an outstanding job.'

'He's done more than an outstanding job,' David insisted. 'He's exposed our whereabouts to put us both at risk, all for your benefit, Liz.'

Distracted by people coming and going, who made no secret of the fact that they were curious to look at the project and chatter in the background, Elizabeth didn't bother to answer. But her attention was quickly jolted back to David when he raised another matter.

'I never did understand why you suddenly pushed me away, Liz.'

Again, Elizabeth brushed his question aside.

'Fuck, don't I even deserve an answer? Is that all you think of me?' he asked. 'Well, get stuffed, Liz, and leave me to finish my work.'

Elizabeth sighed. 'You know as well as I do we were vulnerable, David, and anxious about Philip. Thrown together and drawing comfort in our need, we mistakenly believed our strong desire for each other a sign of being in love.'

David shook his head. 'I'm sad to hear that to be your interpretation, but most definitely not mine. You make it sound so cut and dry.'

Impatient to end this conversation, Elizabeth again became aware of the constant buzz of a group discussion surrounding the latest talking point at the Cove. But, determined to air his grievances, David refused to let the matter rest. 'Then that handyman suddenly comes back on the scene and drags our name through the mud.'

Elizabeth bristled when he accused Forrester of being the bad guy in all of this.

'You took your rage out on poor old Phyllis,' David said.

'Poor old Phyllis? Well, there's a statement I never expected to hear coming from you. Have you forgotten she's not all that old, and almost murdered your brother?'

'Seems he's your brother as well, I hear. And I happen to know Phil is genuinely upset that you don't appear to give a rat's rear end about him. He doesn't deserve that.'

Her head now aching, every sound and even the birds were beginning to grate on Elizabeth's nerves. 'I'd just learnt my father betrayed my mother and got his own sister-in-law pregnant. Do you expect me to be overjoyed about that, David? Philip was so insensitive that he wanted to pull the cork out of a bottle of Moet and celebrate.'

'Wrong again, Liz! Philip believed the fact that you were his sister the real cause for celebration. And if you hadn't been so wrapped up in blaming him for something he had no control over, things could have been different. It's always someone else's fault in your mind, Liz.'

Elizabeth edged David back against the wall. Lowering her voice, she was mindful of staying calm. 'I've had enough trouble of late, David. But since you started this and have tried to inflame the situation, I make no apology when saying I came here to have a civil conversation. There's no excuse for what you and Philip have done, and I felt ashamed of the pair of you. So once this job's completed and the money is in your account, you can get the hell out of my life ... is that understood?'

David ran his hands through his hair. 'I feel I don't even know you anymore, Liz. You're a hardhearted woman with no compassion. And one of these days you might alienate everyone around you.' He then turned and leant forward with the flat of his hands against the stone and gazed down at the ground. 'Phil and I will finish your precious bookstore and garden, but always remember, the next time you push someone away, you may well live to regret it.'

The sound of a truck grabbed their attention and when David stuck his head around the corner, the driver shouted, 'Got a delivery for y'mate ... a load of pittosporums.'

It was easy to see David wasn't impressed when cursing under his breath. 'None of the plants I ordered were supposed to arrive for another two weeks.'

'Too late, brother! I'm just paid to do what I'm told and am certainly not takin' 'em back.'

Elizabeth looked at David and said, 'We'll see about that! I'll have a little chat to the man.'

Three minutes later the truck was leaving with the full load on board.

Shocked, David asked, 'What did you say to him?'

'Nothing much! I simply told him I thought it might be a good idea for him to bring them back in two weeks.'

'How did you manage that?'

'You may think I have no compassion David, but sometimes there's a need to stand up for what one believes to be right. In the short term it can get tricky, but in the long term, I usually find it hasn't done me any harm.'

58

Making Amends

Three months had passed when Elizabeth decided it was high time for her to make peace, not merely with Phyllis, but those around her who she had treated harshly.

Balinese windchimes softly tinkled on the breeze as she made her way through the garden. The prayerful statue of a Buddhist monk – legs crossed, hands joined, and head bowed – sat in the same position where he had taken up residence so long ago. As always, his presence amid the leafy surrounds generated a calming effect that Elizaeth felt much in need of right now.

Armed with a potted orchid and fully repentant, she had spared no expense when selecting this exotic bloom.

A peace offering of sorts, Elizabeth hoped that Phyllis would see it as such and be willing to forgive her. She also hoped that the wretched black eye she had inflicted on her so long ago would be well mended by now.

Peace seemed to be the key word in her vocabulary today, as there hadn't been much of it since her return to Mariners Cove. Yet, seeing the garden left to run wild and the birch grove spilling over with rambling pockets of nasturtiums, the scene did little to settle her nerves.

Raising her face to the sunlight, she breathed in a welcoming blend of nature's delicate perfume and recognised the place had not lost its appeal.

It had taken a while for Elizabeth to think about apologising to anyone. She felt she had every right to be angry. But strangely, it was David Anderson's cutting remarks that had struck a chord and played on her mind all this time and finally prompted her visit. Intent on judging others, perhaps she had enjoyed feeling sorry for herself and even relished playing the victim – "poor me!" having become a convenient catchcry.

So, was it any wonder when knocking on the backdoor of the farmhouse, that she wasn't expecting a friendly reception? Far from it, in fact. Because she was not exactly a figure of virtue in all of this since socking Phyllis in the eye. Then when thinking back on Gary, poor guy, she had shunned him when he'd done nothing but profess his love for her and made one rash decision that had harmed no one. Forrester, she had accused of murder and so undeservedly treated him with a high-handed and snooty contempt. Even Tilt, her best friend and a person who had saved her life, had come under attack. Not forgetting the Andersons who, irrespective of their past, had since proven true to their word. And lastly, the most hateful words of all, she had directed at her aunt who had given up everything to take care of her.

Things were about to change. Elizabeth was about to change. The St Thomas Bookstore & Gallery was due to reopen, and she wanted to wipe the slate clean. A sight to behold, the sculptured statue being the focal point outside that stately window – the walled garden, the hedging and French lavender setting such a romantic scene in the cobbled courtyard, Elizabeth couldn't believe what had been accomplished. The new building being every bit as perfect as she'd been hoping.

Without a hint of a bruise, the look of shock on Phyllis's fully healed face said it all when seeing Elizabeth. 'Goodness, you are the last person I was expecting, and I'll bet you're probably thinking I might slam the door right in your face.'

'The thought had crossed my mind,' Elizabeth replied.

'Well, I don't for one minute intend to do that. And as it's not my birthday I really must say if that pot plant you're holding is for me, I can't accept it.'

'Please, Phyllis, before you start telling me what a hateful person I am, I just want to say you caught me at a bad moment. I'd just received upsetting news and wasn't myself.'

'That's strange, because I thought you were being exactly yourself.'

'No, this is who I really am. I've come here to apologise. I'm sorry for what I did, and I am sorry that it has taken me so long to say so. My behaviour was inexcusable. I haven't forgotten that you were so caring towards me when I became depressed, and you didn't deserve to be treated like that. I'd like to make it up to you and ask your forgiveness.'

'You want my forgiveness? After what I tried to do to you with that confounded spear I managed to plunge into Philip? I'm surprised you ever spoke to me again.' Phyllis stepped aside and ushered Elizabeth into the kitchen.

'Now don't say a word, young lady, because I want you to take a seat right there and listen to what I have to say.'

Elizabeth relieved herself of the orchid and looking a bit confused, she waited to hear what else Phyllis seemed so keen to tell her.

Filling the kettle and popping it on to boil, Phyllis went about the business of setting out the mugs, teabags, milk and sugar before being seated herself and only then did she continue. 'Look, love,' her voice softened, 'I know that I've misjudged you and been an interfering old fool. We've had this discussion before. I also know you defended me when asked if you were against me working for the Andersons again. You agreed that I deserved a second chance. You did that for me Lizzie, after the way I treated you. I've never forgotten that.'

This was not going at all the way Elizabeth had expected with Phyllis now actually doing the apologising.

'So, here's the deal!' she said. 'I think, and you know I do think a lot, that I deserved a bloody good whack to knock some sense into me. You know why, Elizabeth? Because I never learn. I should have backed off, respected your request and given you space.'

'Gosh, Phyllis, you were worried about me that's all. As for the spear, you were unwell, and I was a total cow, so wrapped up in my own world and too insensitive to understand all you had suffered. Now, please say you'll accept this orchid and let's put all this behind us,' Elizabeth said, watching Phyllis pour out the tea.

A tear ran down Phyllis's cheek as she came around the table to hug Elizabeth. 'I think myself lucky you know!' And when she had sat back in her chair and taken a sip of her tea, her eyes lit up to see a white envelope being pushed across the table towards her.

'It's an invitation to the grand opening of the bookshop. I want you to be there, Phyllis.'

'I'm speechless. Well, I'll be needing to check my diary,' she joked.

Aware that Phyllis was secretly delighted at the prospect of being seen at the opening, Elizabeth said, 'All you'll be needing to do is lash out on a lovely new dress and book your appointment at the hair salon before everyone else gets in.'

'You know, Lizzie, I've never been one for holding grudges,' came this brand new voice of reason, 'and I truly appreciate you have thought enough of me to take the trouble to come here and say you're sorry.'

'Thank you, Phyllis. I wasn't expecting that things would turn out quite so well to be honest.'

They both laughed as they sat at the table together. Phyllis who had appeared to mellow since her stint in prison, again repeated, 'I promise I'll only mention this once more, but I can understand why with all that pent up anger you may have been eager to punch me.' Phyllis paused and looked down at the invitation. 'You haven't had it easy either when losing your parents. We all want to blame someone for those things we can't fix. But I never should have blamed you, that was quite wrong of me, and I feel ashamed for wanting to take my revenge out on you.'

Elizabeth reached out and placed her hand on Phyllis's arm.

59

Making Amends (Part 2)

On her return home from her visit with Phyllis, Elizabeth felt confident that any adverse kinks in their relationship had been successfully settled.

Next came Gary, she thought, as she kicked off her shoes and pressed his number in her contact list.

Detecting a measured tone in his voice when he answered, 'Liz …this is a surprise.'

A pleasing surprise or unwanted surprise? She settled on the latter.

'Is everything okay?' he asked.

'All's good thanks, Gary. What about you?'

'Yeah … apart from the fact that my best girl left me and broke my heart, I suppose I can now say it's taken a while, but I'm gradually getting my shit together.'

Gary, being a guy who usually watched his language, was obviously still bitter about their break up, and a moment of silence followed. 'So … how's life at the wonderful Mariners Cove?' he then added, with an exaggerated emphasis on the *wonderful*. Or had she simply imagined it? 'How's that church of yours coming along?'

'The building's completed!'

'No way! That's fantastic,' he replied.

'Yes, I'm pinching myself right now because I can't quite believe how amazing it looks. And one of the reasons I'm calling is to ask if you're free, or able to juggle your flight roster on the 29th of next month, I would love you to come to the Opening.'

With no immediate response, and to save any further embarrassment, Elizabeth quickly added. 'No stress if you can't, of course. I completely understand if you'd prefer not to.'

'Truth is, it could be a bit tricky to get the time off and even a touch awkward, Liz.'

'That's a shame. Because I happen to know that a certain friend of mine might be delighted if you could make it. You see, Tilt's already told me she's run into you a few times on her trips to Melbourne.'

Run into, sounded like a far better way to describe their friendship than anything of a more personal nature. Yet, moments of protracted silence were becoming far too frequent. The invitation was not going down well.

'Are you still there, Gary?'

'Look, Liz,' Gary's voice cracked. 'Let's not pretend that …'

'Forget it, Gary!' Elizabeth cut him short. 'I should never have called in the first place. It was wrong of me. But the real reason I wanted to speak to you, was to tell you I'm sorry … I'm truly sorry for the way I treated you. You didn't deserve that.'

'I could say no hard feelings, Liz. But I would be lying. You had your reasons, and I wasn't exactly blameless. I knew I was losing you on the day you left for Mariners Cove. Just couldn't face the fact. I still hold out the hope that we can get back together. Yet I can't pretend these meetings with Eileen haven't had an impact on me. Are you certain you're okay with that?'

'Absolutely! Plus, I know that Tilt's been on the lookout for a handsome pilot to escort her at the opening, and I thought your presence would be a lovely surprise for her.'

Gary forgot his woes for a moment and seemed a whole lot happier at the mention of Tilt's desire to see him. 'Sounds like an offer too good to refuse. Just not sure I can handle the situation, if you get my drift. I can't promise you anything, but text me the details and I'll give it some thought.'

Gary's response didn't sound at all encouraging. Only time would tell if he'd ever truly come to terms with the fact that she had turned his proposal down. Elizabeth wasn't even certain how she would react when seeing him partnered with her best friend. But at least she had tried and hopefully made her peace. It was all up to Gary from here.

With the next person on the list being in no position to challenge her, Elizabeth then stepped out into the garden and cut a bunch of flowers so that she might square up with Aunt Margaret. She then made her way to the cemetery and carefully removed the weeds that had sprung up around the gravesite before swapping over the withered contents in the jar for the fresh blooms. 'We both know I was pretty mad when I last visited, so please don't think I'm trying to bribe my way back into your favour,' she said. 'It's just that these flowers are probably the last I will ever pick from our garden,' Elizabeth sadly sighed. 'I've sold our house, Aunt Margaret.'

At that moment, it felt like she was about to cry. But she quickly regained her composure and explained, 'It was wrong of me. So wrong of me to sell our home. I did it to save the church and reopen the bookshop. I had no other choice as the insurance pay out fell far short of the amount I needed to rebuild after the fire.'

Elizabeth lowered her voice when becoming aware of another couple tending a grave across the way. 'Oh, and one last thing. Whatever the reason for your involvement with my father, it was not my place to judge. Perhaps, like me, you had no other choice either. And in the heat of the moment, I should never have said what I said … about hating you, I mean. It's so untrue.'

Satisfied that Margaret would hear and forgive her wherever she was, Elizabeth's mind quickly turned to Philip and David Anderson. Of course, she needed to include them in her bid to become less judgemental. Then there was Forrester to consider. He had taken up her offer to stay with her since his return to the Cove. So, it seemed, with the final exchange of contracts fast approaching, he was taking her to dinner tonight to discuss something of importance to do with his future living arrangements.

Tired of the hotel, he had hinted that Graeme Jenkins had a room on offer and had offered him the use of it whenever he came to town. Disappointed, Elizabeth hoped that since they had become closer and there was never any mention of changing his lifestyle, that he had agreed or at least found a convenient alternative nearby.

60

A Defining Moment

Seated in the dining room at The Cove, Elizabeth checked the specials of the day.

Lenny looked up from the menu and asked, 'How about we share the fisherman's basket?'

'Are you serious? I love seafood … you know that. But it's the most expensive dish on here.'

'It's your favourite, and tonight I feel in the mood to celebrate.'

With an icy cold Carlton Draught already sitting in front of him, once Lenny had ordered their meal, he raised his glass and reached it out towards Elizabeth.

She then picked up her own glass of white wine. 'What are we celebrating, Forrester?'

'New beginnings! How does that sound?'

'New beginnings it is,' Elizabeth said as they clinked glasses, and Lenny didn't waste a moment washing down the frothy white head from the top of his beer. He then sat back and began to enlarge on his reason for choosing to celebrate. 'I'm a little surprised but pleased those Anderson guys have done the right thing and that church of yours is about to be up and running again.'

'It's a relief, I can tell you, Forrester. Especially when worried about being the loser in all of this. But now, maybe this proves they really are intending to change their ways.'

'Yeah, I'd like to agree but have a bad feeling about those guys. They're a bit too shifty for my liking. Smart, but I just don't trust 'em,' he said. 'Anyway, enough about them, because the reopening of the bookshop is not the only reason why I brought you here for dinner. I'm glad we could make it early coz I've been hanging out to show you something before it gets dark.'

'Is it Jenkins' place you want to show me?'

'No way would I subject you to that, Elizabeth. Bugger moving in with Jenko. He's a good mate, but I couldn't see meself sharing a bathroom with him. I've wanted to keep this a surprise, but if you promise you won't laugh, I can't keep this a secret any longer.'

'I'm not surprised. Secrets are boring if you don't tell anyone. But why would I laugh?'

'Well, you might think it a bit unusual, that's all. Y'see the truth is, I've been thinking for a while now about buying a house.'

Elizabeth laughed.

'I knew it! I told you not to laugh.'

'Sorry! But did I hear you correctly? You're actually thinking of buying a house? Because if that's what you said, let's face it, Forrester, you just don't do houses, and I can't see you settling down anytime soon.'

'A bloke's allowed to change his mind y'know, Elizabeth. An' what with you moving out of your place shortly, I've been looking to have somewhere a bit more permanent to … well, y'know … hang me hat … as the cowboy said to the hooker.'

'But you're no cowboy, Forrester. And do you even own a hat?'

'Course I own a frigging hat. I thought you'd be more interested in asking about the hooker.'

'I've never really heard anyone use that expression before. What's a hooker got to do with the hat?'

'Forget about the hat. Coz another thing I've been meaning to ask is, when you do move out, what in the hell are y'planning to do with all that furniture?'

'Most of it'll go into one of those storage bays, until I get around to finding a place to live. Why?'

Lenny downed the rest of his beer. 'I didn't wanna say straight up, but I've had an offer accepted on this house, and I'd like your opinion about the place before I sign on the dotted line.'

'So, what's all this got to do with the furniture? Do you want to take it off my hands?'

Buttering a bread roll, Lenny hesitated before moving on to answer the question. 'No, no, not exactly. But I do have a question and don't want you to get the wrong idea, Elizabeth. What I've been thinking is, well let's just say if you like the place, maybe I could return the favour, and you could bunk in with me for a change. Just till you find somewhere you like. You could then stack all your stuff in the garage 'n' that'd save forking out extra for storage.'

'Lenny Forrester, what is this? Are you asking me to move in with you? Is that what you're suggesting? I'd have to seriously think about that.'

'What's to think about? You were the one who seduced me remember, and considering what's been going on lately, I'd like t'think we're a bit more than just good friends.'

'But are we, Forrester? Because I've got my eye on an apartment close to the bookstore. With you always travelling, I'd like to base myself in town.'

'That mightn't always be the case. I'm not going to be an itinerant worker for ever.' Lenny's face clouded over right when the fisherman's basket was placed on the table.

'Is everything okay, Mr Forrester?' the waiter asked.

'All good, thanks, Max,' Lenny replied with a distinct tone of disappointment in his voice.

'You're not mad at me are you, Forrester?' Elizabeth asked. 'Because I couldn't stand that tonight just when I've been wanting to tell you how sorry I am.'

'For what?'

'Accusing you of murdering Margaret, for starters. And then there's the times when I've been a bit less than kind to you.'

'If you're trying t'make me feel bad, Elizabeth, you're doin' a great job of it. We came out to enjoy ourselves t'night. New beginnings … remember?'

When dinner was ended and it came time to leave, Elizabeth noticed that Lenny had gone unusually quiet, and as they drove out of town, she placed a hand on his knee and thanked him for the delicious dinner. Then as that little show of gratitude didn't seem to have the desired effect, on a brighter note, she asked. 'Where is this house of yours, Forrester?'

'Just up the road a bit.'

'Well at least it's comforting to know you've decided to live nearby,' Elizabeth said as she stared straight ahead. 'Are you sure you're going the right way? We seem to be heading in the same direction as home.'

When Lenny didn't answer, Elizabeth knew for certain his mood had shifted since she hadn't jumped at his offer. She felt sure this was the real reason he had shut her down so abruptly when she ventured into saying sorry. And now, it was clear he had changed his mind about showing her the house as he turned down the dirt road towards home and pulled in at the front gate.

'So, you are mad at me, Forrester … is that it? I cannot believe you're treating me like this and now it is you who is spoiling our evening all because …'

Lenny didn't wait for her to finish. Instead, he got out of the car, opened the gate, got back in and then kept driving. 'Say something, Forrester! Why aren't you taking me to see the house?'

'You're looking at it, Elizabeth. This is it!'

'That's not even remotely funny.'

'It's not meant to be. I've never been more serious in my entire life. I've already paid the deposit and as you know, due to sign the contract in a week or two. It's meant to be a surprise.'

'What! You mean to tell me you're the mystery buyer? You and Jenkins cooked this up between you?'

Lenny nodded. 'Well Jenko did the easy bit, and I didn't count on the idea being such a disappointment. But I couldn't let you sell. Always did love the place, an'I'm sick of bedding down in cold old rooms that a bloke can never call his own. You're not too upset, I hope. I'm buying it for you as much as me, Elizabeth. And as I said at dinner, I kind of hoped the two of us could live here.'

Elizabeth gave him a puzzled look. 'What … like as in together, you mean?'

'Well yeah. We've already been doing that, haven't we? We could tie the knot, like in a marriage of sorts if you wanted to make this a more permanent arrangement.'

'Lenny Forrester, am I to believe this to be a proposal … of sorts?'

'No pressure, Elizabeth. I can see you wouldn't want to be stuck with a guy like me, and the house is yours even if you don't agree to marry me. I want you to have it. It's yours. I'll sign the contract, pay it off and get out of your life if that's what you want. That's how much I love you.'

'What did you just say, Forrester?'

'I reckon you heard me right the first time. Don't make me repeat it, Elizabeth, as I don't want to make a dick of meself. All you've gotta say is, not interested. But I'm warning ya, I just lied a minute ago. I won't be giving up so easy. I'm planning on stickin' around and will keep on asking until you change y'mind.'

'I'm speechless! To think you would do this for me. How can you afford it?'

'I've wanted to buy this place since the first day I stepped foot inside the gate. Besides, I've got nothing else to spend me money on way out here in the sticks. Then I met you. Will you say yes, Elizabeth?'

Elizabeth's eyes filled with tears. 'Are you crazy, Forrester? Just try and stop me.' She said, throwing her arms around Lenny and smothering his face with kisses.

<h1 style="text-align:center">61</h1>

<h1 style="text-align:center">A Dream Fulfilled</h1>

Elizabeth felt the troubled years that had led to this moment of happiness in her life were now behind her. But also, she was wise enough to know that this ending merely heralded the beginning of yet a brand new chapter.

But there was no denying she had had her doubts initially when it came to selling the house and learning of the unusual request by the buyer whose identity wished to stay hidden until the settlement date. Elizabeth had thought to seek Jenkins' advice. He in turn agreed to consult the agent and promptly came back to assure her the buyer was genuine, and it was safe to go ahead. So, now that all had been revealed and the contract due to be signed, Jenkins copped a bit of flack about the part he had played in keeping the vendor in the dark about the identity of the mystery purchaser.

'It wasn't easy! And with a background in conveyancing law, I wasn't aware of a precedent to this effect, I can tell you, Elizabeth. You must have had your suspicions about this being someone you knew. Especially when I had to get you into the office and cover Lenny's name on the document.'

'Well, Graeme, all I was concerned about was that it might be someone I didn't like. But, never would I have suspected it would be our friend Forrester here.'

'Well probably more your friend than mine now, Elizabeth, considering you've agreed to marry the bloke.'

Elizabeth, who couldn't wipe the smile off her face as she looked at Forrester and squeezed his hand, replied, 'The reason I can forgive him is that it was an offer too good to refuse. Forrester has not only saved the house, but I wasn't expecting a marriage proposal. That wasn't part of the deal. And what could I say. I really love that house.' Elizabeth laughed.

'He's not as silly as he looks and has got you over a barrel. I can well understand why you can hardly refuse. But I would have to add, I'm a bit let down by it all as God dammit, he's beaten me to the punch. I was going to ask you the same question myself.'

As if everyone had forgotten he had a voice in all of this, Lenny said, 'Well, you guys can talk about me all you like, but it's too late for you, Jenko!' he laughed. 'You've missed y'chance. She's mine now mate, 'n' I'm not letting her go. I'll be calling on you to draw up a replacement document so I can add the name Mrs Elizabeth Forrester back onto the title.'

'Bloody hell, you like to complicate matters, Leonard my man. It's a bit unusual I'd have to say. But I think I can manage the legal side of that request,' Jenkins smiled, as he came around from behind his desk to offer his congratulations.

With everything falling into place and the building finished without any hiccups, Elizabeth found the whole saga quite extraordinary and knew it was time to make her peace with the Andersons.

Philip and David, the two supposed villains from hell, appeared anything but when she entered the study with an altogether different expression on her face than the last time they had met. 'Okay guys, the final instalment has been paid into your account. And I've come here today to tell you both I've never been happier in my entire life.'

The relief on their faces gave her a good feeling as she paused and directed her gaze at David. 'I'd also like to apologise for the way I acted on that day we spoke about the landscaping. You made me realise what a bitter person I'd become.'

Aware that her face must be glowing, Elizabeth could feel the warmth radiating from inside as she flopped into the armchair and couldn't stop talking.

'Tilt and I are so excited. The entire building both inside and out is a masterpiece.' She stopped and nodded as though they had performed a miracle. And then went on to say, 'As is the glass cabinetry and polished woodwork you've built to display the books and giftware. The paintings and soft furnishings will also attract the buyers who will never want to leave.' Elizabeth paused to draw breath. 'The customers will want to relax and enjoy the green oasis and tasteful displays in the stylish surrounds. I just cannot find enough superlatives to describe it. You must feel very proud, as I do for choosing you both to carry this project out and see it through to the end.'

The look of surprise on the Andersons' stunned faces was so obvious when Elizabeth handed them the details of the grand opening. 'You both must be there. In fact, you've got to be there so that everyone can see who drew up the design. I really cannot understand when the two of you are so gifted why you would have had the need to … aw well … we've already covered that subject and I'm confident you've turned the corner and life is about to improve from here.'

With not one word from either of them, Elizabeth pecked them on the cheek and swept out of the room as breezily as she had swept in.

Seconds later she popped her head back around the door. 'Are you alright? You both seem so quiet.'

'Yeah! We're cool,' David replied. 'Couldn't get a word in, that's all. Thanks for everything, we're so happy that you're happy. That's all that really matters.'

'Great! Oh, and I meant to ask, what's with this pile of boards you've got stacked up outside?'

'Leftover timber from the old storage area in the church,' Philip said. 'Jack was pitching them away, and we thought a few planks might come in handy for a little job we've got in the pipeline.'

Elizabeth couldn't help feeling puzzled about why they would want to use old timber. 'Well don't work too hard. I want you to be in good shape for the opening.'

'Just one thing, Elizabeth,' Philip said. 'Can you spare a minute before you go?'

'Sure!'

'Seeing as how we're all pleased with the church, and the circumstances under which you left the last time you visited, do you think a hug might be in order?'

Elizabeth's expression softened as she rushed back inside and noticed that Philip appeared a little emotional when clinging to her for just a touch longer than expected.

The early evening of the opening could not have been more pleasant, as the weather was perfect. The entire garden and building had been dressed by an interior designer from Melbourne. No expense had been spared as willowy bowers were placed strategically in tall vases and candlelight flickered to gladden the senses. Champagne glasses on silver trays awaited in readiness.

Unable to hide her delight, Elizabeth found it difficult to believe that, apart from the hosts, Gary Cartwright was the first to arrive at the opening. Tilt's look of surprise was all telling when seeing him dressed to the nines. Even Elizabeth herself was pleased when noticing he had put on weight and the colour had come back in his face. She'd forgotten what a handsome catch he was, but then so too her precious Forrester.

Tilt turned to Elizabeth and mouthed a quiet word in thanks before greeting her favourite man with a kiss.

'My God, I'm supposed to be psychic, but had no idea you were coming.' Elizabeth overheard their opening remarks to each other.

'Couldn't keep me away, Eileen. You look stunning in that dress ... by the way.'

Only then did Elizabeth step forward to say hello, closely followed by Lenny who shook Gary's hand. 'I believe we've already met, mate.'

'And wasn't that a night to remember?' Gary replied.

'I had no idea that you two knew each other. When did this happen?' Elizabeth asked.

'Young & Jackson's pub, would you believe. But hey, that's another story,' Gary said with a quick change of subject. 'What I can't believe, Liz, is this transformation that you've managed to pull off. Wow, wow and triple wow!' He whistled as he admired the feature floor to ceiling window. 'This looks like a space out of the Melbourne Art Gallery.'

'I'm glad you like it, Gary. That's just the reaction I had hoped for,' Elizabeth smiled as she purposely veered him away from the group on the pretext that she wanted to show him something he may have missed. 'Sorry for dragging you away,

I just wanted a moment alone with you to say how grateful I am that you've come.'

'I won't pretend it's not hard seeing you again, Liz, when knowing we are never going to get back together. The idea of losing you just kills me and if ever you need me for anything at all, don't hesitate to contact me. But having said that, I have made a good friend in Eileen.'

'I'm truly thankful for our time together and will keep your offer in mind. But it looks to me that Tilt means a bit more to you than just a friend. So, don't let me keep you from her,' Elizabeth said, making her excuses when seeing Graeme Jenkins arrive with Phyllis clinging to his arm.

This unexpected partnership did raise eyebrows and, of course, Phyllis was positively gushing with pride when able to hold her head up in company again among those important people she so admired.

Jack Cooper, the project manager in charge of the building, then entered with his wife, and the list just kept growing to include former customers, local identities, dignitaries, business owners and the bank manager. Even Elizabeth's dear friend and fatherlike figure, Bernie Blackwell, her boss from the publishing house, had made the effort to travel from Melbourne.

'Well, I see you didn't finish up with your pilot, Liz. A great guy as far as I can tell. But this decision hasn't done you much harm. You are looking on top of the world, and I'm happy to see how this venture has come together. The space is truly outstanding both inside and out, and the gallery a grand addition to enhance the loveliness of the church.'

Elizabeth hugged Bernie and thanked him not only for his kind remarks, but for all the advice he had given so generously when at her lowest.

The clock ticked around to 9 pm, but strangely Philip and David didn't appear. And, with no response on their mobile phone, 'I can't understand it.' Elizabeth nervously alerted Tilt. 'How are we going to begin the formalities without them? Something bad must have happened.'

Minutes later, Constable Madden made a belated entry with a stranger by her side. Following the necessary introductions, she then informed the intimate circle around her that Detective Steven Barker, formerly from the fraud squad, was conducting a search for two persons of interest.

'Oops!' Tilt pulled Elizabeth aside and whispered in her ear. 'Don't like the sound of this.'

The detective said his hellos then went on to add that the investigating team had received a tip off about their whereabouts. 'Seems they were last spotted at a remote coastal hideaway. And it would now appear the pair have played a significant role in the restoration of this very same building.'

'We expected them to be here tonight,' said Madden. 'But when Detective Barker paid a visit to Misty Headland, the house was boarded up. It's deserted, Elizabeth, with no sign of either brother. Do you know anything about this?'

Elizabeth shook her head. 'That's news to me, Constable Madden. They were supposed to be attending the opening, and I've heard nothing to tell me otherwise. Are you sure you're searching for the right people, Detective?'

'I'm sure alright!'

'It seems they've completely vanished,' Madden again stressed while giving Elizabeth a knowing look out of the corner of her eye. 'But I'd be the first to admit, the two have done an amazing job here. And all credit must go to the builders as well, wouldn't you agree, Detective Barker?'

But the detective was no longer standing by Madden's side. He had his back to her and could be seen gazing up at the commissioned statue of St Thomas who, surrounded by greenery, dominated the courtyard scene through the central window.

'This is an impressive place you've got here,' he said when turning to face Elizabeth. 'You're one of the lucky ones. Those blokes are no dunces. They're educated in fact!' The detective kept shaking his head. 'Sadly, it makes no difference! They're a couple of con artists and renowned for fleecing trusting home buyers of their hard-earned savings with no intention of ever completing the job. Hate to say it, but the two of them are probably lazing on a tropical beach somewhere under a coconut tree in the Bahamas by now.'

Later when it came time for Elizabeth to make a short speech, she apologised and informed the guests that much to her regret, both Philip Anderson, the architect, and his brother, David, who landscaped the garden, had been suddenly called away. But Elizabeth did take pleasure in congratulating and thanking the builder, Jack Cooper and his workers. Her final words being that she was happy to officially announce – 'The St Thomas Bookstore & Gallery will be open for business at precisely 9 am on Monday.'

62

An Unforeseen Development

The following Monday morning, Elizabeth returned to the bookstore to discover Tilt had arrived early and let herself in. She handed an envelope to Elizabeth saying she had found it slipped under the door.

Recognising the handwriting, Elizabeth impatiently ripped it open.

Dear Elizabeth,

So sorry that Dave and I had to leave in a hurry and couldn't be with you for the grand opening. Please don't think too badly of us and remember not all was a lie. We got the nod that some detective was hot on our tail from a most unlikely party who had our best interest at heart but shall remain nameless. We will set up shop where nobody knows us and repay any money outstanding as promised. We can't do this in a jail cell.

Don't concern yourself about the house at the Headland. That's all taken care of and rests in the capable hands of an acquaintance of mine who will tie up the loose ends.

To see your happiness with the completed rebuild has made our sudden departure worthwhile. Unfortunately, this little exercise did expose our whereabouts and any attempt to change our ways would most certainly be overlooked had we turned ourselves in. Will catch up again one day when the dust settles. Until then, David and I will miss you. Pass on our regards to Phyllis and be sure to tell that friend of yours, Forrester, he'd better take good care of you, or he'll have me to answer to.

Your time to shine starts now, Elizabeth. That won't be hard for you. In my view you have always had a special glow and I'm confident you'll make a great success of this venture.

With all my good wishes dearest sister (this part is true).

Your loving brother

Thomas xx

'Who's it from?' Tilt asked as Elizabeth reached for *The Book of St Thomas* and placed the letter inside.

'I think you already know, Tilt.'

'We all knew, darling! Or those of us who matter. I've never been a fan, but as the Andersons decided to do the right thing by you, we each agreed they deserved a second chance when that detective hit town and started poking around. Even Constable Madden couldn't make secret of the fact that she deliberately delayed his visit to Misty Headland.'

Tilt took Elizabeth by the hand and said, 'Close your eyes and come with me now. There's something I want to show you.'

Leading her back outside, as soon as they appeared at the doorway a band started playing and she opened her eyes to see what appeared to be the whole of Mariners Cove represented in the crowd as a cheer went up and balloons were released into the air. Everyone applauded. A local schoolkid came forward with flowers and a banner was raised to wish Elizabeth the best of luck on the first day of business and newly reopened premises.

Lenny stepped up and shouted above the noise to Elizabeth and Tilt. 'I think you're going to be rushed off your feet today, as everyone here is planning to buy a book. So, hop to it ladies, Phyllis and I have volunteered to lend a hand.'

With the four busy behind the counter, 'What do you reckon Thorny would say if she could speak to you now, Liz?' Tilt asked.

Elizabeth didn't hesitate as she looked beyond the customers to capture a glimpse of a white haired lady, and she thought of Beatrice Barry's words. 'Always remember, you are not alone.' Elizabeth replied in a faraway voice.

'You got that one right, what with all this lot clamouring for service.'

'I believe Margaret wanted to impress these words on me when I first arrived and felt abandoned. She delivered the message through a sweet old lady who called herself Beaty.'

'I remember you telling me that,' Tilt said. 'Always thought it strange, as Beatrice passed away before you arrived.'

Elizabeth's world went silent for a moment as she glanced across at Forrester and he smiled. In that defining moment she knew she had picked the man she truly cherished and quickly gave thanks that together they would share in a future at Mariners Cove – the home where she belonged.

Unbeknown to Elizabeth there remained one last piece of disturbing information she hadn't counted on. This news was to be delivered in a follow up visit from the detective who sat patiently waiting in the small office discreetly hidden behind the gallery.

Elizabeth had arrived early the next morning and with all the vacant shelves staring her in the face, she was eager to place more orders and restock the bookstore as quickly as possible. This would have to wait however when Tilt indulged in a bit of quiet sign language to make her aware of the detective's presence.

Pointing in the direction of the office, she picked up a metallic envelope opener and pretended to slash it across her throat. Elizabeth thought this action somehow comical if she hadn't been so confused. Tilt then gave her a puzzled shrug. 'Didn't say what about,' she whispered.

'For God's sake, Tilt, I never was any good at charades. Who in the hell are you talking about?'

'The detective!' she whispered. 'He's been snooping around and now waiting to speak with you.'

Elizabeth raised her eyes to the ceiling and sighed. Then making her way to the office, she looked back at Tilt whose face was distorted in some pained expression, to be quickly followed by an encouraging thumbs up.

God, she hoped that Gary would never entice her most valued friend to ever decide to join him in Melbourne. No one could ever replace her, and life would be far less interesting.

Detective Barker rose to greet Elizabeth with a polite, 'Good morning.' When they were seated, he said, 'I know how busy you are, so I'll get straight to the point, Ms O'Connell. Or can I call you Elizabeth?'

'Yes of course, Detective.'

'Well, as you are Margaret Thornton's next of kin, I do have some relevant news to convey. You see, following the death of Senior Sergeant Ian Henderson, new evidence has come to light surrounding the circumstances of your aunt's death. A death which led the accused to mistakenly believe himself the guilty party in her murder.'

Elizabeth frowned and cupped a hand over her mouth.

'An investigation was immediately re-opened, and we now have reason to believe it was neither a heart attack, nor a blow to her head that caused her death.'

'Oh my God, how can that be? Henderson virtually admitted to the crime.'

Detective Barker cleared his throat and dabbed at his forehead. 'My guess is, he panicked when believing he'd fatally killed her. She may have even momentarily stopped breathing, and in his haste to clear away any evidence of his visit, he hurried away to leave her lying unconscious.' The detective then asked if he might have a glass of water and after taking a few sips he proceeded.

'Margaret wasn't dead, Elizabeth. And there is good reason to believe that someone other than Henderson finished the job.'

'How can you know all this?'

'Currently, I'm not at liberty to divulge the source from whom this information was received. Except to say, there is enough proof to put the murderer behind bars for the rest of his days. For unbeknown to the perpetrator of this crime, there was an eyewitness.'

'But surely this is one person's word against another?'

'Of course, you're right, Elizabeth. This is precisely why the witness has been reluctant to come forward in the past.'

Elizabeth considered the detective's answer for a moment and asked, 'So why now?'

'The informant believes the senior sergeant was wrongly portrayed as the murderer and wanted to set the record straight.'

'And the person of interest who has been accused of this horrible act … do you know his name, Detective Barker?'

'I do.'

Elizabeth held her breath.

'I find it interesting that you use the word *his*, because the accused is a male who fits the description and is known to you. I'm sorry to have to burden you with this, but it's for your own safety. Because in his past dealings he has a record of preying on older, single ladies, when calling himself by the name of Simon Taylor.'

Relieved, Elizabeth said, 'I don't know anyone called Taylor, Detective.'

'Oh yes, I think you do, Elizabeth. I think you know him extremely well. But because *Taylor* is not a name with which you are familiar, *Anderson* is so much more relatable. It is just one brother in particular who I am eager to apprehend. And that man is no other than the one you described in your speech as being a landscape gardener, I believe.'

Elizabeth shook her head in denial, and rising from the chair she gazed at the detective with a cold and calculating look of intense dislike. 'You are not welcome here. And whoever has come forward with this story, I consider it to be an outrageous lie.'

The detective made his way to the door. He stopped and said, 'My intention was never to upset you, Elizabeth. But more so to warn you. Should he ever try to contact you in the future, please keep in mind the suspect's name is David … David Anderson.'

Epilogue

Life could have turned out differently if only her aunt hadn't died.

But her aunt had died. That was the painful truth of the matter. And Elizabeth now refused to be swayed by the allegation that David Anderson had murdered her. No, she would not allow the detective to spoil her renewed trust in the two people her aunt had believed in.

Her thoughts interrupted, Elizabeth looked with love at Lenny as he appeared beside her holding two glasses of wine. He placed one in her hand and led her to the spot where they had at first exchanged fiery words. A peaceful place, Elizabeth breathed in the freshly mown grass and admired the finely clipped hedges.

'Do you believe in fate, Forrester?' she asked.

He shrugged. 'I prefer t'leave that kind a stuff to the experts.'

'My grandfather must have been one of them. You see, when I was a kid and lost my parents, he told me that fate has a habit of stepping in to determine one's destiny.' Elizabeth turned to look directly into Lenny's eyes. 'I used to hate that thought and wanted someone to blame. But now I honestly believe that fate has given me you.'

'Could be just luck,' Lenny laughed and squeezed her hand.

'Perhaps that's not as funny as it sounds. But then again, perhaps I should simply give credit to my wise old grandpa, a man who may have always known the answer.'

Elizabeth also thought about her aunt; the one person at the centre of her story who had stepped in to wipe away her tears, fill the empty void and comfort her in the night. It was her aunt who tended and cared for her. And it was her aunt who had loved her like her very own child.

'You know, Forrester, speaking of luck, there's not a doubt in my mind that Margaret was an angel who I truly loved. The thing that saddens me being those among the people of Mariners Cove who will choose to think of her as nothing more endearing than my wicked aunt.'

'There's nothin' sad about that, Elizabeth. We each have a bit of wickedness in us. I reckon Margaret would've loved t'be remembered by that name. I can hear her laughin' right now.'

'Really?'

'Yep! There's no way she'd wanna be thought of as someone who had her nose stuck inside a book all day. That lady had a wicked sense of humour, a playful spirit and knew how t'enjoy life.'

'You know, I've never thought of it quite like that before. I think you're right,' Elizabeth smiled as she looked to the sky. 'How about we make a toast, shall we, Forrester?'

Lenny placed his arm around Elizabeth and they both raised a glass as her fond farewell echoed across the valley. 'Here's to you, dear Margaret. My darling, wicked aunt.'

Acknowledgements

With thanks to the following:

My husband, Bill, who has urged me to finish this novel and been willing to cast an eye over the pages to provide help wherever needed. Without his encouragement, I may never have completed this story or enjoyed the bouts of laughter as he teasingly joked with his mates about me having difficulty writing the sex scenes.

All too frequently, when panic sets in and dozens of expletives can be heard coming from the normally quiet confines of my computer room, I call on my technical adviser and fixer extraordinaire. My daughter, Lisa, immediately recognises from the tone of my voice it's crisis time in Mum's writing world again, and drops everything to ensure my PC is returned to normal working condition.

My friend, writer and author, Joanne, who has not once wavered in her belief in my stories. Every author needs such a person in their life. And Joanne is mine!

The talented members of the Telltales Writing Group: Kara, Kerry, Sue, Anne, Dianne, John and retired member Richard, who have offered their advice about many of the chapters of this story throughout the past five years.

Rebecca Cannizzaro, my editor, who has helped to get this story as perfect as it could be before it reached the final print.

Kev Howlett, Les Zigomanis and of course Oscar, who always offers a friendly hello whenever I visit Busybird Publishing. Their warm and welcoming friendship, advice and expertise in publishing all three of my earlier novels and now this the fourth and most ambitious of all my books. You really do make it all happen!

Pablo Picasso – "Everything you can imagine is real."

Stories – a source of entertainment for all eternity.

About the Author

Having lived in Briar Hill, Victoria, for most of her adult life, Colleen's journey in writing began twenty years ago and she has been a member of a writing group ever since. Completely immersed in storytelling, this, her fourth published novel, is claimed to be the most ambitious of all and has taken the longest to complete.

Apart from writing, Colleen's love of family, friends and spending time together is all important to her. Enjoying many creative pursuits, sporting activities, travel and gardening to name just a few, Colleen is grateful for every precious gift in life and hopes to live till one hundred as she has many more tales to tell.

Previously published books:

Curly O'Callahan is a salt-of the earth philosopher who longs to make a bold statement. He decides to write the stories of his eventful life, following the advice he once learned from Kermit the frog, that the first belief is self-belief.

Colleen Noonan's tales of Curly, written with humour and gentle assurance, take the reader into familiar and not so familiar realms of the human heart.

– Carmel Bird

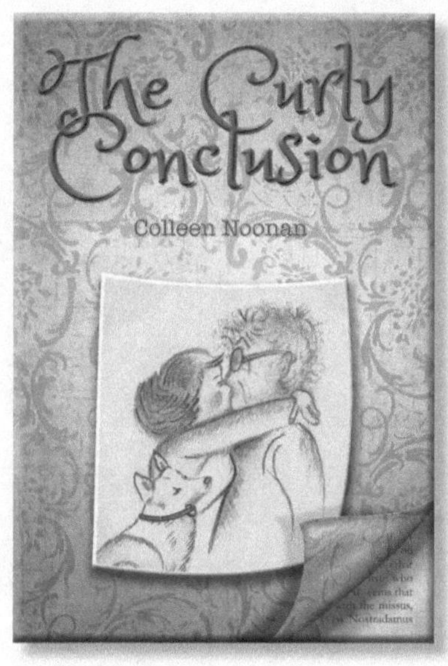

Curly has some new challenges ahead, along with several important decisions to be made in this the final chapter. A practical joke, lies and trickery are high on the agenda. And what of Penelope? When it comes to romance, shall Curly be a willing participant? What promised good fortune might the ladybird bring? Is Curly likely to publish that much sought after bestseller? Does Smudge continue to come up with the correct answers, and what changes will Curly be prepared to make which might affect his future? These questions and more will be answered in the long awaited sequel to the 'The Curly Collection'.

Unlike Curly, Mackenzie was fully aware of her actions as she tapped in a second sentence.

Several lines of mumbo jumbo made up of repeated letters, dots and dashes confronted her. But even more distracting were the hands spinning wildly out of control on the clock.

The hourglass suddenly took flight. It lifted off the desk and floated through the air. Mackenzie watched in amazement when, as smoothly as a glider on water, it landed on top of the filing cabinet. Undisturbed the sand continued to sift through the neck of the hourglass.

Laughing Emojis flashed across the computer screen as if to make fun of Mackenzie as she again attempted to write another sentence.